SIMSBURY PUBLIC LIBRARY

3 2509 11738 8936

JUN 24 2010

ED

DATE DUE

D0813660

SIMSBURY PUB
725 HOPMEADO
SIMSBURY, CT 06070

ED

DISCARDED

FIGHTING CASTRO
A Love Story

BASED ON A TRUE STORY

KAY ABELLA

WingSpan Press

SIMSBURY PUBLIC LIBRARY
725 HOPMEADOW STREET
SIMSBURY, CT 06070

Copyright © 2007 by Kay Abella
All rights reserved.

No part of this book may be used or reproduced in any
manner without written permission of the author, except
for brief quotations used in reviews and critiques.

Printed in the United States of America

Published by WingSpan Press, Livermore, CA
www.wingspanpress.com

The WingSpan name, logo and colophon are the
trademarks of WingSpan Publishing.

ISBN 978-1-59594-146-6

First edition 2007

Library of Congress Control Number 2007924403

THIS BOOK IS DEDICATED TO ALL THE
CUBANS
WHO NEVER MADE IT HOME.

AND TO THOSE WHO STILL WAIT.

Surgieron del abismo
De los tiempos
Con un dolor de rejas
En sus rostros
Y en los ojos . . .
el destello lacerante
De su Cuba esclava.

They emerged from the abyss
Of time.
In their faces
The agony of prison bars.
And in their eyes . . .
The lacerating glare of their Cuba enslaved.

-Jesús R. Beruvides

Beruvides was a young farmer from Matanzas imprisoned by Castro from 1961 to 1978. He learned to read and write in prison and became expert in the tiny lettering needed for smuggling documents out of prison.

PREFACE

This story is true. If a person or their memory might be hurt by words in this book, a name or detail has been changed, a character disguised.

Obviously most conversations are not recorded, so they have been reconstructed based on people's memories. Incidental facts have been assumed where the real ones are long forgotten. I do not believe this has affected the basic narrative or meaning of the story.

The only untrue thing is the scope of the story. Emy and Lino Fernandez are not the only ones who stood with courage against Castro's attempts to destroy them. There are so many more. I only wish that they could all be brought into the light.

Kay Abella
Connecticut
2007

Note: An overview of Castro's Revolution is included in the back of this book, for those born after the events or those who may have forgotten exactly what happened.

ACKNOWLEDGMENTS

What a long complex journey a book turns out to be. You try to recollect all the people who helped. You only hope to remember them all and to thank them with the worthiness of your storytelling.

Most of all, my deepest gratitude to Lino and Emy who opened their hearts and their memories, sharing deeply of their very personal journey, even the parts that made Lino shout and Emy cry.

Tony and Irma Abella opened the door to this book by bringing me together with the Fernandez. I am indebted to them as well for sharing their own experiences of leaving Cuba and for their advice at every stage of the book's creation. Special thanks to Tony for the hours spent restoring and enhancing the photos used in the book.

My delightful husband Luis first introduced me to the exuberance and warmth of the Cuban people and the strong bonds of Cuban family. He has my loving thanks for being the cheerleader who encouraged, pushed, and cajoled me through the long process of getting the story right.

The extended Abella and Alejandre families gave me the greatest compliment by treating me as a Cuban from the start. Sofia Abella embodied for me the fathomless love in a Cuban family and the richness of a way of life that will not disappear. Rosita Abella instilled in me the important of holding history up to the light and of remembering. Maggie Khuly kept an eagle eye on my Spanish.

My daughter Caroline. The richness she has brought to my life allowed me to understand the depth of Emy and Lino's sacrifice.

My sister, Sue Singleton, taught me that if you're going to use language you'd better get it right, then agreed to give the manuscript the last look – to be sure I'd learned my lessons.

Natalie Bates introduced me to the basic building blocks of writing that I didn't even know existed and taught me that good writing is crafted step by step, not created in a flash of genius. Liana Scalettar set a dauntingly high bar for excellent writing and never let us be satisfied with just good.

The members of the Friday morning writing class, Doris, Julie, Lauren, Tom, Celia, Jack, and Darlene, were my spirited companions on the road; they kept me moving when I flagged. They gave their generous feedback, and they weren't afraid to tell me when the writing didn't work.

Thank you all.

INTRODUCTION

On February 24, 1996, Armando Alejandre and three other Cuban-Americans, in small planes looking for rafters fleeing Cuba, were shot from the sky by Cuban fighter planes. Armando was my cousin.

We were at the house that night, watching the television tensely as grief grew and hope faded. Aunts and cousins, in-laws and friends streamed through the house, each hoping to hear it had never happened.

As we rose to leave about 10 p.m., Rosita, an elderly aunt, herself an exile for almost 40 years, took us aside in the hall. Dry eyed, in the measured dignified language of the intellectual she is, she said,

"This is a tragedy. But do not forget – every day there is a tragedy for a Cuban family. Only today it is **our** *tragedy."*

♦ ♦ ♦

I had been part of a Cuban family by marriage for 15 years. But it was not until that night that I knew I would write about these tragedies. I wanted to bring to life the wrenching pain shared only in family circles, the unique personal story that fades when it is only one in a long list of lives mutilated and destroyed by the Castro regime. I wanted to give a face to what Fidel has done in the service of his ego and his estrangement from the concepts of justice, family, and human dignity.

As it turned out, the story I have told here is not a tragedy, only because those who lived it would not allow it to become one.

I don't know what I expected when I met Dr. Lino Fernandez and his wife, Emy, one sunny February afternoon in 2000 in Coral Gables, Florida. But, knowing what they had been through, I was certainly not prepared for their centered warmth, their recovery from the long years of deprivation, their complete lack of bitterness for the irretrievable years stolen from them. Lino looked like he had never lived any life but the one he had now, professionally respected, dedicated to family and medicine, open to every pleasure of life – and not surprised to get it.

Emy gave you the impression that you were exactly the person she had hoped to see in her house this day. Welcoming, genuine, slightly surprised that you would be so interested in her story.

It was only as their story unfolded, as I probed relentlessly month after month for every detail and feeling of those years, that I truly saw why they had survived as they did. Beneath the gentle exteriors were cores of psychological steel. A refusal to die within themselves, no matter what savagery Castro might unleash. A sureness that they could not have acted otherwise, that their sacrifice was not a tragic mistake but a set of inevitable decisions dictated by their beliefs.

I had begun writing the story intrigued by what I saw as the central drama: Emy's choice and her and Lino's struggle to survive the consequences. But as I got to know the Fernandez better, I realized that her decision, although dramatic, had been only one moment in eighteen years of everyday courage on both their parts. I was in awe. I understood for myself what heroism is.

Midway through my writing, I was surfing the internet for the hundredth time, looking for some detail of Castro's revolution. I came across a grainy black and white photo of a body sprawled gracelessly on the ground, a bullet hole in his head, eyes still open in death. He had just been shot by a firing squad. I stared at the photo. This image must have been in Lino and Emy's heads through the long years of uncertainty and violence. This could happen to Lino. Any moment of any day. Without warning. And yet they went on. With courage. With humor when possible. And most of all with love. In the end, it was enough.

I wasn't sure that I could ever capture all the details and nuances of a story so convoluted and so far from my own experience and my own heritage. So I felt a great satisfaction when I sent the finished manuscript to Lino and Emy and received this e-mail from Lino.

You have recreated something you have not lived. It is as if you were there in our lives. Remember I was not there, I was in prison. For the first time in all these years I get acquainted with my Emy's life and suffering and the whole cadre of the ordeal, not only ours but of the whole nation.

Lino

PROLOGUE
1958

It was her favorite time of day, Havana cooling down after a sultry afternoon. Emy Fernandez, her curly chestnut hair pulled into a barrette, put her baby daughter, Emilia Maria, into a yellow dress with ladybugs on it. Then she went downstairs to meet her husband who stood, relaxed and animated, talking to the doorman of their building. Dr. Lino Fernandez had just finished his long day of clinic work and office hours. Now he had another hour or two of house calls, and Emy and the baby were coming with him. He loved the company, and they saw so little of each other. Without this time Lino might not see Emilia Maria before her bedtime.

Their small Plymouth had one of the newest inventions - air conditioning - a boxy gadget that sat between the front seats. Emy put Emilia Maria's bottles in front of the machine to keep them cool as Lino drove through the broad avenues of downtown Havana.

"The man I told you about, who was so sure he had tuberculosis? Well he was back today."

"Does he have it after all?"

"Of course he doesn't," Lino chuckled. "He never did. But now it's malaria. Nothing will convince him except a blood test. I think the real diagnosis is lack of attention at home."

"Well this little one isn't suffering from lack of attention." Emy took Emilia Maria's hands and waved them in the air. "Tell Daddy about the little giraffe your grandmother brought you. And how you cried when you saw it."

"Well, wouldn't you cry if a giraffe came into your bed?" Lino grinned at the baby and stroked her tiny wrist. "Wait till we take her to the zoo and see the real thing."

When Lino stopped to see a patient, Emy waited in the car, chatting with Emilia Maria as she fed her, or reading a book she had brought along. Women heading home from the market lingered in the tantalizing cool breeze of evening to talk to neighbors. The throaty voice of Celia Cruz came wafting from an apartment window.

Almost every entrance had a collection of potted flowers, flamboyant shades of red and pink trailing onto the sidewalk punctuated by spots

1

of iridescent blue. Emy tried to decide what to plant in the squat glazed pots she'd bought for their terrace.

When Lino's calls were finished, they stopped for a treat at their long-time favorite cafe in the old section of Havana. The luminous coral of the lowering sun glowed against the pastel houses. Glinted on the windows of the shops and apartments. Two boys on bicycles trailed each other aimlessly up and down the street. The usual jumble of men surrounded the coffee window, shouting and teasing one another long after the tiny cups were empty.

Emy and Lino perched on the wrought iron stools at a high wooden table. The café's owner, a chubby mulatto lady with white hair piled thickly on her head, came rushing over the see the baby.

"*Ay*, Adela, you used to come over to see me." Lino feigned disappointment. "I think I've been upstaged." Adela waved him off and whisked Emilia Maria away to show her to the waitresses.

They considered the usual choices of vanilla, chocolate, and strawberry ice cream and then the café's specialty, a lavish variety of tropical fruit sherbets. They prolonged the choosing, enjoying the anticipation. In the end, they ordered their favorites - mamey sherbet for Lino and mango for Emy. They talked about the day when Emilia Maria, and other children to come, would sit on their own stools chattering, ice cream smeared across their little hands and faces.

"We'll be very strict," Emy said, a smile spreading into her smooth round cheeks. "Ice cream only on weekends."

"Oh no we won't." Lino pulled her to him and hugged her, kissing her temple. "You're such a softie. They'll have it every day if you're in charge."

They would never find out.

1
1959

*"We have come to give all Cubans the life they
deserve - a life of freedom - freedom to
prosper, freedom to learn, and most of
all, freedom to live without fear."*

The great booming voice of Fidel Castro went on and on - smug
with its practiced seduction.

*"We want only what is best for the people.
And we welcome all those who are willing to help
us - whatever their background or their ideas."*

The crowd roared approval. Lino felt a shudder of disgust. He
had an irrational urge to throw out his arms and bellow at the crowd.
"Outrageous lies. Hear them? Familiar. Tempting. But still lies!" His
careful disciplined nature won out - for now.

On this hot September night, the Plaza de la Revolución was a
masterful stage setting. "Saint Fidel" was illuminated by blazing military
lights that made the curly iron street lamps on the surrounding streets
irrelevant. Behind the podium a humongous banner of Che Guevara
stretched across an entire block of buildings.

People, more than 400,000, crowded into the enormous plaza. True,
Fidel was a mesmerizing speaker. But even so, Lino was sure most
people had been brought in buses from their workplace, to swell the

3

crowd. After three hours they continued to stand in their assigned groups, perhaps weary of listening, but alert to signs that they were supposed to cheer.

Circulating among the people were militia in the now famous mufti-green uniforms, carrying rifles or machine guns. Some pushed their way through the crowds, barking orders at anyone who strayed from their group. These untrained self-important young men were the victors of *la Revolución*; they wanted everyone to know they were in charge. Lino knew that highly trained security troops were on alert in the surrounding area, but they were not visible here.

Lino frowned. The people's militia. What a joke. They didn't give a damn about the people. A massive statue of the 19th century patriot Jose Marti dominated the Plaza. Marti would certainly be disgusted by what he saw tonight.

Dr. Lino Fernandez looked like the aristocrat he was not, graceful and confident, handsome in the traditional Latin style. He was actually from a modest background, the son of a small-town pharmacist, and had gone to the prestigious Belen boarding school as a scholarship student. His assurance came from having known early what he wanted to do, become a doctor and try to improve the social system in Cuba. There was much to be done.

Now he leaned against the wall of the National Library, arms folded across his tall frame and a cynical smile on his face. He didn't care who saw it. He wasn't courting Fidel's favor. With him was a friend from medical school Dr. Antonio Martinez.

After the last hysterical cheer, waves of people, released from their roles as adoring fans, swarmed eagerly towards their buses, afraid of being left behind.

Lino felt a deepening weariness as he and Antonio walked silently across the Plaza and into a dark side street.

Fidel certainly knew what Cuba needed. But did he have any intention of delivering it?

In spite of the looming nightmare, nothing appeared to have changed at *El Carmelo*. The bright buzzing restaurant on the corner of Calzada Street still served anything from an ice cream sundae to a plate mounded with arroz con pollo at any hour. The two men threaded their way through the wide bustling terrace and went inside. The small room was crowded with couples and, in spite of the late hour, family groups spilled over two or three tables, children fidgeting in their chairs. Eventually they spotted a small vacant table next to a window looking across at the Victoria theatre.

Lino greeted Juan, a tall middle-aged waiter who'd been at *El Carmelo* forever. He had their table tonight, and he was his usual blur of motion. He snapped his fingers at the busboy, took their order for coffee and pastries, and rushed off to another table, almost before they had time to sit down.

Lino stretched out his arms and shoulders, then visibly relaxed as he sat down in the familiar wood chair. His face showed the pleasure of dipping back into the Havana he loved, the Havana he was afraid would disappear.

Antonio and Lino exchanged news of their families; Antonio's second son had just been born. He began stacking and restacking the spoons on the table. At length he said, "You'd never know from these crowds what's brewing outside. Do they still think he's going to save this country?"

"Well I certainly haven't seen anything encouraging." Even with an old friend, Lino kept his tone low-key. Then he fell silent.

"Everyone says we should give him a chance," Antonio suggested cautiously. "But it's been almost nine months . . ." He let the sentence dangle. He shook a cigarette from a pack of *Partagás* and Juan was instantly at his side to light it. Lino waited until Juan was gone. God, he was tired of watching his back..

"Come on Antonio – we've got no choice. But honestly, what the hell did you expect from a guy like Fidel?"

Antonio was a little surprised at Lino's frankness, especially in public. He looked quickly to see who was at the next table. An elderly couple was just settling in, fussing over where to put the man's cane and paying no attention to the men's conversation.

Lino pulled his chair closer to the table, his voice lowered but intense. "Let's face it, the guy's a thug."

Antonio raised his eyebrows.

"I don't broadcast it, but I went to Belen School like Fidel. He was only a kid then, and he was already a bully. Got what he wanted any way he could."

"Oh great, just what the country needs." Antonio's sarcasm was palpable.

"Same at the University. Part of those student groups that were really just gangs." Lino accepted a cigarette from Antonio's pack and lit it. "Fidel was hell-bent on controlling student politics at the University, but he was never elected." Lino's voice turned bitter. "He seems to be having better luck bullying all of Cuba."

Antonio leaned in towards Lino. "He keeps saying he's not a Communist. What do you think?"

"An opportunist for sure. Communist. Who knows?" Lino rubbed the back of his neck and stretched his spine. "I don't care what label you give him; I don't like what he's doing."

Juan appeared with their pastries and disappeared again. Lino took a big bite of éclair and chewed it slowly. He let the familiar pleasure distract him for a minute before continuing.

"The ludicrous public trials, executions on TV for God's sake! Sure, some of these Batista guys are guilty, but this stuff makes us look like a bunch of savages. In every civilized part of the world the accused is considered innocent until proved guilty. Except here."

Antonio put his fork down. "You have to admit, some of them deserve what they get." There had been graft and violence in the Batista regime Fidel had overthrown. Although Batista had left most people alone, behind the scenes there had been a ruthless police machine.

"Oh absolutely. They do. But look at the way it's being done. One of the lawyers is a friend of ours. He's been at the trials. You should hear his description."

"Like what?" Antonio put out his cigarette and motioned to the waiter for another coffee.

"Like something out of Robespierre. The courtroom has all the right props: judge, lawyers. All that. But the atmosphere's a circus! Pure histrionics. People shout and jeer at the prisoners. They applaud those stupid revolutionary statements, then barge in when lawyers try to speak."

Lino shoved his plate away. "And the judge does nothing. He's a good guy, but he knows what Fidel wants from him. Nobody's getting a real trial."

Antonio smashed the rest of his eclair with his fork, then swirled the cream around on his plate. "What about the guys who get no trial? You know they got Juan Rodriguez? Executed him. No trial." Lino winced; he hadn't known. Rodriguez had been a respected journalist.

Antonio paused while Juan took their plates away. What he said next, almost in a whisper, chilled Lino. "I had an interesting visit myself on Monday. Guy from the Ministry of Health."

"Oh?"

"He was very friendly to start with - how important doctors are to the campaign for rural health - all that stuff. Then he got to the point."

"Which was?"

"I would be very 'unwise' to support informal meetings of doctors."
Lino felt weary.

"I asked him why, all innocence, and he said that meetings like ours
demonstrated bourgeois pretension. Lack of support for the Revolution."
Antonio drew his knife savagely across the tablecloth. "Who is Fidel to
tell me when and where I can meet with other doctors, for God's sake."

Lino raised his eyebrows. "He obviously thinks we'll talk about more
than medicine."

"Exactly. The little weasel's attitude seems to be, 'if you've got
something to say, go ahead, but not where anyone can actually hear you.'
I don't like it. In fact, that's where I draw the line." He stopped, looking
surprised at his own vehemence

"Well, why do you think Fidel banned political parties? Before he even
took his boots off." Lino imitated Fidel's pompous tone. "'A temporary
measure to let the government get organized.' Who's he kidding?"

Antonio's cup clinked into the saucer. "'A temporary measure.' In
other words, enough time to make sure they've got their hands in every
pocket. Control every power spot."

Lino noticed a waitress standing nearby doing nothing - listening
maybe? He made a mental note of what she looked like, in case he saw
her again, then waited for her to move away before he spoke.

"Remember how he went on and on about all the rebel groups
sharing power? No matter who entered Havana first. Well guess what?
He doesn't want input from anybody." He shrugged his shoulders. "And
if you tell him what you think anyway, you might just disappear."

Antonio nodded sharply, as though just now coming to a conclusion.
Or maybe just deciding to share it. "Mark my words, Lino, there'll be
no elections - and no coalition - unless we fight for them." He drew out
the last three words.

The two men finished their coffee in silence and paid the bill.
Lino decided to walk home from Calzada Street. He'd always loved
strolling through the crowds and the busy streets, then into the quiet
neighborhood where he and his young wife Emy had found their first
apartment when they married two years ago. But the area was already
changing, a palpable tension in the air. People didn't linger to talk in
groups like they used to, especially in the evening. Militia members were
always around. The whole atmosphere of the city had changed.

Just a few days before, Emy had lamented how she didn't see so many of the lively *billeteros* anymore. The lottery vendors normally dotted the city, selling tickets from their hanging displays, usually at a corner where they had stood for years. Now they took a low profile, especially when the militia was around.

Lino had felt sad when she said, "I've always loved that singsong cry of *Tengo ocho y tres, lucky numbers, get them from me now - no espere.*"

"Si si," Lino had agreed. "Selling that eternal dream of the big one."

When Lino got home, Emy had waited up for him, wrapped in her pale blue cotton robe, dark curly hair free around her face. He kissed her softly. He couldn't believe he was really married to this smiling green-eyed girl he'd courted so long.

Tonight her tall figure was tense - she hadn't wanted him to go to the rally.

"Who did you talk with? Were there other people you knew?" When she heard about Lino's conversation with Antonio at the restaurant, she reminded Lino to be careful what he said. "Just don't call attention to yourself. Things get repeated. And if they want to pick you up, they'll use any excuse."

"*Mi amor*, don't worry. Antonio and I've known each other for years. We went through medical school together."

Emy looked straight into his eyes, to make sure he was listening. "And lots of acquaintances have parted ways over politics in the last few months. Lots of acquaintances have become informers. So try to be a little less outspoken, *mi vida*. Promise?" Lino nodded.

Lino could see how worried Emy was. They had started out with so much to look forward to. Now he deliberately hadn't told Emy the details of his conversation with Antonio. She would only have worried more.

Trying to pretend she was less worried, Emy smiled at Lino as she left to check on the baby before going to their own bedroom. She doubted he would pay any attention to her warning.

When she had met Lino Fernandez more than six years before, Emy was still a schoolgirl of 16 and he was finishing medical school. He seemed almost unaware of his elegant looks, his dark wavy hair combed straight back in the Cuban style of the 50s. But he knew what he wanted. He made it clear very quickly that he intended to marry Emy. Soon he was almost a member of the family, eating supper many nights at the Luzaraga's gracious old stucco house, charming her mother and engaging in long discussions with her father about politics and agriculture. Chaperoned by her mother or an older brother, the couple would sit after supper on the terrace and talk or go out in a group with friends.

In the beginning, Emy had felt intimidated by Lino's intensity when he talked about social issues or his studies. She soon found that in personal relationships the intensity turned to enthusiasm; he was gentle and committed. He was right for her. More than anything she loved his certainty and his strength.

As their lives got more complex and Cuba slid into violence, Lino had made it very clear where he stood. She had known he would, that he wouldn't put on an act. God, what kind of world was this? Where you have to pretend who your friends are, watch who you talk to, about what. Worry if your husband doesn't come home after work.

A close friend Rogelio hadn't come home on Tuesday night. No one had heard from him. In today's Havana that could mean only one thing; he was in the hands of Fidel's police. If he was alive.

In the baby's room Emy opened the window shade so the moonlight fell on Emilia Maria's little body, scrunched in one corner of the crib. Her hair was damp from the heat. She thought of the new baby on the way.

Lino had been urged to come to meetings just like the one Rogelio was on his way to when he disappeared. *When would it be him?*

2

Ana Martin huddled just inside the door of the *Ten Cen*. She was flushed and her eyes darted from side to side, as though one of the people streaming by might drag her away. The minute she saw Emy, she ran to hug her, starting to sob.

"Gone, they're gone." Emy could barely understand the girl's words through the crying. She was an old friend; Emy couldn't remember ever seeing her so upset. Emy's stomach tightened.

"Who? Ana, who's gone?"

Ana took in great gulps of air, trying to stop crying. Emy moved the shaking girl to the side of the crowded store entrance and put her arms around her, speaking softly but insistently.

"Ana, what's going on?" No response. "Who? For the sake of God, who is gone?" A chubby older woman stared openly at weeping Ana, then turned left into the cosmetics department.

Ana finally managed to speak, her voice halfway between a whisper and a sob. "Felicia." She looked behind her nervously and continued to sniff. "I went to see if she'd come with us." Felicia Vargas, Ana, and Emy had been friends all through boarding school, first as inseparable children, then growing up with their lives still intertwined. Assuming their futures would be too.

Ana hurried on. "The house was totally deserted - you know how Señora Vargas was always home in the morning. No one. Even on the terrace." Her eyes started to brim over again.

Emy handed her the handkerchief from her purse, and Ana blew her nose, then wadded the handkerchief up in her palm. People were turning to look at the two as they hurried in and out of the store. They probably thought this was all about a breakup with some boyfriend. Emy wished it were. She steered Ana towards a quiet area where only one woman was looking through a pile of striped canvas sandals on a counter.

She turned Ana to face her and spoke firmly, "Was anyone there at all?" she asked.

"I didn't think so - I mean, not at first." Now Ana seemed eager to tell the story, stumbling over her words. "But then that young maid Graciela - remember her, the little one with braids? From Pinar del Rio?" Ana took a deep breath while Emy waited patiently. "She came out when she saw it was just me. She said the family was all gone."

"Where?"

"To the U.S."

Emy's mind was racing. "Did she know why?" She wished she'd been able to talk to Graciela herself.

"Well, first she said they went to see Felicia's brother at school, in Virginia."

"It could be true." But even as she spoke, Emy knew they wouldn't go to Virginia without telling anyone.

"No, no." Ana shook her head rapidly. "After a while she admitted they aren't coming back. Said they told her to come and go like everything was normal, for as long as she could. You know . . . so the militia wouldn't see they were gone." She stopped to blow her nose again. "But they came anyway. They told Graciela to get out by the end of the month." Ana seemed calmer now. She picked up a red and white rubber sandal and turned it over idly, bending the sole almost double.

"Poor thing. She must've been petrified." Emy remembered Graciela as a young country girl who said little. She'd certainly be terrified at having to talk to soldiers.

Emy struggled to take it in. The Vargas. That rambling colonial house full of kids and music and action. All the vacations spent there when there wasn't time to go all the way home to the mill. Theirs was the house where she'd learned to play gin rummy, where she'd first hated Felicia's brother, then been sure she was falling in love with him.

Anyone could guess what'd happened now. Lots of families had left. Half her class was gone. But not the Vargas, not like this, not without telling their best friends. She leaned against a counter stacked with shampoo. She felt like hurling the bottles through the plate glass window.

Ana's voice broke into her thoughts. "Emy, she showed me inside the house. The family took **nothing**." She threw the sandal back onto the counter as though it disgusted her, and her voice turned plaintive. "Not even photographs. Or that beautiful shawl on the piano. You know, the one from Spain that Felicia loved."

Emy's mind was racing, trying to think what could have happened to make them leave so fast. An open threat? An arrest? She knew Señor Vargas had been high up in the finance ministry, and he hadn't been happy with what was happening there. She'd even overheard him once with his wife, mocking the incompetence of Che Guevara, Fidel's Finance Minister who insisted on signing official papers just *Che* as though his fame was enough. *Maybe Señor Vargas had been warned to get out - fast.*

Ana, seeming calmed by Emy's silence, went on. "Graciela showed me everything - I think she was happy to talk to someone. Untouched. The closets and the china cabinets - even their books and paintings. That goofy gorilla Felicia always sat on her bed? Still sitting there - all alone." She thought for a minute. "It was a ghost house Emy. Like all the humans had been siphoned away by an evil force, and everything else left untouched. Creepy."

Emy didn't want to think about the house. Besides, it was more important to find out what had actually happened. "How did the Militia find out?"

"One of the soldiers told Graciela it was a neighbor. Remember that Francisca Sanchez in the back, the one who always objected to the dogs?" Emy nodded. She remembered the tall thin woman who used to yell at them when they played in the garden. "Supposedly she told the police she was 'worried' when she didn't see Felicia walking the dogs like she always did in the morning." Ana tugged at her pony tail. "What a lying snake that woman is."

Emy thought of her own neighbors, whether one of them would do that to her. She couldn't imagine it, but then so many people seemed to be in disguise these days, the old civility now just a mask covering a new cunning. You couldn't count on anything.

Emy thought back, searching for a clue. "I just saw Felicia last Friday. She seemed so normal . . . Do you think she knew then?" Ana shrugged.

Round-faced Felicia, her long dark hair pulled into an unruly ponytail. The eternal tomboy. Then all at once, blossoming. Worrying about how she looked. Boys hanging around her house, trying to get on the good side of her mother. Felicia had adored Emy's little girl, always teaching her little songs. Not anymore.

Emy's own eyes were brimming now, partly with tears for her friend not trusting her, partly from the realization that she might not see Felicia again. Felicia wasn't the first friend, but certainly the first close one, to leave. And she probably wouldn't be the last. Emy felt her world shattering, one pane at a time.

Ten Cen was the Cuban name for Woolworths, and its lunch counter was where everybody met to eat and gossip. Emy and Ana moved toward the crowded counter and slipped onto the plastic seats of the only two empty stools next to each other. Emy ordered her usual, *una Coca Cola y una orden de croquetas, por favor.* Ana made a face, she didn't like the little ham and potato fritters, and ordered *una hamburguesa.* The skinny young girl in a pink uniform nodded and moved off. They agreed without words not to say any more about the Vargas with so many other people around. Instead they talked about news from friends and about Ana's wedding in six weeks, but the conversation was flat, falling into silences. Even the wedding plans had been simplified. "Papi says it's not a good idea to give a big party. Too visible." Emy nodded. Even two years ago, before Fidel took over, her own wedding had been subdued because of the uncertainty of the situation with the guerillas.

As she hugged Ana goodbye and started her walk home, her heavy sadness began to sharpen into a blade of fear. Her thoughts went back to the Vargas. Was this the future for them all? Leave their country? Let Fidel take everything? Lino never would.

The alternative had been made pretty clear. Don't criticize the new order, and besides that, be enthusiastic, get involved. Emy's neighborhood recruiter for the new National Women's Federation had called her again on Tuesday.

"Señora Fernandez," she had begun sweetly.

"How nice of you to call." Emy had heard from her aunt about the cloying posturing of the meetings. Emy wasn't very good at pretending, so she had just not gone.

"We were so disappointed that you didn't make it to the last meeting."

Oh I'm sure, Emy thought. Didn't meet your quota. To the woman she said, "Oh you know, with the baby. And my husband counts on me to be near his office . . ." she let the sentence drift, not knowing what else to say.

The woman's voice turned harder. "Señora Fernandez," she said more formally, "*la Revolución* is counting on you too. Every one in our district needs to show their support."

Emy hated hearing herself say, "Oh I understand."

"I strongly urge you to attend next time. People like yourself - a doctor's wife - you need to be sure people don't wonder about your enthusiasm. You know what I mean?"

Emy hurried to say goodbye politely, fighting her temptation to hang up on the woman.

At first only Batista supporters had left. And rich people. But now it was normal working people, the ones that made Cuba run. One evening, her mother's friend Rosita had come over. Rosita was a spirited intellectual, a librarian at the University of Havana. She spoke in her usual precise Spanish, pronouncing each syllable.

"You know. I am not a political person. The only anti-Fidel thing I ever did was leave little notes under placemats in the cafes so people would find them. You know the kind of thing. 'No to public executions' or 'Elections now!' Hardly open insurrection."

"But you're not happy the way things are?" Lino asked. That wording had become code in Havana for "Will you be leaving?"

Rosita leaned forward in the caned rocking chair and paused for a long minute. She was clearly choosing her words carefully, "Lino, I am 100% Cuban and I love my country. I never dreamed I would leave it. But let me tell you what happened, what made up my mind for me." She took a slow dramatic drink from her tiny coffee cup and replaced it in its saucer. "A few weeks ago, I had lunch with my friend Blanca. We were sitting in *La Casa Potín* and talking about everything; we've been friends for years. Of course we talked about the government. How could you not these days? Since I am never one to measure my words, I said some things against Fidel that she didn't like." Emy smiled to herself, imagining how unmeasured the words had been.

"But then she told another friend of ours, Rita, what I had said. Rita called me immediately and told me, 'Rosi, you must be careful. You can't say what you think. People will go to someone in power and say you're against *la Revolución*. And that could be the end of you. Certainly the end of your job at the library.'" Emy knew how important Rosi's work was to her. "When I heard that," Rosi continued. "I knew that I couldn't live like this, hiding what I think, constantly looking over my shoulder."

Neither Lino nor Emy asked exactly what she meant. But by the end of that month, Rosita was gone. Emy eventually heard that she'd had to lie to her maid, telling her she was going overnight on the train to her sister-in-law's in Varadero. She left her house and car just as if she would be back the next day, for fear someone would alert the police and she'd be stopped at the airport, the treasured mementoes and photographs she had tucked among her clothes taken away. No one knew what was going to happen to her house. Most unoccupied houses were claimed right away for the government to use.

Almost home now, Emy turned the corner into her street. The *viandero* was still there, pushing his small cart filled with fruit and vegetables. One part of her world that stayed the same. She asked if his wife's arthritis was better, and he asked about the baby. Then she bought fresh salad greens for supper. As he lumbered off behind the cart, she heard him call out his distinctive jingle to announce he had mangos, *mangomangofrescosdeliciosos.*

She felt the tightness in her shoulders loosen.

3

Lino badly needed to talk. He decided to walk across town to see Padre Llorente at the University. The outgoing Jesuit priest, originally from Spain, had founded the *Agrupación*, a men's religious service organization and residence where Lino had lived at the University. They'd had many long philosophical talks over the years, and the priest had strengthened Lino's already strong concern for social justice.

He sat with Padre Llorente in the peaceful courtyard of the residence where he'd spent so many hours as a student. A few students passed through now, nodding at the priest, but it seemed quieter than Lino remembered. Still, the peace he had hoped to find there eluded him. He could hear his voice get more strident as he told Llorente about his experiences. As an internist and psychiatrist, Lino had been asked by the new government to help at Havana's notoriously neglected mental hospital, Mazorra.

"I agreed partly so as not to rock the boat, but really because I hoped to see things improve. Instead I'm sickened. Fidel's cronies in jobs they're not remotely qualified for. Good people pushed out because their politics aren't right."

The bells in the church began to ring and then to chime six o'clock. Lino stopped to listen to the soothing sound.

"Padre, it's just like before. Do the minimum and take all the money you can get away with. When I pushed the idea of working actively with some of the long-term patients, it was clear that not only were my opinions not welcome, they could hurt me."

"So what are you going to do?"

"Well, my child-wellness project closed a week ago and I just didn't show up for a few days, hoping they'd forget about me."

"Did they?"

"Of course not, I'm stuck now. They want me to represent the hospital at a big conference in Mexico. Meaning represent Fidel. The head guy actually used the word 'dangerous' when I talked about refusing."

"Do you think that was wise? You don't want to stand out." Padre Llorente waved to another priest crossing the courtyard.

Lino waited until the second priest was gone before he let his frustration burst out. "All those years we spent trying to throw Batista out, and we end up with Fidel instead. And you know what? He's actually worse; he's openly threatening normal people just because they don't go along with his contorted claims. Don't people see where this is leading?"

Padre Llorente put his hands on Lino's shoulders. "Lino. Lino. Don't let things get to you so much." He knew Lino well and he respected the strength of his beliefs. But he didn't want to see him dragged off to prison. "Listen, you can't blame people for wanting peace for a change. That's why they want to believe in Fidel's promises. Remember the day his army arrived in Havana?"

Lino snorted. "Of course. My neighbors were all there - very excited." Lino didn't try to hide his disgust. "They talked about it for days."

"Well then you heard. Flowers everywhere. People posing for pictures with the soldiers, on the tanks. Why do you think they did that?"

"Obviously they didn't know what was coming. They were fooled."

Padre Llorente put his hand up. "More likely they're just tired, of violence. And uncertainty. They want the government - some government - to work; they just want to get on with their lives."

Lino broke in, "But Padre, that's the whole point. Instead of something better, we've got all the old crap. Plus some worse stuff: control of the schools, veiled threats about what happens if you don't go along." Llorente put his hand up to stop the torrent of words, but Lino ignored him.

"You know it's true. It's happened to you, even in the church; and it's happened to me." Lino knew Padre Llorente hated what was going on as much as he did. And of course he could trust the priest. But he had hoped Llorente would share his outrage, show some readiness to take action. Any kind of action. The priest only shook his head.

17

"I understand. But Lino, give it some time. And please. Don't say these kinds of things in public. I worry about you when you get wound up."

Lino took the priest's hands firmly in his own, leaning in close to the older man. He enunciated each word. "I am getting very tired of hearing that."

On the crowded *guagua* coming home, Lino smiled as a young couple ran behind the bus. The girl jumped on and hung out the window while the boy continued to chase the bus, blowing her kisses.

Some things even *la Revolución* couldn't change.

4

On a Monday night in mid-November, the phone shrilled well after 11 p.m. It was Alain Molina, an internist Lino knew from medical school. He asked to come over; he didn't want to use the phone.

When he arrived, he accepted a whiskey gratefully. He was sweating through his thinning sandy red hair.

"I got a call from a friend in the militia. Antonio Martinez has been arrested. He's being held at G-2 headquarters in Miramar."

Lino's throat went dry. G-2 security police did all Fidel's dirty work. He was sure they were the ones who had taken his friend Rogelio when he had disappeared off the street a month before.

"What for?"

"No one knows for sure."

"Of course not."

"He's been pushing this National Medical Association. Hasn't even tried to hide the fact they've been meeting."

Lino felt a passing bitter pride at his friend's honesty. Antonio would never give in, on principle. Lino crossed to the terrace door and looked out. The trailing hibiscus from the upstairs patio was sending long branches down like a curtain. He turned back to Molina.

"Unfortunately, Antonio's also been very outspoken about the elections never happening." Lino looked out into the darkness in silence. "And so far he's right."

Molina got up and moved toward Lino, as though someone were listening from inside the wall. "That's the trouble. Fidel hates public defiance."

"So he could decide to make an example of Antonio?"

"He could. Anyway, his wife's frantic - she asked me what to do."

"What did you tell her?"

"Nothing's official. And I can't implicate my contact in the militia."

"So she's supposed to pretend she doesn't know."

"More or less. I told her to wait a day and then make inquiries. Her brother can help her. I've got to stay out of it. And you should too."

Lino had to stay calm. He wanted to leap to Antonio's defense, rush to G-2 headquarters, and drag him out of their hands. But Molina was right. It would accomplish nothing.

Lino hated that nervous voice within him that wondered. *Will Antonio give out names? What will they do to make him tell lies about other people? What might he say about me?*

When Molina was gone, Lino washed out the glasses and put away the whiskey. When he went to lock the window, he could see the shadow of a soldier at the building entrance.

A few days later Molina appeared again at the apartment after dark. He said he could only stay a minute. "Antonio's wife hasn't been able to see him, but the G-2 did admit they have him. They said the family could arrange a lawyer."

"Any trial date?"

"No, no word on a date - not even what he's accused of." Molina promised he would keep Lino informed and then he was gone.

"It's good about the lawyer." Lino told Emy with more hope than he felt, when Molina had gone. "If the whole trial is a sham - which it usually is - they assign a public defense attorney, just a puppet. With his own lawyer, Antonio might have a chance at a fair verdict. That is, if anyone does."

But the next week's events sickened Lino and made him fear for people like Antonio Martinez. Forty-four Air Force pilots from Batista's forces were tried in a highly public session as war criminals for bombing guerilla troops during the Batista regime. The court found they had acted properly under military orders and were not guilty. They were released.

When Fidel heard the verdict, he was outraged and addressed the nation on television in his usual paranoid fashion. "This verdict is a disgrace. It only shows us how the gangsters of the old regime still try to control *la Revolución.*"

Castro took a long dramatic breath. Lino, sitting next to Emy, was holding his own breath. "These criminals who attacked their fellow Cubans are guilty. And they will be punished." Lino snorted.

El Máximo Líder, as Fidel liked to be called, had spoken. The pilots were re-arrested, retried, and in spite of no new evidence, given long prison terms.

Even more sinister, the man who had presided over the first trial was found dead in his car, supposedly a suicide. Many of the witnesses and lawyers for the defense were arrested.

Lino felt his gut tighten with fear when he heard about the sentences and the "suicide." He and Alberto Rodriguez, another doctor he had trained with for years, were in the parking lot at San Juan de Dios Hospital.

"Clearly, whatever Fidel wants, he gets." Lino's mouth twisted bitterly. "Forget about truth. Laws. Those can always be contorted and broken to conform to our glorious leader's wishes."

"Careful Lino." Rodriguez looked around.

"I don't want to be careful, Alberto. You know I'm right. It doesn't matter how good a lawyer Antonio - or anyone else - gets." Lino spoke every word slowly and distinctly. "Today, there is no rule of law in Cuba."

Alberto unlocked his car and put his jacket and a stack of journals on the backseat. Finally he turned back to Lino. "Lino, remember this is one incident. Maybe such an obvious injustice will actually turn people against Fidel - it's so blatant."

When would people stop trying to whitewash what was happening? "Alberto, don't you see? Fidel has seized absolute power. None of us imagined his speed, his audacity. And he doesn't care if we like it or not."

Alberto wiped his brow with his handkerchief. "But Lino, surely some good things have come out of all this Revolutionary fervor."

Lino glared at Alberto. "Like what?"

"Lower rents. Land for farmers who've never had any." Alberto's voice was almost pleading.

"That land thing was a sham - part of Fidel's spectacle. *Reforma Agraria.* What a great idea. Give land to people who work it. And how did it end up? Taking land from farmers and passing the property to the State."

He left Alberto with a silent shrug, unlike their usual warm embrace. Lino was already in another world. He had passed through some moment when the truth became undeniable. Fidel had betrayed the movement; he had no intention of giving Cuba democracy.

Lino drove home the long way, along the Malecon, where the city and the sea met. He stared a long time across the bay harbor. He was baffled by people who, once they saw what was happening, quickly abandoned the essence and shape of their lives, left their goods as ransom, and crept off to Miami or somewhere else.

He had no intention of walking away from this country, the place where he belonged, the life he had built here. Those who wanted a real democratic government - and he was one - would have to fight again.

A few evenings later Emy and Lino sat on the balcony of their apartment, Emy holding their new baby, Lino Jr., who they called Po, on her lap. Looking out into the tranquil palms and bougainvillea of the common gardens, they could almost believe life was going as they'd planned.

They knew it was not. A thousand dangers threatened their lives. Some were minor; some could destroy them.

Lino sat close to Emy on the sofa, reaching to stroke the baby's head. His arm around her shoulder, he spoke gently but without hesitation.

"*Mi amor*, life under Fidel will never be what we want for ourselves and our children. Our country's being crushed. And our future with it. Nothing will change until someone fights back at Fidel." Emy could tell he was weighing his words carefully, willing her to understand, to face this reality.

She looked away, out at the brilliant green lizards criss-crossing the garden wall. Of course she had known. There had been undercurrents of violence and corruption for as long as she could remember. Lino had always hated it; they had tried with others to make things better from within the framework of their lives. But this was different.

"How long my darling? How long will this new violence last? When will we take back our real lives - the ones we dreamed of?"

He could not tell her.

She began to sing a lullaby softly, although the baby was already asleep. Then she stopped. She knew he was going to fight. Whatever the cost. What would happen to her? Would she be able to protect her family?

Lino pulled her closer to him as she struggled to keep back her tears. He looked down, straight into her eyes.

"I don't know what's going to happen, *mi amor*. But I won't let anything break the bonds between us."

They remained silent for a long time, Lino stroking Emy's cheek. He was so sure. She wondered if it would be enough.

Within weeks, Emy and Lino became active in the resistance movement. Remaining as invisible as possible, they urged others to commit, to take action against the Castro regime. They drove people who were already working underground, within Havana or to other cities, and asked no questions. They found safe houses for people already on the run, and took them food. They never asked why or who was involved. It was better not to know. It was only a matter of time before they themselves would become the hunted.

The watershed commitment came that winter with Lino's helping to form the Movement to Recuperate the Revolution, the MRR. Many of the men were from all over the country, people who had organized against Batista and were frustrated at the course being taken by Fidel's followers. Some Lino had known at the University or in medical school: Cesar Baro, Jose Almeida, Pelayo Torres, Manduco Zaldivar, and Andres Cao.

Others quickly joined the MRR, many working class people and farmers, some professionals, and plenty of middle class citizens with a social democratic philosophy. It was solidly Catholic. It would become the largest and best organized of the organizations opposing Castro.

In March the CIA made contact with the MRR. They wanted to bring former Batista officers into the organization. When the MRR refused, they asked again in May with more insistence. The CIA's need for control made Lino nervous. Why did they want to use Batista survivors when there was a strong resistance movement already in place? Why were they so anxious to be involved in the decisions of the MRR?

One night a few weeks later, Lino walked into the apartment from the clinic late. Emy was on the sofa in the living room, arms crossed, clearly seething. She jumped up when she saw him. "They've taken the mill," she almost shouted. "Just walked in with machine guns and took over." She took a deep breath and said more quietly, "Lino, Papa's devastated. He put his heart and soul into that place."

Lino held her close. This wasn't really a surprise. "*Mi amor.* We knew this might happen. How did he find out?"

Emy didn't answer, instead pulling away and continuing to rant, "There's no logic, no rules. If you have land, if you own a business - you're evil. So they take away the property of people like Papa, who give people work, treat them well. Like he was one of those big absentee owners. It's not the same."

Lino's body was tight with the effort of not just telling her the brutal truth. This was only the opening move; Fidel was out to crush the middle class.

They packed up the children and drove to Emy's parents' house. Her father, Jacinto Luzarraga, seemed drugged by grief over the loss of his family's sugar mill; he had run it most of his life. He was tall and thickset, with the dark eyes and hair of his Basque ancestors. He'd always been a hard worker who did things the way he felt was right. Now, even though he was retired, he clearly found the seizure a personal insult. He could only stir his *café* slowly and defend himself.

"I'm not a parasite."

"I know, Papa."

"My father built that mill out of nothing . . . you know, Emy. He worked like a dog. Right beside everyone else . . ."

"*Sí, yo me acuerdo, Papa.*" She leaned over him from behind and squeezed his shoulders.

"We didn't even have a nice house till years later." She sat down across the table and took the coffee her mother handed her.

Emy thought about growing up with her two younger brothers and younger sister at Enrucijada, the sugar mill on the north coast. It was a dusty rural place with none of the sophistication of Havana. But she'd loved the freedom and familiarity of such a small community. Before they'd gone away to boarding school, the kids had all gone to the local school and played with the workers' children in one rough and tumble group. Later on, as the oldest, she'd often gone with her mother to visit houses where someone was sick or there were family problems. Her mother wasn't gushy, just solid and principled, and she'd passed on to Emy her own awareness of responsibility for the lives of the workers. Emy believed her parents had given those people a good life.

"No one who knows you - or our family - could ever say you're a parasite, Papa. That's just propaganda. You know that."

He did not react. She could hear her mother singing to the baby in the living room.

She tried again. She couldn't change what had happened, but she could try to soften how he saw it. "Look how your workers still stay in touch, how they urge you to come visit, bring the grandchildren." He continued to stare into space; Emy wondered if he'd even heard her.

After that, Jacinto never spoke of the seizure except with his family, the only people he could still trust. In public, he walked away from political discussions. But the sadness in his eyes stayed with Emy. Her parents were now labeled "outlaws" in their own country.

Summer arrived in Havana. The usual cloying humidity covered the city. But this summer was different; the city was bound in an intricate tangle of brutality, deception, and fear. People didn't voice political opinions out loud, unless they agreed with Fidel. The people of Havana, normally sociable and outgoing, kept to themselves. Normally people loved to argue; now they just kept their heads down.

Closely knit families were being torn apart by opposing views of *la Revolución,* no longer sure how far they could trust each other.

People were reeling from 18 months of unrelenting shocks: a house seized, a father arrested, a school shut down. Every day a new loss to absorb. A cousin loses his farm, the *viandero* stops coming with his vegetables, the barber on the corner is given a choice: give his business to the government or be shot. A whole way of life gone.

Emy and Lino had never hidden their political feelings or their commitment to a democratic system. But now they and their comrades learned to lie, to steal information wherever they could get it, and do whatever they had to in order to protect each other.

They were careful to look normal, to appear to have typical lives, in spite of their support of the underground. As far as the government was concerned, Lino was still a respected doctor. So he and Emy had no trouble traveling to the U.S. Lino had to go while he still could. He had to find, one way or another, arms and support for the internal resistance, especially the MRR. He also wanted to protest to MRR exiles who were appointing resistance leaders in exile, thus confusing and undermining the internal resistance and making it easier for the G-2 to infiltrate.

In June of 1960, they flew to Miami for a week, supposedly to visit Emy's sister Juani. In spite of their cover, Emy was nervous as they passed through customs and searches. She was afraid her growing hatred of this government would seep out and leave a visible stain for all to see.

Lino found the Cuban exiles in Miami naïve and misinformed. Over and over he heard them brush off talks of resistance with breezy assurances that "the U.S. will never allow a threat like Castro just 90 miles away" or "we'll be in Havana for Christmas."

He met with the CIA, after they contacted him through Manuel

Artime, the MRR head outside Cuba. But Lino didn't sense the CIA was committed to the MRR work inside Cuba. How could he make them see that, not only did a strong internal resistance movement exist, but that it would be essential to the kind of mass uprising that could defeat Castro? All Lino got were vague promises of help. The CIA finally agreed reluctantly to begin dropping arms to underground troops training in the Escambray Mountains to the east of Havana, but Lino wasn't sure they'd come through.

Friends urged the Fernandez to stay in Miami where they were safe. "This is becoming a real Latin city. You could easily start a practice here. Bring the children over, start a new life."

But Lino was shaking his head before they got to the second sentence. How could he bow out when his country's future was at stake? He was stunned at the ease with which Cubans in Miami were willing to sit back and let matters take their course. Just walk away from their country.

"What are your plans?" Ricardo Carvajal, a wealthy exile, asked him a few days before their return to Havana. "Surely you're not going back?"

"What do you mean our plans? We'll go back to Havana, of course. Cuba's our home." He knew Carvajal had declined to contribute to the resistance.

It's supposed to be your home too, you know. But apparently only when things are going well.

"Just stick around. In a few months everything will change, and we'll all go back." Carvajal spread his arms in a welcoming gesture.

"And how can it change? If we don't fight, who will? I want to be sure we get our country back."

Carvajal just shrugged.

Already discouraged by the reactions he had seen in Miami, Lino pushed away frightening thoughts of what might lay ahead. The flight home felt very long.

5

The return to Cuba brought a wrenching decision for Emy and Lino. Even though Emy was pregnant again, they agreed they couldn't stay at the edge of the fight much longer. It was becoming impossible to balance their resistance work with a normal life. They would have to put aside the life they had hoped to build. Go underground. Disappear.

Emy had to be honest with Lino "The only part that hurts is the idea of being separated from the children."

"I know *mi amor*. We're fighting to regain a normal life; but to win it back, it seems like we have to give it up. God, I hate all this."

Emy told herself she shouldn't blow things out of proportion. This was only temporary. And she could still see the children, just not every day. How long could it last anyway? The sooner people like them put all their energy against Fidel, the sooner he'd be gone. The anti-Castro movement was growing; surely they'd all be together again in a few months, before the new baby came.

They decided that when the time came to go underground, they would put Emilia Maria and Po in the care of Emy's parents who would give them a stable environment. Emy took consolation in the fact that her parents had always been a huge part of their grandchildren's lives.

Emy's mother Emilia, tall with Emy's same chestnut hair, was sociable and intelligent - and unusually open-minded for her background. She usually heard people out, and she didn't judge now when her daughter told her their plans. Emilia Maria and Po wouldn't have the upset of their parents' constant comings and goings, wouldn't sense their worry. Emy's father held strong beliefs and one of them was family. He had come to respect and trust Lino and would support whatever he and Emy decided.

At the end of June, all of them, including Emy's parents, moved to a rented apartment in Miramar owned by a wealthy banker who had left Cuba but still supported the underground. Emy told herself that Po, six months old and Emilia Maria, one-and-a-half, would be fine there for now. Surely by the time Emilia Maria was ready for school they'd all be living together again. She couldn't guess that her children were beginning a life with their grandparents that would last their entire childhoods.

After four or five days, when they felt everyone was settled at the new apartment, Emy and Lino spent a peaceful day at the beach with the children, letting them go to bed a little later than usual. Emy read Emilia's favorite story, *El Ratoncito Miguel,* to her.

"Remember how Mami said she and Papi would have to go away for a little while?" she began, when Emilia Maria was tucked in.

"Uh huh." The girl's tiny face held caution.

"Well, that's why we won't see you tomorrow or a little while after that. But you'll be here with *Ma and Pa.* They'll take good care of you."

"Juani?"

"No, we're going somewhere different this time. To visit some friends. They need our help."

"Ana?"

"No *mi corázon.* Not Ana. These are different friends. You've never seen them. But they really need us to help them. So will you be good and stay here with Ma?"

Emilia Maria had not answered, just pulled the covers up and closed her eyes. Emy couldn't bear to ask again. *I have to trust she knows I'll be back, that she and Po will feel safe, that it will be enough.*

Then she kissed the sleeping Po in his crib, held her parents in a long hug, and drove with Lino to San Carlos, a working class neighborhood where the first of many "safe houses" waited. Emy, her eyes glistening in her flushed face, told herself over and over the separation wouldn't last long. Their real life of Saturdays in the park and early suppers with the children would soon return. Realistic or not, that was what she would think.

Lino was now the Military Coordinator for Communication for the MRR. His job was to encourage new resistance groups and convince existing groups to send supplies to resistance forces training in the Escambray mountains near the South Coast.

The country was in chaos. New regulations and prohibitions came out every day, many contradictory or illogical. Professionals were leaving Cuba in droves. New resistance groups formed as fast as the militia broke them up. By now the G-2 troops knew of the MRR and were on the lookout for its leaders. Still it was easy to hide; Lino always used the code name *Ojeda* with his contacts.

He and Emy moved constantly from one safe house to another as Lino met with members of the resistance to arrange for supplies and recruits. Her presence was essential. In the countryside people noticed strangers and traveling with a woman was less suspicious. Emy's being pregnant again made their disguise even better. No one noticed a young woman asking for directions or leaving a note at a café. They pretended to visit friends or relatives, often changing cars so people wouldn't notice how often they criss-crossed the country.

When they were first married and Lino was absorbed with clinics and his new practice, he and Emy had seen each other only at the end of the day. Weekends they had spent with extended family, especially after Emilia Maria and Po were born. Now they found themselves with long drives and time to talk. Lino had been afraid Emy would be depressed being away from the children. He knew that, even though she was a good Catholic, she worried about bringing yet another child into their fragmented lives.

But she took one day at a time, pushing away her longing for her children by sharing her pregnancy with Lino. They spent hours one day thinking of names and laughing over silly possibilities. They talked about the life they would build someday with their growing family. One day they detoured to the sugar mill where Emy had grown up, remembering how they met each other there for the first time when Emy's cousin brought Lino home on a school vacation.

But traveling for the underground, even in the light moments, they needed to be alert. They couldn't afford to overlook a figure that shouldn't be there, a casual remark that hinted at danger. Emy became keenly aware of Lino's strength and determination. It seemed as though Fidel's tyranny was a personal challenge to him.

Arriving one day in late summer at the Martinez' house in Maneadero, a small town in the province of Matanzas, Lino and Emy carried out the usual charade of pretending to visit family. Neighbors watched everything; the Martinez had been careful to talk up the visit of their "cousin" from Havana.

"*Bienvenidos queridos!*" Lourdes Martinez gave Emy a warm hug on the porch of the small white bungalow, even though they were strangers. "It's been such a long time. I'm glad we convinced you to come at last."

Lino and Fernando Martinez, a local mechanic, exchanged bear hugs, pounding each other on the back. "I see congratulations are in order!" Fernando gestured to Emy's rounded abdomen. "You've been keeping this one a secret."

Once inside they dropped the pretense. Lino and Fernando fell into deep conversation while Emy and Lourdes made coffee in the kitchen and talked about raising children in such scary times. Lino was grateful that Emy related to people so easily. Looking at the two women, he would have sworn they'd been looking forward for months to this chance to catch up. Her ease and patience made it easier to concentrate on what he had to do.

After dark two more resistance members arrived, with more faked effusive greetings. The four men continued the conversation in the tiny living room. Even indoors, their tones were hushed.

Emy and Lourdes served a simple meal of beans and rice with chunks of fried pork. The men ate without stopping their talk. About 11 p.m. they took off for the house of another member of the resistance. As they left, they made a show of stumbling down the steps as though drunk, shouting at each other.

Emy, asleep on the sofa, never heard Lino come in and drop to his floor mattress in exhaustion. The next morning he was up early, full of energy, and they were off again. Although the emotional goodbyes were staged for the neighbors, Emy and Lino did feel truly connected to the Martinez, as they did to all those who wanted to help the resistance. Fernando Martinez would be killed less than a year later fighting in the Escambray Mountains. They would lose touch with Lourdes when their own lives fell apart.

Emy found herself drawn to the many people they met and stayed with. She began to see Cuba in a wider way, to feel profoundly tied to it as she never had before. She learned to listen and hear beyond the words of the people she talked to. She lost count of all the trips, but each one strengthened the web supporting her belief in what they were doing.

They tried to vary their routine to allay suspicion. After leaving the Martinez, they started toward Playa Pinon, a seaside town where they would check into the Hotel Caribe and pretend to be vacationing for a few days.

The road was little traveled and the sun was brilliant. They stopped at the tiny cafe in La Roca. The place had only two tables, so the workers at one table joined the men at the other to make room for the Fernandez. Lino ordered cold drinks and sandwiches. Then he spoke loudly to the owner.

"*Señor*, I'm afraid my wife is not feeling too well. All this driving I guess. Would you have a room where she might lie down?"

"*Seguro, Señor*. We have a room upstairs that isn't rented right now. Here, I'll show you. You can tell me if it works." The two men disappeared upstairs.

"Are you going directly to Playa Pinon?" Mario whispered when the door to the upstairs room was shut. "There's a group about an hour east of there that might be able to help. Want me to set something up?"

"No, not yet. Maybe once I'm done in Playa Pinon. But that's my first priority. Do the people there know what hotel?"

"Yes, someone will be there as planned, once I confirm. We always reconfirm in case there's a hitch. You were later than we expected. I was worried."

"Then get word to them. We'll be there by three." Lino grasped the man's hand and thanked him warmly.

A few minutes later, Mario's son took off on his *velomoto* toward Playa Pinon.

"Actually, *mi amor*, I'm feeling a little better after the food." Emy smiled at her husband. "Let's just continue on to the hotel. I'd rather get settled and relax." The café owner nodded sympathetically.

Within months, it would be impossible to check into a hotel without bringing the police to investigate. But by then, Lino would be deeply involved with the fighting in the Escambray Mountains.

That afternoon, once Emy was settled in their room at the Hotel Caribe, Lino sat in the lobby reading the paper. An older man in elegant slacks and an open necked shirt sat down next to him. They appeared to strike up a conversation, and the gentleman, Jose Montana, offered to show Lino the fishing port where he owned a small fleet of boats. The two men spent several hours in the port and on the beach. Their conversation appeared spontaneous and congenial, as they ran into friends of Montana. But most of their conversation took place out of earshot of other tourists and of Montana's workers. By the end of the day, Lino was pleased with the setup in Playa Pinon; he felt confident about two key players - Montana and Reyes, the captain of one of Montana's boats.

"You must have gotten good news here. You look smug," Emy teased him when he returned to the hotel. "Sometimes I think you enjoy this visiting big-shot role you get to play."

"I always feel good when I find boats we can count on, people who know the coast." He hugged her. "And you know something, sometimes for a moment I can almost forget the problems and the danger. I'm here with my beloved wife, my almost baby, and dealing with people who really believe in what we're doing. We're gonna get those communist *bandidos* - wait and see."

When Emy and Lino had talked about her joining him in this travel, they had agreed it would only be worth the risk if they didn't let the tension corrode their world, if they could enjoy the good times in between.

In the years to come, Emy would think often of those months together and treasure them. Lino found that the soft-spoken girl he had married four years before was changing. He had worried about her being overwhelmed by the constant tension. Now he soon realized she was as strong as he, in her own way.

In early September they traveled to the rolling hills of Villa Clara on the north coast to attend a wedding. The Perez were supposedly their "cousins" and the Perez' daughter Patricia was the bride. They lived near the capital of Santa Clara, in a beautiful hacienda on their large cattle ranch. Here the hardships of Revolutionary Cuba were not yet so strongly felt; Lino was glad for Emy to have some luxury for a change. The Perez were warm and hospitable, even though the mother, Eva, was wrapped up in the details of the wedding. Emy, as flexible as ever, threw herself right into the arrangements. She always amazed Lino with her ability to slip right into the lives of others.

Soon she and Eva were conferring on the length of the veil. Patricia was a fragile-looking girl with dark hair down to her waist, barely 18 and full of plans. Emy found it nice to be away from the constant talk of supplies and strategy. She found herself relaxing in the novelty of laughter and excited talk about the wedding.

Her own wedding seemed centuries ago. She had been married at *La Coronela*, a retreat house near Havana where the small chapel opened onto an airy courtyard. She remembered how she had forgotten to bring the marriage license, and her mother had to go home and get it before the ceremony could start. Her mother had been so worried about whether the sleeves on Emy's dress would be too tight. Emy smiled now at such small worries.

Raul Perez and Lino retired to his library. "My wife's not happy about mixing the wedding and politics, but I told her it was too good a chance to gather lots of people without suspicion." He offered Lino a cigar from a mitered mahogany box. "Besides, these are not times when we can worry about social niceties." Lino wondered if Raul's wife might not be right. It would be hard to keep track of so many people, to be sure no one saw anything suspicious.

"Well your son tells me your parties are famous." Lino accepted a cigar but did not light it. "I'm sorry I can't just relax and enjoy it."

The next day, when everyone returned from the wedding Mass and the wedding dinner began, Lino and Raul circulated in the large interior patio lit by wax torches and iron candelabra. Raul introduced his "cousin" to other guests. At one point, Lino stooped down to talk to the bride's two young brothers, asking them if they thought their sister looked pretty. The sight made Emy ache to see Lino with his own children. How long would it be?

Then, while people were distracted by the champagne toasts, Lino slipped into the library where Perez had an elaborate transmission system set up inside a locked liquor cabinet.

As the evening wore on Emy enjoyed playing the role of old family friend. She moved through the crowd of people in her blue taffeta dress, her hair pulled back in a twist. The last time she had worn this dress was at Ana's wedding, when she was pregnant with Po. Before all this sadness and turmoil. She struggled to keep her spirits from slipping into melancholy.

Sitting between two neighboring ranch owners at the long carved table, she ate little, in spite of the platters of suckling pig and rice and black beans. She loved listening to the musicians and the local gossip of the guests. She did yield to her sweet tooth, accepting two pieces of wedding cake.

She watched smiling as Patricia moved among the guests with her new husband Alfonso. She wanted to freeze this moment in her mind. When would there be another like it? It was hard to believe young men like Alfonso were being shot not so far away in grey stone prisons. Families like this were losing everything, even bitterly splitting up, all because Fidel thought he knew best.

At one point she noticed a heavyset man in the main hall, frowning as he leaned against the wall near the library door. His glass was empty and he seemed to be staring into space. Was he anti-social or was he listening for activity inside? She decided to interrupt him and be sure.

"I don't think we've met. I'm Emilia Fernandez. My husband and I came down from Havana." His expression did not change. Finally he spoke, in a slow monotone.

"Oh yes, I think I met your husband earlier. A doctor isn't he?" He looked around. "I don't see him now." The man introduced himself but didn't elaborate on his connection to the Perez.

"Yes he is. He was enjoying the party but we had a long drive and he works so hard. I think he may have just slipped up to bed." She couldn't tell if the man believed her. "What a shame. He loves to meet new people."

He made no response. His lack of warmth made her suspicious. So she twittered on about the party, asking about other guests, trying to mask sound from the library. After a polite interval, he excused himself and moved back to the tables. She continued to keep him in sight until he left about an hour later.

Late into the night Lino used the transmitter to contact resistance groups in Pinos and Campera, putting them in touch with each other, arranging contact with new recruits. When most people were too busy with cigars and brandy to notice, guests began disappearing one by one into the library for meetings with Lino. It was almost dawn when the last guest departed, and Lino and Raul reviewed the progress over strong Cuban coffee and *pan tostado.*

Lino told Raul he felt good about the night's work. "Personal contact always brings bigger commitments of help. I got some new contacts I'll follow up on in the next few days."

Raul nodded grimly. "The movement is definitely growing, but so is Fidel's power. There isn't much time."

"I know." Lino suddenly felt very tired. "Anyway, I understand it was a great wedding." He touched Raul on the shoulder. "I hope we didn't make you too nervous by being here."

"It's fine." Raul spooned more sugar into his coffee. "We loved having your wife with us. And I'm glad we could do things right for Patricia. It may be a long time before any of us will be so carefree again."

Shortly after the wedding, on September 28, Castro established the watchdog neighborhood groups, Committees for the Defense of the

Revolution or CDR. Hiding got much harder; every block had people watching their neighbors, asking, "Who did you see on the block? What did they do? When did they leave?"

Emy and Lino traveled less, but each trip became crucial. They couldn't remember all the apartments and bungalows and haciendas they had slept in. They learned not to panic if the militia stopped them and searched their things. Their hiding places and invented stories became second nature. It was hard to recall their spacious apartment and the time spent with family.

When they were near Havana, Emy longed to see the children. She knew it was dangerous. Did the militia know who she was? She never knew if she might be followed, might lead the militia right to her family. Still, she cautiously met her mother with the children at different spots: the ice cream shop, the park, the beach.

It was hard to explain to the children why she came and went. Harder yet to hold their little bodies and then have to let go. If only she knew what the children thought, how they felt. They were so small to be in such a tangled world.

In the fall of 1960 Lino's second-in-command, Andres Cao, was captured and sent to prison. Now Lino had to travel to the Escambray to connect with people and arrange for supplies to be sent. Emy waited for him in a small safe house on the beach at Santa Maria del Mar outside Havana. She knew he was in greater danger with every trip. She slept a great deal, always waking to the silent beach sky.

6

A small wiry man stood in the doorway of his *bohío,* a hut of palm trunks with a thatched roof, set on the edge of his tobacco fields. He moved cautiously toward the six men, shading his eyes from the strong September sun with his hand. The man, Dominguez, was a *guajiro,* a peasant with a small farm. He was part of a covert support web that kept anti-Fidel guerillas alive in the Escambray Mountains. His farm was near Cumanayagua, on the highway from Cienfuegos city to Manicaragua.

As Lino approached with the driver and gave the password, Dominguez seemed to relax. Lino introduced himself only as *Ojeda.* The four other men, Plinio Prieto, his aide Mario, Enrique the radio operator, and Manduco Zaldivar of the MRR, all dressed in heavy jackets and boots, introduced themselves with false names as well. Plinio Prieto's name in particular would have been instantly recognized. A tall slim man with a military carriage, he had been a young teacher when he joined *Organización Auténtica,* one of many groups that fought beside Fidel against Batista. He had become Comandante of the OA. Once he realized Fidel's intentions, however, he had defected and led the OA in a new direction, fighting against the man who had once been his ally. He had just returned from the U.S. where he had been trained by the CIA.

"*Hola,* you made it." The peasant's gruff voice showed no emotion. "Which guys are going in?" Lino gestured to the four other men who nodded.

"Well, it's almost dark. We can't wait any longer - militia's all over the place. I'll give you water. Something to eat that you can carry with you. You'll need it soon." The farmer turned away toward the *bohío*.

The driver was anxious. "*Ojeda*, we gotta get back." Lino hugged each of his companions and walked away quickly toward the hidden car. No need to tell them how important this trip was - or how dangerous. Most perilous was Castro's new Law 923. The death penalty for anyone guilty of armed action against his regime. If you carried arms, you were guilty.

All but Mario had been trained on the outside for this duty. Plinio, a commander, and Manduco, a lieutenant, had both fought against Batista. Enrique, the radio operator, was a Cuban Marine who had deserted, gone out of Cuba for training, and snuck back in with Plinio.

Lino was glad to have Manduco with the group; the two men had been in medical school and the *Agrupación* together. Manduco was intense, always on the move, with a one-track mind. He would keep the group focused.

"What's next?" asked the driver as they reached the car. He was from Havana.

"Hopefully those men will be picked up after dark by somebody who really knows the area. There'll be a whole chain of guides who'll take them into the Escambray."

"Why at night?" The driver was straining to see the road.

"Because they have to bypass Cumanayagua on foot. Fidel has at least 16,000 troops there.

The driver nodded.

"Once they actually get to the mountains, they'll be under cover of thick forest."

Lino wasn't worried about the guides. They'd be men who'd used these trails all their lives and could take the men to the concealed guerilla camps without running into the militia. But his people would need stamina. The narrow trails in the forest were perfect for hiding, but trudging up the rocky winding paths would be hellish. They had no choice. Lino's job was to get Plinio safely into the Escambray where he could lead a joint operation with the MRR.

Perhaps more importantly, the four men were carrying the first radio equipment to go into the area. Almost 3,000 guerillas were training there in small groups, and more arrived all the time. Plinio and his aide knew how to use the equipment, and radio contact was critical to the arms drops the CIA had finally promised. Messengers were useless when you needed split-second coordination.

As he drove toward Havana, Lino felt a rush of excitement and relief. With Plinio in place, the internal resistance would become a major fighting force against Fidel. Serious military training could begin. With the promised arms drops, the fighters would not only be trained but have arms to defend themselves. He'd worked months for this.

Fidel was no fool. He already had 100,000 militia in the Escambray, sent to surround the area and cut the lifeline of the guerillas. Thousands of soldiers were camped on either side of the roads bordering the mountains from Cienfuegos to Trinidad. But once inside the mountains, Plinio would be safe. The farmers in these villages hated Fidel for taking away their land. No worry about informers.

Almost everyone living near the Escambray was part of a network supporting the guerillas, especially taking them food. The farmers had pigs, chickens, even milk cows. But it was more practical to leave dried pork or hard yellow cheese and canned foods in caches in the woods. There were plenty of wild rabbits, but it was too risky to hunt or build fires. There were always *galletas,* the large flat crackers fishermen had used for years. Once in a while, a farmer-guide would bring real food: fried pork, sweet fried bananas, maybe black beans and rice. Filling canteens was easy; the hills were criss-crossed by streams running from the peaks down to the coast.

Lino had discussed the whole operation with Plinio before they left Havana. "Our strategy is different, but the logistics in the Escambray are probably a lot like your old operation against Batista." Lino knew it took about two hundred people to support a hundred fighters: food, equipment, medicine. All brought in over those same paths during the night.

Plinio had nodded impatiently.

"You'll be constantly on the move. We won't initiate radio contact until three days after you leave Cienfuegos."

Plinio had nodded again. He'd travel with little more than a hammock and the radio, sleep wherever night found him. He'd done all this before.

Three days later Lino tried to contact Plinio at the arranged time, Saturday night at 11 p.m. He hoped for an arms drop soon, and he wanted to make sure everything was set on Plinio's end.

At the hidden radio setup inside a resistance member's house in the Havana suburb of Miramar, the transmitter sprang to life. Lino in Miramar, Plinio in the Escambray, and a third communication center set up in Guatemala should all be connected by radio. Lino received Plinio's message perfectly. Lino radioed back, "Radio working. Message received." Silence. Then from Plinio, "Please acknowledge you received our message." Lino repeated, "Received your message. Are you receiving?" The Guatemala center also radioed Plinio. No response. Then there was another message from Plinio asking for confirmation.

Lino clenched his fist and lowered his head to the table. *Shit. Plinio was not receiving their transmissions. The radio was receiving nothing!*

He tried for over an hour, sending messages out to Plinio, waiting tensely for an acknowledgement. Nothing. Plinio continued to ask for confirmation that his messages were being received. But no confirmation could reach him.

Lino was distraught. The group in Guatemala continued to report the same results; no radio messages were penetrating the Escambray. He felt a weight like a steel blanket fall on him. No working radio. No arms drop. No military force. He was back where he'd started. He radioed the Guatemala contacts to continue trying; Lino would go back to the Escambray with a new radio. He sent a last message to Guatemala. "Tell Plinio, if by some miracle you reach him, that a new radio is on the way."

Plinio never got the message to stay put. Knowing he was useless without a working radio, he tried to slip out of the mountains, along with Mario and Manduco, to find one. In Cumanayagua the three were captured.

The militia officer recognized Plinio as the defected OA head from the anti-Batista days. He sent him with Zaldivar and ten others to trial in Santa Clara. Plinio was declared guilty and shot in the head immediately. The radio operator Enrique escaped and returned to the MRR underground.

Lino was paralyzed with shock and grief at Plinio's execution. He couldn't believe that Manduco and Mario weren't shot too, although they received 30 year sentences.

"Didn't Plinio know how valuable he was?" Lino almost shouted at Emy. "He knew how Fidel thinks; he knew every corner of the Escambray. His kids are so young . . ." Lino's voice broke, torn by frustration and grief, near tears. There was a long silence. Then he looked Emy in the eye and said fiercely, "I **will** get that radio in. I'll substitute for Plinio. I'll take the damn radio in myself." Emy felt a shiver of fear. There was nothing more to say.

Plinio had been a critical link in the plan to organize and expand the internal resistance forces. Without him they needed more support from outside, and Lino had to get it. He also needed to know why the arms drops promised by the CIA during Lino's June visit to Miami remained just that - promises.

Lino went with Emy to the United States one more time in late 1960. They took advantage of the ongoing confusion in regulations and information to go and return without anyone realizing who they were, posing again as a young couple going to a family reunion in Miami.

Again Lino was disappointed though not surprised by the naive views of exiles and Americans alike about Castro's future. There was a string of excuses for the delay in the arms drops. Joint efforts between the CIA and the internal resistance were going to be tricky, if not impossible. Lino's perspective - the facts he offered - seemed to fall on deaf ears.

He returned to Havana with serious doubts about whether help would come from the United States, and more determined than ever to build the strength of the internal resistance.

7

On January 10, 1961 Lino returned to Placetas, on the northwest edge of the Escambray Mountains. For eight nights, he slept in a safe house in Santa Clara. For eight days he nosed around Placetas, trying to contact the *30 de Noviembre* guerillas. The group's name was an ironic reminder that Fidel had launched his supposed fight against despotism on November 30, 1957. Now Fidel was the despot, and new guerillas were fighting for the freedom he had promised and never delivered.

The *30 de Noviembre* group was now led by another veteran of the fight against Batista, Cesar Paez, a tough young man who at 21 had already been a *Comandante de la Revolución* in the fight against Batista. The group had contacts with the MRR in Havana, but it took time to get word to the Placetas underground. Resistance cells were strictly compartmentalized; even a tortured prisoner couldn't give up information he didn't have. Lino moved slowly, making careful inquiries that could incriminate no one. Long days passed with no sign. At last he reached the right people. Guides were arranged.

On January 18 Lino left the Dominguez farm headed for Fomento. With him were the same radio operator, Enrique, and a new radio to replace the one that had failed Plinio. For escort they had eight *30 de Noviembre* guerillas commanded by Pedro Franginals. Their local guide for this first leg of the trip was Alvaro, a short thick-haired farmer's son.

Alvaro was deferential but emphatic. "We'll travel at night, in total silence, without lights."

"The whole way?"

"Well, at least for the most dangerous part, crossing right through the militia lines. All you can carry is your arms and radio." Lino gestured to his equipment and nodded. "You left everything else in the jeep, right? In Placetas?"

"Right." Lino knew the precautions were important, but he was impatient.

Alvaro continued. "Two other columns of the *30 de Noviembre* are also on the way to Fomento, including some new recruits. But we'll all take different routes. That way, one group's capture can't put anyone else in danger."

An hour later, Lino, climbing the faintly marked paths up a steep incline, was glad for his heavy leather boots. He had never been in this deep forest of towering mahogany trees and cedars mixed with heavy pines. In another life, he would have been fascinated. Thick prickly jacanda bushes made passage even harder. Little moonlight penetrated - perfect for hiding. A person two feet from the path was invisible. Lino concentrated on keeping up. There was no talking.

After a few hours, Alvaro motioned them to stop and spoke in low tones to Lino, who was happy to catch his breath.

"Mongo should be here any minute. Up to here we've been in my country, but beyond this point I'd be as lost as you. Mongo's good. You won't even know he's here until he wants you to."

Alvaro was right. Mongo appeared suddenly; Lino never heard their exchange of passwords. The new guide was a large cheery man in his forties, clearly used to life in these mountains. The rest of the night they climbed, the wind growing colder as they got higher.

Leaving Placetas, Lino had felt weighed down by his heavy socks and shirt and the leather jacket he wore on top. Now, as the temperature dropped, he found himself shivering whenever he stood still. Only once did they stop for more than a minute or two. They were near a stream for drinking and took just enough time to silently chew the dried meat and crackers they carried and relieve themselves in the woods. Lino smiled for the first time in days when a *majá* snake crossed his path. "I think you make more noise than Mongo. He's a better slitherer," he whispered to the snake and smiled to himself.

By morning, they had gone 15 kilometers from Placetas. Mongo showed them how to hide near a clearing, each man digging his own narrow hole and crouching there as best he could, waiting for dark. Mongo came and went, looking for the next guide.

At last he approached Lino's hideout. "Bad news. The militia got a bunch of people at the farm. Somehow they found out about our columns and they overtook Martin's group."

Lino cursed. "*Y ahora?*"

"We'll wait for the next guide. Franco will know a lot more." When Franco, a lanky young peasant, arrived, he asked who was in charge and then addressed his comments to Lino.

"Look, I can sure as hell take you the next step, but government troops have surrounded the region and cut off the highways. The next guide in line, Guachi, might have found a way to sneak you through. But he was captured last night."

Lino felt like he'd been punched. "So, what do we do?"

"Go home. You'll never be able to cross the big highway from Manicaragua – you'll never make it." There was no way to reach Cesar Paez. No way to deliver the radio.

Franco left to see what more he could find out, while the rest of the group stayed where they were that night, then hid all the next day, hoping for better news. During the morning, Lino thought he might have heard the noise of military jeeps on the road. At sunset the second night, Franco came back. The operation was a failure. "The army's combing the area," Franco said. "You can either take the offensive and engage some of Castro's troops - pretty dangerous - or you can try to sneak back to Placetas. Neither one's gonna be easy."

After more discussion with Franco, Lino called the men together. "It seems like our best bet is to try to sneak out by walking through the Falcon River."

"The deep gorges on either bank may hide you if no one is specifically searching." Franco added. "It'll just be a matter of luck. It's flowing pretty strong. Hopefully the sound of the water will mask any noise you make."

Lino pulled Franco aside. "Here are the keys to the car we left in Placetas, an old Ford. You know Rogelio's garage there?" Franco nodded without hesitation. "The password is *gato con tres patas,* three-legged cat." Franco nodded again. "Get the car and wait for us two blocks before the bridge over the river. We'll be there in the morning, around 9, 10 at the latest. If we don't come, take the car back to the garage and tell Rogelio what happened. He'll know who to tell. Got it?" Franco repeated the instructions precisely and stuck the keys into his shirt. Lino thanked him and slapped him on the shoulder. "Be careful." Franco disappeared into the woods.

Lino's group waded into the river about 10 p.m., hoping the soldiers would be partying or sleeping. They held their guns and the radio in the air to keep them dry. Instantly their arms were numb, locked into the painful raised position. They could hear soldiers shouting and laughing on the bluff above the river. They kept trudging. The night was not cold, but their soaked pants clung to their legs, making them shiver until their legs too went numb. Long after midnight, they heard some shots. Lino's heart sank. He looked around, waited for a groan, a splash. Nothing. Probably some soldier taking shots at a rabbit.

He stayed in the rear, afraid someone might stumble. He was taking his turn at holding the radio up. It felt like a cement block; his arm throbbed. God, if he could just let the radio slide into the water for one minute. If only he had a scalding coffee, strong and jolting.

By 6 a.m. they were almost to the bridge where Franco would wait. Franco had told Lino where he might find stolen militia uniforms hidden in a stone cellar. At 8:20, dressed in militia fatigues, the group crossed the village. Their hearts were pounding. If even one real soldier was in the area, he'd know they weren't really militia; they'd be dead. The storekeepers and housewives in the street didn't even glance at them. They started to breathe again.

Franco arrived at exactly 9:00. Seven men crammed into the car and drove 30 minutes to the outskirts of Santa Clara. It was not only crowded but nerve-racking to have that many people in the car. They knew they looked suspicious, but no one stopped them. Everyone arrived exhausted but relieved to have made it. Lino told the others to take the car and continue without him and Enrique.

After they were gone, Lino contacted the MRR underground in Santa Clara, and they drove the two men back to Havana. Enrique fell into an exhausted sleep while Lino brooded. They were damn lucky they weren't picked up. How many times could they count on luck? So damn many troops out there. He unfolded his map and began thinking about a new plan.

When they got to Havana, Enrique pulled Lino aside. Both of them had circles of exhaustion under their eyes, but Enrique was also sweating and red in the face.

"Look I can't do this anymore. I'm a nervous wreck. I wasn't trained for this kind of operation. I'm just not a strong guy physically."

"I can understand. But you did fine. It was a hellish trip. They won't all be like that - at least I hope not."

"No. Please. I'm afraid I'll end up getting everybody in trouble. I just can't do it." Enrique was trembling, his voice plaintive.

"O.K. don't worry," Lino patted him on the shoulder. "You're damn good with a radio."

Five days later, Lino had a new plan. The western slopes of the mountains were crawling with militia. He would try from the east, near Sancti Spiritus. On January 28 he started out a third time with a guide, radio equipment, Francisco Castell the new radio operator, and Gabriel Riaño a prominent member of the underground. He hoped to rendezvous with a group led by another veteran of the fight against Batista, Merejo Ramirez.

They got to within four miles of Sancti Spiritus, to the house of a farmer who was their contact. The farmer shook his head. "I guess Ramirez got spooked. He came very close to losing a big group - they almost surrounded him."

"Well where the hell is he?"

"He must have headed further east till things quiet down." The guide shrugged his shoulders. "That's what they told me."

Lino took a deep breath. "O.K., no sense risking our necks any further."

They returned to Havana. The baby was due soon. He wanted to be with Emy, but the problem of putting a radio into the Escambray had to be solved. One part of his brain was constantly wrestling with how to do it.

In Havana, he met with the next highest in command, another founder of the MRR, Rogelio Gonzalez Corzo, code-named *Francisco*.

"I think we've got to go with the Yaguajay plan." Francisco said. For several months, there had been preparations to open a new front near Yaguajay Mountain, just north of the Escambray mountains but outside of the area surrounded by militia. .

Lino agreed. "If we can set up a front there, concentrating troops and arms, we'll have a chance of making a real impact."

Francisco nodded. "And if all goes well, we should be able to have a ship waiting there with arms."

"Even if the ship doesn't make it, we can receive an arms drop there a lot more safely than in the Escambray." Then Lino added. "In any case, we can surprise them; they won't expect us from the north. We might be able to fight our way through into the Escambray - finally."

Anticipating success, Lino and *Francisco* established a tentative plan for an arms drop as soon as Castell was in place. Lino would leave with Castell as soon as the baby was born.

8

When Lino returned to Havana he and Emy enjoyed a few calm days together. As soon as Emy went into labor, a friend brought her car to Santa Maria and took them to the hospital. Emy's doctor, Alexander Saker, an old friend, met them at the *Hopital de Nuestra Reina de Los Angeles*. Saker was very nervous about the hospital; he was afraid someone on the staff would betray them and have Lino arrested.

Saker told Lino "Listen, I don't know who those guys in the hall are, but I've never seen them before. I think we have to get Emy out of here." Lino nodded. Saker had good instincts. The doctor looked around once more. "I don't trust the staff here. Let's put Emy in my car."

"Isn't she close to delivering?"

"Pretty close. If she delivers in the car, that'll be O.K. Better than staying here. It's too big a chance."

Saker told the nurse on duty he thought the labor was a false alarm and he was taking Emy home. Then he whisked Emy into his car before the nurse could check her records.

The three headed for *Centro Médico Quirúrgico*, a small hospital where Emy's uncle was the main physician and the head nurse knew them well. The baby was born just after they arrived, at 7 a.m. on February 6, 1961. She was immediately christened Lucia.

By 8 a.m. Lino would be gone. He knew the doctors would take good care of his family, but it was wrenching to leave them. He had one hour with Emy, the first hour of Lucia's life.

He tried to memorize Lucia's tiny red face. From where he sat, his arm around Emy and holding the baby, he could see into the garden of the hospital. The peacefulness seemed impossible in such a world. He thought of how it should be: he and Emy walking out through the garden, taking Lucia home to her brother and sister.

Instead he was going to war. They were executing people in the field; not many of those captured made it to prison. He knew this hour with Emy might be the last time he ever saw her. This first hour with Lucia might be the only one he would ever have.

Looking out the window, he could see *Francisco* by the hospital gate, leaning on an old magnolia tree. He was smoking a cigarette. Then Lino saw him throw it on the ground. *Francisco* looked up at Emy's window and jerked his head toward the street. It was time.

"My beautiful Emy." His voice was thick and slow. "This is a time for spoiling you and instead I can offer no future, only memories." He handed her the baby and buried his face in her shoulder.

He could hear the warmth of Emy's smile in her voice. "We cannot lose faith now, *mi corázon*. I'll be well taken care of. And you. You must do what we have chosen. Promise me you'll only think about all we have together. And believe that we will have it again." He nodded, unable to speak.

He couldn't have imagined the hell he would pass through before he would again sit next to his Emy. That he would see Lucia again only as a grown woman, the week before her eighteenth birthday on a small airstrip outside Miami.

9

By the time Lino arrived at Yaguajay, hundreds of peasants calling themselves *Las Guerillas de Yaguajay* waited to join him. These recruits would make their way down the other side of the mountains in small batches; Lino and his group would travel separately. Castell the radio operator would set everything up at the drop zone until the permanent radioman Pablo, trained in guerilla warfare in the camps of Guatemala, could get there. Pablo would then take over from Castell and run ongoing radio operations in the Escambray.

Lino and Castell walked all night with their guide Chino into the mountains where the drop would be made. The terrain was hilly, and this time they carried no food or water. The moon gave the only light. Just before 3 a.m. the group stopped to rest. Lino, aching and edgy, stretched out on the cold ground and looked up at the stars lining the sky.

What the hell am I doing here? My wife and baby are alone. My children don't know me. I may never work as a doctor again. I've been defeated so many times.

He had no answer.

What's the message here for me? Am I stuck in some kind of John Wayne mentality? I cannot fail? I will do this at any cost?

What other choice was there? He closed his eyes and tried not to think.

After they rested a while in this high part of the mountains, Chino told them he couldn't find the next guide, so the three started back down the mountain. After three hours they were a mile and a half from the north coast of Las Villas Province. They could see the highway and the sparse traffic, even the patios of the houses close by. They couldn't walk anymore; they had to crawl most of the time behind the fences.

With relief they saw the sugar cane fields of the Nela sugar factory. In the predawn dimness, they arrived at a harvested sugar cane field with a wide depressed area on one side. Castell and Lino, exhausted, could hide there in a hole. They had no water or food. No arms. Just the radio equipment. Chino left to try to make contact with the other guides. Overwhelmed by exhaustion and anxiety, the two men stayed hidden the rest of the day. The searing sun hovered over the dry field like the tongue of a devouring dragon.

By midnight it had been 29 hours since they left the town of Remedios, and they were still trying to make contact with the guerilla support group. It seemed like they had climbed a mountain and come back down the other side, stumbling through rocks and thick masses of thorny bushes for nothing. A bad beginning.

Just after midnight, they were rescued by the main guides and taken to their house. After gulping down jugs of water, Lino and Castell left again for a headquarters camp, the same place where Camilo Cienfuegos had camped when he was fighting Batista years before. It was three o'clock in the morning on February 9, 1961 when they arrived at the site. It was Lino's third wedding anniversary.

The next morning, after sleeping *como los muertos* on a slope overlooking the camp, Lino and Castell organized the details of the arms drop and then sent the coordinates for the site to the communication center in Guatemala.

The core group of *Guerillas de Yaguajay* had arrived the same morning, and Lino organized the command and sent the first guards to their posts. Four days later Pablo arrived and took over the operation, checking the set up and equipment. The arms drop was confirmed for February 16 at 1 a.m. There should be a moon, but with or without the moon, the drop would go.

On that day, peasants congregating nearby were led to the site to receive the arms. They couldn't hang around long. Even in this northern part of the mountains, there were signs of militia everywhere. The site was a closed gulch where a drop would not be easily visible. It was a dangerous place to be caught, but if they were found after the arms were dropped, they could at least fight their way out.

By day's end more than 500 local farmers were painstakingly carving out wide shallow holes to hide the arms. Lino was ebullient. A radio setup and operator were in place. This drop would go forth; others would come after. Things were falling into place just in time. He and Castell were no longer needed; they could return to where they belonged - in the underground.

After dark, Lino and Castell hiked out of the mountains to the edge of the farmland. Lino caught his sleeve on a branch that left a deep jagged scratch on his forearm. He didn't stop to clean it out; he just wanted to get out of there. A jeep met them. Too conspicuous near militia lines, the jeep could take them only far enough to rendezvous with a car coming from a nearby town. The car should be waiting on the side road to Zulueta. It wasn't there. They drove back and forth trying to spot the car. On the fourth pass through, they slowed near a clearing and Lino peered into the dark field. Maybe the car had pulled off to be less visible.

He saw movement out of the corner of his eye. With horror he realized a troop of soldiers was bearing down on the front of the jeep. The road was narrow - no way to gun the jeep past them. Should he try to escape on foot?

He never had a chance to try. Already soldiers had reached the jeep, whooping as they dragged the three men out. Castell yelled as his shoulder caught on the door and his arm twisted backwards. Soldiers shouted at them, beating their rifles against the men's heads and jamming rifle butts into their testicles. Blood running down his legs, Lino felt one of the soldiers settle his FAL rifle on Lino's shoulder and fire into the field. Pain erupted inside his skull. Lino's eardrum was shattered. His shoulder burned fiercely from the rifle kickback. More militia rushed from the fields.

Felix Torres, commander of the troops, seemed both incredulous and furious to have stumbled over Lino's group only by chance. His thin nose angled to the right, giving his sneer a lopsided look. "*Cochinos.* Dirty traitor pigs," he shouted. "You'll be dead by dawn. I don't need a fucking wall. I'll hang you by your dicks from that tree!"

He called off the beatings. "Assholes! Leave 'em in one piece until after they tell us what they know. Then you can have all the fun you want. Show 'em what happens to fucking traitors!" He gestured to three of the soldiers. "Go on, stand 'em up. Stick 'em in the car till I'm ready." The three were roughly searched for weapons and then shoved into an old Chevrolet militia car.

Bleeding and shaking, Lino spoke quickly in low tones to the others. "Look, obviously we're carrying maps. We can't say we have no connection to the resistance." His voice broke as a wave of pain overwhelmed him, forcing him to wait before continuing. "But we can't give any hint about the drop - or the new front - no matter what they do." His voice was jagged, his tone ominous.

"So what the hell do we tell 'em?" Castell whispered. He checked the car window to see if anyone was coming.

Lino spoke more slowly, clearly straining to sound confident. The blood had started to crust over on his face. "We'll admit we're anti-Fidel but we'll play dumb. Just say we were told to wait in Zulueta - at the hotel - for people who would carry us inside the Escambray. We don't know who was coming. We don't know where in the mountains we were going. We know nothing. They may not believe us, but we have to try." Lino kept his neck rigid; the slightest movement set his ear aflame. He was amazed he could actually hear.

"I don't have any papers. Should I lie about who I am?" asked the jeep driver, Miguel, in a shaky voice. He was a sturdy kid who looked about 18.

"No! Tell the truth. Don't give them any excuse to shoot us." The boy turned pale. Lino touched his shoulder, pausing to quell his own panic before he spoke.

"Look, you're young. We'll try to convince them you just picked us up on the road. Just act scared and don't antagonize anyone." The boy swallowed and nodded.

In a few minutes, the car door was jerked open with a grinding sound and a short soldier with thin hair yelled at them. "Get out!"

They were roped to tree trunks. The soldiers smirked as they made sure the ropes were tight enough to cut painfully into the prisoners' skin. Castell and Miguel were each led in turn to face a glowering Torres. From what Lino could hear, they stuck to their stories; Torres seemed satisfied. Then Lino was untied and dragged over. Torres asked his name. "Fernandez, Lino," he replied without expression. "From?" Torres snarled, shoving his face in Lino's. Lino wanted to vomit on him. "Havana," he said instead.

He held out his driver's license.

"Ahhh . . ." said Torres with mock admiration. "Doooctoooor Fernandez. We have a *Señor Doctor* here. Now why would a rich doctor wanna leave his city life and camp in the mountains?" he asked mockingly, turning to his lieutenants. "Could it be he's not really *El Señor Doctor?* Could it be this isn't really his driver's license? He looks pretty damn filthy for a doctor."

Lino ignored the baiting comments. If Torres was busy with gratuitous insults, he probably had no suspicions, didn't realize he had *Ojeda* in his hands. If he did know, he would've already shot Lino.

More sarcastic questions. More insinuations. He didn't rise to Torres' bait.

At every moment he expected to hear the order to line them up for a firing squad. It took enormous effort not to sink to the ground; he was exhausted and the slightest movement worsened the excruciating pain in his ear. He was thirsty and hungry. Above all he was thinking about how it would be to die. He told himself he would keep the vision of Emy's face before him at the end. He would leave this world thinking only of his time with her.

Dawn was breaking on the edge of the fields. Torres, looking tired and pissed, gave a sharp order to load the three into a car and take them to G-2 headquarters in Santa Clara. Had he decided they weren't worth shooting? Or was he taking them to the professionals who really knew how to get information?

They had been captured at 1 a.m., exactly when the drop was being made. Doubled over with pain, praying, and dreading what they would do to him in Santa Clara, Lino tried to cheer himself with the thought of the drop made that night. Whatever happened to him, they'd finally be able to fight back. Luckily, he wouldn't hear what actually happened for many months.

In the gulch, Pablo and the farmers waited besides the gaping holes in the dirt. No sound. After about 20 minutes a plane arrived over the area and circled several times as arranged. Then it started to move north, turned, and circled once more, dipping low.

Pablo was screaming. "What's the matter with that idiot? The shape of signals is just what they asked for. Why don't they drop?"

The plane dipped its wings again, as if in regret, turned slowly, and headed back toward the coast. Pablo was apoplectic. "We're risking our goddamn lives here - you bastard! You're just looking for an excuse! Who the hell's side are you on?"

The sound of the plane's motor faded. "Shit," was all Pablo could say.

Militia troops were closer than Pablo and the others realized, close enough to follow the sound of the airplane. Minutes later, they streamed into the gulch and captured 487 people. For hours, they marched groups of prisoners to the highway, to trucks that would take them to army headquarters at Santa Clara. Pablo, the core group of guerillas, and some of the farmers would end up in prison at *Isla de Pinos* with Lino. The rest were sent to Santa Clara prison and released a few months later. Their loyalty to Lino would be intense. He was the one who had done everything in his power to make their sacrifice worthwhile.

Midmorning the following day, the sun at the drop site was warm on the soil piled high beside the deserted pits. A vertical bank of dirt cracked a few inches. A larger piece of earth shifted. An arm emerged from the soil and scraped away at the dirt. Another arm emerged, then a torso, a head, and lastly, filthy legs and boots. Three other piles came to life. Four of the farmers had dived into the dirt piles when the militia attacked. Overwhelmed by so many prisoners, the soldiers hadn't even glanced at the dirt. Four farmers had been luckier than Lino.

10

Emy and baby Lucia left the hospital in mid-February, entering a world of unknowns. She was in limbo, not knowing about Lino - if he was still free, alive, executed. Was the government watching her? Did they even know who she was? She needed to be careful where she went, who she saw. Her children needed to be safe.

She took refuge with an old school friend, Doyle Caballero, living now with her husband in Havana. She could recover her strength and decide what was next. Time to think.

The gentle days in Doyle's house were a gift, a cocoon of warmth and memories. Two old friends in the darkness of night, feeding and rocking Lucia, gossiping, hiding out from life.

Reality crouched nearby. Lino gone, Emy's spirit hovered close to her parents and children. When she left Doyle's, she moved the whole family to the safe house where she and Lino had stayed, in the sandy isolation of Santa Maria del Mar, 30 minutes from the city. Even in tropical Cuba, this was not beach season; only two houses were occupied on their stretch of coast. The house was a simple rectangle of stucco and tile where life was lived around the courtyard patio, a palm frond shelter protecting them from the sun.

This house was a haven for the new outcasts of Cuba. Resistance members and their families, or the wives and children of those already in prison, came for the day. Whole afternoons to forget the turn life had taken, to let go and play in the surf as though life were still as before. For Emy time was frozen, waiting for news of Lino.

The first week of March, the news came, and life was changed forever. A part of Emy would live in this moment for the endless years to come. She was at a retreat with women from the Congregation of Mary, led by Padre Llorente from the *Agrupación*. Ironically, the retreat was at *La Coronela*, the Jesuit retreat house where she'd been married four years before. The simple open architecture and the intimacy of the small chapel brought Lino to her mind as clearly as if he was beside her.

It was the first day of a three day silent retreat. After lunch each woman rested or prayed in her own room. When Emy answered a soft knock on her door and saw an older friend from the retreat standing there, she was puzzled. This was a silent retreat. As soon as the woman spoke, everything was clear.

"Padre Llorente would like to talk to you in his office."

A wave of fear crashed over her. But of what? So many things could go wrong. She'd lived so long in uncertainty, in a world where she'd lost control, that her fear was free floating, unfocused. She crossed the courtyard to Padre Llorente's office.

The stocky Spanish priest waited in the hallway. She watched his short stride as he came towards her, walking quickly as always. But his usually animated face was still.

Padre Llorente, who knew her and Lino so well, had long been a part of their lives. He had known Lino as a student at Belen and later at the *Agrupación* where Lino had lived. He had married Lino and Emy in this very place.

In the office she sat down quickly and waited.

"Emilita my dear. We've been notified by the wife of Patricio Suarez - I think you and Lino know him - that Lino has been captured." He paused. Waiting to see if she would collapse? "We think he is in Santa Clara. Patricio is in custody there. I'm afraid there are no other details."

Cords seem to pull tight in her chest, a corset to keep her heart from cracking open. She wants to wail her overwhelming sadness, a long keening lament.

I have lost him. Our life together is over.

But she is silent, forcing herself to concentrate, to do as Lino would: analyze, plan, find a way to cope.

He is alive. A miracle. Executions are a daily thing, with no pretense of consistency or of looking for the truth. No relationship to the seriousness of the crime. He was not shot at once; the first raw danger is over.

Then desolation assaults her. Lino is not coming home, for evenings of talk, of love snatched between hurried meetings and abrupt departures. No more surge of relief at hearing his voice or pressing her body into his. She is alone. Maybe forever. Her mind see-saws, lifting and letting go, relief and desperation. He is still a presence in their lives. While he is alive, in whatever grimy stone cell, he is a force in her universe, the foundation of her family.

He hasn't been tried yet. They would have told her; they are never loath to deliver pain. Surely if they haven't shot him right away, he is safe in prison. She knows nothing is that sure. But she clings to her idea.

Her hope is like the sand forts the children build, so safe by day, standing far back from the water. But with the tide, the waves come and wipe out everything. Hope sinks, dissolves, until by morning, nothing remains. But that would mean no hope. And she cannot, will not, lose hope.

She stands. "All right. Is that all? Thank you." Padre Llorente looks at her with his dark sympathetic eyes and touches her lightly on the shoulder as she passes. Compassion? Pity? Perhaps just understanding. He cares for Lino too.

She walks slowly to the chapel, the very same space where she and Lino bound their souls and futures together. She remembers the comforting new capsule of their vows, the first moments of their marriage. The simple reception in the gazebo, the freshness of the garden around them.

Now she feels Lino close as she prays for him. When he left, she put him in God's hands. And that is where she must believe he is today. She prays too for herself. And for all the others.

She feels as though she is watching herself from afar. How unprepared she is; you can't prepare, not until it happens. Now it's here; she must find the strength to confront it.

God will give me what I need.

A sudden shift in thought: consider the implications. What will happen to the people around him, around her? Her friends could be interrogated. Anyone she has seen or been with will be checked out, interrogated, hassled.

She must give no further fuel to the police. Say nothing. Return to the retreat. Silence is easy. Her mind is in chaos; she cannot even form a sentence.

She finishes the retreat, her mind twisting and coiling with emotion. On the last day, the group picture is taken. She tries to look serene, manages only a thin uncertain smile. The others might know, but she says nothing.

The retreat over, she drove home to her family at the beach, pensive and sad, dreading the conversation with her parents, the one that would make Lino's capture real. The idea of Lino's arrest had lurked about them all for months, half-expected every day. Still, it was agonizing, arriving home, to say the words out loud.

Shock and fear spread over her mother's face; she immediately began to cry, holding Emy close. Emy could see her father begin to crumple, then force himself to stand tall.

"It could be rumor - you never know."

"At least we know he's alive."

"I'm sure we'll hear more soon."

After the first shock, they reacted as she knew they would: reassuring, full of concern for her, holding their own pain in check. They struggled to be resolute for her; she did the same for them.

She felt fiercely drawn to her children, kept them close to her that night and in the first long days of dread. Their father was powerless, gone from their lives. They must get out of Cuba, be protected from the evil seeping in everywhere.

Her parents were in danger too. Her father, already branded as a capitalist and a traitor, would never be allowed to work; he might even be arrested. All of this swirled in her head, but no decision came to her.

She wasn't sure what she was waiting for. Lino's execution? no matter what happened, he certainly would not be with them for a long time. She and Lino had talked about the possibility of capture, and Lino had told her he would probably not survive, would most likely be shot. They had made no plans for this kind of agonizing uncertainty.

In the first months she seldom left Santa Maria, but many resistance people still came to visit. For them a day at the beach was a respite from the endless violence and suspicion of Havana. Even Emy could let go a little on those days, enjoy her children, help to make a meal of whatever food people had been able to bring.

If these people asked, she told them simply Lino was in custody. She never told them her source - better to say as little as possible. To outsiders who asked about Lino, those she trusted less, she pretended nothing had happened, saying only, "no news is good news" or "we think he is fine."

There really was no news, until one day when Padre Llorente came to the house to tell her about a cursory letter Patricio had smuggled out to his wife. *Lino and I shared a cell for two days; he was in good spirits and appeared not to be injured.*

That was all. She should be grateful; someone's life had probably been risked to get that information out. But she wanted to scream, aching for more information. How had they gotten him? Where was he now? What would happen next? But of course no one could answer that.

The one person she took strength from was her friend Raque de la Huerta. It was as though Raque's determined spirit counteracted her own feeling of drifting, waiting, unable to move ahead. Her husband Rene, one of Lino's professors at medical school, was not in the resistance, but was open about not supporting Fidel and was feeling heavy pressure to become involved with Revolutionary politics in academia. Raque never faltered in keeping up a normal life; nothing seemed to faze her.

One day she appeared with her six children at Santa Maria, tall and collected, her blond hair pinned up elegantly as always. Emy was delighted; it had been a hard few weeks, and she looked forward to Raque's warmth, her sensible encouragement and her willingness to listen.

"Here you are, c*ara,* the baby clothes I promised for Lucia. She should just have time to grow out of them before I'll need them again." Raque was expecting her seventh child; Emy was cheered to see how she seemed to relish each new baby even as her family's future grew steadily more precarious.

"You remembered. Thanks so much, Raque." Emy felt like a bright awning had been opened over her glaring airless day. "How can you stay so calm and organized?"

"Nothing to it - the trick is to never stop moving." Raque grinned and gave Emy, with baby Lucia in her arms, a long encircling hug.

The day was warm, even for early spring. They left the younger children to nap in the house with Emy's mother and made their way down the long sloping ground to the beach. They settled under one of the thatch-roofed shelters that had dotted the beach for years; from there they could watch the older children play near the water.

She told Raque about the letter from Patricio. Raque knew about Lino's capture, but they hadn't seen each other since then, and Emy was looking forward to a long talk about it.

"God, Emy you seem so calm. Are you still in shock?" Raque leaned over to calmly retie her daughter's bathing suit, but Emy could tell she was concerned.

"Maybe I am - God I don't know. What else can I do?"

Raque made a face. "Be human. Go crazy like anyone else would. It wouldn't be a disgrace, you know, to just howl and weep."

If anyone else talked to her like that, Emy would feel threatened and close herself off. It felt dangerous to test this thin layer of calm that was getting her through. But she knew Raque wouldn't push her further than she wanted to go.

"Oh Raque, what good would that do? But you're right. I thought I'd collapse if this moment came, hearing he'd been captured."

"I'd have been surprised if you had. You're not the collapsing type."

"But I never had to face anything quite like that. You can't imagine, those first few hours . . . I had to feel my way . . ." She looked up at the protective thatch of the shelter. The wide white beach was deserted, all theirs, as it usually was in this season. The horizon disappearing into a blue haze in the distance was a balm to both the eyes and the spirit.

Emy went on. "But as I got used to it, I realized - odd as it sounds – that nothing changed when I got that news."

"Come on, Emy. You can't tell me that everything isn't different now that you know Lino is in their hands."

Emy welcomed Raque's directness. She didn't hide behind sentiment or pity as many people did. It didn't mean Raque didn't care, and it made Emy feel less like a victim.

"But Raque, it didn't really start with Lino's arrest. It all started the day Fidel took over - that's when we lost control of our lives." She opened the old thermos and took a sip of lemonade, then offered it to Raque who shook her head.

"Oh Raque, remember when Ana Maria turned six? Not even two years ago. It was warm for fall. We all drank lemonade on your terrace and the children ran wild. The patio was so cozy and secure."

"And the bougainvillea had really taken off. Spreading wildly over the stucco. All those scarlet flowers."

"And then wham. Nothing but fear and confusion. All of us deciding what we dare to do, or dare not to." She thought of the long months of traveling underground with Lino, of leaving her children for weeks at a time, the slow decision to stand and fight.

The two women were silent. They could hear the children

screaming as they leapt in and out of the lucent green water, chasing the retreating waves.

"So God, yes. It makes me sick to think of Lino at these people's mercy. They're sadists, and they answer to no one." She shook her head. "But it's not new, not a shock."

Four-year old Javier padded up and leaned on his mother, smiling shyly at Emy.

"It takes a while to realize: nothing protects us anymore. You grow up thinking you're a certain person: your family, school, who you love, what you contribute, who counts on you. You assume your life will go a certain way. If you stick to what you believe in, follow the rules . . ."

Emy stopped, thinking about all Lino's work at the neighborhood charity clinics - her own work tutoring kids through the church. "And then somebody says that none of that counts -"

Raque broke in. "You mean some jerk tells you that you can only have the life **they** think you should have. You have only the rights **they** decide you can have." Emy had seldom heard Raque sound so bitter. When she spoke again, she sounded more like her own self. "What happened to all those things we took for granted? It seems like they slipped away when we weren't looking."

She wrapped Javier in a giant towel and pulled him into the hollow of her lap.

Emy sighed. "But I'll tell you, if Lino were here, he'd say we still have one thing. Ourselves."

She glanced at the children a few yards away, now engrossed in digging a shallow trench across the sand. She was glad they all hadn't come demanding attention. She needed this time with Raque.

"Lino has this steel will. He never loses his belief in himself. I'm sure that's how he's getting through this. If he is."

Raque stayed silent, trying to absorb the idea that Lino might already have lost his battle.

But Emy continued, "People yell at me, tell me I'm a traitor and a coward - a lowly worm. But they can't make me into something I'm not."

She shaded her eyes and looked across the water. She and Lino had spent their honeymoon at a beach like this one, walking in the same gentle surf, imagining a new life emerging, a life that instead had been pulled out by the roots.

"I am so many things: my past, my family, everything I've said and done and believed. I am part of that Cuba - the one that formed me, not Fidel's Cuba. I grew up at a sugar mill, where people took care of each other, for heaven's sakes." She stopped, feeling a little embarrassed at her outburst. "I'm just beginning to realize how strongly I feel. Whatever Fidel says, I love my country."

Raque's voice was discouraged. "And all you can do is watch it be destroyed."

Emy crossed her arms over her chest, hugging herself protectively. "God, it feels like that. But Lino and I said from the very beginning we wouldn't go along. No matter what. I shudder to think of what that may mean for Lino."

"And you? The children?"

"I'll have to get them out somehow. Oh Raque, I'm afraid of waiting too long. But I just can't face it yet. I keep hoping . . ."

Raque said nothing, just watched a tiny grey and white bird racing a wave across the sand. She spread out the towel and laid Javier down to nap. The silence grew long but not uncomfortable. Emy seemed engrossed in burying her right foot in sand. Raque spoke softly.

"How lucky Lino is, to have you here for him. I wonder if he knows how strong you're becoming."

Emy lifted her foot and cracked the sand cover open. "Oh don't worry." She gave a half-chuckle, trying to lighten their mood. "He's seen me stand my ground a few times in our marriage. I'm not that easy to push around."

She shook her foot vigorously and brushed the sand off with her hands. "God Raque, if only I could see him for one single minute. Tell him I'm here. That we'll be O.K. All of us."

She stood up and called to Emilia Maria not to go any further into the water.

11

In late March, Rogelio Gonzalez Corso arrived unexpectedly at Santa Maria. Lino's closest collaborator in the MRR, he had been the one waiting in the garden to take Lino away the morning Lucia was born. Emy had known him since school days, a large robust man who had lived at the *Agrupación* residence with Lino. They were both very fond of him, and he had recently become engaged to a school friend of Emy's.

He appeared, worn and wary but smiling for her, on a sunny spring morning. He brought a gleaming cherry wood cradle for Lucia, beautifully carved with soft metal screening to keep bugs out. Emy was overwhelmed; there was still kindness and beauty after all. In all the chaos of his life, Rogelio had taken the time to find this cradle and bring it all this way to her.

"Oh Rogelio, this makes me feel so comforted and cared about. I'm so cut off from Lino."

"You are cared about, Emy, by all of us. This baby too. She deserves all the good things she would have had if this awful violence hadn't come."

She had given him a warm hug when he left and wished him God's protection.

Her blessing didn't work. Three weeks later he was captured, taken to *La Cabaña* prison, and executed there three days later. Emy was devastated, her heart perforated with grief. She pictured the horror of his death, his cooling body sinking to the ground. This caring man, young, full of principles, so ready for life - destroyed. Is this how life would end for Lino?

In a strange way the horror of Rogelio's death gave Emy a new strength. Her fear of the regime seemed to curl up and transform itself into outrage and determination. Lino's vulnerability would always frighten her; she would need to act cautiously to protect him. These monsters could do to Lino what they did to Rogelio.

But she would fight them every way she could, until the end - the unthinkable end, if it came to that. Fidel wanted to destroy men like Lino with humiliation and isolation, the grinding threat of destroying their lives and their families, convincing them they couldn't beat Castro's system. She wouldn't let it happen.

In mid-April, learning about the invasion at *Bahía de Cochinos*, the Bay of Pigs, and hearing planes fly over on bombing raids, Emy, like a million others, had a moment of wild hope. This could be the end of the nightmare, the return to sanity. But it was not to be. Fidel crushed the invasion in days. Emy was devastated. Why had it been such a total failure? She knew the resistance had been strong and ready, but they were never pulled into action. Maybe Lino would understand.

After the invasion, the militia, ever more belligerent, set up cannons on the beach below the house in Santa Maria. They installed an anti-aircraft gun manned by two old men who sat next to it every day, hour after hour in the sun. Life took on an eerie banality. Emy's father would get up very early to listen to Voice of America, now a criminal act. Then he would wander down to take *café con leche* to the two old men by the gun, and they would chat about this and that, as though they weren't from two different worlds.

When the wife of one of the men began coming along to keep him company, Emy invited her to come to the house to use the bathroom if she needed to. People were still people. She wouldn't let this sick regime pull her into its sour system of suspicion and fear.

Sitting on the patio one fresh April evening after dinner, she was delighted to hear a familiar breezy voice from the house.

"*Buenas Noches, Señora*, how are you?" Then without a pause, "Is Emy on the patio? I'll find her. Thanks. Oh, is that the baby? I have to hold her. I'll be right back."

And there was Vicki, full of energy, banishing the drabness of Emy's thoughts. Emy put Po down and ran to hug her. Vicki Andrial was a younger friend from Emy's Catholic women's group, a tiny woman, just a girl really. Her dark bouncy hair seemed to mirror her enormous enthusiasm for everything she did. Vicki had always told Emy she had the perfect life - a handsome young husband, beautiful babies. But of course that was before. No one had a perfect life now.

Vicki had studied economics until the University of Villanueva was shut down. Now she worked at one of the foreign embassies, always on the move, full of life, even in the exhausted paranoia that had overtaken the country.

She'd been dating Manduco Zaldivar only a short time before he joined the MRR with Lino and was captured with Plinio Prieto. But there had obviously been a strong bond already; she visited him in prison as devotedly as a wife.

Emy's spirits always lifted when Vicki came. She simply didn't take no for an answer. If you didn't know what to say, she'd be there to fill the silence, or to say just the right thing, help you talk your way out of something. Emy loved her irreverence, her sense of mischief.

The two talked in the darkness until neither could keep her eyes open. Then Vicki, in spite of Emy's entreaties to sleep over, took off in her little Fiat and returned to Havana.

There was no official word of Lino. Emy had been startled to hear from his father that he'd been allowed to visit Lino very informally during the Bay of Pigs crisis. Lino had by then been moved to *Topes de Collantes*, a mountaintop prison in the Escambray Mountains, and his father said he seemed well. But Emy had no official status; probably couldn't visit until after his trial. And there was no word of that. All she was allowed to do was leave a package for him at the prison, a grocery-bag-sized rattan carryall called a *jaba*.

She knew from other wives how desperately the prisoners needed everything: food to boost their meager diet, blankets, clothes, things to read, and paper to write letters. In the first *jaba* she put a small picture of the children, and then added some underwear, a quilt, powdered milk, and a candy bar tied with a bright pink bow. She was not allowed to leave a note, but she wanted him to feel the brightness of her love.

She made the long trip to *Topes* for the first time in early May, leaving the children with her parents at the beach. It was a two-day journey with her decrepit old Opel, and the first day she drove as far as Santa Clara where she stayed in a hotel. She knew people who lived nearby; it would have been comforting to be with them. But now Lino was officially a criminal and a traitor; she didn't want to taint anyone with her presence.

On that day, she had two flat tires. People were very kind, stopping to help and, in one case, giving her a ride to the garage in the next town.

In the back of her mind, she hoped she might be allowed to see Lino once she showed up at the prison. It didn't happen; the soldiers just took the bag and turned her around immediately. The only thing she learned was that *Topes* was a high forbidding place where cold winds blew even in May.

She returned on the coast road from Trinidad to Sancti Spiritus. Thousands of militia lined the road, camping while they organized their sweeps into the mountains to capture guerillas. Like packs of jackals ready to pounce. She drove through a sea of green uniforms. The guards, standing every few kilometers along the road, glared but did not stop her.

She was a woman alone on this road, only 22 years old. There were no friendly townspeople as there had been on the way out. No one knew where she was; she hadn't dared tell her parents of such a dangerous trip. She couldn't invite her friends that were still in Cuba; they had their own problems, often a prisoner to visit in some other part of the island.

If she had a flat tire here . . . She didn't want to think. She doubted these soldiers would help. She simply prayed and concentrated on making it each mile closer to home. To keep her fear at bay, she let her thoughts drift to her life with Lino, before fear became a part of every waking moment.

By nightfall she was back at the safe house in Santa Maria. Was the trip worth it? Would Lino even receive the *jaba*? Would he feel the love packed inside, the unwritten message that she was there, concentrating all her force and determination on keeping him safe?

Things were closing in on her family. Emy was just finishing breakfast with the children, Lucia in her arms, one overcast June morning. Without warning, a group of six militiamen barged into the patio. Armed, they made no attempt to be pleasant or even to acknowledge that they were in her home. She could see her parents in the doorway leading into the house, waiting to see how to help.

The leader, who seemed barely old enough for the thin mustache he was trying to grow, brusquely told her, "Army's orders, *Señora*. You've got 24 hours to vacate this house. It's a key security installation now." He frowned at her, attempting to look fierce, and seemed disappointed that she did not cry or shout in protest.

In fact, Emy did not speak at all. She simply handed Lucia to her mother, took her *café con leche, and* slowly walked a few yards down toward the beach where she could think calmly. As she left, she heard the militiamen shout that they would be back tomorrow morning, then roar off in their jeep.

Her mind whirled. She had felt safe in Santa Maria. There had been no sign of the Revolution's poison - or its minions. Where had the orders really come from; did they know who she was; had they been watching her? It could have been much worse. They might have trumped up some charge about sabotaging strategic property or being spies for beach landings. They might have simply dragged her or her father off with no explanation, like thousands of others, calling them "a threat to the security of the state."

No, no. Focus on the now, not on the maybes. Best to just go, melt back into Havana as best they could. With Lino in prison, there was no reason not to return to her old apartment. She was a fifth class citizen, vulnerable like any Cuban to harassment and discrimination, but she was no longer underground. She would take her chances.

12

Emy decided to move her parents and children to her aunt's house temporarily while she reopened and cleaned her Havana apartment. Her mother's sister Julia and her husband had plenty of room: their own daughters had already gone to Miami.

The next day she left everyone at Aunt Julia's and returned to the beach house to pack everything up. Her heart fell when she saw that an ugly industrial padlock sealed the front door. It was as though even the beauty of this place had been sullied, its peace ripped away.

She had become quite good at the mix of dignified pleading and haughtiness that seemed to work best with the brutish young militia recruits, and she managed to convince the young soldier on guard to let her in through the back.

When he opened the back door and stepped aside to let her enter, she let out a gasp. The house had been stripped bare. Every single possession of theirs had been carted away, even their dirty laundry. The furniture, which had not even belonged to them, was gone as well. The soldier looked serious.

"I am sorry to report there has been a break-in," he said. "Thieves have taken everything."

"Thieves are taking dirty laundry now?" she asked him with heavy sarcasm.

"*Si Señora,* I guess they are." He had probably missed her sarcasm, but she appreciated his respectful tone. This boy had once been a civilized young man in a cultivated Cuba.

In spite of her sickening feeling of loss, she almost smiled at the irony. *Not everything,* she thought, remembering the arms hidden in the false ceiling of the cedar closets. *I wonder if they'll ever find those.*

All the things she wanted to do - scream, demand justice, even slam the door in the boy's face - would be useless. Dangerous. Steeling herself not to show her pain, she strode back to her car; there was nothing to do but return to Havana. Driving the familiar roads, she tried not to let her mind stray to what was lost - that comfortable green skirt, Po's favorite bear - all gone. Would she ever get used to this unexpected wounding, this helpless cry that had to be swallowed because you had to move on, had to concentrate on protecting what you still had?

The noose of vulnerability tightened when she went the next day to their old ground floor apartment to get it ready. Shortly after Fidel's takeover, she and Lino had moved to this larger apartment so her parents and two younger brothers could live with them. As the tension had grown, many families like theirs had drawn closer together for comfort and security.

Once Lino and Emy had gone underground the summer before, it wasn't safe for anyone to live there. Her brothers had gone to Miami, and the apartment had sat empty from December to May: bright and cozy, still filled with the furniture they had collected, their books and photos, even their Christmas lights carefully stored in the top of a cupboard.

Señora Delgado, a neighbor who knew Vicki, had called Vicki just the day before to say that the militia had been hanging around the building. But Vicki wasn't able to reach Emy to tell her.

Emy crossed the lawn to the entrance of the building. The pots of trailing flowers were still in place but looked uncared for, crinkled dead flowers hanging below the few fresh buds. The entrance was deserted. She remembered Rafael, the tall dignified doorman who had loved to talk to Emilita and Po. She got out her key and opened the door. She was aghast at what she saw.

Alarmed by hearing a key in the lock, two militiamen in rumpled uniforms had come into the entry with machine guns. Four more were in the living room talking, sprawled on the sofa and chairs. Cushions and framed photographs, pieces of broken ceramics were scattered on the floor. The coffee table was covered with remains of food and dirty plates. One of the green living room drapes hung crookedly, half-ripped from its hooks. Two more soldiers sat on the patio. She could see from here that her round glazed pots no longer held any flowers.

Señora Rivas told me she would water the flowers. Did she give up? Did someone rip them out? Maybe she's gone too.

The two soldiers in the entry - one looked like a schoolboy, the other older and enormously fat - snapped to attention.

"Lieutenant," they called to the living room. "Perhaps you should come here." A middle-aged officer with unwashed dark blond hair, his uniform collar undone, got off the sofa and moved unhurriedly into the hall. He looked pleased at the interruption.

"Well, what have we here?"

"What are you doing in my apartment?"

"I'm asking the questions." He glanced at his subordinates with a smirk. "But let me give you a hint. This isn't your apartment any more. It's been requisitioned in the name of *la Revolución.*"

Emy felt encased in a sarcophagus of inexpressible rage. The very core of her life with Lino, of her children's future - ripped away spitefully like a treasured toy from a child. *You have no right to this. You have not been found in favor.*

She stood for a long moment, feeling the officer now becoming impatient, perhaps disconcerted at her silence. She wouldn't argue. It would only make things worse.

Instead she said, "May I take a few personal things? Some photographs? A few of my children's toys? Those are of no use to *la Revolución.*" She couldn't help but pronounce the last words with a shade of mockery.

She wanted to slap the man, push him out of the way, bolt into her bedroom and lock the door. Lie on her own bed and weep. She felt slightly sick when she thought about who might have been sleeping in that bed.

The officer appeared, with exaggerated gestures, to consider her request. Then he sighed. "I'm afraid I have no authority to allow that. Besides, how do I know you really are the former resident?"

You could ask the neighbors. That is, if you haven't already stolen their apartments as well.

"Well, I can describe the photo in that dark wood frame there."

The officer didn't answer. With an irritated look, he gestured roughly silently to the guards. They moved closer to Emy. She was on very shaky ground; better back off, say no more. She tried to smile pleasantly so she would look cooperative, or at least harmless.

Finally he spoke. "My soldiers will take you to officials who can explain your situation better. They'll tell you what options you have."

He spoke in low tones to a younger officer who had come in from the living room, and she was escorted to a blue Chevrolet parked in front of the building.

They drove a few blocks to an old mansion the government had taken over near the Country Club. The soldiers said nothing about where they were taking her or why. She would learn only later that this building was G-2 Security headquarters.

She was taken to a small room, a former pantry by the looks of it, and told to sit at a narrow painted wooden table with four chairs. Two officers, with neat uniforms and very serious faces, entered and began to interrogate her aggressively. One was much younger than the other, but they seemed to be of the same rank.

They prowled the room, first one speaking and then the other. "Who are you? Where is your husband? Why were you at the apartment? Why have you been holding meetings there? Where are you living? Where were you yesterday?"

After her first shock, she realized they were just fishing. They had probably not expected her to show up at her apartment. Now they felt they had to press their advantage. Perhaps they would uncover something important and impress the higher ups. But they clearly had not yet connected the name Fernandez with Lino's code name *Ojeda*. They did accuse her of having illegal meetings at the apartment, which she denied.

In her travels with Lino and her months alone, Emy had learned how to keep people in authority from getting to her. She was very precise, pleasantly answering exactly the question asked and no more. She was dressed, as she usually was, in a dress with high heels and stockings. She presented herself as a cool collected lady. She knew her best defense was to appear dignified, all the while praying she could hang on to this calm demeanor.

She knew the dangers of dealing with the urban militia who had been given power without any real training or military discipline. You were totally at their mercy; everything depended on which officer was in charge at the moment. If one of them decided you were a danger to the Revolution, you could be hauled away to prison, no questions asked. Emy's aunt was always saying you should tell several people where you were going, so they'd know where to look if you disappeared. This awful unpredictability, this unrelenting vulnerability, would follow her for the next 18 years.

After what seemed like hours of pointless interrogation, another man entered, leaving the door open, and spoke in low tones to the older of her interrogators. She heard a familiar voice in the hall. Could that be Vicki? She did work nearby at the Egyptian Embassy. Emy was incredulous.

She heard the voice say, "Well, his Excellency the Ambassador is certainly going to be surprised - and none too pleased - to find one of his key employees has been taken into custody. I hope you have a very good reason for him."

There was a murmur of male voices, then Vicki's voice again, louder than before. "I assume you have no objection if I get his Excellency on the phone. He will certainly want to talk to the person in charge." Her voice faded as she apparently went into another room, and someone closed the door.

Within a half an hour, Emy was released, with no explanation or further questioning. Sure she was being watched, she began walking calmly toward the bus stop. Vicki was waiting for her on the next block. She grabbed Emy in a fierce hug, and then looked at her.

"God, I was frantic. Señora Delgado called me about the militia being around, and I decided I better go check it out. The place was crawling with those little tyrants." Vicki's voice was a mixture of relief and disdain.

"How did you know where they'd taken me?" Emy wanted to sink to the sidewalk in relief.

"Ah, that's another story," Vicki grinned. "Let me just say that those militiamen aren't always very bright. Didn't you realize who these guys were? That you were at G-2 headquarters?"

"No," Emy said. "Why would I? I wasn't doing anything wrong." She waited until a young woman had passed them and was out of range. "I just thought they were taking me to some kind of housing office to tell me I'd have to share an apartment with three other families or something."

Vicki explained that she had called the Egyptian Ambassador, Omar El Asmani. El Asmani had never met Emy, and Vicki was only able to give him a few coded words of background. But he had assured the officer in charge on the phone that Emy was an indispensable part of the Embassy staff. She must immediately be released.

Emy felt her hands trembling with delayed fear. She'd been so defenseless. They could have accused her of anything, dragged her into the bottomless pit of captivity; she'd have been powerless. One of the disappeared.

The next day she went to the Embassy to thank El Asmani and was escorted to his office. He was an imposing man, almost six feet tall but with a gentle manner.

Emy introduced herself. *"Señor,* you saved me yesterday with your phone call. I can't thank you enough. I think we both know what might have happened."

He smiled. "You're more than welcome, *Señora Fernandez."* He offered her a chair and she perched on the edge, feeling like a nuisance. "Now, to make this look legitimate, you better come here every day like you're coming to work. I'm sure we'll eventually find a place for you." His smile held sympathy, not duty.

She was stunned by his generosity. Only later would she realize the true enormity of his gift. He was offering her a place to go, a place to belong while she was a persona non grata in her own country. The Embassy and its people would become a source of great strength in the years to come.

She had begun to build her waiting life in Havana.

13

Their things at the beach house, the apartment and its contents - everything was gone. After the initial shock, Emy didn't flinch at these losses. She was learning to let go of possessions, discovering that wealth would come to her in very different forms.

She and the children were invited to stay with Raque and her family while Emy's parents stayed at her aunt's house and everyone decided what to do next. The de la Huertas lived in a beautiful old house in the suburb of La Sierra with their seven children and an unmarried aunt. Emy was welcomed without question and without limits to make this house her home. There she would be free to concentrate on the future.

One afternoon, sitting in the de la Huertas' sunroom, she was struck by how lucky she was to be in this lively loving home when she needed it so much. The children, hers and theirs, were busily building a playhouse out of rocking chairs. Raque was having her hair cut. Raque's oldest son Luisito sat lost in a book. Her husband, a respected professor, was gentle and kind, but sometimes strict with the children. Today in the midst of all the activity he was in another world, listening to a recording of *Swan Lake*. It was as though nothing had changed in the gracious life of Havana.

Raque ran the household with energetic precision. Every Sunday all the de la Huerta children, the boys in suits and bow ties and the girls in smocked dresses, marched off to Mass at Iglesia Santa Rita.

Living now with Raque, Emy admired her even more. She often found her bleary-eyed at 5 a.m. boiling milk - everything had to boiled - for a household of four adults and ten children. Raque never seemed discouraged; she just survived. Food was already scarce, and Russian cereal was often the only alternative. Raque blithely did her best to strain out the bugs, saying, "don't worry, it's protein."

She and her sister Marta were both involved in the underground, finding safe houses and driving people to and from them. They had often driven Lino and Emy when they had been underground.

Emy's children were delighted at the de la Huertas. So many children to play with. Awash in their mother's and their grandparents' love, still very young, the three did not yet feel the real effects of the Revolution. But Cuban parents were in shock as the government began to talk of *Patria Potestad*, a declaration which would give the government an authority overriding that of parents. If it was enacted, children could be sent to Russia or other countries, or within Cuba to camps or schools where they would live permanently separated from their parents. The thought of her children in Fidel's hands felt like an electric shock running through her body.

Emy had been hearing about *Operación Pedro Pan*, church-sponsored flights evacuating Cuban children to foster homes in the United States. She felt her own determination swelling. If parents, unable to leave Cuba themselves, were willing to send their children to strangers rather than have them under the power of this government, how could she and Lino keep their children here?

In Cuba, her children would be outcasts, their father a criminal, their grandparents traitors because they had owned a sugar mill and had supposedly exploited workers. They would be taunted, denied education, even sent away. There was no question; they could not remain.

At the end of the summer, she heard from the wife of Vicente Guitterez, who was in prison at *Isla de Pinos*, that he had seen a gang of prisoners being brought into the prison and was 99% sure one of them was Lino. But still no official word. No permission to visit.

She told herself that the delay in his trial might have saved his life, at least for now. Last winter, a paranoid trigger-happy army had shot many captured resistance members on the spot. If an officer felt a "moral conviction" you were guilty, that was all it took. You got a bullet in the temple.

Now, after the Bay of Pigs invasion, the regime seemed more confident. Did it have less need to show off its power with gratuitous cruelty? Or was she clinging to false hope?

When they had learned about Lino's capture, Emy's parents had begun the painful gathering of permits for all of them to go to Miami. They would join Emy's sister Juani and Emy's three younger brothers, Jorge 10, Pepe 12 and Kiko, 17. Emy's mother talked often about how much better things would be in the U.S.; Emy and her children would be surrounded by family and friends.

But once in Miami, there would be no news of Lino - and no way to send messages to him. One day the children might know their father. If he survived. If he could be their father after a long punishing prison term cut off from everyone. She shook off the thought of Lino alone in a Castro prison.

One day she and her mother were in her Aunt Julia's kitchen when her mother spoke openly for the first time about the decision Emy faced. She looked up at Emy from the peppers she was chopping.

"Emy, your father and I will be fine no matter what happens. We've always shared the lives of these children; we'd do anything for them."

What a relief. Mama understood.

"We're not old for grandparents; we can create a new life if we have to. But they'll need you. You're their mother. And you'll need them. They're all you have now."

She wanted to push away the reality of her mother's words. But she forced her mind to open and knew her mother was right. If Emy were in Miami, she'd be the children's touchstone. She'd guide them every day, work problems out as they came along. She tried to feel good about her strength, about being there for them. But she could not put Lino out of her mind.

My children will be fine no matter where I am. They'll have many people there for them. Lino will have no one. He cannot survive with no one to care.

A few days later, as she walked with her father towards the pharmacy in Obispo Street, he said, as though reading her mind, "Emy, have you thought that if you stayed in Cuba, you could be a liability to Lino? As long as they have you, they can hurt him, force him." His voice cracked and he paused. Then he pulled her to his side. "With you away and safe, he'll feel less vulnerable. You do see that, don't you?"

She nodded. She understood what Papa was saying. She knew he believed it and that Lino would agree. He'd always been adamant about protecting the kids, not putting them in harm's way for what he had done. Her mind swirled with the seesaw of thoughts about what was best for everyone.

One afternoon, while she was putting Po down for a nap, Sofia Llarena called. Sofia's husband Eduardo had been in school with Lino and in the resistance. He had been in prison for just over a year.

"Sofia, how are you?" She had thought of calling Sofia but didn't want to complicate the woman's life. "I've thought of you so often since I heard about Eduardo."

"We're okay - still worried about his parents. They should get out, but they feel like they'd be deserting me." She sighed. Then her voice rose. "But Emy, I really called to invite you and the children for early supper on Friday. My two girls will love it. They're at that age where they adore little ones."

"That would be lovely. If you're sure you want that many little ones at one time. How old are your girls?"

"They're ten and eleven. They especially want to see the baby, Lucia isn't it?"

They made arrangements for Friday. Sofia's husband was at *Isla de Pinos* prison; maybe she'd had word of Lino. But no, surely she wouldn't make Emy wait if she had news.

On Friday they sat in Sofia's cool covered patio and ate a simple supper of *jamón* and *ensalada*. In spite of the heat, the children ran around the courtyard while Lucia slept on Emy's lap.

"Have you had a visit recently?" Emy asked. Prison visits were the central focus of anyone with a husband there.

"Next Thursday. We were lucky. We got plane tickets to the island. It helps a lot with the girls. The boat ride is so long for them - and so filthy." She grimaced and began collecting dirty plates and stacking them on a side table.

"How much food can you take?" Emy knew food was the most important thing you could take prisoners.

"Oh the rules change all the time. But now - they forbid bringing meat. Those guys desperately need protein, but they won't allow it. They say it attracts mice." Sofia looked disgusted. "As if Eduardo would ever keep meat for more than three minutes. He'd devour it on the spot!"

She gestured to the iced tea pitcher and Emy held out her glass for a refill.

"It must be so hard, to know they need it and not be allowed."

Sofia sipped her own tea and thought a minute. "It is, but we don't give up. Jose Maria Amaril came up with an ingenious idea. We're going to grind up chicken as fine as we can and then cook it into a banana pudding. The banana should disguise the chicken taste, even if the guards taste it, which they usually don't."

Sofia's face had a look of mischievousness mixed with triumph. "Jose Maria has a friend who tried it, and it worked perfectly!"

"I imagine it tasted a little bizarre," Emy chuckled as she shifted Lucia to a more comfortable position.

I should get the recipe for doing that. Lino likes ham but it might not work as well because of the color.

"Believe me they'd eat any combination we brought them. And fruit. They crave fruit, any kind. I take anything I can get."

Sofia pulled her cardigan around her and sighed. "Last month, a cousin got me some dried fruit - God only knows where. It's great because it doesn't go bad. But no luck this time."

She twisted her gold wedding band and smiled. "God, I can't wait to see Eduardo. The look on his face when he sees us arrive . . ." Sofia's eyes were unfocused, staring into the garden.

The kids invaded the patio, looking for sweets. As she got up, Sofia turned to Emy.

"How are you coming with your exit visas? Are your parents going with you and the kids?"

"Nothing is settled," Emy replied. She put Lucia over her shoulder and got up to help Po climb onto a chair.

Sofia assumed she was leaving.

And at that exact moment, she knew she was not.

If she went, she could never return. Lino would be without contact, without her presence for all his years in prison. Never even their little jokes about her cooking - nothing. It was unthinkable. And if he was executed in the end, he would face it alone. In her heart Emy knew she could not do that to Lino.

Tucking the kids into bed that night, she replayed in her mind the conversation with Sofia. She had spoken of visits like a crusade, totally focused on what could make life bearable for her husband. The possibilities seemed much more concrete now. She could do this. She had to.

A few nights later, at her Aunt Julia's house, she asked her parents to come sit on the terrace with her. She began speaking quietly.

"These last weeks I've been in a kind of retreat within myself. I've thought about everyone, all of us who've been dragged into this nightmare. You, Lino, the children most of all."

She looked from one to the other.

"And I've realized I must stay in Cuba."

Her mother gave a low cry of protest and then covered her mouth with her hand. Emy resisted the urge to go to her. Instead, she put her head in her hands for a long minute before speaking deliberately.

"I am a wife and a mother. I have to consider what is best for everyone. The children cannot stay here, and Lino cannot leave. So I must send them and I must stay."

Papa put up one finger as if to argue; Emy hurried on.

"We can each put ourselves where we're most needed. Together we can keep this family strong. Even when we're apart, we'll be a family." Her voice was almost pleading.

She got up, crossed to her mother, and gave her a gentle hug. Then she sat down beside her, determined not to cry. They sat without speaking for a long moment.

Her father's reaction was strong, his manner gentle as always.

"*Mi Emilita*, I'm just afraid of seeing you trade a rich strong life helping your children grow up - for a life spent in a useless gesture of support. Lino might never even know you're here. You're still waiting for a first visit."

Surely he wouldn't try to dissuade her.

He hurried on as though wanting to get the words over with, say them before he lost his courage. "But if you're determined, *de acuerdo*. Stay. I'll stay with you. Your mother can go with the children. You can't be here alone."

"No Papa, I've thought about this. It isn't safe for you here. And even if it were, Mama can't go alone and face making a home for Pepe, Georgie, and Kiko as well as my three."

Her father gave an anxious sigh. The silence that followed was filled with sadness and regret.

"I won't fight you Emilita. If you believe we're the ones who can best take the children, we'll do it as well as we know how. God knows I love those three." He swallowed hard and looked away.

Her mother nodded in agreement and stretched her hand out to hold Emy's. No one spoke.

Then Emy shared with her parents what she had heard about the families' visits to prisoners. The government made the visits as complicated and physically exhausting as possible. The timing was whimsical, with little advance notice.

"But imagine, Papa, Mama. Those visits are the lifeblood of the prisoners. It's all they can live for."

She thought of what Sonia had said about Eduardo's eyes. "Lino will be able to touch me. He can share his pain and his hope and his ideas. He'll hear about how I live in Havana. And in some way, I'll share what he's enduring, his reality."

"Will you really be able to visit?" Her father's voice was not challenging, only wanting to understand.

"That's just it, Papa. Even when there are no visits, the idea that someone is out there will be a lifeline for Lino. Someone connected to him is waiting, caring, trying to make his life better."

She tried then to take a lighter tone. She repeated Sofia's description of the elaborate system for smuggling letters in and out with visitors. Families sent photos, love letters, food. Most important, they cared: that was what the prisoners needed to survive. She told them about Sofia's banana-chicken pudding. At least that made her mother smile.

"He'll know I'm here. He can send messages out and someone will be here to get them." Her parents began asking how all this subterfuge worked. She saw them slowly begin to understand, to accept.

Every day of the next 18 years, Emy would thank God for this gift, that she had parents who could do this, who could allow her to stay with Lino and not sacrifice her children's happiness. She would not think of her own loss. She would leave it in a far corner of her soul.

Leaving her aunt's house, Emy still twisted and turned her parents' reactions in her mind, gauging their distress. She left them with words that left no doubt of her strength. "If a moment comes when I must leave Cuba, I will. But as long as Lino is alive, I want to be here."

She lay asleep for a long time that night in her room at Raque's, relieved that her parents had agreed, but haunted by the soft breathing of these children who would so soon be gone. In the end the answer had come so clearly. After lingering so long as a wrenching possibility, it had hardened into a bruising certainty, painful to the touch.

She tried to lie to herself. Fidel wouldn't last. The family would be together again within months; this terrifying time would be over. But what if Fidel kept his lethal grip on their country? Then at least he wouldn't have gotten her children. They would be in a place of promise, far from the despotic will, never to be force fed the ideas their parents abhorred.

She was incredulous when people assumed she would go with the children to the United States and wait. Meeting her friend Ana for a coffee, Emy didn't tell her for sure she was staying, but tried to explain why she was hesitant to leave.

"Of course it'll be hard at first in Miami." Ana told her earnestly.

Hard? No. More like rats eating away at my soul. When had Ana become so naive?

"But you're so warm and caring, Emy, you'll get involved with people. You'll build a normal life, for your children. You have to."

Emy was aghast at how little her friend understood. Ana would never use the word 'remarry', but clearly she thinks I wouldn't live alone forever. She thinks I could go on without Lino. My God, how little she knows me. Knows us.

Choked with disappointment, Emy couldn't answer Ana. She made her excuses and hurried away. She stopped telling people about her plans. Did other prisoners' wives hear these things? She was baffled. Why can't people understand my children **are** Lino? That I'm not protecting them if I desert him?

Her decision made, she felt heavy-hearted but anchored. Resolute. Her parents kept their pain inside and did everything they could to support her. They never questioned her decision again, but her mother, talking of their plans, often turned away so Emy couldn't see her face.

14

The children's leaving reared up before Emy like a jungle cat, ready to spring. At the same time, on the brink of panic, she wanted the awful moment to come, wanted them whisked away beyond Fidel's grasp. Only then would they be safe from this perverted system where crime meant not agreeing with people in charge. To survive her pain, she needed to know that these small beings would grow up without fear, flourish in the kind of lives she and Lino had wanted for them. Her greatest fear was that they would somehow be forced to stay.

It took ferocious determination not to fixate on the moment of goodbye, not to constantly imagine that last hugging of their little bodies, trying to imprint them on her. If her own dread and longing leaked out, the children might feel it. Instead she turned her back on the beast, ignored its approach, and chose to simply relish the emerging spirit of each child. At three, Emilia Maria was quiet but strong-willed and very protective of her brother Po. He had gotten the nickname because Emilia Maria thought the new baby looked like a friend's puppy, a *perrito*. Po, going on two, was in constant motion - happy-go-lucky and always ready for something new. Raque and Emy often laughed at Po's constantly hanging diaper.

"Do you think it's the way he walks?" Raque suggested, laughing as Po toddled by. "Two minutes after you set him down, there it goes."

"I don't know - Emilia Maria certainly never did that. But it definitely spoils his macho act," Emy chuckled.

Her throat tightened.

My God, I won't be there when he learns to give up diapers.

Lucia was too young to crawl, but she seemed to enjoy all the action and noise. She was a good baby except she was the slowest eater any of them had every seen.

"My arm is falling off," Emy said to Raque's aunt one morning when Lucia was still only half way through her bottle after 40 minutes. But in truth she loved this time when she could stroke Lucia's hair and marvel at how much she looked like Lino. Soon enough her arms would ache to hold her.

The de la Huerta house was a haven, a jumble of movement and play. Emy's children had become so used to changes and new people; they settled right in. They didn't object when the older children dragged them into their plays and make-believe games.

Emy imagined them growing up: learning to read, ride bicycles, swim. She was thankful they were so young. If they were older the separation would be much harder on them. And anyway, if she waited, they might not be able to get out at all.

They would ask to go to parties. They would ask where babies came from. They would ask why their parents were not with them. Who would answer them? What would they say?

She wondered about the future but she didn't worry. She'd always been close to her parents. Both were gentle accepting people. When she was growing up at the sugar mill, they had been open and fair - and most of all, loving. She saw them now every day with her children, saw how they nourished each child's budding personality. She knew they would do the right things.

Lino was like a son to her parents. They understood why he was in prison and they respected his choices. Their admiration and love for her and for Lino would come through when they were absent. She was sure her parents would convey to the children how much their parents loved them and why they couldn't be with them.

Emy had six more weeks with her family, weeks just to get exit papers and then a long wait for reservations on a flight. She had time to get used to the idea that her children would really go. She was working at the Egyptian Embassy, but only part-time. Her time at home was full of decisions, solving old problems, worrying about new obstacles. She was glad to keep her mind busy.

With a last rush, the flights were set. The documents signed. Only four days left. In the shocking certainty of a date and time, Emy was forced to confront her parents' pain, up to now obscured by her own. She was sending her own children to sanctuary; they were leaving their daughter to a perilous future, all rights denied to her as the wife of a traitor. She could be thrown in prison. Lino, like a son to them, could face a firing squad. The ultimate nightmare loomed; they might never see Emy or Lino again. Maybe she was asking too much.

Two days before the flight, her mother brought her a small package. Taking off the shiny blue paper, Emy found a studio photograph, in a small silver frame, of the children.

"Mama. This is so perfect." Emy, trying hard to hold in her looming grief, was near tears. From the gift. From its intention. From knowing how much she would need it.

"I put them in the clothes they'll be leaving in," her mother almost whispered. "That way a part of them will be staying with you." Her voice was husky, strained.

Emy drank in every detail of the photograph. Emilia Maria sat with crossed legs, her round face crowned with little pixie bangs. She wore a sundress with three little rows of ruffles at the neck and again on the skirt. Her arms encircled Lucia's waist from behind protectively, as though she knew how her sister would need her. Lucia, in a smocked dress and bare feet, looked wide-eyed and a bit confused, her miniature mouth forming a perfect O.

Po looked as though he were trying to stride right out of the picture, a little tough guy in a linen one-piece suit with round collar and a buckled sash.

How much they've grown just since Lino's been gone! And how many stages we're going to miss before we find them again.

The picture would become her touchstone.

On August 16, early in the morning, she gathered the children around her in the bedroom at Raque's. She sat quietly, gathering her courage and trying to dissolve the tightness in her throat. She spoke softly, leaning towards them.

"*Queridos*, you're all going on an exciting trip with Ma and Pa. It'll be quite an adventure. On a real airplane." Emy's throat muscles tightened, and again she had to stop until they released. Lucia smiled in response to the cheer in her mother's voice. Emilia Maria listened carefully as she always did. Po wandered over to the window.

"And when you get off the airplane, you'll see your uncles, Pepe and

Yoyi and Kiko - and Tia Juani too. They'll be so happy to see you. And you'll get to stay at their house for awhile." Emy chose her words carefully, praying that Emilia Maria would not ask if her mother was coming. Emy didn't know if she could lie. But Emilia Maria did not ask.

They're so used to moving around and things changing. What troopers they've been. Will be.

Now her whole face felt frozen. If she tried to smile, she was sure her face would crack open. So she just sat on the floor. She stroked Emilia Maria's arm, then pulled Po toward her, holding him until he shook her off and waddled over to pick up a wooden train engine. The minutes ticked away.

They rode to the airport, divided between Raque's car and a taxi, getting there early as instructed, though they knew the plane wouldn't leave for hours. She was determined that the leaving be low key; otherwise she and her parents would never get through it. She had insisted she could handle going to the airport alone with her family, but Raque insisted on coming. No discussion. She would leave Emy alone with her family to say goodbye. But she would be there when Emy turned away the last time.

Even with the looming dread of saying goodbye, Emy's biggest fear was that, at the last minute, her parents would be yanked from the plane. Permission to leave was a government weapon. Any official might decide that her parents were traitors after all and pull them off the plane. Then her children would be trapped in Fidel's vise. The iron fist of the Revolution would squeeze all the freedom and joy out of their lives and replace it with violence and mistrust.

They went through the initial check-in and searches. Hours passed. Emy wanted to scream from the endless tension. She wanted this not to happen. She wanted this to be over with. They all popped up and down from the sticky plastic chairs, watching over the children as they explored the drab airport lobby.

They spoke in low tones about trivialities.

"How lucky that no government official showed up to usurp our seats."

"I wish we could have brought Po's barnyard set."

"It looks like they're loading the luggage."

Words blowing back and forth aimlessly, without impact, like old leaves across a frozen field. In the end, they sat in silence, the crushing sadness ever harder to keep at bay. Emy noticed for the first time emerging folds of age in the skin of her mother's neck. *My God, this is an old woman. How can I ask her to do this?*

Then without warning, officialdom seemed finished with them. They were told to pass into the holding area. Passengers only.

The unthinkable moment had come. Emy rose. She had to get through this without breaking down. She couldn't let the children take in her desperation. She took Lucia in her arms, enfolding her whole pudgy body against her chest and crooning softly. She held the baby's dark hair against her palm, feeling the pulse in her skull. Lucia was always ready to cuddle, but Emy knew that, no matter what she did, her tiny daughter would never remember this moment. In the end, she handed the baby to her mother. A guard stood rigid, holding the door open.

Po squirmed as always when Emy picked him up in a bear hug, pretending to growl to cover her cracking voice. "My big boy." She whispered. "Always in motion like your daddy." The daddy he would grow up without. The moment Emy put him down, Po bolted away, trying to see out the window. How much easier it was like that. Racing ahead. No clinging.

Emilia Maria was last. Emy knew this was her child who would most remember, best hold the feel and sound of Emy in her memory. Maybe. She wanted to sob into her daughter's neck, tell her how sorry she was. But Emilia Maria understood the most too, was most alert to signs of alarm. So Emy did not sob, just kept her voice calm. "My beautiful Emilia Maria. My big girl. I'm so proud of you." It worked. Emilia beamed and gave Emy a wet kiss, as though she were off on an adventure she would relate to her mother as soon as she got back.

Now the last goodbye. Emy faced her parents. No hug could be long enough or tight enough. She held them both at once, Lucia squeezed in the center. She would miss them desperately; her heart would be an open wound, unprotected, stinging at every touch. Her strength felt fragile, like a palm with shallow roots, easily flattened.

Abruptly the five of them were herded away by the guards, moving through the double doorway into the *pecera*, the glass fishbowl of a room, where they would wait until the very last minute. Emy's hand trembled as she returned Emilia Maria's cheery wave. She saw her father emerge behind the glass with Emilia Maria and Po by the hands.

It hit her like a bomb blast, obliterating the walls of her determination.

These three little beings, only steps away, could no longer be touched by her. They were beyond her care. For years to come, they would be impossible to reach, to clasp, to hug. Just like now. No. Worse than now. They would be at best shapes in a photo, a scrawl on a sheet of paper. Perhaps not even that. She felt ripped open by loss. She was seized by an irrational urge to run after them. *No I've changed my mind. I can't do this.*

Then she saw her mother, sitting in a plastic chair with Lucia on her lap. Lucia's tiny feet, her little *piecitos*, were sticking straight out. Her short hair stood up in spikes. Emy's mother was kissing Lucia's neck. *This is my baby. She is where she needs to be, where she will be safe.*

Emy could only mouth through the glass the words, *gracias.* She could not have spoken, even if they might have heard. She took a step backward, afraid the sight of her tears would upset the children. She gestured cheerily to them and blew them kisses. Her body formed smiles and waves, even as tears slid down her cheeks untended.

Emy and Raque waited in paralyzed silence as the five bodies disappeared into the plane. Then the plane taxied, turned and took off in a sudden rush, as though it knew Emy needed this moment to be over. Her whole body went limp when she saw that this precious cargo was really beyond Castro's grasp, that at least today he would not find a way to wound her family further.

It was time to go home to supper.

Raque silently put her arm around Emy's shoulders as they walked across the desolate parking lot to the car. The touch felt soothing, like cool lotion on searing sunburn. Raque was still there, with whatever she could give. Emy could be herself, could cry or not cry, talk or not talk. She slowly let her body sink into the seat of the car, abandoning herself to a silent whirl of remembrance, grief, and relief.

When they got home, seeing Raque's children was a great balm for Emy. She hugged each one in turn, so long that they looked at her oddly. She was so fond of them. Surely the warmth she gave these children who were in her arms would be given to her own children by others.

She was glad for the maelstrom of Raque's family routines that allowed her to sit quietly, unspeaking, a spectator. After dinner, she excused herself and went alone to her room. She stood a long time looking down at the children's empty beds. Then she put on her nightgown and climbed into her own bed where she lay motionless in the dark.

Where were they sleeping? Who had read their bedtime story? How long would they remember her?

There would be few letters. Even if there were, nothing would ever satisfy her wish to know every moment of her children's lives. She felt a surge of panic that her grief might overwhelm her, might overflow, that she would be unable to contain it in the days to come.

She got out of bed and forced herself to move slowly to the open window where she knelt to peer out into the garden. The hibiscus flowers glowed coral and pink in pots on the terrace. The slow rhythm of the frogs croaking sounded peaceful and wise. Like Lino.

She had to let go. They were with people who loved them - safe and free. They were in her heart; they could not be in her life. Her life would center on Lino, on his survival. God willing she would see him soon.

15

Lino stirred on the metal cot covered with stained canvas. Bright sunlight pounded at his consciousness, but a dark red throbbing in his head made him resist opening his eyes. He turned his head slightly to avoid the glare, and his ear exploded with a tidal wave of pain. He felt hot and feverish all over. Throbbing pain in his genitals, his shoulders, his back. His clothes were stiff with dirt and dried blood.

Consciousness finally won out, and his spirit crumpled as his full memory returned. He was a prisoner; the madness of the Revolution had him trapped like an animal. He was at the mercy of Fidel's thugs, these sadists the Revolution seemed to spawn everywhere.

At least he was alive. The militia had not put a bullet in the back of his head while he knelt in the dust as they had done to Plinio Prieto. Had not ripped his chest apart with rifle bullets in a dark cellar as they had so many. But as soon as they realized who he was, figured out they were holding *Ojeda*, he would be shot without trial. He was powerless in the hands of people to whom law and justice meant nothing.

He tried to remember every detail of their capture, the beating, the long agonizing drive in the militia car to G-2 headquarters in Santa Clara, being slammed into a dark cell. He supposed he had simply collapsed or passed out on the cot.

Moving his head as little as possible, he looked around the small cell. The floor and three walls were cement. A fourth wall, of bars, opened to a corridor. Small windows high in the back wall let in bright sunshine. There was a bucket in the corner.

With a start he realized he was not alone. On the back wall was another cot where a short dark-skinned young man was curled in sleep. Lino did not recognize him. From his clothes and hands, he looked like one of the *guajiros* who were so often guides and food couriers in the Escambray. He was rumpled and unshaven but seemed unhurt.

What about the men he'd been captured with - Castell and the young jeep driver Miguel? Were they alive? Surely they hadn't been shot if he was still alive. Were they in a cell nearby? Had they been taken somewhere else to break them, beat what they knew out of them? Thank God neither knew much, but under torture they might say anything about him to save themselves. Betrayal was always a possibility, a lurking fear.

He hoped Miguel had taken his advice and told the truth. They might let him go; he was so young and played such a small role.

Lino lay motionless for over an hour. The slightest movement brought searing pain. His mind was clearing a bit; he wanted time to think before facing his captors. They certainly wouldn't offer any medical care, nothing to make him feel better, more likely insults and physical abuse.

The young man on the other cot stirred and looked up. He smiled tentatively at Lino.

"It looks like they beat you up bad. *Cómo te sientes?*"

"I'll live, but don't ask me to do any push-ups." Lino tried to speak without moving any muscles, without intensifying the pain.

"I'm Mario. Rodriguez. Moto really, that's what everyone calls me. Can I do anything to help?"

"Thanks but no. I'm Lino Fernandez. Have you been here long?"

"Two days. They nabbed me when I went to meet some guys I was supposed to take into the Escambray."

"Bad luck."

"I don't know how they knew the signal, but they did. I walked right into their arms. I'm going crazy sitting around all day. The food is really bad. I'm glad to have company."

Moto suddenly seemed to feel he was talking too much and he stopped.

"I'm glad for company too." Lino looked around. "Is this G-2 headquarters?"

"I don't know at all. Nobody told me anything. I came in at night, and I've been here ever since."

Lino liked the young farmer, but he realized he would learn nothing from him.

He struggled to sit up, pausing twice to let the worst of the back pain pass. Why did his ear hurt so much? He remembered a gun fired directly over his shoulder. Was his eardrum shattered? He wasn't deaf; he could hear noises, people stirring in other cells.

Through the window he heard traffic noise and people shouting. Those were the voices of people who could still walk anywhere they pleased. He wanted to scream with the frustration of being out of the fight. Maybe out of luck, out of time.

He had known this could happen. "This is real," he had told Emy just weeks before, at the hospital after Lucia was born. "I'm going to war. These are savage people. With prisoners, they don't play by the most basic rules. If I'm caught, I probably won't live long enough to see prison." He had wanted to be honest in this - perhaps the last - conversation he would have with her.

"I know." Emy, holding tiny Lucia, had looked right into his eyes. "I know you, and there's no other choice. Let's just pray you'll beat the odds, *mi vida*."

Lino had taken both her hands in his and kissed them. "How I do love you."

Where were Emy and the baby now? Thank God her parents were there to watch out for her and the children. And friends. So many people cared for Emy. He cared for her the most, but he had left her alone.

He was startled by a grinding screech in the street, followed by angry shouting. He thought of Emy out in the harrowing world Cuba had become. Something could have happened to her parents. What if she'd been arrested? What if they hadn't believed his story? Would they beat her to get the truth about him?

Stop! He couldn't think that way. He'd go mad. He had to trust God wouldn't let that happen. He could only believe and pray.

If she were here, he would tell her how much he loved her, how he prayed every day for his beautiful little family, begun in such a time of hope and youth. Prayed for the slim chance he might live to bring them up.

Now the fight would go on without him; but it would go on. Fidel had lied. His brutality had crushed every attempt at peaceful opposition. Lino urgently wanted to live to see a real government in Cuba, maybe not a perfect one, but one that would at least try to bring democracy and justice.

"Have you been questioned?" he asked Moto abruptly.

Moto had been watching him all the time. Now he spoke eagerly.

"Not since the night they brought me in. I guess they know I'm small potatoes. Maybe they'll just let me go," he said, a question in his voice.

"I wouldn't count on it," Lino said. Why was he being left alone so long? What were they saving him for?

Loud clanging came from down the hall. Lino's damaged ear protested. His skull felt like it was being cracked with a hammer. He tried to struggle to his feet but gave up and settled for sitting gingerly on his cot, looking toward the sounds. He tensed himself for what was to come, pushing the physical pain to the back of his mind. Moto seemed unconcerned.

It was only a tall soldier with close-cropped hair, his rifle dangling awkwardly off his shoulder, dragging a large metal trash bin filled with some kind of liquid. Wearing the rumpled green uniform of the Army, he stopped at each cell, ladled some of the liquid into wide flat aluminum mugs, and shoved them through the bars, spilling liquid on the floor. Lino tried to make eye contact; maybe he could get some information. But the guard moved on quickly.

"God, I hope that's water - or coffee." Lino's throat burned with thirst.

"Believe me, it's not like any coffee you ever drank. More like dish water. Just before you throw it out," Moto answered with a gloomy look. "Here, I'll bring yours."

"Thanks Moto, but I want to see how much I can manage on my own." After several tries, he inched toward the cup on his knees, unable to straighten to more than a half-crouch. The cup was only lukewarm but it felt comforting in his hands. He sipped. Tepid water. Sweet. A vague taste of coffee. If it had sugar, he better drink it. He'd need any nourishment he could get. Even moving the cup to his lips made his muscles protest. When he finished, he lay back down, on the floor this time, head swimming.

He lay there as Moto told him everything about his capture, then about his family and his farm where he and his father raised goats. Moto's voice was a nice diversion and Lino felt himself drift off. When he awoke, the light was fading at the window. He felt a little less stiff, even on the floor. He limped slowly back to his cot.

These hours were helping him gain his strength back before the G-2 got hold of him. Usually the longer they did nothing to a person, the better off he was. Unless, of course, they found out you're a guy they've been looking for.

Just as the light softened towards dark, the same guard reappeared with another watery concoction, glutinous with a little rice and some unidentifiable green and yellow clumps in it. Lino stared into the mug.

"Whatever you do, don't smell it." Moto said with a lopsided smile. "You don't have to worry about taste though. There isn't any."

He watched as Moto demonstrated by gulping the slop down. At Lino's first sip, the texture made him want to gag. But he drank it slowly, forcing himself to keep it down.

Long after dark, a loud strident voice came from the hallway, and Lino painfully rose to sitting position again. Four soldiers, the oldest one the owner of the loud voice, entered the cell. Moto jumped to his feet, but the guards ignored him. The oldest, a man with mottled skin and hair down to his collar, told the others to watch Lino closely, and snarled at him to follow him down the hall.

The day of rest had helped. He was able to get to his feet and walk slowly behind the man. Any movement of his head was still agonizing. But he found that if he turned his whole body, not his neck, to look in a new direction, he could minimize the washes of pain.

They left the corridor, crossed a deserted anteroom, and passed through a grey metal door. He was having a hard time keeping up with the pace set by the soldiers. When he slowed, he got a shove in the back, which sent pain radiating from his back into his legs. At the end of a second hallway, the soldier opened a door and gestured him inside.

The room was medium-sized, totally without decoration. The paint, originally white, was now a dirty ivory color. A large window showed only darkness. Must be a courtyard. A dark carved wooden table, once quite elegant, took up most of the room. Two wooden chairs stood at angles to the table.

Lino sat in one of the chairs without being told to. He was afraid he would faint otherwise. He sat very still, to minimize the pain that came with movement. His testicles hurt from rubbing against the cloth of his pants, like someone was scraping them with sandpaper.

Maybe when they get through with me tonight, this pain will seem like nothing. The thought chilled him.

He tried to get his breath and regain his calm. A short trim man entered the room and crossed immediately to look down at him. The man's uniform was immaculate. Even at this hour, he looked like he'd just shaved.

"*Buenas Noches, Señor,*" he said with mock courtesy. "I hope you don't mind the late hour. The days are just so busy with other matters." Another smug smile. Lino wanted to punch him in the gut. "I am Commander Suarez. I have been asked to talk with you about your activities." His pseudo politeness grated on Lino. He was sure it wouldn't last long.

Sure enough, after reviewing how and where Lino had been captured, Suarez' voice took on a new urgency and he began rapid-fire questioning about Lino's background, his connection with the guerillas, and the plans of the rebel groups in the Escambray.

As Lino answered, Suarez took out a cigarette and gave a sharp command to a guard who came forward with a match to light it.

Lino kept to his prepared story and prayed Castell and Miguel had done the same.

"I'm a doctor. I've admitted I was on my way to try to hook up with one of the guerilla groups in the Escambray."

"You and who?"

"We were in a group of seven or eight, nobody I'd every met before. They told us to make our way to the Via Godon near Zulueta and wait. But no one every contacted us, and we two got separated from the others."

Suarez gave him a look of utter boredom. He threw his cigarette on the floor and ground it into the dirty cement. "Go on."

"We were cold and hungry so we decided to go back to the town, get something to eat, and go to the hotel where they'd contacted us the first time."

"So you were trying to join a group you didn't know the name of, and you didn't know how to find them?"

"More or less. They told us the less we knew the better. I don't think they trusted us." Lino tried to sound slightly miffed. "Maybe that's why they didn't show up. All we knew was we wanted to be trained to fight and they said they would do that."

Suarez crossed to the window and looked silently into the darkness.

"So you decided just to hang around and see what happened?" Suarez's tone was unnervingly conversational. *What the hell's going on?*

"Not exactly. We were exhausted. So when we ran across Miguel with his car, we convinced him to take us to the hotel. He didn't really want to do it," he added, hoping to give Miguel some help. "That was when we were stopped by the militia." To his surprise, Suarez said nothing more, simply gestured to the guards. Lino was returned to his cell.

He repeated this story many times over the next two weeks. His captors tried every psychological trick to bring him around. There were interrogations in the middle of the night, even three or four sessions in one night. He was never tortured or beaten, although the guards who brought him back and forth never missed an opportunity to shove him, twist an arm, stomp on a foot. In his condition, the simplest whack took his breath away from pain.

Meanwhile, in the long dark evenings, Moto taught him more about raising goats than he had ever hoped to know.

More prisoners arrived as time went by, and there were sometimes as many as six in the small cell. Some of the people Lino knew, but because there was always the danger of a planted informant, those who knew each other talked only about the most general subjects. One man, Patricio Suarez, who he had known a long time, said he had a way to get word to Emy. Lino could only hope it was true.

In his interrogations, officers traded off, using a bad cop-good cop routine. One officer would treat him with great respect and sympathy, another with brutality.

One night, Suarez said, "Look, don't be stupid. Just cooperate with us now and we'll send you back to Havana. You can resume your life. We'll find a nice spot for you, maybe in the State medical system. You'll have the good life: a new car, a nice house, maybe in Miramar."

Probably stolen from one of my friends, Lino thought. He kept his face blank as he replied evenly.

"But you see I **have** a car, a rented apartment. I already have a profession. I'm a doctor, and that's all I want to do."

Suarez' face showed nothing as he lit a cigarette and inhaled leisurely.

"In fact, at the beginning of the Revolution, I was a volunteer psychological advisor for the Mayor of Havana, working on the child care units. I just want to return to this important work." He felt like a bad actor. He hoped he didn't sound like one.

The same offer was made night after night, and he gave the same response. At every interrogation he waited for Suarez to say, "Give it up, *Ojeda*, we know exactly who you are." But he never did. And after the first two weeks, Lino was left pretty much alone. They would find out who he was. It was just a matter of time. And a lot of things could happen before that.

16

On April 15, 1961, without warning, Lino was transferred with six other prisoners, the core group of the Yaguajay guerillas, to *Topes de Collantes*, a large hospital prison in a poor rural area high in the Escambray Mountains. Castro was using it both as a military hospital for his troops and as a prison.

The hospital was neglected and poorly organized. Lino's group was put in a shoddily constructed overflow building in front of the main hospital. It was spring, but at this altitude there was a constant bitter wind. The building was unheated and uninsulated; Lino could never get warm.

He was put in a six by ten foot cell with eight others. He was happy to find himself with Cesar Paez who'd been captured in a massive round-up shortly after Lino was caught. A compact sturdy man with black hair and very white skin, Cesar would be a good cellmate. He was talkative and social, generally happy. But he could be tough when he needed to. Now he looked around the cell.

"I don't know how you're gonna stretch out in here Lino. This is one time I'm glad to be on the small side."

Lino agreed. Anyone over six feet tall would have to curl to fit the width of the cell. He could have fit stretched out the length of the cell, but then the nine men couldn't lie side by side with enough room to at least turn over. There was no bedding, just a cement floor.

Two days after arriving at *Topes*, they learned why they'd been moved. All that day, April 17, there was a vague dread in the building, tension in the hallway outside the cells. The guards were distracted.

The radio in the soldiers' duty room usually blared popular music. Now it was only voices, talking urgently about fighting between Castro's army and an invasion force.

The prisoners were transfixed, straining to hear who was fighting and where. Was an invasion under way? Lino thought of the MRR troops who were probably involved. Even though he didn't know what role they were playing, he felt pride in the group. He thought of the men he knew, men who might be dying right now.

If an uprising succeeded, this could be the end of the savagery. Cubans could get back to building a country they could be proud of. They wouldn't be in the grip of these monsters.

And he would be free. Free to return to medicine, his family, the life he'd hoped to build. He dared not even whisper the thought, so fragile was his hope.

The afternoon dragged on. News from the radio was ambiguous. There was the usual bragging that the invaders didn't have a chance, that Castro's army was performing valiantly. But you could hear an undercurrent of confusion and concern in the announcers' voices.

About four o'clock a soldier came to Lino's cell and escorted him to an office in the army headquarters. The only person there was Edmundo Betancourt, the head of the G-2 in *Topes de Collantes*. Betancourt began questioning Lino. What did he know about the invasion? Lino could truthfully say he knew nothing. Betancourt didn't seem surprised, or even to care much. He told Lino frankly that he didn't know much either. *Why was Betancourt having this conversation with him?*

Betancourt gestured to Lino to sit and he did the same. "Hopefully this invasion business will clear things up, and people can get on with their lives."

If we get rid of Fidel, then people can do exactly that, Lino wanted to say. But he was sure the officer knew where Lino stood. He asked Lino a few more minor questions, the answers to which Lino was sure he already knew.

Lino decided to be civil until he knew what the guy was up to. Betancourt was actually a pretty decent person; he seemed to have more education than most G-2 officers. And he clearly wanted Lino to warm up to him.

"Hey, I'm not really a military guy. Or wasn't until *la Revolución*. I'm just a regular Cuban like you. If I can make things a little better, why not?"

It clicked. Betancourt was covering his butt. He was obviously afraid that the invasion might succeed. If it did, if the prisoners were all free by tomorrow or the day after - not only free but in charge - this officer wanted someone on his side. Someone to help him slip away, or at least to say he'd done what he could to help.

Betancourt suddenly changed the subject. "Listen, Fernandez, I know who you are and I know you have a future. Let me tell you something." *What the hell was he trying to say?*

But Betancourt continued without explanation. "You should tell Cesar Paez not to talk about anything important in his cell. The guy in the hammock above him is a spy." Lino nodded without speaking. Betancourt was taking no chances; he wanted the resistance people to feel grateful to him.

Betancourt continued. "And tell him not to try to seize the arms stored outside. It won't be necessary." Now Lino was really surprised. It seemed as though Betancourt expected the invasion to succeed.

Betancourt paused now, seemed to measure his words.

"Fernandez, I have brought your father here to see you. He's just outside. You have a few options right now. One is to escape through that door - I won't stop you - and take your chances in the mountains."

Lino was speechless by this time.

"Or you can go to the room next door and speak to your father. Then go back to the cells and wait for the situation to develop."

Lino did not speak right away, but his mind raced. *I have to see my father. He needs to see the way I am now. Strong and free in spite of being in prison. He will reassure Emy and my mother.*

Finally he turned to Betancourt. "Well, let's go then. I don't want to keep my father waiting any longer."

Lino followed him to the lobby of the garrison. His father stood at a table. Lino gave him an enveloping hug and began asking questions.

"Tell me about Emy, the kids. Are they alright? Have they been bothered by the militia, the army? Where are they living?"

Lino's father smiled. This intensity was so like his son.

"They're fine. Don't worry. Of course they're worried sick about you. They get some news from the grapevine, but not much."

"But where are they? How are they living?"

"They're with the de la Huertas. From what I know of that family, they're well taken care of."

Thank God. Someone was taking care of her.

"Emy calls me as often as she can. She says a house with so many children is just what she needs to distract her. She'll be so relieved when I tell her I saw you."

"Are her parents still here?"

"As far as I know. She's careful what she says on the phone."

Lino sunk into a chair in relief. What good friends they had. He should have known they wouldn't turn their backs on his family.

"And the invasion? What are you hearing?"

"Rumors everywhere. But they don't give us any facts. Just the usual proclamations of victory over the enemies of the Revolution."

Lino's father came closer and looked down at Lino.

"It's my turn to ask questions, Lino. What the hell's going on? This militia guy just appeared at the house in a jeep at the crack of dawn and said he would take me to see you."

Lino smiled. Why would his father think **he** would know what was going on?

"And you know who it was? Burrito's son, Mario! What a crazy world. He wouldn't tell me what was going on. Can you imagine? A kid I've known since he was born? Treating me like a stranger."

Lino's father sighed and stared at him. "Tell me the truth. Is this some kind of last visit or something?" His lips quivered.

"No Papa," Lino smiled gently at his father. "I don't think so. We're just reaping the benefits of some people being nervous about the invasion." Lino hugged his father again and explained in a low voice what had happened with Betancourt. "Let's just enjoy what time we have."

The two men talked about the family, and Lino told his father what little he could guess about what the future held for him if the invasion failed. He tried to sound optimistic but he didn't want to get his own hopes up. It turned out that his father knew even less about the invasion than Lino had learned through the prison grapevine.

Thirty minutes later the same soldier came in.

"*Nos vamos. Lo siento.* Time to go." His politeness was a far cry from the guards' usual rudeness. Betancourt never appeared.

"Don't worry Papa," His father's eyes were moist. "We'll all get through this." He wanted to send some very special thought to Emy, but he ended up simply saying, "Tell Emy I love her and miss them all terribly, but I'm O.K."

Lino hugged his father. "Give my deepest love to Mama, to everyone. *Dios sabe cuanto los extraños.* God knows I miss them all. "

He hadn't meant to say that, but hugging his father he remembered how much he wanted to hold Emy and the children. He hadn't realized how painful a visit could be. But it was still better than no visit. He looked closely at his father's face for a long moment, trying to memorize it. Then he was escorted back to his cell.

Morning came and Lino waited anxiously with the others in their cold cells. The barracks seemed quieter than usual. There were no new sounds, no victory noises. He tried to imagine jubilant guerillas coming down the hall emptying out the cells.

The usual guard arrived that afternoon with their food. The prisoners said nothing to one another, but Lino had a bad feeling. When he asked the guard what was going on, he received only a shrug. Later Betancourt's senior officer appeared at Lino's cell.

"Well I hope you weren't planning to dine out soon in Havana," he sneered. "Your friends didn't quite make it. Their pitiful little attack never got off the ground. In fact, the beach at *Bahía de Cochinos* is covered with their bodies, rotting in the sun." His smile was pure malice.

Lino was silent. He didn't want to hear any more from this man. He knew enough. But once alone in their cell, the men talked for hours, trying to guess at the news. Clearly an invasion had been launched and had failed. But who and where? What had happened?

A few days later, they learned how the invasion had been launched by the Cuban expatriate brigade but switched by the U.S. at the last minute to a new location. Even if the new location had worked, there had apparently been none of the promised support from the U.S. military.

Lino felt outrage bubbling up with explosion force.

"How the hell could this have happened?" Paez' face was red with disbelief and fury.

"I should've seen it coming." Lino slammed his fist against a pillar. "We kept sending people out to train, but they never used them the way they were supposed to, to strengthen the resistance, to coordinate with the invasion. I told them over and over. We're strong. Well-organized."

"Obviously they didn't believe you . . ."

"Or they didn't give a damn."

Lino rubbed his temples with his fingertips, as though he could rub out the reality of what he had heard. "All the CIA needed to do was support our resistance, not cook up their own. At the absolute least, we should have been a key part of any attack they dreamed up. That was the whole point of all our preparations."

Paez shrugged his shoulders. "The CIA wanted to be in control all along. Remember in '60 when they wanted us to take in those old Batista loyalists?"

Lino nodded. "Yea, I remember."

Lino leaned forward with his palms out. "For months, they had us risking people's lives for stupid errands. Then when something important is set up, they let us stand out there in the open, digging big obvious holes, with militia all over. And they decide the weather isn't right, or we aren't really who we say we are. I'd like to strangle somebody!"

Paez broke in, "I don't think it had to do with us. They just got fixated on this expatriate army idea. Then they abandoned them at *Bahía de Cochinos*. Just left them sitting for Fidel to blow up."

When new prisoners were transferred in a few weeks later, Lino learned the resistance had never even been informed of the invasion, let alone called to participate. Obviously the CIA had only wanted to work with the resistance inside Cuba if they could control it totally. And they couldn't.

He turned the events over and over in his mind. They should never have trusted the CIA. There'd been lots of signs. But to not even inform the internal resistance of the plan - that was not only monstrous but stupid! The CIA were fools - arrogant fools. Thousands of men had died in the Escambray, and more at *Bahía de Cochinos*, and for what?

Lino alternated between despair and fury. "We needed arms. And we got an insane suicide mission."

17

Within a week, Lino and his cellmates were transferred to the former game room inside the main hospital. Lino looked around for people he knew. A gangly man in his fifties with a shock of black hair gestured him over.

"You better find a space. There isn't much. I'm Leon, and this is my mattress. It's only three feet wide, but half of it's yours if you want it." He smiled. "Lot better than the floor."

The man knew nothing about Lino, but he shared everything he had. One plate, one spoon. He ate. Then Lino ate with the same plate and spoon.

"You're very kind to a stranger," Lino handed back the plate.

"You're not a stranger. You're a soldier in the same army. And I know you're not gonna rob me, cause the criminals are the guys on the other side."

Lino chuckled and laid back on his narrow half of the mattress. It was a lot better than a stone floor. Later Lino found out Leon was a member of the Masons, and he knew Lino was a Catholic. On the outside it would have mattered; here it didn't. Lino felt the first stirrings of the deep connection he would develop in prison with people he would never have met otherwise. The only things that counted here were loyalty and strength, not who you were before.

Lino was appalled at conditions in the game room. There were nearly 200 prisoners; many of them guerillas wounded in battle or during capture. They had been lying for days in their filthy wet clothes on the cold damp floor. Even those with severe wounds had gotten no medical attention.

One young man, a thin blond boy named Mercio, was lying on the floor with an open head wound that had never even been cleaned. The wound had started to become gangrenous - maggots were crawling in it.

Lino was repulsed. Not by the wound but by the callousness of guards who could stand by and watch. He couldn't believe the prisoner group had four physicians, one a surgeon, and all they could do was stand helplessly by.

He sought out one of the surgeons. "Surely they can give us something to clean this boy's head. That's part of the Geneva convention, isn't it?"

The surgeon laughed bitterly. "Oh yea, let's complain when the commission comes by to check on us." His face grew serious. "Lino, we've asked for weeks and weeks. Bandages, antibiotics, even permission to use the hospital facilities. Nothing. They don't even answer our requests."

Lino was gritting his teeth. "Well I can't just stand here." He moved through the room, looking and asking for any kind of alcohol and a razor blade. Hoping against hope. But there was nothing he could use to clean away the infected flesh. His only consolation was that the boy would probably die anyway. But his own helplessness was agonizing to Lino.

Slowly he became aware of something much more disturbing. The prisoners, many sick or injured, most uncertain and scared about what would happen to them next, spent the days haphazardly, without any real organization for using what little they had. They felt powerless but they weren't. Their best resource was themselves - a room full of courageous intelligent men - and they weren't using it. True, Fidel's people could be cruel, but they did leave the prisoners alone as long as they didn't cause any trouble.

"There're a lot of us in here," he told the other prisoners, assembled in one corner of the game room. "We need to be a community that respects everybody, keeps everybody healthy and out of trouble. Otherwise these goons will break us."

He proposed some basic rules. Everyone quiet after 8 or 9 at night. One person would distribute the mail, when there was any. They would share any resources. Lino committed to call everyone out in the morning before 7 so no one would be beaten or put in isolation for being late to roll call.

"I'm not in a monastery here. I don't need rules and people to tell me when to take a shit." The speaker was a hot-tempered plantation worker. He said he respected Lino, but he would take his chances organizing his own life.

A few of the worker's friends agreed and moved off to another part of the room. But within a few days, when they saw the system working, they gave up their boycott. The plantation worker became one of Lino's most able helpers in treating the wounded.

One day, Orlando, an older man who slept near Leon and Lino, peered at Lino's face. "What on earth is going on with your mouth?" he said. "You look like a monster."

Lino looked sheepish. "It's my tooth; I've had this abscess festering for months, since just after I was captured." He thought of those around him who were suffering much more. "I guess it looks pretty bad, but it's not a big deal."

"The hell it isn't. It looks dangerous. I was a medic. If those poisons start spreading through your system, you'll be in real trouble."

"I know, I know." Lino fingered his jaw gingerly. It was rigid with pressure from the infection inside.

"I'll fix it - and quick." With that, Orlando pulled out a needle he kept hidden under his collar, sterilized it with a match flame, and jabbed it ferociously into the abscess. Thick gray-yellow pus, putrefying under pressure for weeks, came shooting out. Lino had been in such pain the needle jab didn't faze him. That was the end of his medical treatment.

The abscess shrank dramatically from its original size but was still swollen and throbbing. Anything was an improvement. The hole would drip pus for months, but Lino would never be sick again in prison. Anemic. Near starvation. But never really sick.

Lino was infuriated at the continued refusal of medical supplies. No matter what they asked for the answer was no. Like they were mangy dogs, not worth saving. They weren't even asking for help - they **had** doctors. They just needed supplies.

"We're in a huge hospital," he said, livid with frustration after trying to clean a long gaping leg wound. "There are operating rooms upstairs, for God's sake! Ready and stocked. And Mercio is lying over there dying of gangrene. Ricardo is going to lose his leg!" He sat down and buried his head in his arms.

The following evening, the surgeon called to Lino.

"You better have a look at Mercio. He's unconscious."

Lino hurried over. He had become quite fond of Mercio and ached to see him get treatment. The young boy appeared to have slipped into a coma.

"The gangrene is everywhere. Just as well he's unconscious. He won't last long now."

He was glad Mercio was not in pain, not fighting for breath. He spent the night by his side, though there was nothing he could do. Even if supplies did come, it was too late. The boy died early the next morning. Lino had never felt so impotent. He stared at the wall as they removed the body, afraid if he even made eye contact with the indifferent guards he would attack them with his bare hands.

Less than a week later a pig farmer from Pinar del Rio, already weakened by malnutrition, suffered a heart attack and was dead in minutes. This time Lino was not silent. A large group had gathered around the body.

"So what? We just sit here like animals waiting to be slaughtered? I vote we use the only weapon we have - a hunger strike."

There was silence. Then Ramon Miravaldez, a *guajiro* who had been a Castro army sergeant and defected, broke in.

"It's worked other places. If we can embarrass Fidel, do something dramatic enough to get attention outside, no matter how hard they try to keep it quiet . . ."

Lino broke in. "It won't work unless everyone's in. It's the numbers that'll make it dramatic."

Padre Francisco, a thin secular priest with a pronounced hunchback, stood up and spoke quietly. "Wait a second. We have to respect that every man here will make his own decision."

The men were silent.

The priest continued. "We each have our own kind of strength, our own needs and fears. If we do this, no one should be judged by whether he decides to join or not."

"*Estoy de acuerdo.*" Lino looked around to see if others agreed as well.

They discussed the idea for a long time, first in a large group and then in smaller ones. It wasn't an easy decision for some of the men. They were already weakened by malnutrition and unhealed wounds. They had signed up for danger, but this was the first time many of them had faced the idea of purposeful death - of consciously dying for this cause.

These men didn't want to commit and then break ranks later. And Lino didn't want them to. But agreeing could mean condemning their families to never seeing them again, accepting the loss of all their plans and dreams. What was the alternative? If they didn't make a gesture dramatic enough to draw attention to their conditions, people would continue to die.

In the end even the most reluctant men realized they'd rather risk death than be treated like expendable mice in a laboratory. They began refusing all food.

The guards just shrugged, which only hardened the prisoners' determination. The very next day the guards came and said the warden, Betancourt, wanted to talk to Lino. The soldiers obviously sensed that he was a leader, so they assumed the hunger strike was his idea. Actually there were four men heading up the strike, Lino, Cesar Paez, Padre Francisco, and Ramon Miravaldez. The four insisted they be seen together by the warden.

When they entered Betancourt's office, a spacious paneled room on the top floor of the hospital, Lino was determined not to blow up. The warden walked over to the group and said in the most casual tone, "Now, could you explain exactly why you're on this so-called hunger strike?"

That was it. Lino exploded at the man's obvious indifference to the lives of the prisoners. "You have human beings down there - human beings who are dying! You have doctors who can fix them. And you can't give us a few cartons of goddamn supplies so we can clean wounds, suture them?"

The warden reluctantly promised to solve the problem and left the room. The meeting was over. The four were roughly returned to the game room, bayonets pricking their backs. The next afternoon they had the warden's response.

Truncheons sounded against the heavy metal doors. Boots hurried along the cement floor. A platoon of heavily armed guards stormed into the game room, jabbing at bodies with machine guns and rifles.

"Come on you slime, you're gonna see what a hunger strike gets you. Get going! *Arriba!* Prisoners were pulled and shoved roughly to their feet.

"Get your stinking things - and don't take all day." They were lined up in groups of fifty, clutching scraps of blanket, hoarded food, extra clothes if they had them. They waited in dread for over two hours, imagining every possible punishment. Then they were herded into trucks and driven to the port of Trinidad on the south coast where they were loaded onto a waiting frigate. The news passed from man to man: they were being transferred to the maximum security prison on *Isla de Pinos*, the largest of Cuba's offshore islands, 90 miles south of Havana province. They'd heard a lot about *Isla de Pinos*. And none of it was good.

18

In the soft light of early morning, *Isla de Pinos*, seen from the sea, looked benign enough, covered with shrubby vegetation, a few beaches tucked in among the rocky edges confronting the sea. The frigate *Ortiz* approached the harbor shortly after dawn on the morning of July 3, 1961.

The 200 prisoners on board were cramped and disheartened, nauseated by the smell of overflowing human waste. They were thankful for the mercy of a cool night passage, but they had slept little. They were still weak from the days of hunger strike, even though they had been given a little thin soup on the trip. Worst of all was the dread. What was in store for them at this remote island prison?

The ship docked at Nueva Gerona, a town of a dozen streets, home to less than five thousand people, mostly farmers and fishermen. Few people even glanced at the prisoners as they were hauled out of the ship and into open metal trucks lined up at the pier.

People were used to seeing these slouching emaciated prisoners headed for the "model prison" as it had been called when the hulking cement buildings were built in the 1930's in the interior of the island. Only two elderly fishermen, getting ready to go out for the day, stopped for a moment, looking at the faces.

The heavyset man spoke. "My cousin in Havana, his brother-in-law was arrested a couple of weeks ago. Maybe he's one of these poor bastards."

"Nothing would surprise me," the thinner man responded. "My neighbor told me he saw a priest come through one day. And would you believe, the guy had been their parish priest back in '49. Can you imagine putting priests in a prison like that one?"

The two men continued to watch, shaking their heads, until the trucks rumbled out of town.

Isla de Pinos was already crowded. Since the Revolution, the prison's 1200 common criminals had been sent back to the mainland and were replaced by more than a thousand political prisoners. More arrived every day, a few by air at the tiny airport, many by military ship like Lino's group from *Topes de Collantes*. The least fortunate came by overnight ferry after an exhausting fourteen hour drive in closed trucks from Havana.

Most of the inhabitants had lived all their lives in *Isla de Pinos*. The prison was isolated and off-limits; few people had any contact. If they saw the political prisoners at all, they hurried on, unwilling to face the proof of what Cuba had become.

A few people were getting to know the prison well. Taxi drivers regularly went there with passengers who'd come for a precious visit with prisoners. The visitors were happy to pay. The trip from the mainland was hard enough without trudging to the prison from the town on foot. Shops in Nueva Gerona had extra customers on visit days, looking for anything they could take to help their husbands and sons.

The women were often young, dressed in their best clothes to boost the morale of their husbands. Older women came too, weighed down by packages for their sons or grandsons. Children, confused and exhausted, were brought to see their fathers. The little ones were uncomprehending and grumpy, but sensed from their mothers this was important.

Most visitors came off the battered overnight ferry from La Coloma, on the south coast of the mainland. They had spent the night exchanging stories with one another, huddled on wet decks or inside the stuffy vomit-smelling main cabin. The mothers herded their children off the ship and tried to calm them with bread and hot milk, if they could get it.

On this morning, the men with Lino weren't thinking about visitors. They just tried not to think about what would happen next, how long it would be before they'd be out in the air again. They knew of *Isla de Pinos*; word traveled fast among prisoners. Many went in and were never heard of. A few came back with stories of filth, starvation rations, and beatings.

This morning's prisoners were tired and jittery. They had already learned that any transfer of prisoners opened up the possibility of new forms of cruelty or trials, sadistic guards looking to show the new prisoners who was boss.

As the convoy of trucks approached the prison, Lino leaned over the hot metal side of the truck to see the compound from the outside, a sight he suspected he wouldn't see again for many years, if ever. There were four huge circular buildings, each five stories high, each separated by 20 or 30 yards from the others.

The buildings were enclosed by a rectangular wall dotted with guard towers and soldiers with machine guns. In the middle of the four round buildings was a large open air pavilion with a lightweight metal roof to ward off the sun. Inside the rectangle at one end were two long cement buildings. One, Lino would soon learn, was filled with punishment cells; the other was a hospital.

The trucks rolled through the guard barrier and stopped near the center pavilion. Two guards approached laconically. The older of the two, a chunky man with a waddle that would have made Lino smile in other circumstances, made a great show of finding a paper on his clipboard.

He read off Lino's name, along with the names of Padre Francisco, Cesar Paez, and Ramon Miravaldez. Paez leaned over to Lino. "Shit. They obviously have something special in mind for us ringleaders."

Lino shrugged. "We knew they'd get back at us, make an example."

The four were told to jump down from the truck. They were herded roughly toward the smaller of the two rectangular buildings, a two-story cement building with high windows and a single door in the long side facing them.

As they passed through an entry patio and entered the first large space, Lino saw that a series of granite cells had been built inside the high-ceilinged room. Each cell was about seven feet high, with its ceiling open to the much higher original ceiling of the room.

The top of each cell was made of cross-hatched metal fencing, the kind used for factories or savage animals. The four prisoners and their guards stopped in the corridor next to the first small cell. The cell door, already open, was barred, but it had metal sheeting over the bars that left only a slit of open space below and above the metal. At a nod from the taller guard, a stocky one, looking not too sure of himself, grabbed Lino's arm and gestured into the cell. Lino felt like an animal being transferred to a new cage.

"What do you want me to do?" he asked, determined to be treated as a fellow human. In answer, the taller guard grabbed Lino. He stuck his face close to Lino's and shouted, "I'll tell you what we want - get your fuckin' clothes off - right now!"

Here it comes, the usual disinfecting, head shaving, bogus "medical" inspection. But once Lino was naked, the stocky guard just pushed him roughly into cell #3, the number splashed in black letters on the floor. The door was slammed immediately. He was alone.

The cell was about six feet square, too small for him to stretch out without bending either his knees or his neck. The only way to see anything in the corridor would be to stretch out on the floor and peek under the steel plating of the door.

Lino stood in one corner and took inventory. A hard edged space - not a single soft surface. No bed, no mattress, a hole in one corner of the stone floor, the tip of a pipe coming out of the wall. No way to turn the water on.

How long would they leave him here? Until the end? A panic rose in him. Is this where the last of his spirit would leak out and dry up? Would his body slowly deteriorate into a living corpse? Would he die here, his last thoughts of the family he loved and the country he had wanted to save?

No, he would not. He straightened his spine and stretched his limbs as far as they would go. He would not allow such thoughts. Cold stone and isolation would not defeat him.

He listened carefully and heard Ramon and Cesar and Padre Francisco being put into other cells close by. He felt a surge of relief; he wouldn't be totally without human contact. He'd be able to hear signs of life, know others were near by. Right now, the noise of locks grinding and the guards yelling allowed him to hear very little. But his cell wasn't completely closed in. The open ceiling would connect him to the world.

One way to shake off panic and depression was to try to put himself in his jailers' minds. Figure out the code. Why had they put them here? What was the significance? Where were the others from *Topes*?

There would be light and air from the ceiling; but there would be rain and sun too.

He wasn't worried about the physical conditions they might impose on him, even torture. But left completely alone? Severed from all stimulation? Desperation hovering, he forced himself to focus fiercely on one thing: *Take what comes and concentrate on making it through. Not will I make it - just how will I do it.*

The first hours all he could think of was the heat, his raging thirst. He begged for a drink without any real hope of getting it. And he didn't. He was outraged to see how normal Cuban men, once they were made guards, could become so indifferent to the suffering of other Cubans, people like themselves. Didn't they remember how a corroding thirst felt? How cold rough granite grated against bare skin? Could the people he knew in his old life be doing this to someone else? How far would uncertainty and raw fear push people?

At length he collapsed on the floor, too exhausted and discouraged to do anything but sleep. In the night he woke up shivering, his naked body curled tightly into a ball on his side with his head on his arm. His arm felt paralyzed, his whole body tensed and achy. But when he tried to stretch out, he felt the cold stone on every inch of his skin and he curled up again. He tried folding himself into a corner to conserve body heat, but the stone seemed to conduct cold, making him shiver even more.

Early the next morning there was a commotion in the hallway, and Lino thought maybe more prisoners would be put in the cells. As cramped as the cell was, he'd welcome having another human being with him. A few minutes later, however, a small flap near the bottom of the steel plated door was opened and a battered aluminum bowl of food shoved in. No words. No contact. The food was disgusting, tepid greasy liquid with a little macaroni pooled in the bottom. He wanted to gag but he drank it down quickly. He had eaten almost nothing in 48 hours and his body was already lacking nourishment from the hunger strike.

Over the next few days a bleak routine became apparent. No bed or blankets. No clothes. Food shoved in once in the morning. Sometimes a metal spoon to eat with and sometimes just his fingers. It was impossible to stay clean; there were bugs everywhere. Whenever he was motionless for too long, rats would nose their way into the cell through chinks in the stone.

Once a day, the small pipe near the latrine hole was turned on from outside for a few minutes - just enough to get a drink and clean the latrine. Sometimes he had to choose between thirst and filth.

The worst was not knowing when, or if, the isolation would ever end. Would he ever again be with other human beings, feel a warm touch, see his family? The other prisoners probably assumed the four of them had been hauled into this building and shot, were already decomposing in some anonymous grave. The thought of Emy not knowing if she was a widow haunted him.

He hoped she had gone to Miami to live with her parents and raise their children as best she could. Neither of them had really expected him to survive if he was captured. And whatever she could do for him here was not worth the hell of staying in Cuba – with or without the children. It was bad enough he'd deserted them; they mustn't be alone, pariahs in their own country.

He prayed for his children, that they would understand. He prayed for his own strength. Most of all, he prayed he would endure - take whatever pain the regime could inflict and not give in. Even if he were executed, he didn't want to leave this world beaten into submission by Fidel and his minions.

Each time he awoke, he shuddered with revulsion at being caged. The guards took sport in yelling at the prisoners, especially if they were trying to rest. The lack of privacy was hideous. If they peered in, the guards could see everything a prisoner did, even squatting above the latrine hole or inspecting his body for sores.

What preserved his sanity was the presence of the others nearby. He soon learned to recognize them by the smallest signs of their existence: Padre Francisco's tuneless humming, Cesar's pacing in the early morning. They were all learning the key to surviving prison life - finding the smallest normalcy, staying human in the most deadening conditions.

The best moment of the day was just before the sun set when the prison quieted down and the heat abated a little. The angle of the sun brought sparkling light through the slit at the top of the cell door. The guards, lulled into indifference, would abandon their posts and gather in the hallway to play cards and gossip.

Then the prisoners' words would flow through the ceilings. They talked not about their pain and their longings but about almost anything else: times past, people they knew, music and books, funny stories they'd all heard before but now brought soothing memories of better times. Other prisoners came and went to the punishment cells for a few days or a few weeks; sometimes they joined the conversations.

After a day of no contact - and no action - it was surprising how much there was to share. Their voices would sometimes give out from talking loud enough to be heard up and over the walls. They didn't care; they'd been silent all day.

Ramon often talked about what would be going on at his farm at this time of year: the temperamental machines, his wife's hopeless attachment to animals she knew had to be sold, the ancient donkey he kept for his children to ride. Padre Francisco would tell about parishioners he remembered and what had happened to them. Sometimes these stories would lead to discussions about faith and scriptures, the doubts the men were feeling.

Lino, the only doctor, found that others liked to hear about cases he had treated, his thoughts about the future of medicine, and especially psychiatry. He revisited difficult decisions he'd made about patients; the others would ask questions and give opinions.

One day Lino began teasing Cesar in jest about being on time. "Aren't you a little late getting up this morning? You better get a move on if you're going to keep to your schedule!" The ridiculousness of watching the time in such a timeless existence for some reason made them laugh.

After that Lino became the imaginary timekeeper. Ramon would yell out, "Lino what time is it?" Lino would pretend to consult his nonexistent watch and call out, "exactly 12 minutes after 3." Or "at the tone, it will be 6 p.m." He spoke with great authority; for some reason this seemed to make everyone feel better. If time passed here just as it did outside, then they were still part of the world. No one could keep them from smiling at their own jokes in their filthy dim cages.

Lino often talked about how much he missed books. One night he started talking about a book and ended up relating the plot in great detail. Everyone agreed it was a wonderful escape. From then on, they "read" to one another each evening from remembered books, sometimes even plays or movies.

They all took turns, but Lino was the favorite storyteller. Sitting on the floor with his back to the cold wall, he told stories that carried them all a thousand miles and years away from that place. His calm rich voice sounded as though he were seated in an armchair reading from a leather-bound volume. He told stories from books he had read, stories he made up, and stories that mixed the plots of several books.

Sometimes he lost his plot or changed a character's name in the middle. It didn't matter. His voice in the soft light of sunset was the soothing moment of their day. A gift before they lay down on the stone floor and slept. One more day endured.

19

In mid-July, the hurricane season began. The open ceiling, such a joy for talking among themselves, became a scourge, the source of nature's tortures. The guards were always happy to make the prisoners' lives miserable; now nature did it for them.

The high windows of the building had no glass, and blinding sheets of water invaded the cells. Lino's corner cell let double the water in. He and the others spent hours, even entire days and nights, huddled in naked drenched misery. The guards made no attempt to protect the prisoners. Then the sun would arrive, the heat at first delightful but soon scorching the prisoners who had no way to escape it.

Lino carefully counted off the days. He believed he was tracking right in his head, but he made scratches in the stone just to be sure. Thirty marks, then forty, careful cross-hatches made with a tiny dislodged edge of metal sheeting. He figured it was August 15 on the day a Captain came into the corridor and spoke through the metal paneled door to him.

"Fernandez, you have a telegram."

Lino was instantly alarmed. Telegrams were only allowed to announce deaths or other catastrophes. Never good news. What could have happened? Or was this one of their cruel tricks, to get him riled up? Must be something they wanted him to know, since they let it through.

He said nothing as the Captain opened the food door and slipped in a yellow folded piece of paper. He grabbed the paper and took a deep breath before he slowly unfolded it and read.

The children will leave tomorrow for the United States with Mama and Papa. I am here with you, Siempre, Emy.

Siempre. Always. Forever. Four years earlier, young and trusting in a white satin gown, Emy had said "as long as we both shall live." His eyes filled with tears - how truly she had meant it. He felt a deluge of regret, of heartsickness. What a joyless life he had brought her. And yet she loved him, had renounced her own right to be a mother every day for the dreary task of watching over him. He had hoped so much for her to go to Miami and live surrounded by family. To rescue what she could from this miserable turn of life.

Instead, she was thinking of everyone but herself. Her parents, even though far from her, would be involved and dedicated, focused on their grandchildren. The children would be loved and watched over. Lino had no agonizing choice to make. Emy had the worst choice and she'd chosen him, chosen anguish for herself rather than leaving him alone in hell.

He stood, reached up to grab the ceiling and dug his hands into the rough metal fencing. He pulled his weight a few inches off the floor, welcoming the distracting pain in his fingers. He wanted to howl in distress and helplessness.

She would have no contact with her children. She would be reviled and without rights. Painful memories everywhere. No real home. No future, nothing to work for, never allowed to belong. She had made that choice to be as close to him as she could, to give him hope. Because she believed she might save his life.

He read the telegram again and again. It was like having a part of Emy with him. He lay awake most of the night. He imagined Emy embracing each child and saying goodbye. Lucia would be sitting up and smiling now, waving her arms, wanting to get down and explore. For her, Lino did not exist. Did Emilia Maria, at least, remember her father tickling and laughing with her? How long before even that memory disappeared? Would she realize her mother too was saying goodbye? He imagined Po squirming from Emy's arms when she tried to hold him one last time.

Where would she find the strength? Maybe she would change her mind, unable to stand the anguish of letting them go.

He imagined her waking each morning with no one near. He saw her taking up her grim vigil in Havana, alone and missing them. Who could she tell how her heart ached? Who would understand and share her emptiness? How would she stand the long months waiting for a visit?

He wanted to scream. *My darling, it's not worth it!* If only he had her here with him, he would hold her, entreat her to go with the children. In his heart, he knew he wouldn't have been able to change her mind. She had made her decision from the core of her being, from the center of her love for him and her family. She would persevere.

Lluvia. Más lluvia. Weeks of rain. In the moist air, the food stank of mold. No matter how disgusting it was, he ate. He knew he was losing weight and was thankful he had been well nourished and fit before his capture. He had always done sports at school and exercised as a young doctor. He had started out with more resistance than many, and he had been a prisoner for less than six months. When he tensed his arm muscles, he could still feel some strength.

Every time he thought of Emy alone, he banished any temptation to just give up. She had not made this hideous sacrifice so she could take his broken body home. She had stayed to give him courage, to preserve the man she wanted to be with. He would not let this squalor and mistreatment weaken him.

In spite of being careful, he developed sores from constant moisture and his body rubbing against stone when he stretched out to sleep or tried to exercise. Blisters formed and broke. Scabs got rubbed off too early; sores started to bleed or ooze again.

He tried to keep his skin clean, but he had nothing to use. The very little water was needed to drink. The constant itching told him he had lice or worse. He felt himself getting weaker - so little food, no way to move about, almost no fresh air.

The random cruelty of the guards reinforced his feeling of powerlessness. After Emy found out through other prisoners' families where Lino was, she brought once a month, as she was allowed, packages to be given to him. He felt heartsick at the thought of Emy making the long trip to *Isla de Pinos* just to leave a package, knowing she wouldn't be allowed to see him.

The guards would find every way to keep him from enjoying the things she brought. If something could spoil, they left it in the sun. If she included something fragile, the guards looked for a way to damage it.

"Hey Lino, look at this beautiful avocado somebody sent you," yelled a smug bearded guard one evening from the ceiling. He held up a beautiful large golden-green avocado, obviously not yet ripe. Lino was enraptured at the thought of eating the soft creamy fruit. It would be full of vitamins too. How clever of Emy to make that choice.

"Gee, it's too big to fit." The guard banged the fruit against the fencing. "But it's our duty to deliver this to the prisoner." Lightening fast, he slashed the avocado into long jagged pieces." Lino twisted his head away. *You've ruined it, you bastard. You know it will never ripen like that. I can't eat it green.*

"So here it comes," the guard taunted. He stuffed each piece of the avocado through the small space between the bars and let it fall to the floor of Lino's cell. The seed wouldn't fit so he gave a mock apology, and then stood there, hoping to savor Lino's disappointment and anger. But Lino's face was still. He sat with his back to the guard and forced himself to think about a warm evening in Santa Maria, watching the waves slide into the sand.

What bothered him most were not these petty cruelties but the unrelenting lack of action, the black void of loneliness. He had to believe this wouldn't last forever, that he would again be part of a community and not end his life alone in this stinking cell.

Everything the regime did to him was one more barrier to survival. But he slowly realized this delay was probably a good thing. If they were going to kill him here in *Isla de Pinos*, wouldn't they have just gotten it over with? Why waste food on him?

He hadn't even gone to trial yet; that would be the moment of real danger. If he got to trial and the government realized who he was, he would be sentenced to death, shot within hours of the verdict.

God, would he see Emy before he was shot? Would he ever hold her again? Would his children have only Emy's memories of him, their father dead before they could know him? Horrifying. Possible. It was happening every day. He tried not to think of those fine principled men already executed, their souls and minds destroyed, their bodies in untended common graves somewhere.

He remembered all the things he had heard about *Isla de Pinos* - the beatings, the sadism, the random dragging away of men to be shot. Even at *Topes de Collantes*, these things had happened. Before his trial, or after if by some miracle he received only a long prison sentence, death could still come any day in prison, at the whim of some sick revolutionary showing off his power.

If he didn't move around, he felt sluggish and desperate from too much thinking. If he did move, his body protested the lack of food, the cold, the wet or the heat. These things he could bear when he was part of a group, with tasks and a survival plan. How long could he tolerate them on his own?

He began to concentrate on his own self-discipline. His mind was the one thing that was whole and clean, only starved for stimulation. He would feed it. He began rummaging in his mind for pieces of poems or speeches he had heard, even parts of the Bible. Then he memorized each piece as he remembered it. His companions started contributing their own remembered fragments.

As he remembered more and more, he practiced delivering these recitations in a low voice, with great dignity, to the blank stone wall. Just this straining to remember, striving for improvement, stimulated him and made him feel more human.

When he was happy with the results, when he had remembered every bit he could and polished his delivery, he would recite the piece to the others. He sent his eloquence flying up through his own chain ceiling and down through theirs. It helped. He was alive inside. He was connected to a world of fine minds and lofty thoughts. He was holding firm.

Then it happened, in the most ordinary way, with no warning. There was no food that early October morning, leaving them all uneasy and alert. A group of six soldiers entered the punishment cell building in the late afternoon. The officer in charge began to yell.

"Get up, you scum, haul your miserable stinkin' bodies out of there. That is, if you can still stand up," he added, obviously pleased at the possibility of their having to crawl out. Lino looked at his scratches on the wall. One hundred days. This could not be a coincidence. Someone was playing with them.

The four men emerged cautiously. Cesar came first, then Lino, both looking tensely around. Then Ramon came silently out, stopping in the doorway to see what would happen. Last came Padre Francisco who was having trouble walking.

The four looked at one another, each appalled at how thin and filthy the others looked. Then they quickly looked away, not wanting to inspire the sadism of the guards, never far beneath the surface.

The guards said nothing to allay the prisoners' fears, gave no clues to what was coming. The officer just gestured to the youngest guard who tossed each man a packet of cloth, loose-fitting khaki uniforms left over from the time of Batista. The four prisoners didn't wait to be told to put them on. Lino knew he should be insulted to wear Batista's colors, but they felt like silk after three months of nakedness.

In an instant he felt less degraded, more human, regardless of what happened next. Being issued the Batista uniforms actually represented a victory. He knew that political prisoners under Castro had steadfastly refused to wear the standard yellow convict uniforms because such clothes would symbolize they were criminals. They weren't; they were imprisoned simply for what they believed. It was an enormous differentiation to the prisoners and to the world that hopefully remembered their existence. If Fidel was allowed to treat political prisoners like common convicts, he could bury them in his system, make them invisible, insist they didn't exist.

Being given uniforms had an even greater meaning in Lino's mind. If the person in charge had decided, or been told, to shoot them, he wouldn't have bothered to clothe them. Why waste a good uniform? Why give a condemned prisoner the dignity of being dressed? Better to let them die in total degradation. Lino's tension lessened a little.

Still with no explanation, each guard took one prisoner and pushed him toward the door. Lino recognized his escort as a perpetually discontented young man who used to shove their food into the cells hard enough to spill some of the precious contents, probably hoping he would get to watch them lick it off the floor.

In spite of the scowling impatient guard beside him, Lino stepped very slowly from the building into the light and stood stock still. He was engulfed by the glare of the sunlight swirling around him, taking away his balance, forcing him to reach out to the doorframe to steady himself.

The feeling of being almost blinded was delicious. The slight movement of air against his skin felt caressing; he turned his head to feel it better. He turned slowly to drink in the luxury of his eyes focusing far into the distance. Even in those long months of longing, he had never imagined the mere outdoors could be so exhilarating. Whatever happened next, he would remember these sensations.

He followed the others, walking as slowly as he was allowed. At one point he put his feet apart, leaned his head back and stretched his arms above his head, gazing at the sky. The guards moved toward him, looking alarmed, but he was only experimenting with the freedom to move his limbs as far as they could go, to encounter no stone or bars, only air and sky, endless free air.

He knew he must be disgusting: filthy matted hair and patchy beard, unwashed skin scraped and pale, ragged nails. He was glad his slack body was now covered with the cotton uniform. Inside, his spirit felt scrubbed, strong, ready for whatever came next. God only knew what that would be.

The group reached the entrance to the building called Circular #2 and stopped. Lino felt a tentative jolt of hope. Were they being put into an open prison block? Not a firing squad or some kind of fake tribunal? Was the isolation over, at least for now? One of the guards shoved him toward the entrance with his rifle butt.

He was drunk with relief. Being out of the stone cell was dazzling. On the one hand, he desperately wanted more time in the sun, to feast his eyes on far views, to move in the air.

On the other hand, inside this circular waited people he knew, people like him; he craved their community. He would still be a prisoner, still in the power of sadists and thugs. But he would be with other men he cared about, share their lives, feel their respect.

20

Lino stepped through the cement doorway and entered Circular #2 on the ground floor, a round covered courtyard fifty yards across with walls of six stories. He stood at the edge of the uneven concrete floor, his eyes and lungs feasting on the spaciousness after his tiny cage.

Looking up at the five circular rows of cells, one on each story, he saw that a balcony fronted each row. Single figures or groups of men walked along or stood leaning over. A square metal guard tower in the middle of the court reached to the sixth floor ceiling, allowing guards to see into any cell. After Lino's 100 days of isolation, the space seemed abuzz with activity.

"Doctor Fernandez, after all this time I meet you."

The speaker was a stocky young man, nicely groomed, considering where he was. Smiling broadly, he shook Lino's hand. "I am Vicente Guitterez."

Lino was delighted. Although he knew Guitterez had been Professor of Economics at Villanueva University, Lino had never met him, only knew his reputation. He was much respected.

"*Ven conmigo.* We have room in our cell and we would be honored to share it with you." Words of such warmth and respect brought to Lino a pleasure that no physical luxury could.

"Someone else will be very anxious to see you, Dr. Pelayo Torres." Lino nodded, close to tears. He suddenly felt he could survive anything if he could be with men like this, men who believed as he did and were here because they fought for those beliefs.

123

Vicente led him up the iron stairs that linked the floors. Lino wanted to fly from space to space, but the effect of long months in a cramped cell was showing. He had trouble walking quickly and had to stop several times.

People who knew him and people who had heard of him, even held him in awe, stopped the two to welcome Lino. He felt weak with the pleasure of shaking men's hands, of finding old friends alive, of just being free to walk within this enormous space.

They stopped at the top of the stairs on the second floor. The tall man standing at the balcony had clearly been looking for them. Pelayo turned around and Lino saw the familiar black hair and eyebrows, as thick as ever, framing his fine features. He rushed to give Lino an enormous bear hug. The welcoming touch of another human being was like a balm to Lino's tired spirit.

"Allow me to give you a tour," Vicente said with mock formality. "Our home is modest, but we're used to it." Lino grinned and looked around. He'd been so involved with seeing Pelayo he hadn't given the cell even a glance.

It was a wedge shape, about eight feet deep by six wide at the largest part, with a two foot by three foot window set into the thick cement wall.

Two narrow iron frame bunks, one above another, were attached to a side wall and supported by chains when unfolded. Another bunk was temporarily hung between them, leaving only two feet between each bed. Now the bunks were folded against the wall to make more room. The only bedding was canvas slung from the bunk frames, its original light color obscured by stains and grime.

"If what we hear about isolation is true," said Pelayo, "this bunk won't feel so bad to you." With a flourish, he folded down the bottom bunk and invited Lino to lie down. Lino stretched out tentatively; it felt like a feather bed after sleeping on stone. He thought he could fall asleep instantly, but he was much too excited. He sat up again. Talk and the closeness of friends was what he wanted most.

Pelayo sat next to him. He was normally reserved, but he seemed energized by Lino's arrival. "Some lucky bastards in here actually have blankets, even pillows their families sent. Unfortunately they often get 'damaged' or disappear during the inspection raids."

Vicente rolled his eyes. "You can imagine."

"But the guy next door, he's held on to his bedding for almost six months. He's a good guy, lends his blanket when someone's sick.

These SOBs certainly wouldn't give you one," he added, nodding to the guard tower.

"And now, the sanitary facilities." There was a small faucet on the wall. Pelayo grabbed it and turned with exaggerated force. "Either there isn't any water or I'm weaker than I thought," he joked. "Actually we do get water; the problem is you never know when. So we just give it a twist every time we go by."

"In isolation, it came on the same time every day. But only for about a minute." The others grimaced.

"Just tell me there's a shower here," Lino said urgently. "I stink to high heaven and I'd give my right arm for some soap."

"Only cold water." Tommy Fernandez, a young student who lived in the next cell, had been standing listening to them at the balcony. "You're probably used to hot."

Lino liked Tommy right away, especially his infectious grin. "Oh yea, definitely," Lino chuckled. "And big fluffy Turkish towels too."

As much as he wanted to be with people, Lino hurried to the showers on the edge of the central courtyard and took a long shower, cold but heavenly. He was amazed when the water kept coming. He put his head directly in the stingy spray and let rivulets trickle through his hair and down over his shoulders. He'd been given a small bar of soap and he rubbed it slowly, languidly over his dry scaly skin. He knew he shouldn't waste the soap, but tomorrow would be soon enough to be thrifty.

He dried himself with a scrap of terrycloth Pelayo had given him and put his new uniform back on. His skin was about four shades lighter and tingled all over. He gave himself a rudimentary shave with a borrowed blade. He felt almost normal, if he even remembered what that was.

When he got back to his cell, the third resident of the cell was there. He was Orestes Garcia, who had been a member of the *Directorio Estudiantil* underground in Havana and a very good student. He had been Guitterez' student before Orestes was arrested and sent to prison at 18.

As Lino talked to Orestes, they were joined by Tomas, another very young prisoner.

"How did you end up here?" Lino asked.

"Militia found us camping one night. I never knew if our sentry was asleep - or maybe he sold us out. Anyway, we spent a week in Las Villas - what a dump." Tomas spat out the words.

"So I've heard. Were you beat up?"

"Not officially. But this one guard was really brutal. You'll see a fellow named Mario when you go downstairs. That bastard crushed Mario's ankle so badly they ended up amputating the whole foot."

Lino winced.

"Then he almost died of infection. Now he uses crutches because they won't give him a prosthesis. Jesus, it hurts to watch someone badly treated like that. One of you guys could have saved that ankle."

"We sure would have tried." Lino said.

"So anyway they beat us up pretty bad, but thank God they had so many prisoners they just wanted us out of there. So they sent us here."

Lino thought of the operating rooms in *Topes*. Medical school had trained them to make people well. And now they had to stand by while men suffered and deteriorated.

Other prisoners came and went from the cell, discussing and comparing their experiences. Everyone wanted to hear what Lino had to say about the fighting before he was captured - who had been arrested and who was still free.

Vicente had been a messenger for the MRR between Havana and smaller cities. "I'll tell you," he said, "Most of the people out in the countryside are supportive, but some of the petty officials are real snakes. Always ready to use the Revolution for their own ends. I was sent to Cardenas with orders for a guy named Diego. When I got there, they had just buried him!"

The others looked baffled.

"Turns out his own sister was married to a guy Fidel had made a judge. A real rabid Communist. The sister knew Diego hated Fidel. So when the militia was attacked in town, she told her husband where Diego was.

"Nice sister." Orestes said.

"He was dragged out of a barn where he was hiding and shot 'as an example.' His family was torn apart. Diego's mother wouldn't speak to her daughter and the father didn't know what the hell to do." No one spoke for a long minute.

Lino broke the silence. "How do we get news from the outside? Have we got a radio?"

"I'll show you tomorrow." A grey haired man spoke from the corner. "I'm Luis. We met at Placetas - I don't know if you remember."

"*Seguro que sí.* I'd forgotten your name."

The thick walls gave each window a wide sill; Lino sat there where he could look out as he listened to the conversation. The windows had no glass, only bars. He imagined they let in cold in winter, heat in summer, and hordes of mosquitoes. But today it was nice to feel the air. The others sat or stretched out on the floor as they talked.

Just after noon, food arrived and was distributed one floor at a time by the prisoners elected to that job. One of them gave Lino an aluminum plate, mug, and spoon. The food wasn't much better than in the punishment cell, but here he had company and distraction. No one taunted him or watched his every move.

The central court, where the food was dished out, was kept clean by the prisoners who gathered up the garbage, though there was nowhere to throw it. Rats prowled the court whenever it was quiet or dark; roaches criss-crossed the gritty floor.

The center of the court received light from the unshuttered windows, one in each of the 93 cells on each floor. In theory the court was only for roll call and meals, but the inmates used it for everything: social gatherings, every kind of sport, meetings. The guards in the tower didn't care what they did as long as they didn't cause any trouble.

The circular had bathrooms, with real toilets. A prisoner could shower anytime. Certain books and magazines were allowed, passed around and treasured. Lino was free to walk around, talk to others, choose how to spend his time. He drank in these small luxuries in gulps. Such niceties had never given him so much pleasure. Comforts unnoticed in his old life had become treasured privileges.

The first evening, a group gathered in Lino's new cell. Vicente, who had been in the circular for almost eight months, explained how things had evolved.

"When we arrived, there were mostly guys from the old Batista regime. They'd taken power, distributing things by rank and favor. There were all kinds of abuses, violence against the newly arrived prisoners."

"With a few exceptions they were real bastards." A prisoner's voice oozed contempt.

"The abuse was something people just wouldn't stand for," Vicente continued. "One of the worst bullies was found dead in the middle of a fight in the courtyard. There were no questions asked."

Lino rubbed his hand across the edge of the middle bunk, thinking about what he was hearing. "So what changed?"

"Well, as soon as we had enough of our guys in here to support us we just said, 'Enough, this is not the way things are going to be.'"

"I'll bet the Batista guys loved that."

"No, it wasn't easy. There were some pretty harrowing fights. Guys used chains from the bunks, anything we had. Naturally the guys in the tower ignored everything; they just let us beat each other up. They didn't care who won. None of us were going anywhere."

Gonzalez' deep voice broke in. Lino Gonzalez was a huge gentle black man that Lino would come to respect enormously. "Hell, once we got those guys under control, we got things moving. We decided we needed a kind of mayor. We call him a *rejero,* you know like a guy who works with grates and bars, because his job is to 'go to the bars', negotiate with our jailers."

Pelayo grinned at Gonzalez. "And guess who was chosen? Gonzalez here tells the guards if someone's sick. He organizes roll call at seven in the morning and seven at night, so nobody gets in trouble for not being in the right place."

Gonzalez spoke up. "The key is that no one else talks to the guards or their officers. If they know the *rejero* speaks for everyone, it gives the prisoners a stronger voice."

Lino, leaning against the cell wall, loved the spirit of strategy and determination he was hearing from his fellow prisoners.

"There are other jobs too, Lino." Gonzalez grinned. "We saved a good one for you - how are you at washing clothes - with no soap and cold water? You can use your science background."

Orestes laughed. "Don't worry Lino, you have to get elected. So all you have to do is screw it up and you're off the hook."

Pelayo looked serious. "Actually Lino, jobs are important. If you're supposed to give out food or mail or clean, it gives you a reason to get up."

Lino had one burning question. "What's the deal with mail and packages? How often? Do you really get what your family sends?"

"It's hard to know." Pelayo was his usual cautious self. "We're allowed to get quite a few things - clothes, blankets, some food. Of course now they've decided no meat or cheese - in other words, no protein."

Orestes muttered, "Those little bastards. I don't know why they don't just kill us now instead of starving us to death."

Tommy from next door broke in. "And then of course sometimes our little friends in the militia see something they like."

Gonzalez plopped himself down in the corner with a sigh. "It depends too on what your family can find - and afford. My wife doesn't get any rations; the CDR on her block sees to that. A lot of guys, their wives were kicked out of their jobs. Most of our families just hang on. And there's less and less to buy, even if you got money."

"You'll love this, Lino." Orestes leaned in. "They actually **sell** us stuff, like cigarettes and oil for lanterns. Fidel the great equalizer becomes storekeeper. But thank God he does."

The discussion turned to the invasion at *Bahía de Cochinos* and its failure. Some of the captured invaders, Cuban exiles, were in *Isla de Pinos*, but none in this circular. The other prisoners knew more than Lino about exactly what had happened. He became disheartened, deeply discouraged, as he heard the details. Could anyone get rid of Fidel now? Had the resistance missed its best chance to topple him, betrayed by its supposed ally the U.S.?

When he stretched out on the top bunk that night, Lino was exhausted and full of doubts, in spite of the stimulation of the day. He missed Emy. If only she were stretched out beside him. If he could only wake to feel Emilia Maria's baby hair on his skin, hear her giggle as she played with his eyelids and tried to wake him up. Good strong coffee at the kitchen table in the morning. Warm rolls from the bakery down the block. He finally drifted off.

21

Lino's two cellmates, plus Pelayo Torres, Lino Gonzalez, and seven others, became an informal *cooperativa*. They shared critical supplies like milk powder and sugar, storing them in the least crowded cell among them. They pooled contents of packages from home and leftovers from meals brought by visitors.

There were many of these *cooperativas* among the prisoners - pseudo-families where prisoners could belong and feel some predictability in their uncertain lives. Lino's group, if they had a treat like chocolate or crackers from home, liked to gather at 9 p.m. for a pre-bed snack and conversation. These were the pleasures that let them feel they had normal, if impoverished, lives.

All four circulars at *Isla de Pinos* were full - more than 1200 political prisoners in each. They were living three and four in cells meant for two. As Lino watched and listened, it seemed as though the crowding and the dragging days were taking their toll on people's spirits.

He sought out Pelayo one night after supper, sitting on the stairs. "I'm worried about these guys. Most of them have never been confined, and now they're separated from everyone they know and care about. Just listen to what they long for: their families, their villages, a *cafecito* after dinner. Just being outdoors, enjoying the beach or a field, for God's sake."

Pelayo shook his head. "Yea, the deprivation is bad." Pelayo could seem uninvolved, but underneath Lino knew he was astute and caring. "But the worst thing for some is not the conditions but the injustice of being here at all." Pelayo leaned over the railing and looked into the courtyard. "We haven't broken the law; all we've done is disagree with Fidel. And for this we've lost our rights even to be treated like human beings."

Over the next weeks, Lino got to know a burly middle-aged man named Manuel, a car mechanic who had left his own garage in Santa Clara to his brother and gone to maintain trucks and jeeps for the guerillas. He'd been picked up in a jeep stolen from the army.

"God, I miss my garage. Santa Clara's a great place. *La conoces?*"

"Only the prison."

"*Si Si.* I was there a few days too. But I grew up in Santa Clara. How 'bout you?"

"Not too far from there, in Esmeralda. But I've been in Havana a long time." Lino wondered why he was using the present tense.

Manuel shook his head. "I'm not really sorry I joined the guerillas. I just wish I knew what was gonna happen to me. My kids are growing up. My wife, Gracia, she brings them to see me when she can. They don't understand. And it's horrible to hold them and then see them just walk away." Lino nodded. Of course kids couldn't understand. He said nothing about his own children.

"Sometimes I wish I would go to trial, get it over with. But then I think of Cinco, a friend from Santa Clara. He was in a group that tried to blow up an armory. He went to Santa Clara for trial in September and never came back. I don't ask my wife. I don't wanna know."

Lino understood. Too many people never returned from trial. Each time a group was shipped out, the goodbyes and wishes of good luck sounded increasingly false.

Lino was a doctor, but also a strategist, someone who thought in battle terms. They needed to organize for the long term, keep up a sense of normalcy, stay strong. He was always talking to people, asking what they were up to and how they were doing. He found a lot of prisoners, those who weren't too weakened by confinement and malnutrition, applying themselves ingeniously to making do with what they had. To Lino, this was the first step in survival.

One day Moya, a taciturn round-faced carpenter who had been with Lino in *Topes*, showed him how he made glue by melting cooked pasta.

"It takes a long time, but see, it holds up this shelf." Moya gestured to a shelf on the wall of his cell.

Tommy Fernandez told Lino how he had made a lamp from a juice bottle, kerosene, and shredded cloth, so he could read late at night. "In a month, half the cells had the same thing," he boasted. Lino knew how important this attitude was. Not thinking "we don't have it" but "how do we make it?"

Lino knew spreading news was critical. He quickly made friends with a mechanical engineer, a lanky practical man in his forties who had defected from Fidel and been caught. Now he'd taken charge of setting up a communication system.

"With this clear line of sight between some of the circulars, a visual system made sense," he told Lino, pointing out the window. "We just adapted the Morse code to a sheet of paper, white if we have it. When the sheet is flapped forward straight down like this, it's a dot." The engineer demonstrated. "Flipped sideways like this, it's a dash. Guards don't notice it; the sun and shadow make it hard to see unless you know just where to look. And if we ever get caught," he gave a sly smile, "I can chew up the paper or throw it in the toilet."

Lino smiled. "What kind of news do you get?"

"A lot of the stuff we send is for prisoners in other circulars, passing on news from visits or warning about new problems. Prisoners who get moved between circulars take our codes with them so their new circular starts using them too."

"I'm impressed. What about intelligence?"

"Oh we have lots of political and military messages - you know, observations about the island, radar, troop movements, and fortifications. That stuff's more dangerous. We translate it into military codes, ones we still have from the Escambray, before we send them."

He gestured down the hallway. "I've got guys who spend their whole days coding and sending messages between the circulars. They're damned good!"

Vicente explained later that, when it was really necessary, they would smuggle military observations in and out with visitors, but it was more risky. Those messages were always coded and used only for the most important matters.

Lino was dying to get a letter to Emy, but he wasn't authorized yet to send anything out officially. Vicente told Lino to write one, and Vicente would send it out the next time his own wife Fina visited.

"They let visitors take stuff out?"

Vicente laughed. "*Por supuesto que no.* But I'll show you how to put together a letter that will get out - I guarantee it."

Vicente told Lino to write as small as he possibly could on onionskin paper. "Don't worry if you can't read it yourself. Emy can get a magnifying glass. Here, I'll show you with the letter someone gave me this morning." Vicente rolled the paper as tight as he could. Then he wrapped the tiny cylinder in a scrap of plastic wrap and sealed it with a burning cigarette. It looked like a soft obese toothpick.

"Now, I'll give this to Fina and she'll hide it on her person the best she can. It can be hidden in lots of places - we don't ask." He grinned and waved Lino's protest away. "When someone is coming to see one of us, Emy can give them a letter for you. Same process."

Prisoners were only allowed a visit every few months. But with so many prisoners, there were plenty of visit days. The smuggled letters were treasures to prisoners and their wives. Best of all, they weren't censored.

At last he could communicate with Emy. His first letter poured out his love and longing for her, his sadness that she was without the children. He didn't write about his experiences in the punishment cells, and he had little room to describe the circular. He needed to send messages of love, and he was sure she needed to hear them.

Luis came to show Lino the radio system, just as he'd promised. He was one of the operators, but he wasn't on duty this day.

"We're incredibly well informed when you think of it. We have one of those great little pre-revolutionary radios; I don't know how the hell we got it in." As they climbed the stairs, Luis pointed out several lookouts that were always on duty when the radio was being used.

They reached a cell on the fifth floor where Luis introduced Lino to the operator on duty, Enrique. He was assembling the radio from several pieces. Each, he explained, was hidden in a different place. "It makes things smaller, easier to hide. And if they ever find one piece, we only have to replace that one- we still have the rest."

Lino examined the tiny radio. *"Cómo está funcionando?"*

"Good. You'd be amazed. We pick up Caribbean stations great, except in hurricane weather of course. Mostly we get BBC from the British islands or Radio Netherlands." Enrique turned away. "Better get to it."

He put in his tiny ear pieces and listened intently, writing quickly on a small piece of paper. His face was expressionless. When he took off his ear pieces, he quickly disassembled the radio parts and gave them to a young prisoner with instructions where to hide them. Then he turned to Luis and Lino with a more relaxed manner.

"Hmmm. Fidel's brother is visiting Asia, 'building positive relations'. What a farce."

Lino nodded and waited for Enrique to say more.

"I wish we could get more internal news. But when you're in here, it's nice to hear anything." He raised his eyebrows. "And of course there's always that tiny spark of hope - FIDEL SHOT! Now that's a message I'd like to deliver." He gave them a salute and took off, clattering down the stairs.

"Now he'll write up a summary of whatever news we get, a copy for each floor," Luis explained as they went back down the stairs. "People can hand it around or listen to it read out loud. There are a lot of guys here who can't read."

"How do you keep the radio going?"

"There's a guy who makes new batteries from pieces of an aluminum bucket and potassium chloride; we steal that from the hospital lab whenever we can."

Lino felt a tug of hope. As long as men like this were on his side, there had to be a way out of this stinking mess.

Luis continued. "The guards know we've got the radio; they're pissed as hell they can't find it. Maybe that's why they're so savage when they do their raids."

Lino had heard about the brutal searches. But he didn't begin to understand until he lived through his first one.

Requisa! Search! The warning shout. Guts twisted with fear. Barely one minute of warning to try to hide contraband, scramble to protect a few precious possessions. Then the roar of the invading horde, the snarling pack of human beasts, viciously beating men unarmed and weak from malnutrition and confinement. A screaming mass of soldiers swarming over the circular, stabbing with bayonets, crushing limbs with truncheons and rubber-wrapped chains. The panic of no place to hide, knowing you'll be beaten harder for trying to protect yourself, stomped on for clinging to a pillar or rail, thrown down the stairs for daring to hesitate. The shame of having to step over bleeding beaten friends, of being stripped naked as you cower.

The indignity of men whining, begging, whimpering before a skull is cracked, a shoulder yanked from its socket, genitals smashed with the gun butt.

Requisa! Men in heavy boots pounding, shaking the metal stairways.

Yelling orders and then beating men before they had time to obey. Razor-sharp bayonets slicing into men as they were forced to run the gauntlet of soldiers waiting on the stairs - jabbing, gouging whatever flesh they could reach. Stretching over balconies and under stairs to deliver one last blow before another soldier grabbed the man and found new flesh.

The ultimate threat: stopping to catch your breath could bring months in an isolation cell. If you looked like you might manage to harm a guard, you got a bullet in the head from the M14 of one of the guards at the perimeter.

And the final indignity, forced to lie face down in the filthy courtyard floor for hours, mouth in the fungus and mud, bugs swarming over you.

"Anybody raise their head, I'll blow it off."

Knowing it was true. Watching it happen. Trying not to breathe in the stench of blood and urine, holding on until it was over.

Afterwards, telling yourself that surviving was the most important thing - you were still alive. Those who might die carted off to the hospital, the rest left to crawl and ache and feel lucky.

Returning to cells and hallways in shambles. The spirit pain of relentless destruction - everything you need so badly. Photographs and letters ripped, mattresses and clothes slashed, heels pulled off shoes, eyeglasses shattered and rubbed into the dirt, toothbrushes smeared with excrement, broken jars and bottles whose contents had been saved in such anticipation. And the food. Chocolate saved for special days now crushed into the cracks of the concrete floor. Powdered milk, the treasured protein source, scattered from the balconies, writing paper left in the toilets, sugar mixed with kerosene.

The long heartbreaking task of discovering what you've lost. Trying to reassemble a broken razor or cup, mend rips. Was it better to lose a child's picture or keep it, even disfigured by a guard's boot print? The unbearable impotence. These guards came to search but also to crush spirit and destroy any hope.

Lino was horrified and heartsick. Nothing could have prepared him for the barbarism of such attacks, the abandonment of any pretense of civilized behavior. In the next months the *requisas* increased in frequency and savagery. Some came in the early hours of morning, catching prisoners in a haze of sleep, cold and unprotected. Men began to throw themselves from upper balconies rather than face the rain of blows and cuts coming down the stairs. Each time more men were carried away with broken limbs or crushed skulls. Lino felt lucky to be only beaten.

He shook with fury as he stood surrounded by pain and blood. His soul screamed at the degradation, the treatment of human beings as though they were beasts to be destroyed. The roared insults - *scum of the earth, traitors, cowards*. All because these prisoners wouldn't crumble, wouldn't say they believed. *Viva la Revolución*.

After each *requisa*, Lino was more outraged. "How can this happen? How long can we survive this treatment?" He urged some kind of revolt, but it couldn't be one man's decision. Another *requisa*, then another. The men argued, debated, searched their souls. Finally it was decided, as one body, they would endure no more.

On a wet chilly morning in January, when the cry of *Requisa!* went out, the prisoners did not rush to protect themselves. Instead they assembled in somber silence at the balconies. Some jostled to be at the front, anxious to see what was coming. Others stood back, almost inside the cells. Were they wondering about their decision? Pelayo and Orestes and Vicente stood very tall at the front of the second floor balcony, their faces composed, watching.

Lino had been designated as spokesman. He stood in the middle of the courtyard. Both guards and prisoners knew Lino from his efforts to give medical care and pool medicines. No one spoke as they waited for the first guards to appear.

When the guards first appeared at the barred door into the circular, they looked with puzzlement at the silent men and Lino alone in the empty court. They stopped, waiting for new orders.

The Chief of Guards, Rosco Molina, appeared at the gate quickly; the faces of the guards fixed on his. His look of anger turned to confusion as his eyes moved over the motionless men on the balconies. Something in their faces made him pause. No panic. No fear. No shrinking back. Just unflinching stares.

There was an eerie silence as Lino stepped toward Molina. Lino looked around at the guards with equanimity. He looked up at the balconies as though memorizing the face of each man. He saw Moya on the third floor make a tiny movement of encouragement with his eyes.

Now Lino spoke in a steely voice, loud enough to be heard by the prisoners in the balconies and by every guard.

"This will not continue." He paused, looked directly at the guards.

"This treatment. We will fight back." No one moved. The guards did not even look at one another "We have nothing to lose and people will be killed. Your people. Our people. For this **you** will be held responsible."

The silence seemed to drag on forever. The guards shifted, tightened their grips on their rifles, waited for the command. Lino did not take his eyes off Molina's face. Molina looked straight ahead, scowling. He abruptly looked up at the balconies, jerking his head in a circle. After another moment's pause, he turned and strode from the gate, his back and neck rigid. These prisoners, all 1200, were prepared to die. And even the Chief of Guards could not go that far. The guards followed him out, still silent.

Before the last guard was out of sight, the groups on the balconies exploded, men hugging one another, talking all at once, shouting to friends on other floors. They didn't know what would happen next, but they knew they had stood up as men. They had made someone listen. One or two prisoners knelt and crossed themselves, then more, and quickly everyone was on their knees. Lino joined them.

Then the men were on the stairs, racing down to hug Lino, slapping each other on the back. *Lo logramos!* We did it! Lino looked up and saw Father Francisco standing silently at the second floor balcony, looking proud.

There were no more armed invasions of the circular.

137

22

The telegram waited. It sat on the de la Huertas hall table when Emy came home one evening in early October. Her hand shook as she opened it. Bad news came in telegrams; but so did permission to visit.

Su esposo Lino Fernandez tendrá visita en Isla de Pinos el dia 12 de octubre a las 9 AM.

"Lino." She savored the sound in her throat. A visit. At last. She would touch him, hold him in her arms, hear his voice. She would see for herself he was alive and all right.

Since his capture in February, she'd heard about him from many sources on the prisoner grapevine. Lino was captured. He was at Santa Clara, at *Topes de Collantes*, then in a punishment cell at *Isla de Pinos*. But she hadn't seen for herself, seen in his eyes all that had happened, everything he feared, the sum of his suffering. He had not looked into her eyes to see the shadows there. She needed that.

Today was October fifth. Only six days to get through. She felt giddy as she dialed her friend Vicki. Would she be going the same day?

"Vicki? I got it. The telegram. For October 12. I can hardly breathe."

"*Gracias a Dios.* I just got mine too - for the same day. Emy, I'm so happy for you - and for Lino. He must be out of solitary."

Emy took a deep breath. "I am so nervous. You've been to *Isla*, right? Were you shocked when you saw Manduco, the first time? I have to be prepared. *Ay Dios!* Do they ever change the day, after the telegram?"

"Whoa. Slow down Emy. It'll all happen and it'll be great. Don't worry."

"Vicki, honestly - I can't even imagine what it'll be like. I'm glad you'll be there to show me how things work. We need to get tickets for the day before, right?"

Vicki chuckled. "You sound like a veteran already." Her voice began to bubble information and plans. "We'll need to get in line first thing tomorrow morning at *Cubana de Aviación*. Everyone got their telegrams today, so tickets will sell out very fast."

"Is there just one flight?"

"One a day. It's usually a DC3, only a thirty-seater. If we don't get tickets we'll have to take the bus and overnight ferry. I haven't taken it yet, but I'm not dying to either."

"*No me importa*, just so long as I get there."

"Calm down, Emy. Just listen. I've heard it's really just a beat-up tugboat. And then you don't get there early enough to be one of the first into the prison."

"Yes, I want to be first - the very first." Emy felt a surge of pure joy, confidence, faith. She was actually planning a visit, really going. She jumped into Vicki's train of chatter. "What time should I get in line?"

"Oh . . . uh . . . early, eight - yes, 8 a.m. for sure. If you go then, I'll try to find some *café* and relieve you at ten."

In the months since Lino's capture, Vicki had been a strong support. She never seemed discouraged by all the random harassment connected to visits. She knew a whole network of wives of political prisoners and always had news to pass on. Emy still couldn't believe how Vicki had rescued her from the G-2 the summer before. And now she would be there to show Emy how *las visitas* worked. Tonight the two women talked only briefly. Telephones were no longer a place to talk about important things.

Raque and Rene were delighted for Emy, and they talked all through dinner about the visit. That night Emy couldn't sleep. She tried to part the mist of uncertainty about the moment she would see Lino again. What would he look like? What would she say first? What would he say about her sending the children away? What could she take him? She wanted the visit to be so special. But of course it would be. She'd be seeing her Lino. How could it not? Would she cry? No she wouldn't. She couldn't. That wouldn't help him.

The Embassy would be flexible about her missing work, two days to travel, visit, and come back. Time to find things to take. Time to get ready. Embassies understood because most had prisoners' wives working for them; foreign governments knew they could count on these women not to be spies for Fidel.

The next day Emy and Vicki spent taking turns at the *Cubana de Aviacion* offices on Avenida 30. The airline was now a lifeline to Lino; the visit was becoming real. Emy began thinking about what to wear. The wives of prisoners were limited in what they could take to their husbands, so they threw their youth and spirit into how they would look. They knew they were symbols of a world outside, a world the prisoners were fighting to see again one day.

She consulted Vicki while they stood in line, and Vicki became even more animated than usual.

"It's great to dress up, even though high heels are not fun to travel in. Wait 'til you see their faces light up when they see us!" Vicki laughed. "Of course it's not like we have to worry about them looking at other women."

Sharing ideas of what to wear, Emy felt like a schoolgirl. "I have the salmon colored dress I made from that beautiful linen Maria Rodriguez gave me when she left last year. Remember - sleeveless with a matching jacket."

"*Perfecto.* I always try to wear bright colors. There is **no** color at the prison. You'll see."

Emy smiled. She would look bright and new for the most important person in her world. Maybe her color could leach into his grey world.

By 3:00 that afternoon, they had tickets for the plane, and they turned their attention to the *jabas*. Each visitor could bring two of the woven carryalls to a visit. Emy liked to think of them as gift bags, but they really held things to keep the prisoners going. It was harder and harder to find anything in the stores, but Emy had been hoarding things for months.

One of the *jabas* would be taken away by the guards when a visitor arrived and given to the prisoner after the visit. It would bulge with the best necessities that could be managed in Cuba: food above all, healthy food that would keep well and help fill the widening gap in the prisoners' nutrition, paper and pencils, reading material when it was allowed, perhaps a towel, a blanket, underwear, soap. Even plastic bags were priceless, to keep food fresh.

And always, hopefully, some little treasure, a chocolate bar, a photograph, a love letter, tucked in the bag. A candy bar might have cost a visitor hours on line to get, but it would fill a tiny corner of the desolate void left when a visitor had to say goodbye.

The other *jaba* was carried in by the visitor and held the food for their picnic together, plus things to share and take away again like photographs and letters. A thermos was like gold and treated with great care, since it allowed visitors to bring hot coffee or cold lemonade.

Emy searched everywhere for fresh fruit. Lino loved it, and she knew he got none. She wanted to take it to eat on the day of the visit. Fruit didn't last long. Besides, selfishly she wanted to be there to see Lino's face when he felt the soft flesh under a velvety mango skin or cut into the bright orange flesh of a papaya with its black seeds like so many exclamation points. Pleasure showed itself so softly in Lino's face. She finally found a mango.

On October 11, Vicki and Emy took a taxi to the airport for their 4:20 p.m. flight to the island. They each lugged their two *jabas* plus an overnight bag. They would stay at *Isla Del Tesoro*, a small hotel Vicki had found. The family that owned the hotel never spoke about politics, but they were always very kind to the prisoners' relatives who stayed there. In the back of the hotel was an unused bar. Visitors could use the under-counter refrigerators there to store food until the visit.

More than half the people on the plane were visiting prisoners. Vicki knew many of the women and spoke to everyone. One older woman seemed surprised at the gaiety and excitement of the younger women. She looked exhausted and discouraged, probably a mother going to see her son. The physical trip was grueling, even for Emy. How sad to end your life trudging to a prison where your son was wasting the life you'd given him. Thank God she was young and healthy and could share her burdens with other wives.

By 6:00 p.m. they were at the hotel. Emy was relieved by Vicki's organization; it left her free to just be excited. They would spend part of this first night waiting in line at the prison, but then return after the visit and spend another night. Many visitors didn't have that luxury.

"O.K., Emy, we have a place in a taxi coming just before midnight. We need to get to the gates then."

"Eight hours early?" Emy knew the gates opened at 8 in the morning.

"Yes. Definitely. If we're first in line at the gate, we'll be first in the inspection line, first to the visiting room, the first to see our guys. Believe me you don't want to waste one minute. It'll go fast enough as it is."

Emy had a flash of sadness. In just 18 hours it would be all over and she would face many more empty days. She pushed the thought aside.

They ate a quick supper and then got ready. There were wives in and out from other rooms, admiring clothes, giving advice on make-up. Being part of a group lifted their spirits and made them feel less alone.

Emy turned and looked at Vicki who was fussing with her hair.

"I'm beginning to feel like I'm going to one of those *quinceañeras* parties when we turned fifteen. Remember, our first long dresses, wondering what the boys would look like in their tuxedos?"

Vicki thought a long minute. "You know Emy, if anyone on the outside heard about this, they'd think it was pretty bizarre, almost ghoulish. Such preparations for a bleak cold prison. But here, in this place, it's just what I want to be doing."

"Me too."

Sonia, the girlfriend of Lino's medical school friend Pelayo, was one of the women who joined them in the taxi. Vicki had used the taxi driver on other trips, and he would stay with them so they could wait in the car. During the long night, the women shifted in their seats, joking, half dozing, and waking with a start at the thought of something they must remember to say or ask in the morning.

Emy was too excited to even think about sleeping. She just half-listened to the conversation of the others. The women tried to dwell on happy memories and news of families who had already left Cuba. But there was also somber news of capture and execution. And there was prayer, to find the men well, for the strength to share and endure as couples, to not lose faith.

At eight in the morning sleepy guards dragged open the heavy metal doors and spent endless minutes preparing the tables in the inspection room. Finally a soldier with long limbs and glistening black skin motioned languidly for the first people in line to come forward.

Emy had been warned about the inspections, but it was still a shock. The guards treated them like criminals and seemed to take pleasure in the discomfort of the women. Emy knew from Vicki no one had ever been attacked here; still Emy could feel the oozing hostility of the guards.

Oddly, the female guard, a tall skinny woman with frizzy hair addressed as Rita by the others, was the worst. She was in charge of having everyone disrobe so they could be checked for hidden contraband.

When an older woman, a prisoner's mother on her first visit, stripped only to her underwear, Rita yelled at her, *"Quítate todo! E*ven that big brassiere - you can hide a lot in there." The woman started to protest. Rita put up her hand. "If you got nothing to hide, show us."

Emy was happy she had been coached what to do by Vicki. She carefully took off her salmon dress and her underwear, trying to hold everything off the dirty floor while Rita frisked through her clothes. She was repulsed by the obvious leering of the male guards, even though they stayed over at the doorway.

A greasy-haired flabby guard standing near the door muttered under his breath, "*Si si, Mami,* show us everything." Emy thought she might throw up.

When her *jabas* were inspected, a balding young guard with a puny mustache took a stick and stirred the rice pudding she had made, to check for hidden weapons, she supposed. As though a pistol wouldn't show in the small porcelain bowl. Then she watched as he took the same stick and poked through the fruit in someone else's *jaba*, probably bruising and breaking the skins. How many *jabas* had that stick been in? Emy wanted to grab it and poke his eye out.

No. Don't let this get to you. Don't let it spoil this wonderful day, the day you'll be together. You're his link with the world. Don't bring the ugliness in with you.

When they had passed inspection and everything was repacked, Emy stopped for a moment and realized she had been holding her breath. But Vicki was already yelling to follow her. She was walking fast, almost running, as well as she could in her high heels toward the center pavilion where the visits were held, 200 yards away. Every second counted. Emy's concern with looking hot and damp and rumpled disappeared. All that mattered was getting to Lino, like a prize offer that might be snatched away if you were late. Arriving at the pavilion, the women had to pass one at a time up a narrow stairway to the main floor. The slow pace was excruciating. Lino was only a few yards away.

23

He waited in the high center hall, freshly shaven, wearing the prison uniform he had washed the night before and ironed with a heated metal can. Manduco was with him, impatient, his hands running nervously through his light curly hair. Both men were silent. Lino hoped Emy would be one of the first. But now that he knew she was so close, it didn't seem hard to wait another few minutes. The anticipation was itself a pleasure.

Without warning Emy and Vicki emerged from the stairway. Lino saw her. She seemed to carry a bubble of warmth around her young frame. Her dark hair was tousled like a schoolgirl, the bright pink of her dress reflected against the freshness of her skin. He loved the softness of this body that had borne their three children.

Then Emy saw Lino. She watched his beautiful face open in a slow splendid smile as he moved towards her. *He's so gray. His skin is a pasty texture. Like an underground animal.* Now she couldn't see him, only feel the rough cotton of his uniform. He was holding her against him so tight she couldn't breathe and didn't care. She let her body melt into his, every muscle limp against him, letting the tension and uncertainty flow out of her and be absorbed by his strength, his steadiness.

"*Mi amor, mi corázon, mi Emilita.*"

After a long moment, they separated just enough to stare into one another's faces, seeking signs of wear and uncertainty, seeing delight and relief. Then he led her, still holding her close, to a table.

The room was 50 yards across, filled with rows of steel picnic tables radiating out in long spokes from an elevated guard platform in the middle. Lino and Emy sat at a table with Vicki and Manduco and others from Lino's circular. It was better to be surrounded by friends, safer to talk, to say what you really meant. But there was no conversation now; everyone understood these first moments belonged to each couple.

When Emy spoke, it was all concern for him.

"*Mi amor.* Are you alright? How long have you been out of the punishment cell? Were you hurt there? You're thin. Is it better in the circular?"

Lino put his finger to her lips and smiled, stopped the wild flow of words.

"I am fine, *mi corázon.* Let's talk about other things."

He was right of course. She couldn't imagine where he'd been, what he'd gone through. But it didn't matter any more. They were together. His health had been her greatest fear, and he seemed O.K. She could feel the vitality in his limbs, even though they were slack and thin from long confinement. Many of her questions were answered just by seeing him, hearing his voice, seeing his face as he spoke.

"You are right, *mi cariño, mi Lino.* God, I have missed you so." This came out in a gush of intensity that surprised even Emy. She felt tears begin to form. She pushed them back. She would **not** spend this time in tears.

Slowly the high-ceilinged room became of sea of protective bubbles, each enclosing people who needed desperately to connect in the little time allowed them. A swarm of urgent conversations created a gentle hum in the room.

A thousand thoughts, held in too long, spilled over. The horror, the funny stories, the bad moments, the moments of love and longing, of uncertainty, of needing to share their pain. The flow of these thoughts from one to another brought enormous relief.

Emy told Lino about making the decision to send the children, her searching for the right way. She wasn't telling him in order to justify her decision. It had never occurred to her he would question it. And he didn't.

"It was so painful, Lino, watching Papa. He was fighting so hard to get the children out. But I knew inside he didn't want to go, to leave me here - or leave you."

"God, Emy, we are the lucky ones. Think about it. We know our children will always be in a safe loving place with your parents. But your poor father has no idea what will happen to you, his own daughter. He can't know if you're afraid, or lonely, or even arrested, locked up."

"And he's worried sick about you too, Lino. They love you so much.

I think that's why, in the end, they were able to leave me here. Because they believe you need me." Tears threatened again and Emy held Lino's face against her so he wouldn't see.

Lino took her face between his hands. "And now, *mi cariño*, tell me every minute of saying goodbye, of leaving the children and your parents at the airport." He needed to hear. She needed to tell. This was for his ears only, and she had held it inside for these long months.

"Oh Lino, you should've seen Emilia Maria with a ribbon in her hair and her little red shoes. She was so good. They were all so good." She showed him the picture her mother had given her of the children in their going away clothes.

"I don't think they had any idea of what was happening. I hope not. That's why I sent them now, so they wouldn't feel that same tearing away that I felt."

She described everything: the last hugs, her emotional thanks to her parents, the terse telegram saying they had arrived and all was well. She told him of returning to the de la Huertas, of how they tried to help, of the first nights in bed alone, longing for her children. He knew she was not blaming him. They had passed through that long ago. This was a joint fight. They each had their battles.

He reassured her, helped her untangle the confusion of what was going on with the Revolution, how she might live on her own in a very changed Cuba. Emy was being forced into a drastic coming of age. Lino softened the pain and helped it make sense.

Lino told her about his arrival in the circular, about life at *Isla de Pinos*. Only the facts she needed to know, none of the horror, no idle laments or regrets. They wanted these hours to be the positive core of their lives. She told him how life in Havana was changing, even making him laugh with her description of the clumsy morose Russians who were appearing all over the city.

And in between the words, touching, laughter, shared food, joking with the others at the table. The luxury of being able to reach over at any moment and find Lino's warm skin and loving touch. No thought of later. Only of this moment and its pleasure. Lino with mango juice dripping from his lips. Lino looking with wonder at the small cake Emy had brought, finding the bits of chicken she'd hidden there. Lino constantly looking at her, smiling, reaching out, his body always close enough to touch hers.

The visit would be over soon. They must talk of the future.

"What do you think will happen now?" she almost whispered.

His longing to protect her felt dangerous, ready to spring. He would not mislead her; he could not. He looked straight into her eyes.

"At best, this will be a long prison sentence. You must know there's no quick solution." His glance fell to the floor, hiding his moist eyes.

"I'm already learning how to wait." Her voice was soft but sure.

Neither of them spoke of the eventual trial, the possibility of execution. They tucked that terror away for now, unable to look too close.

"If you decide you need to go to the children . . ."

"No." She cut his voice off. "I am where I need to be. We are both where we have to be." Her mouth opened as if to continue, but she stopped herself. Lino wondered what was left unsaid.

When the bell rang for the end of the visit, people dawdled, desperate for extra time. The bubbles slowly burst, releasing people, their hunger only partially sated, wary of surfacing too fast. Emy was surprised at the dignity of people's parting. No hysteria. Gentle private separations.

The guards began to tap their gun butts on the table, "*vamos, vamos.*" Even this gesture seemed kinder than usual, as if they knew what they were asking. Now the delay to enter the narrow stairway was savored. One more moment of contact.

She found herself with still so many words to say. They tumbled out. "We'll be together again soon. It won't be so long this time. Now I can come often."

Lino took her hands. "*Mi amor*, we **are** together. Now. And after you go. And when you reach Havana. Always together. Remember that."

Emy waved once but didn't look at Lino as she entered the stairway. She wanted him to see her solid and straight, strong enough for whatever lay ahead.

In spite of the ripping pain of leaving him, Emy felt an unexpected relief, a serenity, an enormous weight off her shoulders. The hours of talk had been healing. Their words and touches dulled the bitterness of the last eight months, brought back to them the strength of melded lives and shared loss.

There would be many years apart. Or worse. But she felt centered. She had shared the deepest feelings of parting from her children, of a future on hold, of her sorrow for her parents. She knew where she stood, and she knew that Lino, however far away, stood with her. Her children were safe. For them the future would only get better and better.

Back at the hotel, Emy felt absolute exhaustion. She was empty of the fear and uncertainty, comforted by Lino's stability and love. She and Vicki talked for hours in the hotel garden, not about the most personal moments, but about every story, every detail of the visit, all they had learned about life in the circular.

Emy had seen the life of *visitas* before her. They wouldn't dwell on the painful, but they would share everything they needed to. It was like a new set of marriage vows. *"Until death do us part"* had become *"Until we can be together again."*

It was hot on the hotel's patio, even under the palm shelter. Emy wished she had a mamey sherbet.

24

All life focused on visits. Sometimes they were delayed; other times last minute, completely unexpected. Out of nowhere - a telegram, a date, and Emy would rush to make arrangements. Always Emy was on edge, wondering when and if the next visit would come.

Life between visits centered around the search to fill the *jabas*, finding just the right thing for Lino. If Vicki heard a rumor that ham was available through the black market, her first words to Emy were, "Wouldn't that be great *para la visita?*" If Dolly, a friend at the Dutch embassy, brought Emy chocolates from home leave, she tucked them away *para la visita.*

The visits created deep enduring friendships. A group of twelve wives, girlfriends, and mothers of prisoners began to travel together when their visiting dates were the same. Maria, the mother of Vicki's boyfriend Manduco, would sometimes come. Emy felt especially sorry for the mothers; they had not raised their sons to end this way. The visits were hard physically for the older women; they didn't have the advantages of youth and optimism the younger women had.

Out of the blue the government decided that only relatives could visit prisoners. That meant Vicki, who had visited her boyfriend Manduco for years ever since his capture, could no longer go to *Isla de Pinos.*

Vicki never hesitated; she married Manduco by proxy as soon as it could be arranged. The wedding took place in the tiny office of a lawyer in Nueva Gerona, near the prison.

Vicki had insisted the ceremony be on *Isla de Pinos.* "If we can't be together to be married, we can at least be under the same sky," she had told Emy with her matter of fact air. She and Emy had dressed up for the occasion, even though there would be no visit that day. The bride and groom would not see one another.

Manduco's father was there and stood in for his son. The mothers of Vicki and Manduco both refused to come. They weren't against the marriage, just against this sham of a ceremony without a priest. Maria had ranted on, "Terrible, macabre, being forced to do things that way." Only Vicki's Aunt Rosa came. After Vicki and Manduco's father pronounced the vows, the lawyer congratulated Vicki and drove to the prison. Vicki wasn't sure he would even be allowed to enter, but he was. When he returned, he described how he strode into the circular, handed Manduco the paper, and said, "Sign here and you're married." Manduco had signed with a big smile, marveling out loud at Vicki's loyalty. Some of the prisoners in the circular threw water on him in celebration. It would be six years and another wedding before Manduco and Vicki would spend the night together.

On visits, many of the women stayed at the same little hotel and shared their sorrows - and their relief. Between visits they kept in close touch, passing on worries and news from the *Isla*. To Emy, this group was an encircling cushion, protecting and comforting. Being with women who faced the same risks relieved the numbing tension of being constantly vulnerable.

These women were already connected by past experiences and the loss of their old lives. They had not been raised for the life they were living, but they were tough. Emy seldom saw tears or drama when visits were over. Each woman took pride in not letting the situation, or the guards, affect them. "*Esto no me lo noten.* It doesn't get to me." Hate was a powerful and nasty emotion, a wasteful one to Emy's mind. Most of the women had chosen perseverance instead. In their minds, if they let hate for the jailers poison their own souls, overwhelm them with bitterness and thoughts of revenge, then the jailers would win.

One woman became especially close to Vicki and Emy. Emy had known Ileana Puig slightly when she was Ileana Arango and they both went to the Merici School for girls. Ileana was a class ahead of Emy and had married a promising young manager at Bacardi a year or so before Emy and Lino married. Since then the two women had seen each other only occasionally at church or receptions. Ileana's husband had been arrested in 1960, and she was a veteran prison visitor by the time Emy began visiting *Isla de Pinos*.

Ileana was a true beauty, tall and slim with blue-black hair and light hazel-gray eyes. She had always been sociable and outgoing in school. Now she had a natural elegance and confidence that intimidated Emy. But when they traveled together the first time to *Isla de Pinos* Emy found her gracious and friendly. Over the years she would learn that Ileana held iron strong principles; nothing dissuaded her from a path she had chosen.

As Emy got to know her better, she saw that Ileana's eyes held a dullness that hinted at something black and painful inside. During the long hours of waiting in the taxi one night, Ileana told Emy a story that chilled her to her core and brought into painful focus the torment that might await her when Lino went to trial.

Ileana explained how she and her sister Ofelia had married two brothers so that the lives of the two couples were closely intertwined. In the fall of 1959, Ileana's husband Rino was arrested for anti-Castro activities. Then in March, Rino's brother Nongo, Ofelia's husband, was arrested and held in the hulking fortress prison *La Cabaña*, across the river from Havana. The charges against him were the now familiar "threatening the security of the State." In his case, the actual crime was meeting with others who disagreed with *la Revolución*.

"As soon as I heard what had happened," Ileana leaned forward in the taxicab seat and lowered her voice. "I told my parents to be ready for the worst."

Only two days in advance, Ileana's family had been notified that Nongo's trial would be held April 17 at *La Cabaña*. The city was in chaos from the bombing before the *Bahía de Cochinos* invasion. There were no lawyers available. Ileana's father, Jorge Alberto, was a respected lawyer, and the government told him that if he wanted Nongo to have a lawyer, he would have to do it himself, even though he had no criminal trial experience.

In the end her father's experience made no difference. "The trial was a mockery, as we knew it would be," Ileana said with barely controlled contempt. "The witnesses were government agents who had been sent to infiltrate the group and uncover 'evidence' of crimes against the State. Of course they found what the government told them to find." Ileana clenched her fists.

"They always do." Emy spoke in a disgusted voice. She was beginning to understand the dullness in Ileana's eyes.

Ileana stared out the window into another time and place. "*Se imaginan.* We never doubted he would be found guilty. But we knew they often chose someone with a big name to execute, and Sori Marin - remember, the man who deserted from Castro's inner circle - was on trial at the same time. Our greatest hope was that they would execute Marin as an example, and Nongo would get off with a long prison sentence." Ileana slowly took off her cardigan and folded it carefully. Emy saw how hard it was for her to tell this story.

"The trial began very early in the day and the room was filled with soldiers. They were yelling, waving machine guns, poking people with their bayonets. As usual, they brought in government people to make noise and intimidate the prisoners' families. It was chaos - like one of those mobs at a public hanging."

Emy shivered as she imagined the scene.

"This crude circus went on until almost midnight. At the end Nongo was given the death penalty." Ileana was silent, then took a deep breath.

"This was when I truly saw the pitiless face of the Revolution. Here was this man I had known most of my life, a sad disbelieving look on his face. He was a young healthy man, a father and a husband; he meant so much to so many people. He had fought bravely for what he believed; there was so much he could still do in life. And they were going to destroy him - put a cold steel gun barrel to his head and blow his brains out." Her voice broke, "For **nothing**."

Ileana stared out the taxi window. After a few minutes, she spoke again. Her voice was louder but remained cold with fury.

"They had him. They had total power over him. Wasn't that enough?" Ileana stared at the other two women. "Couldn't they feed their sadism with putting him in a dungeon somewhere? No. They had to destroy this fine creature - take him from us and give us back a rotting corpse!"

Vicki winced and took in air through gritted teeth.

Lino's face with its slow loving smile flashed in Emy's mind. She willed it away but it remained. This could be destroyed. This beautiful mind - that loving heart she knew so well - could be shattered. Horror and despair washed over her. This could be her reality; she had never felt it so piercingly before. She had not let herself.

She wanted to say something consoling to Ileana but knew there was nothing. The light of dawn was creeping into the cab when Ileana spoke again.

"When the death penalty was announced my sister was frantic. She rushed toward Nongo. We all knew she would never see him alive again. And you know what those bastards did? A soldier stepped between my sister and Nongo and stuck a bayonet in her face. He yelled 'Against the rules to approach the prisoner!'"

"**Against the rules?**" Ileana was almost shouting. "Is it against the rules for a woman who is never going to see her husband again to embrace him? To tell him she loves him? To ease the pain of going to his grave?" Ileana took in a deep breath, almost a sob. "This is not cruelty. This is pure relentless evil. They never let her touch him. She could only stand powerless, inches away, as he was dragged from the room."

Emy couldn't breathe. Never had their vulnerability been so raw. She had heard about the executions, knew people who had been shot. But now the act had a face, a searing picture in her brain. If she moved, she would shatter into a thousand pieces.

Ileana's voice held misery now. "My father is an old fashioned Spanish gentleman. He loves the law, and he loved his part in it. In my memory, nothing had ever touched his dignity, his serenity. That night I saw him cry for the first time in my life."

Vicki touched Ileana's arm. "I know your father. How awful for him."

"He had been forced to participate in this travesty of justice. Worse yet, he had been powerless to defend this man he loved. He would have to tell Nongo's mother he could do nothing to save her son. He had seen hell. We all had."

Ileana's voice took on an odd flatness. "Of course, there was an 'appeal.' Minutes after the verdict. In the chapel. My father had to go. The judge was drunk. He flopped on the table and said 'Let's get this over with. It's late and I want to go home.' He never looked at anyone who spoke and never addressed Nongo. In less than five minutes he confirmed the sentence. He sent a man to his death without ever looking at him."

"He was shot immediately." Ileana spoke more quickly now, as if she wanted to get the story over with. "We asked to send a priest. They refused. We asked them to tell us when the bodies would be taken to the cemetery. They lied. Nongo was only kept from a common grave by the luck that another family we knew was there. They claimed his body. They've buried it for now in their own plot."

The three woman sat silent, each with her own grief. Vicki was a

153

strong Catholic, and this callous disregard for a person's desire for last rites was surely intolerable for her.

"And your sister?" Vicki asked presently.

"She's not doing well. She told the children what happened to their father. But there's something terribly wrong. She did it like a robot. Now she tells my father that Nongo is really in a concentration camp in Siberia and he'll be back. She's not doing well."

Ileana's voice broke with these words. She shook her head. No one spoke.

Whenever visits were suspended for whatever unexplained reason the wives continued to take *jabas* to the prisoners, making the long trip to the island to stand outside the prison and hand over the packages. Emy found it somehow comforting to see the buildings, to know Lino was nearby, even if she couldn't see him. In her heart she always hoped she would catch a glimpse, reassure herself he was well. Maybe he would see her through a window and know she had come.

One cold winter morning when she had traveled with Vicki to the *Isla* to leave off their *jabas*, a guard stopped her and asked her to wait a moment. Her heart sank. Was something wrong? Had something happened to Lino? The guard told Vicki to stay in the entry hall and led Emy to a small room where a young officer waited, a slight young man with thin perfectly combed hair and pale skin. Her palms were sweating; she sat down tentatively in the chair he pointed to.

"Señora Fernandez, I am Captain Garcia. We've decided to allow you an extra visit, while you are here." He smiled. "You see, we are not as insensitive as people think."

She gave a weak smile and said nothing. What kind of manipulation was this? Why would they give Lino a visit and no one else? She willed herself to not care about the pleasure a visit would give.

"Please wait here and a guard will bring your husband." The officer closed the door on his way out.

She stared out the window which faced one of the circulars. She scanned the windows. Prisoners always knew when a visitor was inside; maybe Lino would be there. She was astonished a few minutes later to see his face appear. He gave a broad smile, then slowly and very subtly shook his head. His thumb appeared below his chin, in the classic downward gesture of rejection.

What was he trying to say? Something wasn't right. She should be careful. Moments later, Garcia reappeared. He took a seat and sighed.

"Señora Fernandez, are you and your husband having problems?"

"No, we are not." She would say as little as possible until she knew what this was all about.

"Are you sure you're the only one who visits him here?" He gave her a mock look of compassion.

"Quite sure." He certainly knew that. Was this another tactic for demoralizing couples, weakening the relationships that kept the prisoners strong?

Garcia looked her in the eye. "I am sorry to have to tell you your husband doesn't want to see you. He asked who the visitor was, and when we told him, he said he didn't want to see you. I am so sorry."

Oh, I'll bet you are. She put on her most serene smile.

"You don't need to be sorry. My husband and I are in complete accord. If he refuses a visit, he has his reasons and I understand."

The officer looked surprised. Disappointed perhaps?

Now Emy wanted to get out of the room, away from this manipulative man. In spite of herself she felt disappointed. There would be no visit. But she and Lino had not played into whatever trick Garcia had wanted to pull.

On her way back to the entry to meet Vicki, she gazed again at the windows but saw nothing. When she told Vicki what had happened, she hugged Emy and sighed.

"I was afraid of that. I've heard about this tactic - telling wives their husbands have girlfriends, even that they've found relationships inside the prison, whatever the hell that means. Anything to demoralize you. Let's get out of here."

In the taxi back to the airport, her mind whirled. She was disgusted at such cruelty but still excited at having seen Lino, even if just for a moment. Pride that she and Lino had not taken the bait. Even if she hadn't seen Lino at the window, she would never have doubted his reasons for refusing a visit.

In a smuggled letter a few weeks later, Lino explained. Just as she suspected, the prison officials had been trying to discredit him as a leader by giving him special privileges; he'd refused them all. He wrote to her, *"Mi cariño, you must know that a visit from you was the hardest offer to refuse."*

25

Lino woke early, jarred by the unaccustomed noise of trucks and soldiers outside. Eight men slept in the cramped cell, two sets of triple bunk beds plus two mattresses jammed in-between. Lino had one of the mattresses. He lay motionless for a long time, his mind moving slowly relentlessly over the facts.

He was 30 years old. By day's end he might be dead.

He would be tried today by Castro's government for treason and crimes against the people. If treason was wishing a government gone, he was guilty. Crimes against the people? No. If they shot him for that, it would be a lie.

This day had been coming for 16 months. He ought to be nervous, frantically trying to come to terms with the choices he had made. He ought to be preparing for the worst. But he was neither.

Lino had slept soundly on the lumpy mattress, even though a heavy slack-faced man was snoring loudly in a top bunk, and a card game was going all night in the hallway. Lino had never had trouble sleeping in prison, except when he tried to quit smoking. Last night he had slept well and woke with a feeling of calm resolve. He might die today. First he would have his say. He might see Emy today, only from a distance. What could he give her from afar to sustain her through the worst?

Julio, a middle-aged balding man on the mattress next to him, stirred and rubbed his eyes. "You look pretty wide awake, Lino. Waiting for your *churros?*" They both knew the only breakfast would be the same stale bread and watery coffee - no milk or sugar. And certainly no crispy fried *churros.*

Lino smiled at Julio. He was a farmer from Las Villas who Lino knew from their months together in *Isla de Pinos*. He could be quick tempered sometimes, but Lino counted on his gentle ironic humor.

A few weeks before the trial, Lino and 85 others had been transferred to this bleak forbidding G-2 prison in Santa Clara, the same place he had been held after his capture the year before. Back then he had told his captors he was only an eager patriot headed to sign up with the resistance. Luckily they hadn't connected him with his code name *Ojeda*. They hadn't realized who he was or the psychological victory to be gained from shooting him in the head.

There was no interrogation now. For a long time, Lino hadn't been sure how much the Castro government had uncovered about his real position in the underground. But on his arrival this time at Santa Clara, Lino Gonzalez, who had been with him at *Isla de Pinos*, told Lino that the G-2 now knew who he was. They were furious that Lino Fernandez had tricked them for over a year about his real role in the "counter-revolutionary forces" as they called the resistance. The G-2's anger wouldn't help at Lino's trial.

Gonzalez had also caught Lino up with his own adventures. He had been sent from *Isla de Pinos* to a smaller prison in Las Villas province and had escaped. He had returned to the Escambray and fought for months. When he was captured again, he was sent to Santa Clara where he waited to see what they would do with him. He and Lino both knew he would probably be shot this time.

Rough yelling came from the end of the hallway. The guards were banging on the cell doors, yelling instructions and telling prisoners to hurry. What could be the rush to get to a sham trial? Were they just impatient for the thrill of ordering prisoners around, shoving them onto trucks, sending them to be condemned?

The other prisoners began to drag themselves up, coughing and stretching, lighting their first cigarettes. Turns at the grubby toilet. Jokes and teasing. There was an odd normalcy, given that everyone knew today would bring death for some among them.

Lino straightened his worn Batista army uniform - standard issue at *Isla de Pinos* - and wished he could take a shower and have clean clothes. At least in *Isla de Pinos* he had the first hours of the morning alone: a cold shower, time to exercise, time to prepare himself for the day.

This trial could easily end with the firing squad. Lino was inclined to think it would. A few days before, he had written a long letter about his decisions, what he had done, and why he had done it. Perhaps it would help his children understand, if they never saw him again. Emy would not need a letter. She already knew.

In the letter he said, "I could not walk away from my country. I could not participate in Fidel's charade of freedom and a better life for all Cubans. He will bring nothing of the kind. The world must know that." He sent the letter to his parents. It never arrived.

The guards entered the cells one by one and herded the prisoners down the long unlit corridor and through a series of metal doors. Outside on the rutted pavement of the parking lot other prisoners waited, and the forty men headed for trial were given breakfast. Then they were loaded in the back of an open truck with wooden slats on the side and driven to the courtroom building.

It was a clear spring day, a day for sitting in a café, walking by the harbor, weaving among the people. A day for rushing to see his patients. A day for building the future and loving the present. It would be none of those. More likely a day for ending a life. A day for Fidel's final victory over him and his family.

But now Lino, trying to keep his balance in the back of the truck, turned his thoughts to what he would say. Today his beliefs - the ones he would likely give his life for - would be heard. He believed Emy would be at the trial; he almost hoped she would not. He wasn't sure he could bear the sight of her, the rush of longing and the knowledge of losing.

The prisoners were unloaded from the truck in the back of the downtown court building and led in through a back passageway. As he came through the double wood doors to the courtroom, Lino was instantly alert. He had only a minute to glimpse the spectators.

He saw Emy near the side about half-way back. He wanted to make a sign but only managed a vague dip of his head before he was pushed along by the skinny kid acting as guard. He didn't know if she had seen him. Was she alone? Hopeful? Frightened?

He felt himself begin to tremble with need. He wanted to fall into the warmth of Emy's embrace, to abandon all thought and sink into languor. Then he forced himself to stand up very straight. He sealed himself away from all emotion and concentrated on the supposed trial. They were closed into a wooden bullpen with walls about three feet high and told to sit on the wooden benches. They were forced to face the judge, unable to see the onlookers.

26

Emy had made the 300 mile trip from Havana to Santa Clara alone over rough poorly marked roads. She had worried about the car breaking down, even though she'd borrowed her uncle's car because hers was even more undependable.

Alone was fine. She had much to think about. At the time Lino was captured feelings had been running high. Resistance fighters were being shot on the spot. Or it would have been so easy to shoot him at *Isla de Pinos*. No need for proof of anything.

Now, more than a year later, she felt more optimistic. Fidel had consolidated his hold on the country. The *Bahía de Cochinos* invasion had failed, and the militia seemed to feel more confident. Some rough order had been established, some rudimentary sense of proportion about death and justice. But plenty of people like Lino were still getting the death sentence.

Whatever happened Emy wanted to be there with him. Share the last moments of his life if need be. She understood that only certain things were possible for her to do. Those she would do. Lino's gentle father had half-heartedly said he would come with her, but she knew he would be devastated if the trial ended in Lino's death. Her friend Mariana had offered to come, but Emy wanted to be free to focus totally on Lino, to live these hours just with him. After spending the night in a modest boarding house, she arrived early at the courthouse because she had no idea when Lino would arrive or whether she might manage to talk to him.

Because so many prisoners were on trial, the room was dense with bodies: parents, wives, children, even families and comrades of those already imprisoned or shot. Emy spoke quietly to a few families she knew, and then found a seat alone further down the room. She sat next to a couple from Oriente whose son was on trial. They seemed confused and disoriented. The mother sat silently, occasionally looking furtively around the room. The father finally turned to Emy.

"How do we know when the prisoners will come?"

"*Es difícil.* I think you just have to keep an eye on that back door. If you like, I'll tell you if I see them coming."

The man thanked Emy. She felt guilty at not having the energy to help them follow what was happening. But she had to invest her strength in connecting with Lino.

The room was large, about 60 feet square with high ceilings. Large windows lined one wall, but dirty shades blocked out any view. The other walls were rough stucco, once covered with a greenish paint, now faded and pocked-marked.

This was a place for real trials in the time of Batista, she thought. But today had nothing to do with justice. Better to have the trial in a prison or an armory.

It was only May, and the heavy summer heat had not yet begun. But the room was heating up, even with five of the eight ceiling fans turning slowly. The light was filtered; the few electric lights had not been lit. Once the judge was seated, small lamps were turned on for him and for the lawyers.

Lino knew he would not have a chance to defend himself. Prisoners were allowed only, if they wished, to put forth their reasons for their actions. Few prisoners did. But for Lino this was an important moment, his time to speak.

The week before the trial, Lino's father had written to him, "Please. Don't say anything at the trial. Staying silent is your only chance of not being shot. I don't want to lose my son."

Lino had written back, "Papa, I don't know if they are going to kill me or not. I'm thinking they will. And I'm not going to die without giving my reasons, without being heard one time." His father had not replied.

One by one the crimes of each prisoner were laid out. Crimes that were not in any law book. Actions that never happened. Eyewitness accounts from people who had never seen the defendant. The audience members did not react to this litany of invented evidence, unwilling to jeopardize their prisoners' chances.

Most of the other prisoners declined to speak. Emy thought with alarm that the judges looked satisfied each time that happened. Or was it her imagination? If only she could speak to Lino, perhaps she could convince him to stay silent. Maybe it was better she couldn't pressure him. She wanted to be as strong as he was.

The day passed in a fog of anxiety. She desperately wanted to give him some signal, some sign of optimism and love. She held herself constantly ready in case she could exchange a look with him, but in the end she could not. She only sat and feasted on what she could see of his familiar body.

There was a short break about 2:00. Most of the spectators went outside to get cool and eat the food they had brought. The prisoners were led out the back passage to the washrooms, quickly given cups of tepid beans from a steel drum, and then hustled back into the bullpen. Emy stayed in her seat and declined an offer of something from the Oriente couple's knapsack.

In the row behind her, Emy heard one woman tell another, "See the lawyer up there, Orlando's his name, the one in the gray shirt? He's from Vedado, like me. There's very bad blood in his family." The speaker warmed to her topic. "His brother hates Fidel - already took off for Mexico. He wants the mother to come to Mexico and Orlando forbids it. The whole family is up in arms."

The story took Emy's mind off the trial for a moment. At least she and Lino felt the same. Hadn't they discussed this moment long ago without knowing it? She'd told Lino even before they were married that his idealism was one of the things she loved. That his passion for justice made his love for her even more precious. That she would not blame him, no matter what happened. Could she be so sure she would say the same now, now that they had created children, now that she had grown to love him ever more deeply?

Lino was trying to calm his mind. His case would come up soon. What if his father had been right? Wasn't it better to be imprisoned but alive to fight again when he got out? Would he even survive prison? Could he live with himself in prison if he gave Fidel the victory of his silence now?" He tried to clear his head of thoughts but he could not. What would life be for his family if he was alive but dead to them? How much could he ask of Emy? But she had known. She had always known.

When Lino's trial began, the lawyers presented information proving he was one of the main organizers of the MRR, which was true. They also "proved" he was a member of the CIA, which was not true. In fact, the CIA's hypocritical failure to help the MRR in any way was an acid memory in Lino's mind. How ironic that they wanted to condemn him for a collaboration he had desperately wanted but never gotten.

Oddly, by the time he was allowed to speak, his anguish was gone. He felt no hesitation. He could not go forward, to any future or any death, without being heard. Standing in the prisoner's box, he could at last see Emy clearly and he felt a moment of remorse for bringing her to this moment. He stared at the judges, the other prisoners, and the families that had come to hope. Finally he spoke in a steady deliberate voice.

"I am not a violent man. I am a doctor. I am committed to helping people live, not die. I admit I do not support Castro. I do not agree with him about what is best for Cuba." He looked directly at the judge before he continued.

"But I did not elect violence. I - and those with me - only turned to violence because we had no other language. We had no other way to give a voice to all Cubans."

He paused and cleared his throat. "Many Cubans who disagree with Castro have simply left. We have stayed. We are Cuban. We too are fighting for the good of our country."

He continued speaking for eight minutes, repeating his horror of violence. He spoke of how he believed the Revolution was poisoning the people and their way of life, his conviction that all the Cuban people deserved to be heard. When he finished there was silence. The judge frowned. Emy wanted to clap. She loved him more at that moment than at any time in their lives together.

Less than an hour later, the verdicts were announced for all 40 prisoners. All the verdicts were guilty; no acquittals. Emy's breath came in short bursts. She had to clasp her hands to keep them from shaking. Was she about to hear the words that would end Lino's life, destroy her world? She bowed her head, but she could not pray. Prayer would come later, to help her bear the worst.

One by one the name of each prisoner was called out, followed by his sentence. Emy felt as though her mind were filled with static - she had to strain to hear each name. The sentences for some men were light, three years, for others heavy. No death sentences. So far.

Then she heard it. She felt as though she were in a bubble, able to hear only one clear voice.

"Lino Fernandez, *Treinta años*. Thirty years."

Thirty years. Not death. Thirty years. Oh thank you God.

Emy let her muscles go slack for the first time all day. She slumped with relief and looked quickly at the bullpen to send a smile to Lino.

Could he see her in all the confusion? If he could, she didn't want him to misinterpret her relief as shock or pain. She wanted him to see her joy. *There would be no firing squad. No death for now. Whatever the future held, it was a future. And he had been true to himself.*

"I am so sorry for your husband's long sentence." The voice was that of the man from Oriente. "We had hoped our son would be released. But then five years is not so bad." His wife was sobbing quietly.

"No, it's not so bad." Emy spoke slowly and smiled. "Nothing is so bad. They're alive." She wanted to hug the man.

As she left the courtroom, she saw that many of the mothers and wives of prisoners were weeping. She walked, almost ran, to the back of the building, determined to see Lino as he was loaded into the truck to return to his cell. Maybe a quick hug, a hurried whisper of joy and relief. The soldiers were keeping people away. She didn't get to touch him, but she saw the lightness of his stride as he stepped up into the truck. It was enough. She saw he understood. *This was bearable. This they could endure.*

She sent a prayer of love towards him. She willed him to think of what they still had. They could smile and touch and speak about their children, about all the good things they had known and would know again some day.

Once the truck drove away, Emy found she could hardly stand. She stumbled to her uncle's car and sat silently in its refuge for a long time. She had so longed to hold him. How could she find the strength to drive back to Havana? She hadn't eaten all day. Some food would help.

She drove toward the center of Santa Clara and stopped at a small outdoor restaurant. She ordered *sopa de camarones,* even though the sun was still hot. People were out on their stoops, talking, drinking, forming and reforming social groups.

What if the trial had ended differently? Would she still be sitting here? Would she be claiming Lino's body, arranging for its burial? Would she be a widow at 24, preparing to tell her children? She stared at the pieces of shrimp in her soup. How intense the color was. Her sky began to brighten, her mood to lift.

Today was May 25, 1962. Lino was alive. *Sopa de camarones* still existed. She might one day fix it for him. For the first time in many months, she thought of herself with excitement as the mother of a growing healthy family. She ached to see her children.

As the prisoners were returned to their gloomy cells, Lino's group was shoving and teasing with relief from the tension and the immobility of the day. He could tell that the two fishermen, who had received only three years each, were trying to be sensitive to Lino and not overdo their happiness.

Julio gave Lino one of his bear hugs. He had received 10 years.

"Well, *Señor Doctor.*" The title was used with great affection. "They didn't fill us with lead. I wish to hell they hadn't screwed you so bad."

"I never expected any less." Lino tried to be light. "The worst is, ten more years of putting up with you!" The teasing fell flat. Julio lay down on his mattress. Lino sat quietly on his, absorbing the liveliness of the voices swirling around him.

Another week dragged by after the trial. Each morning Lino was flooded with relief that he had escaped execution. Now he was anxious to return to *Isla de Pinos*, to the community that nourished him.

At one time he might have hoped to return to regular visits with Emy at *Isla de Pinos*. But a few months before the trial, the prisoners had gone on strike, refusing all visits. It had begun when the prisoners in Circular #2 had looked out the window to see guards building a set of chicken wire fences in the visiting pavilion. The two fences were one foot apart so visitors would be forced to see one another across that distance. No touching. No physical contact. No meals together. The prisoners had been outraged and refused any visits. The fences sat, half-built, a testimony to the determination of both prisoners and prison guards. And all visits had stopped.

The director of Santa Clara prison was Lieutenant Edmundo Betancourt, the same man that a year before had brought Lino's father to visit him at *Topes de Collantes*. One afternoon a few weeks after his trial, Lino was taken to a visiting room where Betancourt waited.

"*Felicidades,* Lino. You survived your trial."

"Now all I have to do is spend the next 30 years in prison," Lino replied evenly. "Thirty years without seeing my children grow up. Thirty years without practicing medicine. Thirty years treated like a caged dog." Lino knew Betancourt wouldn't punish his truculence.

The officer ignored the outburst. "You'd be a lot better off here at Santa Clara. Much closer to your family. More visits. We treat prisoners pretty well, wouldn't you agree?"

Lino said nothing. What was going on?

"I can try to arrange it. No promises, but I'll do my best. Of course, you have to promise not to make trouble."

"I'll save you the trouble of worrying about my behavior. Just send me back to *Isla de Pinos*. That's where my comrades are. My home."

Betancourt gave him a long look and sighed. "O.K., I tried."

Before he fell asleep Lino tried to remember the words to a poem he wanted to send to Emy. He knew they'd come back to him eventually.

27

"*Gracias a Dios.*" Manduco had tears in his eyes when he saw Lino return to the circular from his trial in Santa Clara. "They didn't send you to the firing squad. He enveloped Lino in a hug. "I honestly . . . I never thought I'd see you again."

Lino hugged his friend distractedly. He appreciated the heartfelt welcome, and he was just as relieved and amazed to be here. But his mind was on the future, on the thirty years ahead. He wasn't going to waste them.

He lost no time. His first night back at *Isla de Pinos*, he told the others in his *cooperativa*, "Look, the invasion at *Bahía de Cochinos* was a disaster. The guerilla movement is weakened. We need to face facts - we may be here a long time." He looked around at the group. Cesar Paez had recently been moved to their circular. Lino Gonzalez was missing; he had been led to execution in Santa Clara a week ago, just as he had feared. *God I'll miss his solid presence, the way he shrugged off the worst indignity.*

Lino chose his words carefully. He might sound preachy, but the most important thing he could do right now was pass on his own resolve to these men. "We have to build a way of life that can sustain us for years, as independent as we can be of the guards and the arbitrary rules." He was trying to make eye contact with as many men as he could. "There's only one way we'll survive - by creating as normal a life as possible. That's how we'll make it back to real life someday, healthy and sane."

"The alternative," Lino said, his mouth set, "is to let Fidel win. And we do that if we accept - no, abandon ourselves - to his power. If he can take away our feeling of worth, our determination to last, then he's won. No question." When he stopped, Lino was pleased to sense an energy that had not been in the group before. No one challenged his point. The discussion turned instead to specifics of how to stay strong.

One thing no one could take away, Lino knew, was social closeness. He had found many old friends in prison - from college, from church, from the Belen school, even from his years as a psychiatrist. There were new friends too, like Eduardo Camaraza, once the owner of a sugar plantation in Matanzas. He had been trained by the CIA and infiltrated back into Cuba, only to end up in prison. And there was Tommy Fernandez, a young man who Lino had learned to count on to tackle any new problem.

Lino had been a leader on the outside; he was also greatly respected here. He had survived three months in isolation. Even those who hadn't known him before sensed his determination and his integrity. Through all the prisons he would be in, his commitment to normalcy and community would remain the steel rod that supported him.

Without the threat of *requisas*, the prisoners found they could organize themselves pretty much as they wanted. The guards, entering the guard tower from an underground tunnel, had almost no contact with prisoners. Within the circular, the cells were open to the balconies, even at night, and prisoners moved around at will.

Sometimes they would be herded into the open air pavilion outside the circular while guards searched the cells. But there was little of the random cruelty of the *requisas*, at least for now. When the prisoners were inside the circular, they were left alone, like an independent kingdom surrounded by hostile but not aggressive neighbors.

For the moment, the guards didn't seem to want to be involved with the prisoners. Most of them were in their early thirties and came from Oriente province, an isolated area far to the east. Those who were new recruits, dreaming of glory for *la Revolución*, were not happy guarding these passive political prisoners hundreds of miles from the action in Havana or even a smaller city. Others were just happy not to be fighting in the army, staying invisible.

"Things could be worse here. It's like we're a small republic," Lino wrote to his father. "We run our own lives. The odd thing is I think we know as much about what's going on in Cuba as you do in Esmeralda."

The confrontation that had ended the *requisas* had shown the political prisoners that, even as prisoners, they had some power. They were also becoming hardened to the pain of isolation from their families and the lack of the most basic comforts.

Nevertheless, the first thing a new prisoner was told was, "Be alert. Even when things seem calm, you're still at the mercy of people who hate you. Never let your guard down."

Most important was keeping things well hidden - radios, medicines, keepsakes, extra food. These were precious and had to be protected. The layout of the cells created an ideal hiding spot. Between each two cells, up against the outside wall, there was a triangle-shaped shaft running down six floors to the basement. It was used primarily for pipes to carry water and waste and could be reached from each cell by a small opening about 18 inches square. The opening was covered with a metal door.

Orestes had told Lino when he first arrived, "I'm telling you, do not forget to keep that door closed. Otherwise the rats will run through the cell all night"

Lino had looked into the shaft. "Oh my God, what **is** that smell?" Orestes had shrugged. "Do you really want to know? *Yo no.*"

The interior of the shaft was dark and humid, with a lively population of rats and insects, sometimes even bats. The guards hated to even look into these spaces. The braver ones might open the door but no guard would put his head inside. Some even pretended they didn't know the shafts existed so they wouldn't have to look. A prisoner could get his whole torso in and hide things by attaching them to the wall or to the pipes. This space was used for the most precious items: codes, letters, weapons, and above all, pieces of the radio. It was a disgusting space but worth using if it would keep things safe.

Besides the Morse code, the prisoners could transmit written messages across a pulley they had set up between two of the circulars. They used a very thin almost invisible wire that stayed up all the time. It couldn't be seen from the ground, even if you were looking.

One day, Moya saw with horror that a small bird had alighted on the wire, his tiny feet resting on what seemed like thin air, like a floating ballerina. He alerted Lino who arrived in time to see the bird stretch its neck out as though enjoying the view, then settle its beak against its wing feathers.

"Oh my God, it's taking a nap!"

The prisoners tried in vain to shoo the bird away without being noticed by anyone on the ground. Nothing could budge it. Inevitably a passing guard noticed the bird, called another guard, and the wire was discovered and dismantled.

As frustrated as he was, Lino had to smile when he wrote to Emy about that tiny bird defying the frantic attempts of a herd of prisoners to scare it away.

The meagerness of the food kept the prisoners on the edge of starvation, slowly weakening them from lack of vitamins and protein. In the morning, guards left large bins at the entrance. Every prisoner received a spoon of sugar in a mug of warm water and a small bun. Even though he was constantly hungry like everyone else, Lino always saved this bun until just before bed. All his life he had gotten hungry at bedtime, and he decided it was worth saving the bun for that moment.

He often thought how Emy used to fix a little tray with their bedtime snack. A colored cloth napkin. Cookies on a china dish. Pleasures he had hardly noticed at the time.

In the middle of the day, guards brought big cauldrons of some kind of lukewarm broth, just macaroni or rice in water. Everything tasted old, tainted. Tommy told Lino he'd seen bags of rice being delivered to the prison stamped "not for human consumption." Lino tried not to believe him.

The prisoners never knew quite what food to expect, but no matter how disgusting it was, they took every drop. About six o'clock in the evening, more cauldrons of thin soup. Every month or so, there would be a big treat - watery bean soup with rice.

Lino wrote to Emy, "I have **never** seen a vegetable or piece of meat in the food they give us." Emy was beginning to understand why the food sent by families was so important. It was the only thing keeping the prisoners alive.

Once every few months - the schedule was erratic - each prisoner could receive one *jaba*, a grocery-bag size carryall from his family. A prisoner tried not to get his hopes up. Sometimes there was no *jaba* for him; sometimes it didn't contain what he hoped. Those who received *jabas* tried to share with those that didn't.

Anything at all was treasured. Families were always on the lookout for a treat that could go into the next *jaba*, especially food that had protein but didn't rot too fast in prison. Powdered milk was a prize; it kept many prisoners alive over the years. Families were very creative: meat disguised as dessert, raw eggs dissolved in juice, chocolate in any form. And news, anything that was allowed: magazines, books, letters. Even the strangest most irrelevant reading material was welcome. Cesar laughed when he found Lino reading *Chinese Military Strategy in the 15ᵗʰ Century*.

Sometimes there were razors, toothpaste, soap, or aspirin - the most basic supplies were luxuries that could make men weak with pleasure. Paper was greatly treasured; there was never enough. Bic pens were in great demand; everyone agreed they were the most dependable and long lasting. Emy got them at the embassy.

The circulars were crowded, but prisoners could put themselves wherever they wanted or could find room. Some cells had room for a third bunk but a fourth person had to go on the floor.

When a new prisoner arrived there was always someone who knew him. "Hey Mario," a prisoner would yell, recognizing the new prisoner from his old life or from fighting together. "Great to see you. Come up here - I'll make room in my cell."

Arrivals were an event for everyone because they brought news: of the struggle against Fidel, of families and friends, sometimes of the world outside of Cuba.

Above the fifth floor was an attic up under the roof, one big space with no cells. When the crowding got bad, prisoners slept up there, in spite of the searing heat.

Lino, an athlete himself, was adamant about people staying fit. Prisoners began hanging from the roof bars, doing chin-ups, and playing baseball in the courtyard with equipment they made themselves. Pelayo especially loved sports, so Lino drafted him to help.

After his experience in isolation, he'd become a fanatic about keeping things as clean as possible: themselves, the cells, the common areas. Each prisoner got up in the morning and took a shower. Being clean was the best way to maintain their health.

The prisoners were allowed to use the center court anyway they pleased: basketball games, meetings, classes. It was supposedly for eating, but it was filthy. Efforts to clean it were frustrating - no supplies. Many prisoners preferred to take their food to their cells and eat in small groups.

The heat and crowding left tempers always ready to explode. Inactivity made it worse. So Lino was always looking for ways to keep the men stimulated, involved in any kind of routines or tasks. If men began to believe these years were being "stolen," of no value whatever, they would become bitter and lose themselves.

When new prisoners arrived, they were immediately pulled into the existing community routine. Coming from capture and often beatings and interrogations, they were generally all too glad to be part of a more sane existence. Only a few managed to stay depressed long.

One morning on his way back from the showers, Lino noticed a muscular young man with thick curly hair, sitting with his back to the balcony railing, staring into space. His clothes and hands were filthy. Lino had seen him arrive almost a week before.

"How's it going?" Lino asked, sitting down on the floor.

"What do you think?"

"It takes a while to get used to things. How did you end up here?"

"The bastards picked us up drinking and messing around on the beach. Accused us of trying to steal a boat. Jesus, what would I do with a boat?"

"Are the others here too?"

"Maybe . . . I think so . . . in some other building. Doesn't matter. What would we do - play checkers?" His tone was caustic, his eyes empty. "I'll pass on the fun and games. Just sit on this stinking floor 'till my time is up - or until they shoot me."

"That's a sure way to make your time here seem endless. And unbearable."

"I don't need a pep talk. Leave me alone."

Lino shrugged and got up. He felt sorry for the kid. He couldn't be more than 16 or 17 and stuck in here. He'd ask Pelayo to try to pull him into a baseball game. Sometimes that worked; sometimes it didn't.

The men in the circular were a mixture of social levels, jobs, ages, and sophistication. The only common denominator was that they were all there for having decided to fight Fidel rather than give in. For the first time in his life, Lino was not in a privileged environment. He'd been educated in the best schools, belonged to rarefied social organizations.

"I feel like I've lived in a golden ghetto my whole life," he told one of the other doctors as they stood one evening, looking over the balcony. Lino enjoyed times like this when he could think about ideas instead of just survival.

"*Qué quieres decir?*" His friend picked at the peeling paint on the iron railing.

"Well, I've been thinking. The Jesuits. They taught us to give back, help those less fortunate. And we did. They pushed us about our spiritual life too, warned against getting too caught up with material things and the good life."

"Then why was it a ghetto?"

Lino thought for a minute.

"Because everything was done 'to' other people, not 'with' them. I worked for social causes; I gave time and money. I worked at charity clinics and tutored kids before that."

"Nothing wrong with any of that."

"But it was all from inside my cozy middle class existence. It was nothing like what I'm learning to do here, living with people so different from me, background, education, beliefs." He thought of Leon, the man in *Topes de Collantes* who had shared his mattress and plate when Lino had needed them so badly.

The doctor gave a low chuckle. "Yea, I keep hearing only the rich people are fighting Fidel, because they don't want to lose their privileges. Then how come we're not in prison with rich people?"

In spite of all his efforts at normalcy, Lino's longing for his family was a constant vein of sorrow running through his life. He thought of Emy first thing in the morning. Most of the year, daylight appeared first as a thin gray line across the stone floor of Lino's cell. He was always awake before the line appeared. He spent those silent minutes with his mind far from prison, far from the present moment. He drifted to other times and places, evening walks with Emy and Emilia Maria and later the baby Po, relaxed dinners talking and teasing with friends, quiet morning coffee before his first patient.

He had dreamed of all this so long that some mornings he thought he could actually feel Emy's gentle hug, the glass of fresh juice in his hand. He liked to return from these trips slowly, before he was dragged back by the rawness of rough stone and tasteless hot water.

This was his favorite hour, the freedom to rise from his stinking bunk at his own will and move quietly down to the center court where three old suspended pipes would soon disgorge a thin stream of cold water. He wrote to Emy:

> *With twelve hundred men in here, you can imagine how crowded it is by 7:30. So dawn is my time. I go early, enjoy the quiet, and sometimes try to clean my clothes - those awful Batista uniforms. I never thought I'd have to wear those!*
> *Your,*
> *Linote*

As soon as the water came on, Lino luxuriated in the trickle, then dried himself on a ripped piece of terry towel. He had carried that gray toweling to Santa Clara and back. It had been ripped when he got it; Lino handled it carefully not to make it worse. He could ask Emy to try to find him a real towel, but he wouldn't. Any request would send Emy off on a frantic search in Havana where finding the simplest object was an arduous treasure hunt. Anyway, if he had a better one, it would just be snatched in a search or lost when he was sent to a new circular.

The knee of his pant leg was wearing through again. He'd have to scrounge around for a needle.

28

L ino wrote to Emy:

> *There are so many doctors here. We have four or five just in my*
> *circular. I'm amazed at how I find doctors in every part of our*
> *fight. I don't see many lawyers or bankers. Anyway, I'm glad*
> *they're here. We need them.*

The doctor-prisoners were encouraged by prison authorities to accept assignments at the prison hospital. Fidel would be all too happy to free up his own army doctors. It would mean extra privileges, a more comfortable bed, maybe better food, less harassment. Lino knew he could treat the hospitalized prisoners better than the army doctors did, but there was no way he – or any of the doctors - would take the job. They could do more good by living with everyone else in the circulars. The ten medical students in the circular felt the same.

One army doctor who offered Lino the assignment was incredulous at his refusal.

"This martyr stance is inspiring, Fernandez. But you want to survive don't you? Want to get home to your family some day?"

Lino flinched inside, but his face showed no emotion.

"I have every intention of getting home to my family. But while I'm waiting, I'm going to treat the men who won't get any help otherwise, the ones who never make it to hospital, who just fade away from malnutrition - or despair."

The offer would be repeated many times. Sometimes Lino would go for a few weeks to the hospital with a prisoner if he thought he was particularly needed. Then the hospital staff assumed Lino would stay; but he always insisted on returning to the circular. Prison guards were apathetic about sick inmates. Prisoners had to know that, if they were seriously ill or hurt, someone would try to help.

Medical resources were limited and erratic. They never knew what they would get or when. Prisoners who received medicine from home kept it with them. When something was needed, Lino or another doctor would yell from the courtyard up to the cells.

"Anybody got some antibiotics? We've got a guy with pneumonia down here." And someone would yell out and bring or toss the medicine down.

Eventually one cell was cleared out and established as a clinic. On Wednesday mornings, the doctors would treat minor problems as best they could. Just the existence of the clinic gave prisoners the impression of normalcy and power. A doctor could say "Come to the clinic on Wednesday and we'll see what we can do."

It became clear that really sick prisoners were better off isolated, and so were their cellmates. The patient could stay in the clinic or even be given a separate cell. Then one of the medical students or doctors would check on him or even keep continuous watch if necessary. Diseases like mumps or bronchitis, normally not fatal, could turn dangerous, given the men's weakened conditions and the lack of medicines.

As time passed, many ailments had to do with malnutrition: skin problems, weak limbs, sores that wouldn't heal. There wasn't much the doctors could do for those problems, but it helped prisoners not to panic if a doctor looked at them and explained why these things were happening. The doctors also gave advice on keeping clean and exercising. The underlying message was an important one, "You are not helpless. You have lots of options. Lots of way to fight back against these conditions."

Lino's training as a psychiatrist became a real gift. Some prisoners arrived with mental problems of long standing; others developed problems over time. Even if a mental problem had been under control on the outside, the pressure and anxiety of prison life could make it reappear.

One night, about a month after Lino came back from his trial, an older man, recently sentenced to 25 years and convinced he would die in prison, hung himself quietly in the middle of the night up on the empty sixth floor.

Lino stood a long moment in front of the body, crossed himself and whispered a blessing. Other prisoners gathered; they passed by the body and crossed themselves. Lino could feel their fear. *Can I be stronger than he was?*

He spoke in a low voice. "We each have our own destiny and our own relationship with God. If a man decides he can't go on, there's no way to keep him. He'll find a way. We can only hope he's made his peace with God. And God has understood."

Lino hated this ultimate victory of Fidel over even one man. He knew there would be some suicides. He couldn't stop them. But personally he felt he had every reason to endure, and he wanted to convey that certainty to others.

As a psychiatrist, he could see that prison was much harder for some than others. Depression could come simply from the stress of being confined. Some people couldn't bear not knowing about their families or even the fear of being rejected, forgotten. He certainly didn't intend to stand by and watch people sink into desperation. After the suicide, any patient in crisis, either suicidal or paranoid, was sent to a special cell on the first floor. Lino would have two medical students in rotation watching the patient, even taking him to the showers and urging him to eat. Lino had the medical students come to sessions with the patient and take part in the therapy so they could learn from the experience.

One patient, a factory manager who also had a beautiful baritone voice, had been diagnosed schizophrenic ten years before but had managed to control the symptoms until his arrest. Once in prison, he went downhill and began using almost continuous compulsive gestures. He became completely disconnected from reality. Lino put him in an isolation cell where a young medical student was assigned to watch him and to work with Lino as they tried to find some root to the man's problems.

In the end, they uncovered a symbolic connection between a red handkerchief the patient had been concealing and his domineering mother. The medical student observed as Lino helped the patient through a dramatic session in which Lino destroyed the handkerchief and the man was able to open up to the possibility of connecting with other people, of accepting their support.

"I learned more this afternoon than from any rotation in medical school," the medical student told an exhausted Lino when the session was over.

"Just don't forget - you can use this approach with a psychotic, but not with a neurotic." Lino reviewed the reasons for this advice. "Why don't you follow his therapy through with me? I guess you can still work on your medical degree in spite of this damn Revolution."

Slowly Lino ended up with a psychiatric clinic and a regular schedule of patients. He found he could do ongoing therapy just as well in a cell as in an office. He rigged up a canvas sling where he sat near the window and his patients sat on the floor. While privacy wasn't easy, his cellmates tacitly agreed to vacate the cell when Lino was seeing patients.

Jesus Villa, a farmer with a deeply lined face, always peered meekly into the cell, as though he thought Lino wouldn't be there.

"*Señor Doctor, tienes un minuto?*" he asked, as though the appointment had not been set up.

"*Seguro,*" Lino replied "*Siéntate.*"

Villa always insisted on a few polite inquiries about the doctor's health before he said what was on his mind. Lino had already learned that Villa was a *guajiro* from the hills of Camaguay. He was finding it impossible to sleep and suffering from debilitating depression.

"I still hear nothing," Villa began. "A guy from my town had a visit, and I hoped there would be a letter. But nothing. Eight months." He shrugged his shoulders.

Lino waited.

"I don't know if Mariana has tried to leave, if the CDR took our house, nothing. If only I could have **one day** to go and see what's happened. She's so alone . . ."

The hour passed, Lino listening to Villa's urgent frustrations and fears, Villa pouring out the horrible scenarios from his imagination, his feelings of deep guilt at being in prison and not helping his wife. Listening was all Lino could do. He hoped it was enough.

Lino described his practice to Emy.

> *I feel so badly for these men. It makes me even more aware of how Fidel is ruining lives. But when I need to cheer myself up, I think of how I could never have such a laboratory of psychiatric projects as I do here. How many psychiatrists have 24 hour contact with their patients?*
> *Your,*
> *Linote*

In fact, Lino was so busy he was rarely in a funk. If he wasn't treating patients, he was writing letters, repairing things, reading, exercising.

Some professionals, friends from the *Agrupación,* encouraged an informal learning project. Anyone was welcome to teach or to learn. Many of the farmers just wanted to learn to read, some to be trained in medicine or study history. A prisoner who had been raised by a French woman taught French. Lino ended up studying English using someone's copy of Shakespeare. Anyone who knew something could teach it. Anyone who wanted to learn could ask someone to teach them. Most classes were held right after breakfast. Hopefully people who had a reason to get up, who felt the accomplishment of learning, would get through the day better.

A library was set up in one cell, a librarian elected, and regular hours set when men could share or borrow books and magazines. Eyeglasses were as precious as books; men took care not to lose or damage them. A new pair was a big chore, sometimes impossible, for a family to get.

The medical students were anxious not to lose time in their studies, and the doctors, wanting to keep their own knowledge up, were pleased to teach them. Even those who weren't medical students could attend if they liked, learning practical subjects like injections and applying dressings.

People constantly came up with new ideas: arm wrestling, acting out plays, studying Freud, chess on primitive homemade boards. Other circulars began to do the same. All these activities strengthened the mood of community in the circular.

There was surprisingly little conflict. If something serious came up, the elected *rejero* would try to arbitrate. Prisoners had to know they were safe within their own ranks. There was too much danger from the outside to allow anyone to create more within their circle of security.

Like the day the dynamite arrived.

Emy and Lino at a picnic at *Santa Maria del Mar* in 1955, during their engagement.

Emy and Lino at their wedding on a gorgeous sunny winter day, February 9, 1958.

Lino and Emy during their honeymoon at Emy's uncle's beach house at *Jibacoa* on the north coast of Cuba.

Emy and Lino with their first daughter, Emilia Maria, at Esmeralda, Lino's hometown. May 1959.

Emy with her three children at the safe house at *Santa Maria del Mar* after Lino's capture. April 1961.

Emy with Raque de la Huerta on the beach at *Santa Maria del Mar* in the spring of 1961. With them are their children, Po, Patricia, Javier, and Emilia Maria.

1961. The professional photograph Emy's mother had taken of the children before they left for Miami. The photograph was always kept in a thin silver frame by Emy's bed.

From the left, Emy, Ileana, and Vicki when they were living together at Vicki's house. Early 1970s

right, September 1977. Emy and the de la Huerta sisters in *Ruinas* park. Left to right, Margarita, Hortensia, Emy standing, and Ada.

left, 1976, Emy with Vicki's mother, Maria Sutter. Emy is wearing a necklace of seed pods made by Lino in prison.

Interior of one of the four circulars at *Isla de Pinos* prison. Guards entered the circular from underneath the central tower, so they had no contact with the prisoners. The courtyard was a common space used by the prisoners for many activities, including baseball.

Exterior of *Isla de Pinos* with two of its four giant circulars visible and, to the left, the pavilion designed for dining but used only for visits.

A group of prisoners' wives and friends who often gathered at the home of Jaime and Rosa Caldevilla, a Spanish diplomat. In the front are Emy and Rosa. Ileana is behind Rosa and Vicki is in the top row, third from right. Mid-1960s.

Emy with a thin but happy Lino relaxing during his first pass home in 1973 at a picnic at *Bucuranao* beach near Havana.

A photo taken in 1978 after Lino's release, by a fellow prisoner who had become a photographer. Lino and Emy wanted to send the children a photo of their parents finally together.

Lucia broke through the barriers to hug her parents the minute they stepped off the plane in Ft. Lauderdale. January 28, 1979. It happened to be Jose Marti's birthday.

January 28, 1979. The reunited family went straight from the airport to the new Agrupacion center in Miami for a Mass said by Padre Llorente. Left to right, Lucia, Po, Jacinto, Emy, Emilia Maria, Emilia, and Lino.

2006. Emy and Lino with their grandchildren. Left to right, Lino Jr, Emily Mary, Gabriela, Claudia, Cristina, Carolina, Lucía Isabela, Nicolás y Sofía

2006. A family party at the Fernandez house in Coral Gables. Left to right, Po, Emy, Lucia, Lino, Emilia Maria.

next page, A May 1967 letter written at *La Cabana* prison from Lino to Emy. Letters had to be written in handwriting so small Emy used a magnifying glass to read it. An excerpt reads:

"*Mi vida*. How much meaning there is in calling you that - my life. When we started loving each other, holding hands, we called each other *vida*, life. And now we call each other *mi vida*, my life. When I read those words, I know you gave me not only your warmth but your whole life. I told you I was reasonably well, but after reading your letter it is so different. I cannot live without you. I have had you every instant inside me, very deeply inside me. I am not worried, but I am dying to see you. The only thing that hurts is not being able to embrace you. I love you so much. Oh my happiness. I don't have just kisses saved for you; I've saved my whole heart. The desire to kiss you never goes away. I would kiss you even in my sleep."

Vida mía: ¡Qué sentido tiene para mí decirte eso! Cuando comenzamos a amar
nos son las nuevas cogidas nos decíamos VIDA, hoy los dos nos decimos
vida mía. Cuando lo vi me diste un solo tu calor amor mío sino sentí que
me llegaba tu vida toda plena. Te dije que estaba bastante bien pero después
de dejarte fue todo tan diferente, no puedo vivir sin ti, te he tenido a cada
instante dentro, muy dentro pero más ahora, no estoy preocupado pero sí
loco por verte eso es todo lo que me pueda doler, no pudiendo abrazar como te quiero ¡Ah mi dicha! No muchos besos guardados, te tengo, te tengo, el corazón. No
se me quitan nunca los deseos de besarte a ti te besaría hasta durmiendo. Así
toda la noche pendidito de tu boca. Me gustas con una pasión, un delirio
una necesidad tal, una ilusión que me asombra cada día nuevo. Mira, MUJER
eso todo llega, y tendré algún día entre mis brazos, y te daré mi Ser porque tú
eres el mío. Se lo daré como siempre se lo he hecho en esa poesía nuestra sólo de
gestos y suspiros que nos quema y nos consume. Yo te quiero mucho, muchísimo, te
quiero porque me enseñaste a amar. Te quiero porque te enseñé a besar a darme y a
darte. Te quiero porque necesito a alguien que me quiera así como tú en ese ansia viva devoradora tuya que nadie sabe tener para querer. Te recuerdo y recuerdo lo nuestro, ojos y besos y risa, y risas y cantos, y lágrimas, y despedidas y
encuentros y picardías y intimidades, y tareas porque todas son tareas, tareas celes-
tes, y humanas, creaciones tuyas y mías, yo no sé ni las que se tengo ni mías. Solo sé
que cada día pequeña de esos pero grande porque son del alma y cuerpo porque son
genuinos. Cada día de esos es el único día de mi vida, si te he recordado mucho
pero más te siento. ¿Lo oyes? Te siento. Todo lo demás es adorno aún lo más que
vida para nosotros. Yo triste lo desagradable, lo bello, y lo feo de las cosas y de los
hombres son adornos de nuestra pasión, de eso que siento de ti, y por ti. Te supe así
bonita del mundo que me gusta porque me gustas en todo y por todo lo que amas
y esta vez porque lo que hacías es maravillosa y nuestros, lo resueltos no son mien-
tra para un día, lo son para la propia naturaleza de uno y la de todo lo que exi-
siste. Nuestro amor merece todo, y eso es cultivar de lo más hondo y bueno de nosotros y eso es para nuestro amor lo mejor. No me importan los frutos, me importa el
intento. Lo demás vivo porque él sabe lo que hace, yo lo vivo contigo a mi mane-
ra y con gusto de medios, pero me sabía contigo, y tú conmigo, tú diste gusto
sin medida diciéndome que por mí también lo hacías. Así yo lo considero por
que te quiero demasiado de vida, y quiero de todo protegerte hasta de algunas lo
cuyas mías. Conoceremos tanto, viviremos tanto solo minutos contigo en too
tan poco vivir de nuevos pero lo quiero vivir toda contigo no solo comun vida
todo, bien que ya sabes ver, yo voy. Rosa roja, pura, delicada; una rosa roja de
carne, por dentro lo eres YO NO SE.... y tú pura lo sabía de antes. Por dentro
lo sabía también pero de otra forma no precisamente intuitiva. Me gusta tu
respiración anhelante como la oí... bailar dos un día y jugueteando ... se-
cundes. Fue todo tan bello ... me siento que me quedé TODO en ti. No me que-
do en ti que no me fui. Te tengo serpentadita aún. He recordado más, muchí-
sima que otras veces, siempre la porven pero como en tu delante dentro vibra veo
y a lo afuera que me gusta mi hoy, lo hace más cada día más. Sobre por
qui.... Es un abrazo... cualquiera de ellos ... sigo con la ansia de verte y sen-
tirlo de blanco ... ah si pudiera !! Siento en mí un deseo y una fuerza de
besar, y de que tú vivas, todo conmigo haciendo igual, te juro que así será.
La sé porque me lo has hecho sentir cuando he llevado abrazado y por ti reci-
bido. En ese momento siento toda la energía del mundo y toda la paz

29

L ino - Juan - Vengan, vengan, rápido!" Lino dropped the shoe he was repairing and rushed to the window of the cell next door. Pedro was watching, sitting in a deep window sill. Someone always watched. It was the only way to pick up any change in routine, any small event that might be significant. On this glaring Tuesday morning in July of 1962, there was plenty to see.

A long line of trucks had begun to snake into the prison, some parking at the door of each circular. On the truck beds were stacks of rough wooden crates labeled DYNAMITE in large red stenciled letters. No attempt to hide them. Lino and Juan Muller craned their necks to watch the guards unload the boxes. *What the hell* . . .

One figure caught Lino's eye - he looked so familiar.

"Hey Juan - does that guy look familiar to you - the one shouting orders?"

Juan shook his head.

"*Ay Dios! Es Julio Garcia.*"

Garcia, now a Commander of the Revolution, had originally been part of the *Agrupación* with Lino. Lino had heard he now belonged to *Directorio Revolucionario*. Garcia was striding back and forth, supervising the unloading and showing the guards where to place the crates.

Without thinking Lino yelled out, "Garcia, up here, it's Lino." Garcia looked up as though he'd been shot. Looking embarrassed, he made a vague waving gesture, then quickly looked away and hurried off to one of the farthest trucks. Lino was baffled. Why had Garcia not at least exchanged a few words, even though the two men had obviously ended up on opposite sides politically? Then he understood.

Of course. He knows. He knows what this dynamite is for. He's helping Fidel get ready to blow us up. No wonder he doesn't want to look me in the face. Lino knew he should be horrified, but all he felt was a deep sorrow and discouragement.

"Hey - get away from there. Inside, you assholes."

Two guards came charging toward the building and ordered everyone away from the windows. When they were gone, Lino returned to the window, but now he stood off to the side where he was less visible. Juan Muller edged up next to Lino.

"What's all that for?" His face tensed with concentration, as he tried to see what the guards were doing.

Should he tell Juan what he thought? He would certainly find out through rumor soon enough.

"It's going under the circular." Lino grasped the stone edge of the window. "Juan, I'm afraid it can only be to blow us up."

"*Pero por qué?*" Juan's voice went taut with panic. "Do you think they're planning a mass execution - the prisoners not worth holding on to?"

"No! Even Fidel cares too much about public opinion to do something that monstrous without a justification."

Juan echoed one of Lino's earlier thoughts. "Maybe just a precaution? Against a breakout or a riot?"

"*Quizás.* Maybe." But as Lino thought about it he felt a sinister wave of certainty that it wasn't a precaution against a mass escape. They had never needed that precaution before.

He thought about the news they got from BBC and other stations in the Caribbean about increasing tension between the U.S. and Fidel. The Russians were getting more involved and more belligerent in Cuba's defense. Lino's mind told him what he didn't want to know.

The dynamite was protection against an invasion from outside. It made sense. Nearly 6000 trained dedicated anti-Castro troops would be a fine prize for invaders - a great way to increase their numbers. And gain critical intelligence. *Fidel wouldn't hesitate to murder 6000 men to keep that from happening.*

Lino said nothing more to Juan. But the morning's events soon reinforced Lino's dread. Boxes of dynamite were opened, emptied, and the sticks loaded into the underground basement space of each circular. The prisoners could not see exactly how it was being installed, but the sheer quantity of explosives made their stomachs churn.

Their lives meant nothing; they had no value as human beings. Their concerns about punishment and food became irrelevant in the face of this new possibility. Mass execution. One cold act.

Orestes came by to join Lino at the window. "Boy, they sure don't care who sees what they're doing." He leaned out as far as he could.

"Well, it's hard to hide those long fuses, even though they seem to be burying them in trenches."

"Probably just to keep the idiot guards from tripping over them. Where do you think they're leading, Lino?"

"Into the hills. Definitely. To some central spot." Lino was surprised at his own calm as he described how, after evacuating guards and other non-prisoners, one official, crouched high in the hills, could detonate the explosives in seconds. Fidel could then lament this "tragic explosion, due no doubt to a prisoner escape attempt." Lino felt a terrible tightness in his chest. He tried to breathe deeply.

For days the prisoners wandered along the balconies slack-faced, like haunted men. No one slept. They talked endlessly, desperately, about how to survive, about the impossibility of survival. They spoke of their lives in the past tense, what they wished they had done, things they might have said. The underlying tone was the same; *it's too late.*

Guards shrugged when asked about the explosives. But the prisoners saw them on the paths making joking gestures of pushing a detonator and watching an explosion. Lino was appalled. These guards were laughing at the idea of blowing up men who might once have been their neighbors. Even, like Manuel Garcia, their friends.

In this massive malaise, Lino's psychiatric patients were pushed almost beyond coping. A young student, in the circular less than a year, told Lino, "I'd rather jump off the roof than let myself be torn to shreds. At least I'd be in one piece. I'd still be a human being." Lino, having no answer, just listened.

The screams of nightmares had always echoed through the circular. Now there were many more. Wary-eyed men roamed in the night. Many came to talk to Lino. Men who had never come before. They wanted to confess, or to vent their outrage, their wish to face their killer as they died. A few just needed to hear they were not cowards, not alone in their fear.

On Friday afternoon, the guards disappeared from in the interior towers. One shift left at 4 p.m. and their replacements never appeared. Repositioned because they might not be able to get out fast enough if

- *when* - the circular was blown up? The only soldiers they saw now were those who delivered meals and messages. These could usually be seen approaching. The prisoners were alone.

Prisoners who had seen combat refused to just wait; they wanted to fight back. For years, they'd tried to convince the other prisoners that they weren't impotent; they could influence what happened to them. Now they intended to prove it. A group of ten people, including Lino, began to discuss ideas.

A young engineer, Antonio Zayas, gathered them in his cell.

"Look, we don't have to just sit here. He leaned forward, almost pleading. "We've got plenty of demolition expertise in this circular, and surely the others do too."

The others nodded solemnly, stretching their minds cautiously toward this faint hope.

"But first I'm gonna try to get into the basement, climb down one of the shaftways, if it isn't too blocked. I wanna see just what equipment and explosives they're using."

One man mimed gagging. "Brave man. I think I'd rather be blown up than go down one of those disgusting shafts." Several men chuckled softly, appreciating the attempt to lighten the mood.

Zayas smiled. "Good point. But I'm going. At least the guards won't look for anybody there."

Six hours later, they met again.

"I managed to make it into the basement. They left lots of extra stuff - explosives, fuses, wiring material. And I had a good look around."

Juan broke in. "Did you see what we need to know?"

"Yea, the stuff tells us a lot. There seems to be both a mechanical detonation system and an electrical one." He held up a section of fuse. "By emptying the TNT powder from some of these, I think we can disable the whole fuse."

There were murmurs of approval. Lino could feel the group's energy surge at the idea of taking some action.

"Since the fuse itself will still be there, any guard who yanks on it will assume it's still in place and working. But if the system gets detonated, the signal won't get through the emptied section of fuse."

Zayas and two other demolition experts, defectors from Castro's forces who knew how the systems usually worked, got busy. Hundreds of prisoners were recruited to help, but each person knew only his part. A man might be asked to guard a section of cells, with no idea what was going on inside. Those who helped pull the extra dirt up the shaft were not told why.

Disabling the electrical detonation system was trickiest. With difficulty, they were able to separate the two parts of the system so that the circuit signaling readiness operated normally but the actual detonation circuit would not. When they finished, they smeared everything with earth again so a casual inspector would assume nothing had changed. Each step of the process was shared with contacts they could absolutely trust in other circulars, via coded messages.

When the group gathered the next time they were jubilant. "I feel a lot better," Zaya said, then laughed at his own understatement. Any man who doubted that their sabotage would work kept the thought to himself.

Lino interrupted the mood. "Let's not rest on our laurels here. It's time to think in military terms as well. Actually taking advantage of the situation." Cesar outlined their plan.

"If they try to set the dynamite off, and it doesn't go, a group of us will need to rush into the underground area and grab the grenades. We won't have that much time. They'll rush back in to see what got screwed up."

"Wait. I didn't know anything about grenades." Orestes always liked to know everything.

"Trust me, they're there." Cesar pointed to the floor. "Plenty of 'em, made from hollowed out dynamite sticks. With those grenades and a well organized force, we should be able to control the prison before it can be re-occupied."

Lino broke in, impatient with Orestes' questions. "Obviously, we couldn't take over the whole island, but hopefully we would hook up with invading forces by then."

In spite of the fear, Lino felt exhilarated at being back in military mode of thinking.

After a lot of discussion back and forth, everyone agreed. They removed two stone pavers from the floor of a ground floor cell, under a bed where the gap was hard to see. This gave easy access to the part of the basement where the grenades were stored.

The final task was to dig an escape tunnel from the basement to a point outside the circular. The dirt removed from the tunnel was stored in the same shaftways between the cells. Everyone breathed easier when this was done.

Lino felt bad not telling other prisoners what was being done. Here were men who were living in dread, paralyzed by the presence of the dynamite. He tried in subtle ways to reassure them that the system might not be as effective as it appeared. But they couldn't risk sharing the plans with everyone. There could always be an informer in the circular; it wouldn't be the first time. The most innocent slipped word might alert a guard and start a search.

Lino was glad he and the others had been adamant about keeping up their military readiness. About ten percent of the prisoners were members of Lino's organization, the MRR. Many more came from other organizations that had fought in the Escambray.

The head of the military organization in *Isla de Pinos* was Cesar Paez. Before his capture, he had headed only one group, the *30 de Noviembre* movement, but he was greatly respected by all those who had fought on the outside. Each circular had a military set-up; four or five lieutenants reported to Paez. Its existence wasn't secret or exclusive; it was just that not everyone wanted to be involved.

The resistance leaders had been sent to the high security *Isla de Pinos* because Fidel knew they were committed and well trained, guilty of *peligrosidad,* or dangerousness, in the government's eyes. These leaders had fought constantly to be separated from common criminals; it was an issue of recognizing their status, but it also kept their communication and training strong.

"Isn't this all a waste of energy?" asked Manuel the car mechanic from Santa Clara one day.

"Not in my view. We might get a chance to fight our way out of here. If we do, we can't stop to get organized."

Lino saw Manuel wasn't convinced. He tried again. "If we get out, we want to be ready. There's still a very real resistance movement out there; we don't know how long it'll last, but we know it's still there now. If we can ever rejoin them, we need to be in fighting order."

Manuel had scratched his neck, smiled weakly, and shrugged.

To Lino, the mindset was just as important as the hierarchy. The military organization held classes and political discussions, constantly reinforcing the idea that they weren't powerless; there were ways to fight back. The dismantling of the explosives had proved what they could do.

As months passed and nothing happened with the explosives, the tension eased in the circular. Some of the guards returned to the watch tower. And then the dynamite threat was overshadowed by a much worse one.

In mid-October, rumors of atomic warheads in Cuba began circulating outside Cuba and among the prisoners listening to their clandestine radios.

"You think this is the reason for the dynamite?" Vicente asked Lino, when he finished reading a broadcast summary.

"Hell no. If Fidel was going to attack the U.S., he wouldn't need dynamite to blow us up. The U.S. would do it for him, along with the rest of Cuba."

He sat down on the wide sill of his cell window and looked out.

"You know, I heard rumors way back in July of 1960. Atomic weapons were being brought to Cuba and we were making fuel for missiles."

"How the hell did you hear that?"

"People working on the inside told me. I tried my best to pass them on to the CIA. Of course they showed no interest. Typical." His voice was bitter. *Were those agents remembering now and wondering if Lino had been right?*

Over the next ten days, prisoners in the *Isla*, like the rest of the world, held their breath at every new development in the brinkmanship of Kennedy and Khrushchev over the missile sites. Lino was sure the prisoners, with their contraband radios, knew more than the Cuban people. When Castro finally went public, declaring a state of war alert on October 22, Lino couldn't bear to think of Emy alone in Havana. Though she might hear some things through the embassy, she would feel alone and frightened, with no idea of what was coming. When Kennedy announced to the American people on television that Cuba had nuclear missile sites, he doubted the Cuban public was told. He was just as glad.

The next morning after his shower, the circular still quiet, Lino stared out the window. He was overwhelmed by a vision of this sky, this sparkling sea, roiling with atomic fallout. Was there any chance he could reach Emy in the chaos? He doubted it. What a terrible end to all the struggles, all the suffering and the bitterness. Humans obliterated. A world lost. Lino broke out in a sweat, something he rarely did.

There was a subdued air in the circular. The prisoners, not bombarded by news every minute like the outside world, appeared surrealistically calm as they waited. It was as though dying in a holocaust with millions of others held more dignity for them than being trapped like rats in a cage wired for destruction. Oblivion could come at any moment. But it would come quickly and absolutely. There would be no frantic grasping at escape or at saving the lives of those you loved. Everything – everyone – would just disappear.

Now Lino was always in the cell when the radio was monitored. He was there to hear, on October 24th, that the Soviet ships en route to Cuba with nuclear cargo had slowed, and then turned around. Tension was reduced, but there was still the possibility of war. On October 28, he was there again to hear that Khrushchev had agreed to remove the missile sites. He leaned against the wall and let waves of relief roll over him. How much did Emy know? How frightened was she? Lino felt a sense of deliverance, as though he and Emy had once again been spared for some future life.

A month later, Lino again felt he had narrowly escaped. Twenty-three leaders of fighting units from the Escambray were sent for trial. All were shot within hours of the verdict. Lino never found out the exact charges or what had happened at the trial, but he was horrified. He knew most of those men. They had done nothing more than he. The bullets in their chest could so easily have been lodged in his own.

He wrote a long letter to Emy that night. His only paper was a 4 inch square. He rote in tiny letters across both sides, then wrote more words diagonally across the original script. He knew Emy would decipher every word.

30

The blond-haired boy lay curled up in one of the small beds across the room. Emy could just see the top of his head under the sheet. It might be Javier. Or Renecito. He didn't stir. Her room was often invaded by one or more of the seven de la Huerta children. She never knew what inspired them to leave their own beds and slip in here, but she was always glad to hear the light breathing and see a tiny form across the room. For a moment she could imagine it was one of her own.

The silence in the house was so unusual that Emy lay motionless, enjoying the garden sounds coming in through the window. She'd been living with the de la Huerta family for almost three years, since Lino's capture in 1961. She'd shared this long spacious bedroom on the second floor with her own children before they'd left for Miami.

She pushed away thoughts of how much she missed them. It did no good. She knew only that the three were safe and growing up. She received few letters. The children weren't old enough yet to write, and her mother wasn't a letter writer. How could she blame her? She had her hands full doing Emy's job. Of course, more letters might have been sent and never allowed through.

She heard the distant clink of metal on metal downstairs. Raque de la Huerta, as always, was up before Emy, starting the endless work needed to maintain a house of four adults and seven children in a city where the basics had become sporadic luxuries. Her current pregnancy hadn't slowed her down.

Emy put on her worn cotton robe and padded silently down the

187

curved staircase, along the long central hallway, and through the stucco archway into the dining room. From there, she could hear Raque talking softly to the maid Estrella.

"*Está bien*, this milk's boiled enough. *Dios mío, Estrella*, I'll have to find more milk somewhere. We're using more than ever. I'll go by Señor Varela's and see what he has." Jose Varela was a farmer west of Havana who had supplied milk and even rich cream and homemade yogurt to the family since before the Revolution. Raque never knew how he'd managed to keep a few of his own cows when his farm had been seized, but he had. Milk was all he had to sell them now - and never as much as they needed.

"And if Jose doesn't have anything, no one else will either," Raque sighed. "The oatmeal tomorrow may have to be with water. But the children need dairy."

"He won't be able to refuse you, Señora. He never can." The tiny mulatto maid heaved an aluminum cauldron of milk off the stove and set it to cool on the battered kitchen table in the middle of the room. She was always respectful, but she spoke frankly. She'd been 14 years with the family.

Emy stood in the doorway. Raque was lucky to have Estrella. Many maids had embraced the Revolution so fanatically that they'd left the families they worked for, on principle. Or they had remained in the house as spies for the militia and later the CDRs.

But Estrella was different. She'd been raised in Raque's family in Matanzas. Her mother had worked for Raque's family, and Estrella had come to Havana to work when Raque got married. She didn't mention politics much, but she made it clear by her manner that she was as mad about what Fidel was doing to Cuba as anyone around her. In the new Havana where almost no one was to be trusted, Raque and Emy never needed to question Estrella's loyalty.

Now the two women noticed Emy, and Raque came over to give her a big hug.

"*Dormistes bien?*"

"Yes, I slept well. I had company. Javier I think."

"Oh he's a wanderer that one."

Raque always made her feel like a valuable addition to the household instead of one more person to care for. She shuddered when she thought of those prisoners' wives who, after being kicked out of their own houses, had been "reassigned" single rooms in isolated suburbs where they were treated like interlopers.

"Rene must have put sleeping pills in the children's supper," Raque said laughing. "I've never known such silence so late in the morning."

Emy sat on a metal stool at the big table and took the weak coffee Estrella poured for her. "Well, it might have to do with being a weekend. Nobody goes around pulling them out of their beds." She made a face at Raque. "And I might point out that it's only a quarter to six. Not everyone has as much energy as you."

After munching a dry slice of bread with her coffee, she began to help Raque set out the children's bowls around the table. A highchair for the baby, high stools for Luis and Lourdes, and the rest in regular chairs, some with pillows or thick medical books to sit on.

What would breakfast have been like in her own house, with her own three children, and Lino getting ready for his first patient? Let's see, Lucia would be out of the high chair, Po would be insisting on a regular chair. And Emilia Maria would probably be gloating over not having to use a cushion.

No importa. It isn't that way. How long till it is? Oh stop. This is the worst thing for you, thinking that way. Just enjoy being with the children who are here.

They heard one light set of footsteps, then another, and presently an army of small feet galloping at different speeds and gaits down the big stairs. Emy went up to get the baby. Raque and Estrella got the children seated and their bowls filled with hot cereal with a thin covering of milk. Rogelio gave Raque a glum face as she filled his bowl, and she returned a warning look. The children had complained in the beginning about this glutinous paste called oatmeal imported from Russia. Raque had made it very clear she wouldn't tolerate whining.

"You know perfectly well I would never give you this if there were anything better. So complaining just shows ingratitude. And don't complain to Emy either because she isn't responsible for it."

The children knew their mother meant what she said. They showed their lack of enthusiasm in their faces but said nothing.

When breakfast was over and the older children had gone upstairs to wash, Raque outlined the day's plan. During the week Raque was non-stop with the children, and Emy worked at the Embassy. But on the weekends, Raque turned her skills to buying on the black market, and Emy usually went with her. She wasn't sure she'd have the courage to do it by herself. Raque was usually enigmatic about how she knew the places to go. Vagueness was the best policy when it came to illegal acts.

Emy began pushing in the stools and chairs with more force than she had intended. *What a world.* If you're caught on the street with goods and can't prove they were bought legally, you could be charged with "acts against the Revolution," imprisoned on the spot. But the Revolution's economy had dried up supplies to the stores so that bartering and dealing with individuals was the only way to get what you needed to live!

Raque rinsed the last of the bowls and dried her hands on a tea towel with a washed out flower pattern. "The woman lives in Calle Damas, down near the piers. We have to be there before 4:00. Wally's coming too." Wally was a good friend of Emy's from before the Revolution.

"Raque, that's a terrible neighborhood. Are you sure you want to do this?"

"Well, I'm sure of one thing. I wanna see what she has. My friend told me this woman has some amazing stuff." She raised her eyebrows to emphasize her point.

Emy smiled and pushed the last chair under the table. "Judging from the places you usually come up with, I'm sure she does."

"Anyway, Emy, it's broad daylight." Raque stopped and turned halfway through the door to the dining room. "One of the few things I don't worry about since the Revolution is being assaulted. Señor Castro and his buddies keep a tight rein on petty criminals - when they're not busy looking for people with 'bourgeois attitudes'."

Well, Emy thought, as she climbed the stairs, if she was going to be arrested, she wouldn't want it to be with anyone else but Raque. She had such a way of picking life up, shaking out the dust, and folding it back up just the way it was supposed to be.

Wally arrived after lunch. The three women had dressed up more than their errand required. They'd found from experience that if they got into a tight spot, being well dressed made a difference. People tended to treat you better; it was an ingrained reaction. If they were ever caught with black market merchandise, looking good might make even soldiers treat them better.

They settled themselves into Raque's big cream and black Plymouth. What a luxury, a car that still worked, and a snappy one at that. Emy replayed in her mind the times when they would have stopped off at a café and had a sandwich and pastries. Even if the café had food today - unlikely - they needed to concentrate on more important things.

As usual, Wally chattered away, recounting her week. Even the most normal things seemed to take on excitement when they had happened to Wally. Emy hoped there would be no excitement today.

Calle Damas was in Old Havana, and the house they were directed to was a typical long low colonial house, unpainted with missing shutters and a broken front window. The woman who answered the door was a black woman who clearly practiced *Santería*, the Cuban version of African voodoo. Tall and very thin but muscled, she was draped with small objects and tiny figures Emy supposed were fetishes. Her wire-like hair coiled stiffly out on each side, but was pulled into a crude bun in the back. She didn't give her name but gestured them furtively into the front room. Emy never heard Raque give any explanation, but the woman was clearly expecting them.

The woman leaned in toward Raque, who had done all the talking so far. "What you want? What you need? I got things nobody got anymore. Look at this." She pulled out a seatless bicycle of uncertain age from a hallway leading off the large central room. "Very nice bicycle when there's no gas. Real rubber tires."

Without waiting for their reaction to the bicycle, the woman started pulling out bolts of cloth, pieces of leather for making shoes, silk stockings, silver and dishes, even a platter from a little fish restaurant called *El Patio* that Emy had visited often. The platter, with a gaily painted red lobster and *El Patio* in large black letters, looked incongruous and lost.

Emy felt like giggling when the woman showed Wally some high heeled green backless sandals and suggested they would be useful for going to nightclubs. But she kept quiet; she was always nervous in these places. She just wanted to grab the good stuff and get out.

None of the three women knew what to get - they needed so much - so they let the woman continue, examining each item she brought out, deciding whether it was worth spending their pesos.

As they talked, dark-skinned men would periodically open the front door, make an almost invisible sign to the woman, and skitter down the hallway to a back room. Five or ten minutes later, the same men would traipse back through, looking clearly like they felt better. Emy watched them.

Boy I wish I could have a glass of whatever they're having. Why am I so nervous? Any place this crammed with stuff couldn't be a police setup. Besides, the Santería people hate the militia. Don't they?

Now the woman began taking out various bottles and cans, most holding liquor or luxury foods which, while tempting, wouldn't feed the family. A tiny can of curried sardines. A fancy shaped jar of brandied pears. Lino used to buy those. On Christmas Eve.

Her thoughts were jerked back when the woman said in a low tone, "Butter? Maybe you want some butter?"

Butter! Of course they would take butter. An unheard of treat. They could make a cake for the next *visita*. Lino would be in heaven. Or cookies with the children. They hadn't been able to do that in years. Most important, just butter for bread. Big slabs of bread with butter could pass as a respectable meal sometimes for the children when there was little else. Butter. Yes. Quickly. Yes. Now, before she could change her mind. The woman disappeared into the hallway and returned with a huge block of butter wrapped in several layers of greasy muslin.

"There must be eight or nine pounds there," Wally whispered to Emy.

"Where do you suppose she got it?"

"I don't know, but she gave me a pinch. It's real."

They quickly paid and climbed into the car with Wally in the spacious back seat. She had the cloth-wrapped butter on the seat next to her with an old blanket protecting the upholstery. It was still hot out, and they wanted to get the butter home before it began to melt.

They were approaching the Plaza Cívica when they saw a man in front of a factory building waving his arms and yelling.

"*Pare!* Stop! A worker's injured. You have to help us get our comrade to the hospital." Even though he was asking for help, his attitude was insistent, even bullying. That seemed to be everyone's attitude since the Revolution. Always telling you what you **had** to do.

"I don't stop for comrades, usually." Wally muttered in the back seat.

Raque didn't slow down. "Well, I might - on a good day. But not when I'm carrying contraband butter. Anyway, they'd find some way to make my driving this car a crime against the Revolution."

They were almost out of the Plaza when a small red and white police car pulled out behind them, siren blaring. The traffic was too dense to try to lose them, so Raque pulled over.

A pudgy officer with dark eyes sunk into pale skin leaned on the driver's side window ledge. His nametag said *Carlos Sanchez*. Raque moved her head sideways to avoid his stale breath.

"*Buenos días, Señoras,*" His tone was full of sarcasm. Raque could see a vein pulsing on his neck.

The three women said nothing, trying to look as dignified as possible.

"Why didn't you do your duty back there? Why didn't you stop to help a comrade? Maybe you don't think you need to obey these rules?"

Raque stared straight at the man, looking indignant. "*Señor*, please. We are three women alone, driving in the city close to nightfall. We cannot stop for some strange man. How do we know he isn't lying?"

Sanchez seemed unsure for a moment what to do. Then he gave them a disgusted look, withdrew his head, and signaled to another officer to get in the back seat. He told Raque to follow the police car to the station.

Emy glanced into the back seat. Wally had covered the butter with a newspaper, but it was starting to melt, seeping into the blanket and the newspaper both. Wally gave Emy a bland look that said: "Butter? What butter?"

When they got to the station, the officer who'd been in the back seat conferred with Sanchez. Two other policemen opened the back door, and took the butter off the seat. The women were told to get out of the car. Five guards circled them, guns drawn. Another policeman stood by the station door, armed with an M16 rifle.

The officers looked at the butter. Before they could comment, Emy took a haughty tone. The best defense was a good offense. "I'm sorry but I have to inform you that I am a secretary at the Embassy of the United Arab Republics, and this butter belongs to my boss, the Commercial Attaché."

Sanchez' voice was more confused now, less sure of himself. "Your boss asks you to get him butter?"

Emy smiled in a patient, world weary way. "No. His freezer is broken and I told him I would keep it in mine." She spoke as if to a child. "You may not realize it, officer, but diplomats get things in large quantities, since supplies are sent only a few times a year from the outside."

Because the Revolution has screwed up our economy, she wanted to add. She made a mental note to be sure to tell people at the Embassy this story about the broken freezer so they would back her up.

"Excuse me gentlemen," Raque's voice had taken on a steely tone. She touched her large stomach. "But as you can see, I am a mother. And I have seven children at home alone with their elderly aunts. If anything happens to them because of this delay, I will hold you personally responsible."

Motherhood didn't seem to impress the policemen, nor did butter belonging to diplomats. The three women were escorted into the police station by the guards and Sanchez. They were taken to a very hot interrogation room where the butter sat on the square wooden table, melting now through the blanket onto the table. Sanchez and two of the guards remained with them.

Emy felt rivulets of sweat on her face but did not wipe them off. *God, forget the butter. Just let us get home. Get our car back. Get out of here with only some insults and threats.*

After a short wait another officer came in, self-assured and wearing a clean pressed uniform. He listened carefully as Emy repeated her story about her boss at the embassy and the broken freezer. She was sure he knew most Cuban women hired at the embassies were anti-Castro. But the officer seemed very calm, and her tension eased a little when he nodded as she spoke.

He looked at the white mound in a pool of grease. "This is the butter?" He made it sound like explosives or handguns.

She took what she hoped was a confident tone and tried to make everything sound like just a misunderstanding. "Yes, that is the butter. The butter that is the personal property of a diplomat accredited to the government of Cuba."

Now Sanchez interrupted from across the room, in a tone verging on panic. He had uncovered a serious irregularity, and he was determined to be recognized for his cleverness. "Your diplomat should have asked for a police escort then, or used an official limousine. There are ways of doing these things," he ended in a note of triumph.

"Yes, of course he should have," said the senior officer. "We'll make an appropriate complaint through diplomatic channels."

As frightened as she was, Emy was afraid Wally might start laughing. Diplomatic channels? Police escort? To move butter?

There was a long silence. Raque looked cool and unconcerned, her right hand resting on her stomach. Wally smiled uncertainly at Emy.

A female guard entered the room and stood at attention near the door, frowning. Her stomach overflowed her waistband and her pants dragged on the floor. *Why was she there?* What if they were actually put in cells? Charged with crimes against the State? The police answered to no one. If they had been watching her – or any of them - they might just be looking for an excuse.

The embassy could probably eventually get us out, but after how long? That guard would love to take our nice clothes away, search us, put us in rough prison uniforms. Emy shuddered at the thought of being in that woman's hands.

Finally the senior officer spoke in a tired voice. "We will have to keep the butter as evidence."

Emy felt her shoulder muscles relax a little. *Ah, that's the deal.* We give them the butter and they forget the whole thing. No cakes for the visit. No cookies. No buttered bread. But they would be released.

"Of course." She did not insist further.

The senior officer disappeared. Sanchez reviewed the papers with the female guard. No one spoke to the three women. Would the police insist on keeping them overnight while they checked their records? *Oh please, no.* The idea of an iron door closing behind her was terrifying to Emy. There was another half-hour of petty posturing and rudeness.

When would they get out of here?

Then, without explanation, they were told they could go.

When they were alone in the car, Wally was furious, but Raque turned to humor as usual. "Ah, we are undermining *la Revolución* with unauthorized butter. What outrage will we perform next?" Wally's sputtering turned to a chuckle. Emy sat quietly, shaken at their close call.

The police followed them to the house of Rene de la Huerta's three unmarried sisters who had been watching the children. As soon as they got there and the police left, Emy set out for the house of her boss, Hamroush, who lived only a few blocks away.

Hamroush was astonished to see her. "Emy, what's wrong?" She had never visited his house before and certainly not at eight o'clock on a Saturday evening. Her face was still ashen, her manner shaky. He immediately motioned her into the entry. These days no one said anything on the street where it could be overheard.

Hamroush brought two cold drinks and Emy explained the incident with the black market butter. Hamroush nodded his head sadly. "Of course, I'll cover for you. I'll back up exactly what you said."

"Thank you." Emy had not doubted Hamroush would help. But now that it was all set, she felt a weight lifted.

"Of course Emy. I would never do anything else. But God, the Cubans don't deserve this. You love life so much." He slid his glass back and forth across the stone table. "And every year things get worse."

Emy walked home through the humid night, her brain a whirl of emotions, relief mixed with horror at how close they had come to being swallowed up by the police machine. How different this street felt from when she had been growing up. Then there had been a steady flow of people, children playing, women lingering to chat. Now there were only soldiers. A sentry for the CDR on duty around the clock. Even though they were embassy employees, mothers, one the wife of a medical professor, the police could easily have locked them up. That awful vulnerability again. Would she every get used to it?

Three weeks later, Emy received a summons for a "hearing" at the same police station. That was a good sign. There apparently would not be a trial in a real courtroom. Hamroush went with her. With his support and presence Emy felt much safer. But of course the officials missed no opportunity to make her feel threatened. The case was resolved with only a warning, a black mark which Emy was sure would be used against her if the government ever needed an excuse.

When they left the police station Hamroush helped Emy into the embassy car and then got in. "Gee, I'm a little nervous driving around with someone who deals in unauthorized dairy products." Hamroush was obviously trying to cheer her up. And she did have to smile at the way he put it. It felt good to have someone else realize how absurd life was becoming.

Emy wondered how she could tell Lino about the butter without worrying him. She would tell him of course. They had made a commitment not to keep things from one another. But she would lighten it a bit, not say too much about how panicked she had been.

She would rather tell him in person; she might even get him to laugh at the absurd parts. But she had no idea when she would see him next. Visits had been cut off for almost a year because of the refusal of the prisoners to see their families through a wire fence. No one knew when they might start again. This was their life - never knowing.

Emy thought again of the butter. In Miami they had plenty of butter. Emilia Maria was probably old enough to learn to make cookies now. Emy's sister Juani was a great cook. She would probably teach her.

31

Fidel had always been nervous about so many like-minded resistance fighters being housed in one place. He tried to keep morale weak by destroying relationships, increasing stress by moving prisoners around constantly and unexpectedly. Every seven or eight months a group of prisoners would be called out, told to gather their belongings, and transferred to a different circular. Then prisoners from another circular would be dumped into the first.

By the time of the missile crisis, Lino had lived already in two circulars and was expecting to be transferred again. It got to the point that someone moved from another circular was usually known at least by name. Those already in the circular were welcoming and eager to help. Someone who saw Lino arriving would realize his letters might get smuggled to the wrong place and would offer to get the word to Emy.

He often told himself the best preparation for prison had been the uncertainty of the underground. You learned to expect nothing, to be afraid of nothing, and not to hang on too hard to what you had. Lino told Emy in a smuggled letter:

> *It's great to see how all this moving people around is backfiring on the regime. It strengthens us because every time we go to a new circular, we meet new people and carry new ideas. Every prisoner takes with him the strategies and tricks he's learned. Now all the circulars are using similar systems, so it's easier than ever to communicate.*
> *Your,*
> *Linote*

In spite of this unity life in *Isla de Pinos* was slowly eroding the prisoners in soul and body. The prison had stopped selling basic supplies like cigarettes and oil to the prisoners. Then the visitors, who'd been allowed to buy things from the commissary for their prisoner, no longer could. The continuing lack of food, particularly protein, was seriously affecting the prisoners' health. Every single prisoner was anemic. Many were hospitalized for that or for internal parasites. It was common knowledge that much of their food was spoiled - not meant for human consumption.

Time stretched interminably before Lino. Already Orestes Garcia and Vicente Guitterez had been released at the end of their sentences. Inside he was screaming to follow them out.

Worst of all there had been no visits in the two years since prisoners had refused visits rather than hold them through a double chicken wire fence. This lack of visits was soul-bruising. Lino had been visited by Emy only three times before the boycott began. He thought of her, waking each morning to a life without her children or her husband. And she made that decision every day, to remain near him.

Even in a prison so crowded, the political prisoners were more peaceful among themselves than common criminals. But sometimes people were pushed beyond their limits. With so much tension and so many guns, violence was inevitable. One day, a guard accidentally shot one of the older prisoners in the liver with a machine gun as the prisoner walked outside the fifth floor cells. The guard said it was an accident. The prisoner lived. Lino was relieved to learn that at least they bothered to operate on the wounded man. But there was talk of revenge.

Lino wrote to Emy, telling her about the man shot in the liver. *Everyone is on edge. I hope we're not starting to come apart."* Emy was alarmed by Lino's pessimism, so unlike him. Prison life assaulted every principle he lived by. How long could he endure?

But it would only get worse.

Isla de Pinos was a brutal holding pen that wasted prisoners' lives while keeping them on the edge of starvation and madness. But in June of 1963, it became a death camp.

Mid-morning of a bright summer Tuesday. The Commandante appeared at the barred door to Circular #1. Grim-faced as always, he appeared nervous, opening and closing his fists as he waited. Because he knew what was coming? The prisoners, herded into the central court, were alert. Change meant trouble. The head guy was there; it would be something major.

The tall stiff-backed man spoke in a monotone. "Starting tomorrow, every prisoner will be assigned to a work gang and taken to the fields to work. Only those who are unable to walk and the medical doctors assigned to their care are exempt. Be ready at 7 a.m." He turned on his heel and left.

Lino glanced over at Pelayo. *What was going on?* The two men, with a group of other leaders, moved in silence up the stairs and gathered in a cell to try to figure out what the announcement meant and how the prisoners would respond. With them were Pelayo, Eduardo Camaraza, and Juan Muller. Lino was the first to speak, his heart pounding.

"This is outrageous! Unconscionable! They're making us into slaves. It goes against every convention, every agreement." He almost sputtered in indignation.

A slight tremor in Eduardo's hands betrayed the anger behind his calm voice. "They know perfectly well we're *presos políticos*, here because of our ideas. They can't treat us like common criminals."

Lino's mind raced. This was a disaster. They had fought for years against just this. If Fidel succeeded in treating the political prisoners as criminals, they'd disappear in the eyes of the world. Fidel could deny the very existence of an opposition, of any other beliefs opposing his own in Cuba.

"Why?" Pelayo asked. "Why now?"

"Because they can." Lino's voice was biting. "And because they haven't been able to break us."

"You mean *rehabilitación*."

"*Seguro.*"

Since the beginning of the Revolution, Castro had offered *la rehabilitación*, transfer to work camps and early release, to any political prisoner who would renounce his views, undergo indoctrination sessions, and swear his support of Castro. Most had refused.

"Because we survive, Pelayo." Lino spoke slowly and clearly, wanting his words to give shape to everyone's anger. "We've created a life for ourselves here; we haven't let them turn us into cringing animals. We don't give in and they can't stand it!"

Camaraza burst out. "Damn cowards. They don't dare shoot us outright - they'll just work us to death. Then disguise it as 'death from natural causes.'"

Juan looked out into the courtyard where prisoners could be seen in small dejected groups. "Die in your harness like a worn-out mule, is that it?"

"And get left in the sun to rot." Camaraza spat. *"Que animales!"*

Pelayo was quiet, opening and closing his fists. "We all know what working in the sun for twelve hours will do to these guys. Some of them already faint at role call, for God's sake."

Lino stared at the floor. He knew.

"They're wasted by malnutrition, parasites, dysentery. Lord only knows what else."

Lino spoke directly to Pelayo as a fellow psychiatrist. "It's not just physical. Think about it. Why have these guys survived so far?"

Lino waited only a second before continuing. "It's the community, the normal life we try to create, the security they feel inside the circulars."

Pelayo nodded. "Everything that made life bearable will disappear. Instead they'll be in the control of sadists who haven't been allowed to beat us up since the *requisas*. They'll be watching their backs - waiting for the next attack."

Before he went back to his cell, Lino walked into the clinic cell. He rearranged their few scarce supplies and wondered who would die first.

The next morning 5000 prisoners from the circulars were packed into a corral set up in the central pavilion. On this morning the prisoners received only the usual cup of hot water with sugar and a small piece of bread. Were they supposed to labor like animals on 800 calories a day?

They wouldn't find out until later that there would now sometimes be a small ration of eggs or meat in the evenings. Once a week the miracle of a sort of fricassee of chicken with rice. Still no vegetables, fruit, or dairy. Never red meat, with its precious iron and protein.

Each man was assigned to a work squad of fifty with ten guards. The guards were agitated, roaming the corral barking orders. Was it nervousness or anticipation of their power? They wore heavy boots, carried bayonets, and had pistols at their waists. Every squad had at least two attack dogs on heavy chain leashes.

The prisoners were counted and recounted, then loaded into open trucks to be taken to work sites all over the island. In the high sierras where only a few peasants lived, some prisoners would work in the mosquito-infested wet land edging Cienega Del Lanier, the large swamp, or near one of the shallow lakes that dotted the island. Others would work in the low shrubby hills with its dense undergrowth and jutting hunks of bare rock. After years inside, the prisoners spent all day in the tropical sun. Those who had hats wore them; others went without, unless their families sent them

Once at a site the work gangs moved in clumps, each surrounded by a circle of guards and dogs, like a movable barbed wire fence. No matter where they were, anyone who tried to escape, even a prisoner who simply collapsed from heat or exhaustion or hunger, could be grabbed and beaten before he fell more than a few feet out of formation.

The first morning some prisoners refused to work. The response was instant and savage. A few prisoners were attacked while still in the circular. Ernesto Diaz Madruga, one of the youngest men in the circular, had decided on passive resistance and descended slowly to the center court where he refused to go outside. On orders from a Captain, he was run through the stomach with a bayonet. Lino felt nauseated as he watched Ernesto's blood flow onto the dirt. He died a half hour later.

Alfredo Izaquirre, the highly respected young editor of the newspaper *El País*, had been relentless in his fight against Fidel. He had come to *Isla de Pinos* only after a death sentence was changed to 30 years imprisonment. He continued to resist in every way, and when forced labor began, he refused from the very beginning.

A slim young man whose dark eyes normally sparkled with enthusiasm, Izaquirre had told Lino the night before he would probably be beaten to death or killed outright. But he had made his decision. He would draw the line.

Maybe because of his enormous prestige before the Revolution, Izaquirre was given several chances to change his mind, but he refused to perform the slightest task. Every time the guards stopped and asked if he was ready to work, he said no. In the end, brutally beaten and covered with bayonet wounds, he was dragged to the punishment cells and left to die. To everyone's astonishment, he did not die and was finally taken to the prison hospital where he lay for months unable to move. Lino was astonished that the fiery journalist survived.

One prisoner in the circular, Mario Cabrera, a man Lino had always considered a blowhard, made a crude poster criticizing those who refused to work, saying they endangered all the prisoners. Lino was furious. A poster was no big deal. But nobody should put down men who were doing everything they could to survive.

He called Cabrera out to the center court, but he didn't appear. Lino sought him out in his cell. His voice was slow and thick with anger.

"Cabrera, that poster is disgusting. The only damn way we'll survive is if we stick together. Nobody needs to feel worse about himself. What right do you have to criticize people, anyway?"

Cabrero stared at the floor, avoiding Lino's eyes, saying nothing.

"Every prisoner here has to make his own decision. And accept the consequences. If a man is brave enough to take a stand, it's none of your business. You should be admiring him - and praying he'll survive."

Lino was disgusted. *I'm surprised he didn't sign up with Fidel. He'd fit right in.*

Cabrero said no more about forced labor. He avoided Lino even in the tight confines of the circular.

The work was back-breaking and endless - no days off. Many squads worked breaking up the long petrified ropes of marabou roots, hard as rocks. These fields had never been plowed because the farmers were never willing to put in the torturous effort of attacking the roots with pickaxes and chopping them small enough to be pulled out.

Other squads broke up rocks or worked in the marble quarries. The "lucky" ones got to plant and harvest fruits or clean out overgrown areas. Backbreaking work twelve hours a day in the height of summer heat. Working as slaves for the Revolution they hated.

Most prisoners in the circular agreed it was useless to openly protest the labor. A confrontation at this point would lead to killings and no gains. Instead they agreed to resist within the work groups, going out to work and pretending to work hard but consistently doing the least work possible.

One man, a former law student, told Manduco one night while he was being treated for bronchitis, that he and his group had managed to spend the entire day spreading manure on just one field. They slit their bags so the manure leaked out too fast, and then claimed the roots and stones made it impossible to dig the fertilizer in.

Other prisoners would work on moving a light boulder as though it weighed 200 pounds. They doubted the guards would take the trouble to check by actually lifting it. It was a risk. If they went too far and the guards felt ridiculed, they would take their revenge with more beatings and stabbings.

During the day, the doctors cared for the prisoners too sick to work, and Lino tried to give psychiatric care. Evenings they tried to repair those who had gone out. The most seriously injured or ill were sent to the prison hospital, but hundreds more filed through the clinic cell. The doctors worked through the night in a routine that numbed their bodies, their minds, and most of all, their emotions.

Lino wrote to Emy:

> *You can imagine my frustration, working every day to undo the damage done by cruel men. The prisoners line up when they return; there is no examination table so they just stand as we look them over. If they can't stand, we go to their cells. We do our best with what we have, cleaning wounds, looking for infection and broken bones.*
>
> *Some of those who come are like zombies; others can't stop quivering with fear. Most just want to shrivel into balls of misery until the next day. Of course a night spent shivering from lack of blankets is little preparation for the agony of the coming day.*
>
> *Men with chronic respiratory problems come back gasping for breath - they've been exposed to dirt and fertilizer and stone dust. Every kind of eye and throat infection. Diarrhea and high fevers with no explanation. We have no medicines for them. And we have no power to do what's really needed, give people time to rest and heal. Probably the most important thing I do is comfort men; they're in a stupor of exhaustion and hopelessness.*
>
> *Your,*
> *Linote*

Lino had fumed for years at the way political prisoners were treated. Now his rage festered as he saw the worsening condition of the men returning from labor.

Even the reserved Pelayo was horrified. "The venomous bastards." He and Lino sat with their backs to the walls of the clinic cell, the last patient examined for now. "They bring men to the brink of collapse, then 'allow' us doctors to treat them - with no supplies - so they can stagger back out the next day."

"Can you imagine the stress of working all day within arm's reach of sadistic guards who want nothing better than to attack you?"

"No. I can't." Pelayo opened and closed the same empty aspirin bottle over and over.

Lino went on, needing to vent. "Knowing that fainting or not working fast enough could bring a savage beating? When men already have some kind of emotional problems, that kind of random attack can put them over the edge."

Pelayo sighed, his palms now over his aching eyelids. "They see no way out - that's the kind of stress that ends up killing people."

"I'm more worried about sun damage." Manduco had come in to join them. "Every guy in here's already got some kind of skin problem - a fungus, a chronic rash."

He lowered himself stiffly to the floor. "Now, after two years of being crammed in here in the dark, suddenly they're in the hottest summer sun, with no protection." His finger began to trace a crack in the cement floor. "I'm surprised we haven't seen more sunstroke."

"Malnutrition, sunstroke - how do you know the difference? These men are half-dead when they come in; then they get a pitiful meal and sleep full of nightmares."

Lino was sickened by the stories prisoners brought of the guards' sadism. They stood behind prisoners as they worked, always ready to pounce with their bayonets. There was never enough water, and it never came when it was supposed to. Even the break for a pitiful thin soup brought to the field at midday was often shortened arbitrarily. Any protest was met with swift brutality. A heavy boot crushing a hand as a prisoner worked. A kick in the head when a prisoner stumbled or dropped a tool. Withholding water just to make men beg for it.

Lino wondered if he would ever feel the same about his fellow Cubans. Why did some show such courage while others turned into monsters? Could all men be this cruel, given such license and impunity? Maybe these guards were just spiteful and tired of being hated, tired of living on this tough swampy island.

The worst was the response to any prisoner who collapsed or didn't spring fast enough when ordered. Guards leapt on them. Slashed with bayonets. Beat their shoulders and backs where the most damage could be done. Then they dragged them into the isolation cells where they would be held for days without clothes or treatment. Lino knew all too well what that could do.

The pain of these senseless deaths struck him full force when Roberto Fardino did not come back from the fields. Roberto was just 19 but had already served in the Revolutionary navy before turning against the regime. Lino had been helping him with his insomnia and had come to greatly respect Roberto's idealism and spark, in spite of his situation. On this day, a Sunday in the fall, Roberto went to the fields, and Lino never saw him again. As night fell and Lino realized the young man had not returned, he felt sick with impotence. All he could learn - from another prisoner - was that Roberto had simply been taken to the punishment cells and shot. Lino went over and over the scene in his mind. Had Roberto chosen to resist? Or was he just unlucky?

32

Lino knew that prison officials often saw him at the center of unrest in the circulars. So he was not totally surprised – but still alarmed - when, in mid-December, two G-2 agents came to get him.

"Which one is Lino Fernandez?" they shouted from the central courtyard.

"Up here." Lino spoke up immediately, his stomach tightening.

Without a word, the two agents handcuffed him and took him away in a G-2 car. He was not allowed to speak to any other prisoners.

"Where are you taking me? Why?" Lino wondered why he bothered to ask, since he was unlikely to learn anything.

"Havana. Orders." Not encouraging. Of course the nearest G-2 headquarters was in Santa Clara, so it didn't sound like interrogation. But anytime he was singled out he prepared for trouble.

He was flown to Havana and spent that night and the next day in a small jail in a suburb. He couldn't help but have a wild hope that he would see Emy. Still no explanation. Then, just before dark, the same agents came back, handcuffed him, and took him back to the airport where they boarded a second military plane. Surely they wouldn't take him to Santa Clara in two stages.

As the second plane banked to land, Lino saw the familiar landscape of Camaguay. His body stiffened. *His family!* They were taking him to Esmeralda, to his parents' house. Would they try to implicate his family in some way? Would they threaten him in front of his family, to force his parents to cooperate? He'd never heard of that tactic, but nothing was beyond Fidel when he wanted something. Maybe something was wrong with his parents. They didn't usually let prisoners go home to help their families. *Why him? Why now?*

But they didn't go to his parents' house. Instead the agents took him into the city of Camaguay and locked him in the city jail. Another night there. Without explanation.

Lino was exhausted and frantic. What was going on? Was he being used as a pawn in some way? If something was wrong at home, if they needed his help, why was he cooped up here?

It was not until mid-afternoon that he and six security guards were put into two cars and made their way to Esmeralda, to his parents' house.

When the cars pulled in, Lino's father came down from the porch where he had been standing and embraced Lino. He broke into great throbbing sobs. Lino could only stand helpless, still in handcuffs.

"What happened, Papa? Why've they brought me here? Is everyone all right? Where's Mama?"

"She's gone *mi hijo*. She died on Tuesday, early in the morning. At the hospital in Camaguay."

Lino felt like he'd been struck by a steel pipe. He fought to get his breath, to stay upright.

"We just came back from the funeral Mass half an hour ago."

Lino managed to take short shallow breaths. He leaned against his father. *Those bastards let me miss her funeral while they kept me in that lousy cell in Camaguay.*

"That's not possible." Lino's voice rose as his shock turned to anger. "She was only 54. She was healthy. What happened?"

"Leukemia," his father said in a low voice, as though he didn't want the agents to hear. "Some kind of very bad leukemia. Fast moving. Only a few months. We couldn't get word to you."

His father looked furtively at the security agents, then back at the house. "God, I'm glad you're here."

"Who else is here? *Estas solo?*"

"No, *Emy esta aquí*. Carlos is away at military service."

Emy was here? He wanted to scream as the guards forced him to wait while they searched the house and then let him enter slowly, still in handcuffs.

Emy was in the living room. The handcuffs were taken off at last. He was able to hug her and ask softly, "How are you *mi amor*? Did you see

Mama before she died? Can you stay a while with my father?" She didn't answer, only held him. She looked tired. It was a long drive from Havana.

Lino's mind raced. His father was alone. His Emy needed him. If only he could have a few days here. Drive Emy back to Havana. The guards listened to everything they said. When Emy tried to follow Lino to the bathroom, just to have one minute alone together, the guard growled, "No. You. Stay here."

The soldiers were getting nervous. Word had obviously gotten out that Lino was in Esmeralda, and 50 or 60 people had gathered outside. Many of the townspeople were pro-Castro, but the Fernandez family was respected in Esmeralda. Lino was seen as a favorite son who had gone to Havana and become a doctor.

After only 30 minutes, the leader of the six guards, a small natty lieutenant, shook Lino's shoulder and apologetically signaled that they had to leave.

By the end of the day Lino was back in *Isla de Pinos*, feeling stunned and powerless. No time to mourn his mother, to even accept that she was gone. There was a part of his life he could never return to. Fidel had robbed him. Of taking care of her, of being her doctor, of even seeing her again and saying goodbye. The torture of seeing Emy for such a short time. He had desperately wanted to stay longer, to console his father, to be part of the family's mourning. Instead he was back here in this hellhole, doing no one any good.

The roundabout time-consuming trip to Esmeralda had been on purpose, he was certain. To worry him. To be sure he didn't arrive in time for the funeral. Deny him the consolation of a real Mass. Why had they taken him at all? Many prisoners heard second or third hand about a death in the family. This was one of Fidel's tactics, keeping you guessing, always off guard. He tried to concentrate on the comfort he had felt at touching his family, even for an agonizingly short time.

Lino told only Manduco what had happened. He felt raw, without protection. Manduco's hug spoke a world of understanding. Lino murmured, to himself as much as to his friend, "It was so hard to leave my father. He looked so small and sad. I don't think he believes I'll ever get out. He's lost a wife and a son."

33

Lino had never felt more discouraged in all his prison years. All the things that had nourished and supported the prisoners were gone. No classes, no games, no discussions or social interaction. Only pain, fear, and exhaustion. How could it possibly continue? But it did. Seven days a week. Year after year.

Beyond his worry as a doctor, he was haunted by the fear that these men, who had fought so hard against Fidel, would start to give up. They were exhausted. They saw no end in sight. Would they just sink into blind obedience, let Castro take over their minds as he had their bodies? Lino couldn't really blame them. But that would truly be the end.

Sometimes it was Lino's job to make up the list of men too sick or injured to go out to work the next day. It was the only mercy the system allowed. He knew the list could only be so long. He longed to put some of the most terrorized men on the list, but the guards challenged everything. Prisoners on the list were ordered to prove their medical condition, even if the doctor pleaded that they not be sent out. Even prisoners back from the hospital after a serious disease like malaria were not given enough time to recuperate before being sent out.

Mental problems were not accepted as reasons to stay in, even though those were the things that led to breakdowns in the field and the horrible consequences. Lino worried terribly about these men; he would rather have gone himself than be responsible for sending them out. But he was allowed no choice. The Comandante found him too valuable as a doctor.

Diabetes was common, almost impossible to control, given the

209

prison diet. The worse cases were grudgingly excused, but the milder cases went out to work. Victor Oramos, an older man who had run a well-known French restaurant in Havana, was badly beaten and later died in a punishment cell after falling into what Lino suspected was a diabetic coma while working in the marble quarry.

Lino agonized over who he might be able to keep out of the fields for at least a day. He worked on the list late into the night, dreading the moment when Rogi, a tall mulatto guard with a shaved head, came for it.

"Where's the fucking list?" He seemed to thrive on trying to humiliate Lino. "If you're padding it, I'll personally take **you** out to the fields. It would feel good to put a bayonet in your ass." Rogi would grin maliciously at Lino.

One morning, Lino added to the list Luis Santray, a man with chronic diarrhea who the guards had taken off the list two days before.

An hour later, around 5 in the morning, Lino felt a bayonet poking his chest.

"Hey doctor asshole." Rogi was standing over him with a sleepy looking guard holding the bayonet. Rogi jerked Lino onto his feet.

"I think you have a very bad memory. This Santray jerk is not sick. I told you that the other day. Just has the runs - happens to everybody. How come he's back on the list?"

Lino looked Rogi straight in the eye. "Because if he loses any more fluids, he'll die of dehydration, and you'll have to carry his body back. Is that a good reason?"

Rogi punched Lino in the sternum. Lino knew he could have done much worse.

"Maybe we'll forget about the list. Just send everyone out. Would you like that, señor soft-ass?"

Lino said nothing. Rogi didn't have the power to suspend the list. Thank God. But Santray went to the field - and he survived, to Lino's surprise.

One night Lino was drinking his tasteless dinner slop alone in the clinic cell, watching the last light of the summer day and bracing himself for the ordeal of treating more prisoners. A thin middle-aged housepainter from Santiago de Cuba came in to show Lino his grossly swollen knee.

"What the hell happened?"

The man lowered his voice. "I injected mineral oil in it. It hurt like hell but I hope it'll put me on the list. I can't even bend my knee, can't support any weight."

Lino was stunned. But who could blame this man for doing whatever it took to protect himself?

"Is it really worth this kind of mutilation, just to avoid the work?"

"You don't get it Doctor. It's not the work I'm afraid of - it's the attacks, being stabbed, beaten, killed in one of those dungeons. It happens every day. I just wanna stay alive."

The house painter was only the first; others began cutting themselves, burning themselves, especially on the feet so they couldn't walk. They found citrus leaves in the fields and rubbed them on their skin, giving themselves a raging dermatitis. It acted like a burning lesion or some kind of radiation, and it became so common that the guards were sent to look for some source of radiation in the fields.

In a pitiful gesture of balance, family visits, one every 60 days for each prisoner, were restored, without the chicken wire fencing. The boycott had lasted almost two years. Amid their wretched attempts to survive in the fields, it seemed an empty victory. At best a mixed blessing.

"I almost don't want to see Emanuela when I look like this." Rogelio, a once handsome lawyer from Santiago, sat on the clinic floor late one night. His eyes were dark pools of exhaustion. He held out his arms where welts were a sickening green color and a slowly healing bayonet wound on his left elbow showed crude stitches. Wounds took months to heal because there was not enough disinfectant cream. When men were forced back into the fields, their wounds inevitably got infected.

"She may not even recognize me." His grin was almost boyish. "This sure isn't the good looking guy she married." His attempt at humor fell flat.

The first visit came in August. It was held in early morning, so the 200 men who had visits could still be sent to the fields afterwards. Lino did not have a visit that day but Rogelio did. After the visit, he stopped outside Lino's cell when he saw Lino was alone. He had talked with Lino several times about his hesitation to see his wife.

"How was the visit?"

"Lino - she was so happy to see me. Her whole face lit up, like this beat-up body was the answer to her prayers. Just to see her waiting in her bright pink blouse, her clean shining hair, the make-up she put on for me."

Lino came out onto the balcony to join the other man. He leaned on the rail as Rogelio continued.

"My God, I'd forgotten how much it means to have someone fuss over you, to show - with every gesture and every look - how much you mean to her. It made all this exhaustion and pain seem so far off. You'll see when Emy comes."

"I can't wait." Lino smiled softly.

"It was like she knew, even though I didn't go into the grisly details. Of course I had written her about the labor and the beatings, but not the killings. We just talked about the most ordinary things, but she stroked these horrid scars as though they were medals of valor."

"They are, Rogelio, they are."

"I never realized how little someone's caring depends on how you look. It's so far beyond that. The world is still out there, my friend. Whether or not we ever see it, it's still there." Rogelio turned abruptly and left.

During one of these visits, Vicki and Manduco managed to have an undercover religious wedding. It hadn't been easy to arrange the ceremony in secret, but the couple, particularly Vicki, was very religious. Though they were legally married by proxy, in their minds, they would not truly be married until the marriage was blessed by the church.

A priest would never be allowed as a visitor, so they got a dispensation from the Bishop of Cuba. A good friend, Rosa, although not a priest, was very involved with the church and would officiate. The two witnesses were Rosa's father and Lino. Emy was there.

Vicki wore a short white pique dress with lace trim and a big white bow in her hair. They managed to conceal the ceremony itself, Manduco and Vicki sitting on one side of the picnic table, the witnesses and Emy on the other, blocking the guards' view. A wedding liturgy was said, and previously consecrated communion wafers were passed under cover of a handkerchief. Emy had been afraid it would be a sad parody of a wedding, but Vicki and Manduco's obvious commitment made it a rich moment for everyone there.

Now they had been married twice, but Vicki once again returned home without Manduco.

When Lino thought things could get no worse, a hideous routine developed, one that made every prisoner afraid to leave the circular. Lino never understood how or why it started, but every Saturday one or two prisoners would be killed at random. Before, the guards had to find some pretense for a prisoner deserving punishment. Now there was no logic; it was as though the guards felt they deserved this "fun." They often waited until the end of a long day of labor, then dragged one or two men off to the punishment cells and shot them. *Why? Just to create terror for the next Saturday?*

Every prisoner had to live now with the sickening knowledge that, no matter what he did, he might be the one who didn't come back. A man never knew if a cellmate would be there on Saturday night. Lino worried all day whether a sick prisoner forced to work would make it back alive. Lino ached at every death, but personal grief overwhelmed him the Saturday evening when Felipe Loren, a friend since the University, was one of two who didn't return. Lino wanted to cover his ears when a member of Felipe's squad came and told him what happened.

Manduco was working in the clinic that night with Lino. Lino let himself be engulfed in a hug that brought no comfort.

"Like a Goddamn rabbit! They shot him like a Goddamn rabbit."

Lino was wary when, one spring morning in 1966, shortly after the work squads left for the day, he was marched with no explanation to an interrogation room where a G-2 officer waited alone. A large man with a square face and straight black hair, he was seated at a small wooden table. He introduced himself as Colonel Espinosa from Havana. He had no papers with him, and he lacked the arrogant posture of most G-2 men. Lino was more than nervous by that time. *God, now what?* But the officer treated Lino with a certain respect.

"Dr. Fernandez. We in the G-2 are aware that things are deteriorating at *Isla de Pinos.*" *What an understatement.*

Espinosa spoke like an educated man. "You've always been known as someone who would tell the truth, even if you weren't sure it was expedient." *What was this all about?*

"I'm hoping you'll tell me what you see here, what's really happening." He looked Lino straight in the eye. "I cannot emphasize enough that I want the truth. We do not want this chaos to continue."

Lino's mind was reeling. *This is my chance. Reach beyond the petty sadists here - tell someone who might do something.* The Colonel seemed, in some indefinable way, to be sincere. But even if it was a sham, even if Lino paid later for his frankness, it would be worth it to share his outrage.

The colonel waited with no sign of impatience.

Lino decided he couldn't let this chance go by, whatever the risk.

"What do you want to know?"

213

With excruciating understatement, Espinosa said, "We know generally that some bad things are going on. So I can be pretty sure that if you tell me what's going on, it will be true."

Could anyone connected to the Castro regime actually care about what was being inflicted on political prisoners?

Lino's voice was calm and hard as steel. "I'll tell you alright. I've seen an old man stabbed 30 times in the back, for **nothing**. I've seen a university professor run through with a bayonet because he moved too slowly. He died in agony on the ground, alone, without care. They didn't even have the decency to end his misery."

Espinosa didn't flinch.

"Colonel, I'm a psychiatrist. I'd been treating a young student a long time for severe depression. One day they decide he's not working with enough enthusiasm, and they take him to the punishment cells where they shoot him. They never ask him anything. They never ask me."

Lino told of the Saturday killings. "The guards are allowed to do anything they want with the prisoners assigned to them. There's no accountability whatsoever. They're like a gang of sadistic kids with a new hunting rifle."

Lino paused to gauge the officer's reaction but his face was blank.

"A man goes out alive and comes back as a corpse; no one says a word. If we protest, there are more beatings, even another murder."

The G-2 officer continued to listen carefully, not trying to stop Lino's litany of atrocities. Eventually he interrupted Lino.

"Dr. Fernandez, you probably don't believe me, but this is not coming from G-2. It is not what we want to have going on here."

"Well, you better do something then. Because in another few months, I believe things will blow up."

"What do you mean? What do you think will happen?"

"Look, these men have already reached the point where they will maim themselves rather than return to the field." Espinosa looked quizzical but said nothing.

"When you're without power, in the hands of thugs who want you dead, at some point you just decide to die with dignity and hopefully take a few of your tormenters with you."

The officer turned in his chair and stared out the window. Then he turned back with an air of resolve. "I don't know if you'll believe me, but we did not intend this to be a place where the lives of prisoners were deliberately put in jeopardy." He grabbed the desk. "Something will be done."

Lino was surprised at the officer's open attitude. It could be another trick; he held out little hope. But he was glad he had spoken up.

Lino never knew the effect of his talk. The treatment did not change, but in March of 1967 the last prisoners were sent out, and *Isla de Pinos* was closed forever. Maybe Castro wanted to break up the political prisoner block once and for all. Maybe the *Isla's* reputation became too embarrassing even to this violent regime.

Lino was not there to see the end. In August 1966 he was moved to *La Cabaña*, an old fortress prison near Havana. He had been a prisoner for five long years. He had endured years of cruelty, privation, and near starvation. He could endure anything.

But *Isla de Pinos* would look like a palace when he got to the moldy dungeons of *La Cabaña*.

34

*C*hange was bad. The credo of the political prisoners. Still, as the five big buses, packed with tired sweaty men, crawled through the outskirts of Havana, the city looked beautiful to Lino. On a glaring August afternoon of 1966, after five years away, he was in the same city with Emy. *Hola mi amor. I am closer to home, closer to you.*

The buses crossed the river and wound their way up to *La Cabaña*, the old Spanish fortress overlooking the city and the sea. The fort had been built in the 17th century and later turned into a prison with few changes. The thick stone walls cut out light and held in humidity all year; cold in the winter and sweltering in the summer.

Although the sea was nearby, it could not be seen from the interior, and little sea air reached the prisoners over the high walls. The stone cells were long arched spaces, *galeras*, with no exterior windows, only small openings into interior courtyards.

Guards started shouting the moment the bus doors opened, half-pulling prisoners out and pushing them roughly towards the huge entryway of the prison. Lino stopped, relieved to be able to stretch his cramped legs. Then he looked up at the giant stone walls in silence. Would he ever see them from outside again?

When Pelayo tried to look around and get a gulp of fresh sea air, he was jabbed with a bayonet and cursed. Women militia officers ordered the men to strip then searched them. The officers yelled profanities and insults at the prisoners, randomly seizing books and photos or letters. Lino felt uneasy.

He turned to Juan Muller. "What's with this brutal reception? I hope it isn't a taste of things to come."

Eduardo Camaraza was furious and he didn't care who heard him. "What the hell contraband could we have gotten a hold of during a trip inside a sealed bus?"

Antonio Garcia raised his eyebrows in a mock leer. "Maybe they just heard we were fine specimens of manhood. Couldn't resist taking a look."

Any hopeful humor died when the saw their new quarters. Entering *Galera* 7, Lino was dumbstruck. On each side of the arched space were twenty-five sets of quadruple bunks, pulled away from the wall so that the top bunk would fit under the sloping walls. Did they really mean to cram 200 men into this subterranean *galera*, eighty feet long and barely twenty feet wide? There were the usual thin filthy mattresses on metal frames. The stacked bunks were so close together a prisoner had to turn sideways to pass between them. Even the center aisle was barely four feet wide.

The effect was claustrophobic - low stone walls, damp and covered with mildew. At one end, a window with bars looked into a large courtyard. At the other end, an arched opening with bars led to the hallway. No other windows, only a narrow slit in the ceiling, topped by thick ventilator shutters. Some air came in; very little light. A hell hole 300 years old. A space made for storage and soldiers waiting to fight. Now a cage for men with no way out.

In the end, Lino counted 186 men in his *galera*. Surely they would only sleep here. During the day, the patio glimpsed through the windows would be their space. They would be free to roam and interact as they had at *Isla de Pinos*.

But no. As the days crept by, it became clear what a palace *Isla de Pinos* had been. Here the prisoners left their *galeras* only once a day for ten minutes, into the corridor for showers, not even into the sunshine. The rest of the time, there was a small bath area without running water. Just a hole for a toilet and space to pour water over yourself from a jar. The space was never cleaned, there were no supplies. It stank. No one wanted the bunks near it. Men took turns standing next to the archway to get air.

The only water was a 300 gallon tank in the hall. Each prisoner had a liter bottle or metal container he filled once a day with "his" water. This had to suffice for washing and drinking. It was hard, on a scorching hot day, not to yield to the temptation of pouring it over your head for one glorious moment.

The noise was horrendous. An eighty foot long *galera* with few openings and almost 200 people. Even the gentlest noise became as unbearable as it was inescapable. The men talked constantly: about people they had known, parties they remembered, what they were reading, what they had read, history, religion. They seldom talked about the things they missed the most: sex and good food. The longing was too sharp, too perilous.

There was nowhere to exercise but the bars themselves, no baseball, no freedom to move around. Lino thought with regret of the open balconies and central courtyard of *Isla de Pinos*.

When prisoners with mental problems got out of control, yelling and banging on the metal bunks, all Lino could do was try to convince them to calm down. His "office" for therapy was his bunk - a top one, where he and his patient would sit face to face, bending to fit under the sloping ceiling. Other prisoners came to see him there too, just to talk, to have some outlet for their fear, their frustration, their tension.

Padre Loredo, a priest who had once run the historic Franciscan convent in Old Havana, was in the *galera* too. The tall blond young man was outgoing and sociable, wonderful with the other prisoners, always available to talk or just calm someone down.

Some of Lino's friends ended up in *Galera* 7 with him. In the narrow space between the towers of beds, groups of men who had grown close would meet in a sort of "clubhouse" or retreat area, sitting on their beds, finding some solace in social interaction with people they could trust. They called these areas *willayas*, after the retreat sites of Algerian guerillas.

During the day, the heat and claustrophobia made men want to hold their breath. When they breathed, only heat and stale fetid air came in. At night, the men tried to ignore the *chinches*, bedbugs that crawled over them as soon as they lay still. Only the single light bulb at each end of the *galera* discouraged the bugs from a massive attack. They had been a problem at *Isla*; but here the constant humidity made it much worse. The thick stone walls provided thousands of hiding places. At least the problem of snoring disappeared as the prisoners got thinner from malnutrition. Lino slept like a stone.

Sometimes before he fell asleep, Lino thought about the stories he'd heard from others held in *La Cabaña* early in the Revolution when executions were common. Lino could imagine the sounds of the firing squads in the dry moat, heckling from "government witnesses" brought in to watch, condemned

218

prisoners calling out "*Viva Cristo*" or "Down with Communism" in strong defiant voices before their bodies sank to the ground.

He had heard that people actually clapped as shots rang out and a body collapsed in a heap. Men dying because of what they believed, and their deaths were applauded. How had his people come to this?

Lino would not have believed the food could be worse than at *Isla de Pinos*; it was. The battered metal cauldrons of thin soup were dragged in by guards and left for the prisoners to ladle out. They ate on their beds; the floor was too crowded.

The guards at *La Cabaña* were the same *hijos de puta*, SOBs, as at *Isla de Pinos*, always eager to humiliate the prisoners. Two weeks after Lino's arrival, the guards announced that prisoners must run, not walk, past the guards for roll call.

"It's an insult to our dignity - we won't do it." Lino spoke to the members of his *willaya* and others nearby. Some agreed; others said it was too much trouble to fight. By the next morning, Lino and 15 others who felt strongly went out first. They walked slowly; no one behind could run if they did not.

The guards did nothing the first morning. But their looks of malice were chilling. The second day, the chief of guards stepped in front of the 16 and told them to run. They had been expecting the command. No one moved. The guards sprang to action, surrounding the 16 and herding them into a closed cell six feet by eight feet. No windows. No air. Too small for everyone to lie down, even sit at the same time. Someone always had to stand.

The guard's voice was sharp with sadism. "Here's a nice spot for you guys to talk about how good it will feel to run. Just let me know when you're ready."

The metal door slammed shut. A barred opening in the door let in just enough light for a shadowy view. The humidity was so high that moisture from the sweating stone walls dripped constantly on them. How could they make the situation bearable? Cesar Paez suggested a rotating plan; each prisoner had a time for stretching out, a time for sitting, and then a time for standing. When a man had his turn to stretch out, he slept. The rest of the time he waited. The system was fair; still the tension grew. Days and nights passed in a constant battle against panic and cramped bodies. During the night there was only dim light from the outer room where the guards sat.

Cesar shifted his weight from one foot to the other.

The man next to him flinched.

"You're touching me! What do you think I am, some kind of queer?"

"Are you calling me a queer?"

"Shut up! You're both queer!" A big man from Matanzas province boomed. "Now gimmee me some peace will you, so I can sleep - I only get two hours stretched out." Day and night, tempers flared and people lashed out.

One morning, Lino spoke in a subdued tone.

"Listen, you know I'm a psychiatrist. And I'm a man. We're being forced to be physically closer than any of us wants. It feels creepy." He looked around, trying to make eye contact with as many of the men as possible. "Sometimes you feel disgusted. Most of all, you feel scared - that there's something weird about you if you can stand this touching, being so close."

Alberto Izaquirre broke in with an exaggerated indignation. "What the hell do you mean IF we can stand it - is there some choice I don't see here?" A few men smiled at his attempt to lighten the mood.

Lino continued. "We're under horrible tension here. That's what the guards are counting on. But touching each other in these circumstances has nothing to do with homosexuality. You're just surviving, any way you can."

The tension abated. A few of the men were able to make feeble jokes. But slowly conditions edged toward unbearable. The ache of standing for long periods. The heat. The claustrophobia. Lino always tried to live day to day. But now it was hour to hour, minute to minute.

On the ninth day Lino made a proposal. "I have an idea - maybe the only way out." The men stared at him, desperation in their eyes.

"We won't ask for water for two days." There was shocked silence. "I know. It's very hot. It won't be easy. But we have to fight back. If we all agree, I think it'll work."

At last everyone agreed and they began not drinking water. After four days, they began a hunger strike. They were sweating heavily, getting weaker. Had he been right to ask this of the men?

Then Lino demanded to see Comandante Hernandez who appeared in a clean starched uniform. There was not a sound in the cell as Lino spoke to him through a scorched throat.

"We have not taken water for four days. A hunger strike preceded by no water will kill people quickly, probably in five days. This is day four. Tomorrow we will begin to die." He stopped to let his words soak in. "We will all die if you don't let us out. Then you can figure out how to explain the death of 16 prisoners under your abuse. Or, you can let us out now."

The Comandante turned and disappeared without a word. The guards mumbled in the corridor. The prisoners waited, slumped to the floor, leaned against the walls. Without warning a new guard appeared and spoke to the others. Then he opened the door and led the 16 back to *Galera* 7.

They had won. Lino was 35 years old and he was still alive. Every day he and the others would walk when they left the *galera* to be counted. Not run.

35

Even the miserable conditions in *Galera 7* at *La Cabaña* slowly became numbingly familiar. Medical classes were conducted, as they had been in *Isla*. Space was very tight, but people, desperate to use their minds, managed to learn. Medical books were slipped into *jabas* or smuggled past the indifferent guards. Each doctor taught what he knew. Lino was the only psychiatrist. He taught the development of personality. A lawyer friend Emilio Adolfo Rivero, who had studied in the U.S., taught Lino English by reading classics with him, English novelists like Somerset Maugham and E.M. Forster.

Months became years. The guards no longer bothered the prisoners but did little to help. They seemed to be wary of the prisoners now. Every few months, the guards opened the barred doors and let the prisoners spend part of a day in the patio, free to wander in and out and mingle with prisoners from other *galeras*. If by luck it rained, the prisoners would strip and stand joyously, letting the heavy tropical rain course over their bodies. They left their clothes to soak in the rain, and then wrung them out. For many, it was the most water they had seen at one time since their arrests.

Because the interior patio was surrounded by the fort, they couldn't see the city or the sea. But what a rush of pleasure - to breathe fresh moving air, walk around at will, see different people, and collect news from recent arrivals. All this had been normal at *Isla de Pinos*. They had not appreciated it.

Lino had learned astronomy in prison and he and Emy had vowed that, whenever they could, they would look at the bright star Aldebaran in the night sky and know the other was looking too. They would relish being under the same sky - the sky where they had been together, and would again.

One anniversary, Emy sent a card she had made, a drawing of two wedding rings and their names intertwined. Lino wrote back,

> *Mi amor,*
> *Your card arrived exactly on our anniversary. How I loved seeing our names interlaced. I thought for hours of that celestial day when we gave ourselves to one another. I am sending you the poem Bright Star by John Keats.*

He had copied the poem out by hand on a tiny piece of wrinkled paper.

The visits from Emy, even in the depressing setting of *La Cabaña*, raised his spirits. The open pavilion where visits had taken place at *Isla de Pinos* looked like a gala nightclub compared to *La Cabaña*. No high airy ceiling, no shared food, no sitting close at tables. Instead, a long hall with a low curved stone roof. The room reminded Lino of a bread oven. The walls reeked of death - how many men had been executed in this room? It oozed hopelessness and lost causes. Men had wasted away in these walls for hundreds of years. Had anyone cared? Did anyone care now?

At *Isla de Pinos*, the prisoners had missed two years of visits because they refused to be separated by a fence. Now there was a double fence; it had always been that way at *La Cabaña*. The prisoners, struggling now in so many other ways, had no energy to make the fence an issue.

At least visitors were not strip searched as they had been at *Isla*. It was much easier to keep things in *jabas* fresh since Emy merely had to cross the city for a visit. Emy sat on a long bench with other prisoners' relatives. Between Lino and Emy were two barriers, a lower one in front of her and a higher one near him. She hated the place, hated seeing Lino there, hated knowing things had gotten worse for him. He couldn't clean his uniform, really couldn't even shave.

In 1967 a visit happened to fall on May 23, Emy's birthday. Who would care at *La Cabaña*? Still, a visit was the nicest birthday present she could have. Emy greeted Señora Bringas when the visitors filed in and noticed the woman hurried to sit next to her. The two had met on several visits. As soon as things calmed down and the guards had sunk into their usual visit stupor, Señora Bringas reached under her wide cotton skirt and pulled out a thick bouquet of red roses and carnations. She winced as she pulled the thorn-laden rose stems across her legs. Then she smiled.

"Oh, that feels better. I never thought about those darn thorns."

Emy was speechless with astonishment.

The woman smiled shyly. "You know, my husband Emilio admires Lino so much; he'd do anything for him. He knew how frustrated Lino was at one more birthday when he had nothing to give you. So Emilio asked me to bring these for you."

It was as though a grey curtain had parted to reveal a peaceful garden of a thousand colors. After a minute, Emy recovered her voice and gave the woman a hug. "Oh my God, they're so beautiful. You can't imagine how much they mean to me. Thank you." How long had it been since she had received something just for its beauty?

"*No me des las gracias.*" The woman smiled shyly. "Do not thank me. They are from Lino, they come with his love, I know."

Emy smiled across at the beaming Lino. Her extraordinary husband. How lucky she was. She quietly passed the flowers to the wives close to her so they could share the beauty.

Lino thought he would go crazy with the lack of any kind of physical space of his own. He wrote to Emy:

Mi Vida,

I am trying to help other people cope. But I find I have to work as hard as anyone to be able to ignore what is around me. I tell myself, 'here I am in my little capsule. Inside my mind.' Everything else is a hum from afar, although it is sometimes a roar. But I won't let it into my capsule.

How I dream of the hours we have spent together, talking softly or sitting silently, playing out our internal symphony of connection. Each of those memories is like the only day of my life and the day I dream of reliving. I hold you with me inside and you bring me love and peace, marvelous and mysterious.

Your,

Linote

36

The prisoners knew the brutality was not over. Castro could not have them visible and vocal. But the worse the conditions, the more determined the political prisoners became. They would not be silenced. Their message to Castro was simple.

We fought Batista because he put himself above the law, used power for its own sake. You said you would end all that. Now you are doing exactly the same thing. And we will fight again.

They had fought the forced labor and now they endured the caged animal conditions at *La Cabaña*. They had won their battle against the humiliation tactics of the guards. What would happen next?

"Get your stuff." March 1968, after almost two years in *La Cabaña*, a new hell opened up. Without warning, a small platoon of guards appeared at *Galera* 7 and read the names of a few men. The men they named were leaders; men who sustained the ideas of the resistance and who were listened to by others. Lino, Cesar Paez, Pedro Luis Boitel, Julio Hernandez Rojo, Alfredo Izaquirre, Padre Loredo, Andres Cao, Huber Matos, Eloy Gutierrez. Twenty men in all were taken from the *galeras* and brought through a dim stone corridor to *Galera* 11, a tiny space with room for twenty beds and nothing else. Lino looked around. No windows. No space to move around. The only door was an iron one to the corridor; it would always be closed. The only ventilation came from a tiny opening in the ceiling. Through this opening they could see a sliver of sky - and hordes of mosquitoes could invade the closed cell. The claustrophobia of *Galera* 7 was magnified - wet walls, dripping humidity. Double bunks with the same moldy mattresses. One blanket per prisoner, just cotton fabric like a worn dishcloth, bringing little warmth, certainly no comfort.

How long would they be there? Until they lost their will, buckled under? Lino felt as though he were slipping once again down the steep sides of a bottomless morass. Every attempt to climb out brought only another terrifying slide.

All Emy ever knew was she was not allowed to visit. The *jabas* she brought were refused. For *Galera* 11, no visits, no letters, no supplies from outside. No daily trips into the corridor to shower. The same grey walls all day and night. The indignity of squatting over the toilet hole so close to the others. He would never get used to that.

Inside this hothouse of deprivation and isolation, even the luxury of reading and work was largely gone. Alfredo Izaquirre had managed to bring in the only three books they had: three volumes of *The History of Egyptian Civilization*. He read them voraciously, often stopping to read to the others or share interesting facts. In spite of themselves, bored beyond bearing, the others would sometimes read with him, hunched on upper and lower bunks to see the pages.

Padre Loredo was a painter. He had managed to keep a few crayons and pastels with him and began teaching the others how to draw. Sometimes they wrote letters in their heads - they had nothing to write with. Anything to keep their sanity, their feet on the ground. At least the small space was quieter - less friction than the larger *galera*. And they had the one thing that really mattered, each other. Twenty intelligent minds determined to keep one another going.

"Jesus, what now?" Cesar Paez stared at the three guards entering *Galera* 11. The prisoners had been in total isolation for ten months. Lino would never get used to this unpredictability of prison existence.

Paez stood with the others, their backs to the bunks. "This can't be good. Whenever we haven't given in to them, I get nervous about what they'll do next." The prisoners instinctively gathered their meager possessions; they'd be prepared for anything. The guards hurried the twenty men out into the corridor. His heart pounding, mouth dry, Lino followed the rest as they mounted a narrow set of stairs and trudged down two long windowless hallways.

A metal door opened and they were on the roof of *La Cabaña*. Their senses were overwhelmed. The wide horizon of the sky after months of darkness. They smelled the sea. Sunlight, a breeze, a view of a few determined shrubs and flowers. The sea stretching for miles into a gathering mist. The guards settled themselves against the parapets, guns across their arms.

"Looks like we're here for a while. I'm going to take advantage." Izaquirre took his shirt off and let the sun dry his sweat.

"Surely this isn't a pleasure outing."

Andres Cao looked skeptical. "Maybe some kind of 'last meal' on death row?"

Lino said, "They wouldn't bother. More likely tempting us by showing us what we could gain if we cooperate."

All the head guard said, in a grumpy tone, was, "Better enjoy it; we're not gonna' be here all day."

Lino had learned not to question. He turned away from the others and simply gazed, drinking up every detail of the view, drawing in great breaths of the fresh wind coming off the sea. Then he decided to capture the sight with the few pastels he still had. In a frenzy of strokes, he created a sea scene which he would keep with him through many more years of prison.

As suddenly as it had come, it ended. As the light started to fade, the guards marched them back to the *galera*. No explanation. Never another trip to the roof. No hidden agenda to explain the trip. So far.

March of 1969. Almost exactly one year in *Galera* 11. Unbowed but relieved, they were thrust back into *Galera* 7.

But the war for their spirits was not over. Just four months later, fifty men were gathered from different *galeras* and transferred to *Castillo de Príncipe* in two groups. *El Príncipe* was another old fort, not as old or heavily built as *La Cabaña*. Its location on a hill in the middle of Havana gave it more air and less humidity. If you had windows.

During their transfer, Izaquirre was nervous. "I believe they're serious this time, desperate to make a point." No one contradicted him.

Their fears were confirmed when the group was led directly to a windowless *galera* with no beds, already occupied by twelve querulous looking common prisoners. Beefy men with scarred bodies, big hands. Was this a punishment cell for problem prisoners? The guards took away their khaki-yellow uniforms and left them in their underwear.

"Here's your *leonera* - your lion's Den. Just you big guys - you can fight it out," The guard sneered. "Cozy eh?"

When the guards had gone, Lino shook his head. "This is just like forced labor at *Isla de Pinos*. They want to bury us, pretend we don't exist."

"We haven't given in so far. Why are they trying again now?" Padre Loredo tried to sound positive.

Paez' tone was scathing. "Because we've been locked up a long time - and *La Cabaña*'s a hellhole. That's why. And now on top of it, we're in real physical danger from these guys. They're counting on these gorillas driving us to the point of breaking down, realizing it's hopeless, getting tired of struggling against overwhelming odds.

Cesar Paez echoed everyone's thoughts. "If we give in so we can get out of here, Fidel wins. If we're killed, he and his henchmen can deny all responsibility."

"We might not survive." Izaquirre's voice was flat, tired. "I think our only way out is a hunger strike - right now. No hesitation."

Everyone finally agreed. The common prisoners turned out to be sympathetic to the hunger strike. They said they would continue eating, but they wanted the political prisoners to know they respected their position and would do nothing to harm them.

There had been other hunger strikes. But this was the hardest. The political prisoners knew - and the guards knew - they were playing for keeps.

As Lino wrote to Emy months later:

Mi Emilita,

You must know it is not easy to face death so closely. For me to think of you alone, of never having you again in my arms, not even one last time. We were weak. Any of us could have been the one to go. We had to come to terms with the possibility of taking this all the way. It was the only way to be strong and to show our strength. We had to inspect our hearts and be sure we could accept it if it came.

After 17 days, El Pavo died. We didn't expect it. He was a big noisy fellow, very healthy. We called him "pavo", the turkey, because he kind of strutted around the galera. I don't know if he knew he was going to be the one to die, the one who would show the ultimate determination. He didn't say anything at the end.

There have been many heroes in this fight. I will remember him as one of those who just kept on in his steady way.

Your,

Linote

The death took even the guards by surprise. They immediately took the remaining political prisoners to a new *galera* by themselves. There they agreed to eat. Lino was bloated and too weak to walk. He had never come so close to death.

Three weeks later, one of the Comandantes from *La Cabaña*, Juan Hernandez, who had come with them to *El Príncipe*, appeared, along with a tall guard. They pulled Lino and Padre Loredo out and marched them into an interrogation room. Without a word, the guard grabbed Lino and tried to force him into the blue uniform pants of common criminals. Lino kicked one pant leg off as the other was forced on. Then they tried the shirt, with even less success. The whole struggle was repeated again and again, with Lino getting in as many kicks as he could. Padre Loredo proved no easier to force into the hated blue uniform.

Lino was incredulous at the ridiculous struggle. What a lack of dignity for the officers. When they eventually gave up, they put Lino and Padre Loredo in a different cell. Later they tried the same thing with other political prisoners, but had no better luck.

As Lino wrote to Emy,

> *Mi Emilita,*
>
> *Somewhere in the middle of this ludicrous scene, I saw how desperate the government had become. They don't know any longer what to do with us. I believe they are baffled, completely out of ideas. I felt a great sense of victory. If they are reduced to this, what strength do they have?*
>
> *Later we found out they had tried to change the uniforms in La Cabaña at the same time. And every man had refused. How satisfying to see such unity.*
>
> *Your,*
> *Linote*

The next day, the fifty men - leaders of the resistance in prison - were moved back to *La Cabaña*. Castro had failed to break them. He had to find a way to uphold his condemnation of these men as traitors, but still give them a way to shift their position with honor. Their continuing defiance - and visibility - was intolerable to the regime.

37

"We got our permit." Raque spoke softly as she came into the kitchen. Emy was rinsing out her coffee cup just after eight in the morning. They were alone.

The news hit Emy like a tidal wave, slamming against her and taking away her breath. Of course she had known all along the de la Huertas would leave Cuba. They had applied for their exit permit almost two years ago, in early 1967. Because of Rene's status in academia, they hadn't been required to do hard labor to "earn" the right to leave, as many people were. But exit permits were given capriciously these days. No one ever knew how long it would take. Or if a permit would ever be issued.

Now it had come. Emy's spirit sank. They would go. One more degree of isolation and vulnerability.

Emy set the china cup and saucer slowly onto the old marble counter.

"Oh Raque, what can I say?" She tried to sound glad, but she knew Raque heard the tremor in her voice, the effort to hold back tears. Raque engulfed her in a giant hug, and the two women stayed like that a long time, silent and connected.

How she would miss Raque, so full of energy, organizing everyone's lives, so sure there was a solution to any problem. Most of all, Raque who had given Emy a place in her busy normal household, had watched over her, and cared so much. Being with her was like being in a warm pool where you could just let go and relax completely. All this would be lost to Emy

"You'll finally get some peace without all these children," Raque's shaky voice interrupted her thoughts.

"But I'll miss them most of all." Emy knew she should say something upbeat and accepting, but no such words came.

Raque spoke gently. "Things have been getting worse and worse for Rene at Mazorra."

Raque's husband was a psychiatrist at the state mental hospital. But he was a constant, if low-key, critic of government policies, known to be anti-Communist. He was persistently harassed and pressured to join in pro-Revolutionary activities.

"He's managed to keep his private practice, but his patients are under more and more pressure to use a psychiatrist more sympathetic to the Revolution. It wears on him terribly."

Emy knew Raque was right. Rene always seemed serene and unperturbed, but he was only human. Although he didn't talk much, Emy had always felt he was there, giving her his support, balancing her aloneness without Lino. Emy would miss his gentle presence.

Emy rinsed out a rag and began wiping off the wooden table. What a great old table it was.

"Do you think you'll get visas for the U.S.?" Emy knew the family wanted to settle in Florida.

"We've heard nothing from the Embassy. I think we'll have to just go to Spain. We don't want to delay any longer." Raque's new baby would arrive in a few months. And eventually her sons would get close to military age, and Fidel wouldn't let them go. Hopefully from Spain they would get visas to the U.S.; at least in Spain they could wait with less pressure.

"Well, selfishly I'll pray you get to Miami. You know me so well. If you ever get to see the children -"

"I can let them know what a loving mother they have - how she dreams of being with them. I'll tell them about her spirit, her determination, and how we stole butter together . . ."

In spite of her sadness, Emy loved the idea of Raque telling her children stories of their adventures. She rinsed the rag out again and hung it to dry. She knew her smile looked forced.

"Have they given you a date for your flight?" She was torn between wanting it to be soon for their sake and wanting time to get used to the idea of being without them.

"No, but they said probably a few weeks. Who knows what that means?"

Much of the preparation for leaving was already done. As soon as the family had applied for permission to leave, the government had considered the house as government property. The family was only allowed to live there "on sufferance" until they left the country. After they left, the house would probably be used to house a government official or as some kind of school.

Emy remembered the *Inventario* that was done way back then. A very rude and suspicious group of three emigration officials had come to the house and noted every object: furniture, china and glass, books, pictures, toys, even linens and ashtrays. When it came time to leave, if anything was missing, the right to leave could be rescinded. So before even applying for permission, the de la Huertas had taken from the house what they didn't want to leave to the government - jewelry, memorabilia, photos, family papers. A few practical things had been given away to friends who were staying. The most precious small items had already been sent out through the diplomatic pouch of the Canadian embassy to Ottawa where friends would send them on to people in Miami.

Before the *Inventario*, a family had to be very careful about taking too many things from the house. The government could challenge them if the house seemed too sparsely furnished. A pro-Castro acquaintance or a former gardener might say he had seen things in the house that weren't there for the *Inventario*. The last thing anyone wanted to do at this point was antagonize the government.

Emy had stayed with Raque during the *Inventario*. She remembered the burning rage she felt as the officials fingered the rugs, examined the artwork, and turned china over to see where it came from.

"Yes," she had wanted to say, "It's really French porcelain. Don't worry. They won't leave anything tacky for some government official to use on his table. And notice how nice they've kept it for you - no cracks or chips."

Raque had conducted herself with great dignity, as though she were watching admiring friends stroll through her house. When the two-day ordeal was over, when she and Emy could sit on the terrace unobserved, Raque's shoulders slumped, and her cheeks were pale with the effort of containing her emotions.

"At least you and your family will be safe." Emy could think of nothing else to say.

Once the *Inventario* was over, the house was technically sealed; nothing could be taken out. The neighborhood CDR stopped by often to check on things. If something broke now, Raque carefully kept the pieces.

Otherwise, she might be accused of selling or giving away something that belonged to the government. When they left, each family member would be allowed to take only clothes. No jewelry, no family or personal objects, no keepsakes.

Emy shuddered at these memories. She was glad it was time to leave for work. Her heart hurt. She needed to get away from this news. And she knew Raque would understand her reluctance to hear any more right now.

"I have a planning meeting for CCD youth group tonight at church. I'll find some supper somewhere on the way." Emy was always careful to let Raque know where she'd be. Raque would surely assume she was at *Reina* church - she went there most Thursdays. But in these frightening times, you tried never to be unclear. If someone didn't know where you were and you didn't show up, they'd be sick with worry. It was too cruel to leave people wondering.

Walking to work, Emy's thoughts kept returning to Raque and all she meant. Emy usually didn't let herself dwell on what she missed. Even on her children's birthdays, she never did anything unusual, never talked about it. That was how she survived.

But she couldn't hold up today; she abandoned herself to thoughts of loss and loneliness. It was so hard when people left. You got so close, trapped together as you were outside of acceptable society. As each friend left, you felt even more defenseless. More exposed.

She would have to move to a new place. At the age of 31, she still had to depend on others to take her in. One thing cheered her; she already knew where it would be. Vicki Andrial and her mother had told her for years that she could come to their house whenever she needed a place. The time had come.

Emy decided to tell no one about the de la Huertas yet. She'd learned that when she felt bitter and critical, it was better for others that she not share her feelings. A friend could be picked up any time, on any pretext, and be forced to repeat what Emy had said.

The church was a great support to Emy, in spite of its tenuous existence. In 1961 Castro had closed all the private schools, most of them church run. Priests and nuns were watched; security agents went so far as to record sermons and go into confessionals and ask priests about their political attitudes.

Emy remembered her horror when foreign priests, many of them Spanish, were rounded up at gunpoint and paraded before jeering crowds brought in by the government. Then they were loaded onto a Spanish freighter *Covadonga* and taken to La Coruña, Spain. The Jesuits in particular were intellectuals and social activists, much respected for their schools and work at the University. Castro had wanted them out of the country. Most nuns were flown to the United States

Now a few churches were allowed to stay open but only for worship at specified hours. Castro didn't dare ban religion outright, but he had other ways. It was illegal to teach religion to children outside of a church. Religious holidays were not recognized. If you were known to be religious, you could lose your job and other privileges.

Emy was grateful for the few Jesuits who remained in Cuba. She and Lino had always been close to the Jesuit padres, connected to them through the Congregation of the Holy Mother and the *Agrupación*. After the Revolution, both groups had been banned. The only church in Havana still open continuously was Our Lady of the Sacred Heart, called *Reina*. It had always been a Jesuit church, and a few Jesuit priests were allowed to stay. They led an austere life, constantly under surveillance, but determined to serve the loyal Catholics left in Havana.

Since Lino had been gone, *Reina* played a big part in Emy's life. She needed the serenity she always felt in a church. The Jesuits there were a Spaniard, Padre Morin, and a few young Cubans like Padre Millares who had just finished his long rigorous Jesuit training. They were thoughtful and always available as spiritual advisers.

Of course she felt great support from close friends like Vicki and Ileana. They understood how uncertain her life felt.

But the deepest sadness and uncertainties she saved for the Jesuit padres and their calm philosophical counsel. Emy was religious in a matter-of-fact way; it had been part of the skeleton of her life as long as she could remember. But the obstacles she faced now led her to depend more and more on her basic belief; God had sent her only what she could bear. Her daily prayer was a short one - the grace to get through, to be able to do what was needed.

On Sundays, she went to Mass at *Reina* and taught the catechism classes afterwards. Tuesday nights there was usually a study class of some kind; right now a class in psychology fascinated her. Thursdays was when the planning went on for catechism or the youth program. Even if she didn't have a meeting, she often went with Vicki who had choir practice.

"Maybe they'll ask you to join the choir," Lino had teased her during an early visit. Emy was known to have *un oído cuadrado*, a tin ear.

She had laughed. "They're not that desperate yet. They'd probably cancel the music before they'd let me in."

She adored the church music. Her favorite celebration was Easter week. In spite of government pressure, Holy Week at *Reina* was a feast of spirituality for Emy, Vicki, and Ileana. While the Gothic style church was all arches and soaring stone, it gave them an impression of sanctuary. The clouds of candles glowed against the stone structure and reflected off the splendid stained glass windows. The Jesuits gave elegant and moving sermons. All of Easter week there were special services that heightened Emy's spiritual involvement and determination. On Easter Thursday, there was the special altar for communion, on Friday a very somber service, and on Saturday the Easter vigil, ending in a glorious celebration at midnight. Emy had never appreciated the explosive joy of Easter morning as much as now, when she felt so isolated in her own country.

So far Castro still allowed them to teach catechism after Mass, but at the last planning meeting Ileana had reported another catechism program dropped, this one at the church in Miramar.

Emy remembered her discussion with Ileana in the hall after that last meeting.

"You know, Ileana, Fidel's no fool. If there are too few churches open, people won't bother to send their kids. Too much trouble."

"It's more than that Emy, kids who go to catechism lose out in so many ways. They are 'mysteriously' never chosen for special jobs, special studies; they become outcasts."

Emy knew Ileana's own two girls, Annette and Ileana, were struggling with this double standard in their grade school.

Ileana stared at the cover of a catechism book she was holding. "What parent is going to condemn their children to be ostracized, unless their faith is awfully strong? Even I hesitate, and you know how important the church is to me."

She had told Emy then that her oldest girl Annette had come home one day excited about joining the Communist youth group, the Pioneers.

"That was such a hard moment. She was so excited about everything she was told the Pioneers did: field trips, rallies, all that. I really hesitated."

"About letting her join?"

"No, about how much to tell her. In the end, I decided I had to be true to myself. I sat her down and explained to her who the Pioneers are and what their goals are.

"How did you explain it?"

"I just told her, 'Annette, the Pioneers are run by the government, they believe in the same things as the people who have put your father in prison. Your father didn't believe as they did, and they punished him. The Pioneers will want you to think like the government. Papi is not with us because he wanted to decide for himself. And I want you to decide for yourself. I won't forbid you to join the Pioneers. It's your decision.'"

In the end Annette had not joined the Pioneers. What a terrible choice for the girl to have to make.

At lunchtime, Emy, still reeling from Raque's announcement, decided to treat herself to a haircut and set at a salon. Beauty parlors were one of the few businesses still open, probably because they needed few supplies, just their own skill. Even so, people sometimes brought their own shampoo if they knew the shop had only the thick gooey products from Russia.

How ironic that she could have the luxury of having her hair done, but she couldn't buy laundry soap to keep her clothes clean.

"Ah *Señora Fernandez*," Juanita greeted Emy at the salon. "I haven't heard from you in so long. No visits?"

"No, I'm afraid not. You are so sweet to ask." Juanita, a big black woman who moved delicately on her feet, was the cleaning lady at the salon. She had, from the beginning, offered to stand in line at the airline office, or anywhere else when it was hard for the wives to do it. And she often did.

She hoped Juanita realized how much they all appreciated her help. There was no gain for her, although Emy did try to slip her a few pesos when she could. But what good would the money do? Nothing to buy. She could try to explain to Juanita how capricious the timing of visits was. But that could be dangerous, to be heard criticizing her husband's treatment. The less said the better.

God, these reactions were becoming second nature. If life ever returned to normal, would she still remember how to be open and natural?

After leaving the hair salon, Emy stopped at her Aunt Julia's house near the Embassy. Aunt Julia was delicate and quiet, but she seemed to appreciate Emy's coming by. Her husband, Emy's Uncle Pablo, had been a much loved surgeon in Havana, although like others he had been pressured relentlessly to support the Revolution. About a year before, he had died of a heart attack unexpectedly. Emy, the only other family member left in Cuba, had handled the difficulties of trying to arrange a funeral Mass. It turned out to be impossible; they were only able to arrange a simple service at a funeral parlor and prayers for him during a regular Mass.

Now Aunt Julia was waiting for permission to join her daughters in Miami. Emy always enjoyed the time spent in her aunt's beautiful Spanish style house. How her own mother must miss her house at the sugar mill where Emy had grown up, the cool patios, the timeless grace of the arches and open hallways.

38

There was a message from Vicki when Emy got back to the office. She called her back.

"Emy, can we go have a drink at Jenny's before we go to *Reina*? We haven't seen her since they got back from home leave."

"They're back? Weren't they supposed to come back next week?"

"Oh I don't remember. I can never keep track of people."

"Well, she was going to try to see the kids. So I thought I had the dates straight. Anyway, I can't wait to see them. Shall I meet you there?"

"Sure. Ileana will come with them from work. About six?"

Ileana, who worked at the Indonesian Embassy, had become very friendly with the daughter of the Charge d'Affaires, Jenny Nordeen. She was about their age, outgoing and natural despite her privileged status as a diplomat's daughter. Vicki, Ileana, and Emy often went by the Nordeens' beautiful apartment in Vedado for drinks and a snack after work.

The only bad part about going to Jenny's apartment was the demoralizing walk to get there. First she had to pass the stores which were still open but had nothing to sell, their windows yawning empty and depressing. Then she went down Avenida de los Alcades. This was an old section of Havana; the houses on either side of a wide center island - once so well kept, bursting with flowers. Most of the houses were set graciously back from the street, built in the old Spanish style, with covered walkways and gardens dotted with pergolas or covered pavilions. Now almost all the families that had lived there were gone. No one maintained the gardens, not even the flowers that had always grown in the stone urns by the entrances.

Emy reached the towering portico of the old de la Rolla's house. Towels and underwear were strung on a line across the open space. She could see from the street a few young people roaming the grounds like wild animals. Some were sprawled on the terrace on mismatched chairs, some drinking beer, others slurping something from bowls.

She felt sick when she went by the Mariendos' house. Señora Mariendo had been a good friend of her mother, and Emy remembered the day she had taken a very young Emilia Maria to the house for her to admire. Señora Mariendo had loved the old stucco house and kept it whitewashed and surrounded by the brightest flowers. Emy crossed the street to avoid hearing the rude language of the people clustered under the archway to the garden.

By the time she arrived at Jenny's, she had to stop a minute and shake off her sour mood.

"Emy, I've been waiting for you." Jenny's voice was strong, but the hug she gave Emy was a delicate one. The Indonesian girl was tiny but in perfect proportion, her dark hair held back by two carved wooden barrettes.

"Come, sit down. You're probably ready for a drink. But I have to tell you right away. I saw the children - and your mother. Everyone is fine." Jenny tried to see the children every year when she went through the U.S. on her way to home leave in Indonesia.

"Emy, you won't believe how much Emilia Maria looks like you. Your mother says she always did, but I see it a lot more now."

Jenny poured out stories of her trip to the house, coffee with Emy's mother, the arrival of the kids from school, supper with the whole family.

"Emilia Maria's **so** serious Emy, especially about school. Oh, here's a note she sent you. I think it's all about her grades. She's so cute, so afraid you'll think she's not working hard enough."

Each question Emy was about to ask was answered first by Jenny. Emy didn't want to ask if she had taken pictures; Jenny would feel bad if she hadn't. But she hoped. Oh please, yes, pictures. Vicki and Ileana came in with Lair, another Nordeen sister who handed Emy a glass of iced tea. Jenny then took a nice plump Kodak envelope from the desk drawer and handed it to Emy. It felt good in her hand, her children all compressed into a series of shiny black and white sheets. She probably shouldn't read so much into the photos she got, but what else did she have?

"This one of Po came out terrible. He looks like he's about to be sick. I don't know why. He didn't look like that at all . . . Look at Lucia

- honestly, she has the biggest eyes. And she's such a flirt. She wants to take ballet lessons; your mother says she's too young. But that doesn't keep her from pirouetting all over the place."

The women all gathered around to exclaim over each picture and listen to Jenny's comments. Emy relished the lively descriptions. She would study the pictures later. Now she let herself drink in every word, wanting to burn into her mind every adjective, every one of the children's words that Jenny repeated. She would remember everything to tell Lino. He would love hearing about Lucia wanting to take ballet. And the picture of Po in his blazer looked so grown up.

Emy knew they needed to leave for Vicki's choir practice, so she reluctantly tucked the photos in her bag and thanked the girls for all they had done to bring them to her.

At the last minute, Jenny snapped her fingers and ran out of the room. She came back with a little paper bag with the name of a Miami store written on the side. "How could I forget this? I hid it when I came through customs and it stayed where I hid it."

Inside the bag was a construction paper drawing of three cats. Scrawled on the bottom was *"De tus tres gaticos. Te amamos.* From your three little kittens. We love you." Po, Emilia Maria, and Lucia had all signed their names, Lucia's printed with little hearts over the dotted letters. Emy ran her hands over the paper slowly and smiled. She handed it wordlessly to Vicki and then to Ileana. Also inside the bag was a little beaded bracelet, with a note from Emilia Maria saying she had made it in Girl Scouts.

A childhood. Her daughter was having a real childhood, just like Emy had had. She wasn't hidden away, afraid. This was just what Emy had wanted for her.

She put the bracelet on her wrist and stroked it softly.

"Un millón de gracias. Thank you so much Jenny. You can't imagine . . ."

On the bus to *Reina,* Emy thought about how strange it was to learn about her children from others. She was lucky people were so kind about bringing her news.

Over the years, the very best source was her boarding school friend Bessie who lived in Colombia. She went to the U.S. every year and never missed seeing the kids, taking them presents she knew Emy would approve of and inviting them out for special treats. Then, through the Colombian embassy pouch, she would send her "report" to Emy.

She took her job seriously; she sent precise notes on each of the children: how they looked, how they had grown, what they were interested in, things they had said, questions they had asked about their parents, and how she had answered.

Emy knew Bessie so well that she knew just how to interpret something she wrote. And she missed nothing; from a day spent with the three children, she could tell Emy so much. Emilia Maria was something of a tomboy. Po hated haircuts - he said cowboys didn't get haircuts. Lucia said she was going to be a nurse. Po and Lucia couldn't sit together in church; they made too much noise.

From everything she learned, all the kind people who visited and brought things back, Emy felt a cautious optimism that they were all right, that they had no deep resentments about the situation. In her latest report, Bessie wrote,

Don't worry Emy. They seem like very regular children, and they speak easily about the situation you are in.

Emy was also encouraged by the contents of the few letters she received over the years. The kids sounded so matter of fact, as though their parents were only absent temporarily. Lucia had written:

Mommy, reading is really hard. I don't like it.

In another letter she said:

We went with Padre Llorente to Disney World. He is pretty fun, especially for a priest. Padre Llorente had gone to Miami in 1968 and had become like a favored uncle since his arrival.

A note from Emilia Maria read:

Dear Mami and Papi,
I can only write a short note because my basketball game is starting soon. I am the tallest girl so they like me to play even though I don't make many baskets.

Emy loved it when the kids' letters came printed in wide circles on the page, or on little notepaper with daisies or puppies. She remembered doing the same, and it reassured her that they were growing up, as she had, open to everything life offered.

They arrived at *Reina* a few minutes late, and choir practice had begun. Padre Miliardes was in charge of the choir, and Emy loved hearing the muffled music from her meeting room, although Vicki liked to say he was too serious. It was refreshing to see a person striving to do something well when the rest of her life was spent with people doing as little as they could get away with.

After the meeting, Ileana left quickly. Her parents always worried when she was out late. Vicki stayed to talk. It was the first time Emy had been able to share the news of Raque's leaving with anyone. She knew what Vicki's reaction would be, but she was surprised by its force.

"Great!" Vicki's face took on a stricken look. "Oh, I don't mean great. I mean . . . I know how much you'll miss Raque. Of course it's not great. I just meant you'll be coming to stay with us, and, selfishly, that will be great."

Emy chuckled. "Don't worry. I appreciate your being so glad, seeing the good side."

"Wait till I tell Mama. She'll have your room shining clean and waiting in one day."

"Vicki, you're so sweet. I already don't feel quite so homeless."

"Well, I don't want someone else to grab you to come live with them." Vicki put on her stern combative face, and Emy couldn't help but smile. She hugged Vicki hard once, then again. "That second hug is for your poor mother, whose daughter is giving away rooms in her house without even consulting her."

"Without consulting? Ridiculous. She's told you herself a hundred times that you have a home with us."

Emy knew it was true. She would be both welcome and safe at Vicki's. Vicki's mother, Maria Sutter Andrial, was a tall imposing woman with wide blue eyes and thick salt and pepper hair she wore braided and coiled on either side of her head. She had a strong character and belief in community. She'd always been greatly respected by everyone on the block, even when it became apparent she was not a Castro supporter.

The next evening, Emy went by Vicki's, a one-story modern house at the edge of a shopping area once filled with nice stores. Now it was almost empty, but for Vicki and her mother the location at the entrance of the beautiful Country Club neighborhood was safe and convenient to everything.

The building had been built in the 50's by Vicki's father who had worked at Bacardi Rum and had died of a heart attack a few years after the Revolution. Like many Cuban houses a large living room was only used for company. There were three bedrooms and in the back a kitchen, laundry room, and the maid's room. The room they used the most was the long dining room with an enclosed patio off one side. Here there were easy chairs and the TV, plus a wide marble table with wrought iron legs and iron chairs to match. Surrounded by other rooms, it felt cozy and far from the prying ears and eyes of neighbors.

Vicki had already told her mother about Raque's leaving, and Maria was smiling as always. She treated Emy as though her coming was a great gift.

"What good news. I mean, for us. We'll be delighted to have you with us. Of course, I already consider you one of my 'girls'." Then she asked, in her usual straightforward way, "Do they have their date yet? When would you like to come?"

"Nothing definite. But they're probably already under pressure to get me out. You know the CDR; they never miss a chance to make everyone miserable." It was nice to have this interior dining room where you didn't have to watch what you said.

"Besides I don't want to drag things out. I'll still be able to see them after I'm here, and maybe it's better to get part of the upheaval over with."

"You're probably right, dear."

"Remember, Rene's aunt lives with them too. She's told me before that she won't go when they do. I guess she'll go to live with Rene's three sisters on Calle Volde."

At the end of the following week, Emy made her way to Maria's with her few things. She hadn't felt like she was really leaving the de la Huertas; she would see them many times before they left Cuba. She had kept the tone of her departure light, and she already had plans to see them over the weekend.

Maria answered the door and led her to the end bedroom which she had obviously worked hard to decorate.

"*Maria, es magnífica.* You've made it so inviting."

"It's small, but the grill over that large door lets in lots of light and cool air." She would put the children's picture on the little table by the door.

Vicki appeared, having obviously rushed to get there to greet Emy. She gave Emy a delighted hug.

"You'll be right next door to me. Of course, I might talk your ear off. But you'll just tell me, won't you?" Vicki's face was flushed with a combination of heat and excitement.

Emy shook her head. "Oh I'm not worried about chatter, not having lived with the de la Huertas all these years."

"Tell me the truth, do you miss them already?"

Maria took Vicki's arm. "Don't bother her; she'll tell us what she wants to."

"It's OK, Maria. The truth is I would feel selfish missing them when I know how important it is that they get out."

Maria crossed herself. "With that large family, and his 'negative' record, they're lucky to go. God be with them."

True. She'd be relieved when they climbed on the plane.

Living at Vicki's was very different. On the one hand, she missed the noise and chaos of the big family. At the same time, she felt pampered and watched over by Maria from the first day. She wrote to Lino:

> *Mi Linote,*
>
> *I felt at home immediately here. I think because I've spent so much time here in the past. I know both Vicki and Maria so well. They treat me with a wonderful blend of warmth but respect for my privacy. I know they are there for me, but I never feel hemmed in or watched. How incredibly lucky I am.*
>
> *Siempre,*
> *Emy*

39

The next time Emy saw her, Raque was fit to be tied. She pulled Emy through the front door into the house where no one would overhear.

"You're not going to believe this; oh, but of course you are.

Emy was puzzled. Raque seldom got this perturbed.

"Remember the electric roaster I got when I got married? Well, we never used it much, but it was quite the newest thing at the time."

Emy nodded, remembering. She had had the same kind of roaster, long ago. Raque led Emy to sit in the dining room.

"Anyway, I'd completely forgotten it didn't work anymore, hasn't for years. Now the famous Señora Gomez of the CDR says it has to be put into working order before we leave. Where on earth am I going to get it fixed? If I'd thought, I would have gotten rid of it before they came for the *Inventorio*."

Emy leaned a little closer to speak, a habit now, even inside people's homes.

"Maria knows a man down in the old city that might be able to help."

"Really." Raque perked up.

"She says he knows this whole stupid system, and sometimes he can fix something just enough so it appears to work. Long enough for you to get out, anyway."

"Terrific." Raque cocked her head and looked at Emy. "Don't you just love it?" Her voice dripped sarcasm. "Señora *Gusano*, Mrs. Traitor-worm, please be sure everything we are going to steal from you is working. We don't want to be left with a lot of junk." Raque's voice rose. "The bastards - they know we'll do anything to get out of here."

"And they're right. Anyway, we have to play the game for now. I'll get you the name of Maria's guy."

"That would be great." Raque looked tired.

Emy had dropped by Raque's after work to catch up. She knew Raque would want to be sure she was feeling O.K. at Vicki's house. It had been less than a week since Emy had moved, but she could already sense a difference in the house. It felt as though its occupants were poised for flight, only resting briefly in these rooms, alert for the signal to move on.

"Here." Raque handed Emy a worn shopping bag from *El Encanto*, an elegant department store now long gone. "I'm leaving you all my old bras. They're pretty well done in, but I know you'll be able to take the hooks and tabs to Señora Garia."

Carmen Garia was an elegant corset maker who had been an institution in Havana for decades. Mothers would take their daughters there to have their first bras made, and later to buy slips and nightgowns for their trousseaus. She had been openly and courageously anti-Castro from the very beginning of the Revolution. It delighted her to help the outcast women in the only way she could, finding ways to make them new bras and underwear when there were no supplies anywhere.

There was a saying in Havana since Fidel. "If you have bras, you don't have panties." Neither one was available often, and never at the same time. Women like Vicki and Emy would save every fastener and strap of their old bras and slips and take them to Carmen, along with any fabric or even a piece of lace or ribbon they still had that might be used for new underwear. In the beginning, elastic had been a big problem. Then a secretary who worked with Vicki at the embassy brought a huge roll of it back from home leave and solved the problem. Carmen did wonders. Emy almost felt guilty at how good it made her feel to have something fresh and new.

Emy took the *Encanto* bag from Raque. "Thanks for thinking of me, *querida*." She raised her eyebrows and grinned at Raque. "Better be careful they weren't counted in the inventory."

Before the inventory, Raque had already given her several old pocketbooks which could be made into shoes. Emy wore a large size and the few imports that came from Eastern Europe never fit her. Raque had also given her bolts of fabric she had saved for new dresses but couldn't take with her.

Before the Revolution, dressmakers had been numerous and inexpensive. Emy's favorite, Raoul, was still in Havana. By having things made in classic styles, she made sure every piece of clothing served many purposes and lasted a long time. Her taste never changed; she liked a low neck but not plunging, little cap sleeves and a gently sloping silhouette that flattered her large frame.

Being well dressed was a great morale booster. It was important for their jobs at the Embassy, but most of all for prison visits. They always wanted to be a treat to their husbands' eyes, not a reflection of the grayness in every other part of life.

"You know," Emy had told Vicki a few nights after she moved in, "I felt so bad when my friend Marcela said she was leaving, and all I could think of was that beautiful green suit of hers and whether she would leave it with me. We're close to the same size. Isn't that pathetic, to lose a friend and only think of what she might leave you? I really do miss her - honest!"

"Did she leave you the suit?"

"She did. And I love it." Emy' eyes sparkled.

Vicki sat on her bed, experimenting with putting her hair into a French twist, the latest style. Emy sat on the floor watching her. "I believe you Emy. But some people might not." She grinned mischievously. "Anyway, you won't be wondering what I might leave. My stuff's too small for you."

"Oh yea, well how about that great silk cape of yours." Emy threw her slipper at Vicki. "I think I'd look quite elegant with it thrown over my shoulders." They both chuckled, knowing either of them would be delighted to leave the cape behind if they could be leaving Havana with their husbands.

On a night like this, talking with Vicki, it was hard to believe their real world was so constricted, so scary. They should be showing off their babies or planning projects at the charity clinic. Instead they were praying their husbands would survive prison and fearing for their own arrest.

The de la Huertas flight to Spain was scheduled for a month later, on a Friday. They had to report to the airport by 10 a.m., although they knew from other people's experience that the plane probably wouldn't leave until late afternoon. They hadn't gotten their visas to the U.S., but Spain was welcoming to Cuban exiles. Doctor friends in Madrid would help them until they could get to Miami.

Three days before, Raque called.

"Rene just got back from the immigration office. They 'summoned' him this morning. Our date's been cancelled."

Emy gasped involuntary. "Oh my God, you must be in shock."

"We are, though Rene is as calm as ever."

"What happened? Do you know? Did someone complain, accuse you of something?"

"They told us nothing." Raque's voice broke. "They said they'd know more in a few days. I just hope they haven't decided Rene is needed too much at Mazorra."

After an anxious 48 hours, another summons came; they were given seats for the next day. But they all knew there could still be problems. Authorities could bring up anything. "The car you left is in bad condition. Something is missing from your house." Even just, "Sorry, the plane is full. Unexpected government officials traveling."

They didn't have to justify. Worst of all, they didn't have to schedule you at another time. You might just have to stay. Emy knew that sometimes people did have to stay, at the very last minute, after everything was given away, the inventory done. Left with the crippling realization they were trapped for good.

Emy went to the airport to see the de la Huertas off; she was the only one.

"You shouldn't come," Raque said. "It'll be so depressing."

Rene agreed. "It's not easy to get transportation. You could ride out with us, a couple of kids on your lap, but then you might be stuck for a ride back."

None of them mentioned the other reason not to go. Showing loyalty to "traitors" who were leaving would put one more stain on her record.

"I don't care," Emy insisted. "I want to know you've really gotten out. I want to watch that plane really on its way."

At the airport, Emy watched, heart pounding, the searches, the inspection of papers, the grilling by officials. She waited for some shake of the head, some shock on Rene's face. But suddenly everything seemed set, and they were told to enter *la pecera*, the glass enclosure where they would spend more hours before boarding the plane.

Emy tried to keep the hurried goodbyes light. "Have fun on the airplane *chicos*. Help Mami." She kissed and hugged each child in turn. So many years had passed since she'd done the same with her own children, in this very space. If they appeared right now, would they recognize her? She couldn't think about it.

"Raque, *cuídate bien*. Take care of yourself. Really rest when you get there." She hugged Raque's very pregnant form, its bulk minimized in a baggy dress for fear the airline wouldn't let her fly. Emy waited through the long hours until the plane had taxied down the runway, lifted into the air, and not returned.

It was time to go back to her own life. Emy felt like a plant ripped from its soil and flung onto a rock to wither and die. She thought about how soothing it had always been to leave the grey outside world and enter Raque's realm, full of warm caring and energy. She had loved hearing Raque's voice ring out: *Bath time! Who wants to help me cook? Everyone into the kitchen please, on the double!* Emy forced herself to smile. The important thing was - they'd gotten out. They'd be fine, wherever they ended up.

Less than a year later, another departure. Ileana's parents, worried about their daughter in Miami whose husband had been executed years ago by Castro, decided they needed to go and help her. Ileana made the decision to send her daughters, Annette, 8, and Ileana, 7, with them. She would stay in Cuba to support her husband Rino in prison. Emy realized Ileana was making the same wrenching decision she had made years before. Her girls were much older. Did that make it easier? Knowing they would remember their mother? She doubted it.

Ileana came to live with Vicki and Emy at Maria's house. Sensing Ileana's stress and grief, Emy offered to move in with Vicki and give Ileana the end room that had been such a welcome refuge when Emy arrived.

Like everyone else, Ileana's parents had an *Inventorio*. Even though Ileana was staying, she could take only what the inspectors allowed. Ileana was still fuming when Emy came to say goodbye to Ileana's mother, Ofelia.

"That little witch walked around **my** room, telling me what sheets I could take - only two sets - which furniture, which towels."

"How awful."

"That is **my** furniture - I brought it from my house when I came to stay with my parents. Now they say it has to stay in the house!" Ileana folded and refolded a small yellow towel, her face splotchy with anger; Emy wondered what she could say to help.

"Oh, I've seen these people, at Raque's. They're brutal. I may have been lucky not to have gone through that. They stole everything, but at least I didn't have to watch, to say goodbye to each thing." The two women were silent, each lost in her own thoughts.

Ileana's mother came into the room and gave Emy a gentle saddened hug. She was an elegant woman, also very warm and genuine. Emy thought of her own mother's pain when she had to leave Emy in Cuba, her ungrudging response to taking the children. She admired Ofelia for doing the same. And Ofelia faced the added burden of caring for Ileana's sister and her other grandchildren.

Ofelia handed Emy a little white box. Inside was a gleaming engraved silver hairbrush with natural bristles. Emy had seen it before on Ofelia's dressing table.

"I hid this in the garden during the *inventorio;* I wanted you to have it. I know how delicate your hair is."

"Ofelia, *gracias.* I don't think they even make these any more. I certainly would never find one here. You're so kind to have thought of me."

"Remember me when you see it. And take good care of my daughter. You've been through all this. Don't let her be lonely." The older woman was near tears.

"Mama," Ileana interrupted. "Emy has her own things to worry about."

"I think it's more Ileana who will be taking care of me, Ofelia. Don't worry. The three of us will keep an eye on each other. After all we'll be living together, going on visits together, no time to get into mischief." Emy gave Ofelia another hug and prepared to go. She was remembering all too sharply her own mother's departure.

40

Early one Thursday morning, Emy dropped Vicki and Ileana near their offices and parked at the lot of the Hotel Capri, across from her office.

"*Felicitaciones*, Señora, I see you've still got that antique of yours running." Fernando, who ran the parking lot, was always full of energy. A tall clean cut man in his thirties, he still wore his hair slicked back in the old style. His appearance and his polite tone always took her back to the old days and gave her a lift. He also was very kind to her, at some risk to himself. The parking lot still had a gas pump, although in theory gas was available only for government vehicles. But tonight when she picked up the car, she knew he would say in a low voice, "You have ten, Señora," or "I managed just five." She would pay him later. God must be sending her these people who made her life bearable.

Normally she and the others took the bus to work, trying to save what little gas they could get for the visits. But today Emy and Ileana were invited to a formal dinner given by a diplomat friend, and she knew they'd be coming home late.

Before the party, she wanted to drive out to Lenin Park to see what the little kiosks were selling. The park was on the outskirts of the city, so the lines were usually shorter. Once she had found a kiosk that was actually selling packets of cream cheese, so small they had probably been meant as part of airline meals. She'd been so ecstatic she'd gone around the line three times to get as many of the little foil-wrapped packets as she could. She probably wouldn't be so lucky today.

Still, she was hoping to receive notice of a visit in the next few weeks, and it would be so nice to have something special for Lino. When he was first moved to *La Cabaña* prison, it had been so easy to visit him since he was right in Havana. There had been fairly regular visits. Then a long stretch with none. Now they had started again, though she never counted on anything.

She left her car on the edge of the park and walked first to the little kiosk by the playground. The swings looked forlorn, more rusted than the last time, the dirt around them bare of grass. The green lawns and tidy flower beds she remembered from walks with Lino were a thing of the past, victims of the Revolution's other priorities. Whatever scrubby bushes survived were left to fend for themselves. Two dusty children were arguing over whose turn it was to swing; others chased each other around the grimy play area. They had never known the park any other way; maybe they didn't care.

At first she thought the kiosk was closed; there was no sign of life. When she got closer, she saw a tiny black woman leaning under the counter. She straightened up and looked blankly at Emy.

"*Hay algo?* Is there anything today?" Why did she ask? If there had been anything for sale, there would have been a long line.

The woman shook her head and held up some empty cartons. They had Russian writing on them. Just as well. If whatever had been inside was Russian, it was probably inedible.

Emy stopped at two other kiosks with the same results. She tried not to feel discouraged, to just enjoy the cool breeze and the antics of the children in the park.

Memories flooded in without her willing it. When she had first been underground, the only way to see Emilia Maria had been to arrange to meet at the park across from the Ursuline school. One of her brothers would bring the two-year-old at a pre-arranged time. Emy would sweep her into arms, nuzzling her, delighting in her first words, telling her stories. She couldn't get enough of the touch of her, the smell of her, the expressions on her little face. Their short time together was so precious.

At the same time, each visit had crystallized for Emy all her worries about being separated from the children, the dangers the family faced, the uncertainty about the future. She had known why they were fighting, but the pain ripped her apart.

She shook off the past. Memories could lead her too close to black thoughts about what should have been. She forced herself to think instead about the upcoming evening. Her host, Jaime Caldevilla, was an information officer at the Spanish Embassy. He had lived in Cuba for years and knew everyone. Technically he had to appear neutral, but he gave every help he could to the wives of prisoners and other outcasts.

His house was a haven for a core group of twelve or fourteen people, mostly wives who were still in Cuba supporting someone in prison. People who were second class citizens for one reason or another. Many Sundays they gathered at Jaime's and Rosa's house for tapas and drinks. It served as a wonderful respite, an oasis where they could speak freely and let themselves be pampered by Jaime and his house staff.

Emy and her friends were also invited to formal dinners at the Caldevilla house. Tonight the party was in honor of a Spanish dance troupe visiting Cuba. All the evenings at the Caldevillas were a delight. But she particularly loved dance and looked forward to this evening when the focus would be on culture, not politics.

She went by her aunt's house to change into her long turquoise silk skirt with a full sleeved blouse of a lighter fabric in the same color. The skirt she had had since before the Revolution and the blouse had been made from a fabric imported from Indochina. They made her feel young and festive.

Emy parked in the Caldevilla's driveway. There were so few private cars now; parking was never a problem. The house had been built in the forties in Spanish stucco style on a hill in Kohly, a residential area near the river. It wasn't large but the location was striking. Emy walked up a terraced path to the entrance. The massive wood door with iron handles was opened by the butler who welcomed her into the entry hall.

To the left opened the living room and to the right the front terrace. Wrought iron stairs led up to the office and library on the second floor, pausing at a balcony mezzanine with more iron trim. She greeted Jaime, a small grey-haired man with a mustache, and hugged both him and his elegant wife, Rosa. Jaime complimented Emy on the color of her blouse.

"You look beautiful. I'm so glad you're here. Is Ileana coming later?"

"Oh yes, she wouldn't miss it."

"Well, I knew you'd be here for sure, since our special guests are dancers. I guess you heard their big concert last night for government officials was quite a success."

"I'm not surprised."

"I do wish I could have gotten you tickets. Here, let me take you out to the patio and introduce you to some of the troupe."

The party had already started on the large patio overlooking the city, where servants passed tapas and drinks. Later, when dinner was announced, everyone passed through wide French doors and seated themselves at one long table in the dining room. The cream colored stucco walls were decorated with wrought iron sconces echoing the design of the enormous chandelier over the heavy wooden dining table. Two archways on one end led to the kitchen. White coated waiters emerged with silver serving trays, serving guests with a well practiced flourish. Emy drank in the easy elegance; years ago she had just taken it for granted.

The best thing about Jaime's house was that she not only met interesting people, but she could be herself with them. The prisoners' wives, and Jaime, were always very open with the guests about their situation. They didn't hesitate to describe the experiences and privations of their husbands in prison. There was little danger of spies; even the servants at the Caldevilla house were from Spain.

On the rare occasion a Cuban government official was invited, Jaime would always warn the wives, and they would watch what they said. In truth, however, even if something said at the Caldevillas was reported back, which was unlikely, Fidel wouldn't dare use a comment made at a diplomat's party to arrest someone. He respected diplomatic immunity, if little else.

It felt good to dress up, to talk to someone who didn't spout political slogans, to be reminded that a world of culture still existed where ideas could be openly discussed. At dinner she sat next to Jose Valdes Garcia, one of the directors of the dance troupe. He was aristocratic, elegantly dressed, and spoke with a beautiful Castilian accent. They talked about the early struggles of his troupe and how they had managed to grow.

At one point, he said, "When you come to Madrid, you must come for a tour of our new theatre." He said it as though it might actually happen. Happy thought. A dream to keep the future possible. Far away for now.

The salmon was brought in by the butler, and everyone admired the enormous steaming fish covered with a golden crust. Her neighbor on the other side was the dancer Antonio Vieques, a trim blond man in his late twenties from Barcelona. They had met earlier over cocktails; now he asked how often she was allowed to visit her husband.

"About every two months. They just started again, after a year of no visits at all." Emy tried not to be heavy handed, but she took every opportunity to make outsiders aware of what was going on. In one sense, that was why she came.

Vieques' eyes widened. "A year?"

"Yes." She explained about how Lino and other "troublemakers" had been put in solitary confinement. "So two months seems pretty short. Letters do get smuggled in. I'll tell him all about tonight - and your troupe."

"That doesn't get him down?"

"Oh no, he loves to hear what's going on outside. He's very outgoing. If he could be here tonight, he'd enjoy every minute."

She imagined the dancer was wondering how Lino felt about her being out without him, meeting new people, eating wonderful food.

She answered the unasked question. "He says I should go out whenever I can." She found herself telling him how Lino often urged her to leave Cuba and go to Miami - and why she would not.

"I think he must know you cannot keep a beautiful woman in a box," Antonio teased her gently. His comment didn't bother Emy. While she knew some of the prisoners' wives were approached by other men to get involved, she never let it happen. Neither did Vicki or Ileana. Maria said she knew why.

"People sense it right away; you girls have a certain air of seriousness. Your manner makes it very clear that you aren't up for any nonsense while your husbands are in prison."

The morning after the party, Emy lay in bed a long time thinking of the conversation and the wonderful dinner. She could still taste the dessert, a cloud of cream with tiny threads of caramel swirling around it, like the rings of Saturn. Sometimes she forgot such things existed. She could barely remember shopping in a bustling market, hugging her children, watching them sleep. Dancing with Lino and listening to his soft hum.

Were all those things still out there? Was it better to dip back for an evening into her old life or never to be reminded of it? Lino always encouraged her to go out. He might be right, but she still had twinges of guilt.

She traipsed barefooted into the deserted dining room and began to write him about the party and all the people she had met.

41

In spite of the heat, a fresh breeze blew off the harbor on a Tuesday morning in January 1973. Emy and Ileana were waiting for Vicki outside the front door of Maria's house to leave for work.

In the years that the three women had lived together with Maria, she had, in her way, created an island of security and support for the three wives. There would be threats from the outside, but in this house, in their neighborhood, Maria watched over them. She managed to find food and treats for the *jabas* they took to visits, coddled the three of them when they came home, and fended off criticism.

Even though Fidel's creation of the neighborhood surveillance system had created bitterness and harassment for everyone, Maria, even though staunchly anti-Revolution, had always been respected. She had continued to be the first to help others in the neighborhood. She willingly shared her vast stores of sewing supplies and her expertise with whoever asked. She was also proud and determined; no one wanted to tangle with Maria.

"Come on Vicki, we're going to be late," Ileana yelled into the house.

"Hold on. I'm performing surgery on my dark blue pumps." Vicki loved nice shoes and these, her favorites, were badly worn.

Emy went back into the house and peered into the bedroom.

"What?" Vicki had one shoe in her hand, the other beside her on the bed.

"Vicki, I think they might be done for."

"No, no, look. I can do one more amputation." There had been no shoes in stores for many years and Cuban women had devised a special technique for saving high heels that wore down until the leather began to fray. They simply cut the heel off, up to where the leather was still nice. Of course, then the other heel would have to be cut at the same height. The cuts were never quite even, leaving a slightly lopsided effect. But a good pair of shoes was worth it.

"There we go. All set."

Vicki emerged from the bedroom victorious, the shoes, more or less even in height, on her feet.

Emy started to smile, then giggle, and finally doubled over with laughter. Ileana had come in, and she started to laugh as well. Vicki's last amputation had made the heels so low that the pointed toes of the shoes now stuck upward toward the ceiling.

"You look like . . ." Emy stopped to get her breath. "A court jester."

"No," Ileana struggled to speak through her laughter. "Like a slave girl from the Arabian Nights!"

Vicki looked momentarily disappointed. But when she looked down and into the full length mirror, she started to laugh too. They had all lowered their heel height this way, but never with quite such comic results.

How great it felt to enjoy a good belly laugh. They continued to chuckle as they left the house, Vicki still in the dark blue shoes. Today they were taking the bus to work. Cars and repair parts hadn't been imported since the Revolution, except for government officials. The three women had three decrepit cars between them: Vicki's 1950 Dodge which they called *Damnit*, Ileana's pink Fiat known as *The Rattle*, and Emy's little Opel nicknamed *Difficulties*.

At best, only one was usually running. A friend from the Canadian embassy, riding in Vicki's car, had claimed it ran only on prayer. "Actually," Vicki had replied earnestly, "we repair it with old soap. And sometimes when the radiator leaks, we stuff a green banana in it to plug it."

Even when one of the cars was running, they needed to save their gas rations for *visitas*, since Lino, Manduco, and Ileana's husband Rino were now in prisons within driving distance. You could reach the prisons by bus, but the car made it much easier. For one thing, the bus left before dawn and the bus station was in an unsavory neighborhood. You never knew exactly when or if the bus would leave. And if it arrived late, you missed part of your visit.

They usually had no trouble taking the bus to work. Their station was the starting point for the Vedado-Malecon line so they almost always got seats. But on this morning, there was no bus waiting, just a large crowd. After a wait of 20 minutes in the strong morning sun, a bus showed up and they were able to get on, but not to get a seat. As the bus inched its way along its route, it became so jammed the driver didn't even stop where people waited. When he stopped between bus stops to let people off, people who wanted to get on would run to catch up, trying to stuff themselves in through the back doors while other bodies exploded outward.

Ileana gave Emy a quick roll of the eyes. "Ah, another opportunity to sacrifice our time and patience to the Revolution." Emy shushed her. She loved Ileana's dry humor, but that kind of talk could lead to bad things.

How ironic that the opinionated Cubans, who loved nothing more than to debate and complain, were forced now to keep their thoughts to themselves. In the old days, excited conversation was part of daily life: people talking in loud voices, gesturing wildly, and exaggerating just to make a point.

Emy remembered how in 1957, not so long ago in time but long ago in spirit, shopkeepers in downtown Havana had protested new parking regulations, claiming they would hurt business. Colorful signs and slogans had been posted; every shopkeeper you met gave you his version of the problem. Shoppers discussed the situation on every corner. In the end the city had backed down and reinstated the old system.

Today those shopkeepers would have been hauled off to prison the first day, charged with promoting anti-Revolutionary values. Emy and Ileana had both known people who made it clear what they thought of the Revolution and ended up arrested on some vague charge like "lack of revolutionary fervor."

Ileana left the bus near *La Rampa*, to walk to the Immigration office. She had been devastated when she got word a year ago that both her parents had died unexpectedly in Miami within three months of each other. Ileana's sister was now alone with her own children plus Ileana's, and Ileana was desperate to go help. Today she had been summoned to the office yet again to untangle some minor difficulty.

By the time Vicki and Emy got off the bus near the Hotel Nacional, their clothes were sweaty and wrinkled. Before they separated, Vicki reminded Emy in a low voice about a rumor that a bakery in Calle Galiano was selling some kind of cookies.

"I'll go on my lunch hour and get as many as I can." Vicki's eyes shone with excitement. She took these expeditions as treasure hunts, a challenge, while to Emy they were just drudgery. "You might want to go too. I'm sure they'll just be those little packets. I won't be able to get more than two or three even if I go around the line several times."

Emy grimaced as she tried to smooth out her rumpled jacket. "After this morning's ordeal, I don't feel like going anywhere else with crowds." But she knew she'd head over to Calle Galiano as soon as she could. Once they had actually had little boxes of butter cookies. Wouldn't that be something to take to a *visita?* Of course that was a long time ago, but you never knew . . .

Emy was a little calmer when she arrived at the Embassy. She said nothing to the people there about the buses; they would understand why she was late.

"*Hola, Señora Fernandez.*" A slim young man got up from her desk chair when she got to her office.

"*Hola,* Antonio. Have you been waiting for me?"

"No problem, *Señora.* Waiting is my job."

Emy nodded. "Yes I guess it is." Antonio Gilbert worked as a courier for the Embassy; his mother was a nanny at the Egyptian Ambassador's house. Everyone adored this quiet thoughtful young man.

"I'm a little disorganized this morning, Antonio. Forgive me." Emy put her bag away and sat down at her desk.

"Maybe you're a little excited. My mother said you have a letter for me to pick up."

Emy felt a flip-flop in her stomach as she thought about the letter she'd get today. She never knew when she would get a call from a prisoner's wife or cousin or sister, saying that they had smuggled a letter from Lino out during a *visita.* Yesterday a woman she had never met had called to say she had a letter and to give Emy her address. You never asked how someone had gotten the letter or how they had carried it. The less you knew the better.

"It's in Altabana. You have time to go? You're sure?" When the letters could be picked up nearby, Emy went herself. But Antonio usually went for the ones further away. Emy always felt she was imposing on him, but he seemed as anxious to pick the letters up as she was to get them.

"*Señora,* I've been thinking all morning about it. And I have to go in that direction for the Cultural Attaché. Give me the address quick, and I'll try to be back before lunch." He took out a small piece of paper and a stubby pencil. "Did you tell the woman I would be the one to pick it up?"

"Yes. She said she'd be there all day." Antonio would probably take extra buses, even walk a long way to find her letter. Emy wished she could pay him. Even if she did, what could he buy? When she found something special to buy, it was always put aside for Lino's *jabas*. Nothing was more important than that.

She suspected that, like many people, Antonio helped the prisoners' families as a small way of hurting the government. People had been so kind. She doubted whether, without the tragedy of the Revolution, she would have ever known such kindness and deep friendship. Every one of the people who helped her was taking a risk. Just stopping to chat with her on the street could become "contact with a political undesirable." Giving her a ride in a delivery truck might be reported as "using government resources to help an enemy of the State." On and on it went. So much energy expended to hurt others.

Just after 11 o'clock, Vicki called Emy, giddy with excitement.

"They do have stuff at Calle Galiano. Russian unfortunately. But still, it's a little kind of butter cake. Small. A man who opened his said they weren't too stale."

"*Y la cola?* - how was the line?"

"Not too bad - I don't think the word had gotten out. I waited only 40 minutes."

"I'm on my way." Emy grabbed her bag and headed down the stairs. How long would the line be by the time she walked the ten blocks? Would the stuff be gone? Damn. She wished she had the car today. She could get there faster, and she wouldn't put wear on her rapidly disintegrating shoes.

She was still three blocks from the bakery when she saw the line. At least it didn't double back, just one long string of people. Rumors were flying up and down the line. "It was cakes. No it was little tarts. No it was only bread. They were almost out. No there was another big box." No one seemed to know how much they would let you buy.

When she'd been in line about a half-hour, the woman in front of her, looking a little unsure of herself, asked in slow simple Spanish if Emy could hold her place while she found a bathroom.

"*Seguro,*" Emy said. "I hope for your sake you don't have to go too far."

"Oh you're Cuban." The woman smiled. "I wasn't sure. You look a little like a foreigner."

"Now what would a foreigner be doing standing in line like a lowly Cuban?" The woman behind Emy joined the conversation.

The first woman seemed embarrassed. "I don't know, your clothes. And your green eyes."

"Don't worry. People often make that mistake." In fact Emy wore a skirt from Holland her friend Dolly had given her. She sometimes got foreign clothes from her Embassy contacts. And she was taller than most Cuban women. She liked to think the mistaken impression sometimes helped her.

The woman went off to the bathroom, and Emy settled her mind down again to wait. She was getting a letter. She wouldn't get her hopes up; it might just be a small note, one side of thin onionskin. But Lino could put so much tiny writing in a space. And even a few lines brightened her existence. Even after ten years and hundreds of letters, he always found new ways to tell her he loved her, to bring up a happy memory and make her feel treasured.

While she waited in line, she ate the little bread and egg sandwich Maria had made her for lunch. A nice change from beans. In the old days, there would have been big juicy tomatoes in the market by now, to put in sandwiches and salads. But these were not the old days.

By the time she was eighth in line, Emy could see the cookies were in fact more like crackers, five to a packet, with Russian writing on the transparent wrapping. What did that funny writing say? It should say: *Warning: these cakes have no taste.*

The woman waiting two people in front of her was refused.

"Get out of here. You were here before. One to a customer." The clerk looked bored.

"No, that was my daughter. Look, here's my identity card. It's my husband's birthday. And there are six of us."

Emy turned away, trying not to hear. She hated seeing people begging for such shoddy goods. How low Cuba had sunk.

By the time she managed to get her cakes, it was after three. The Embassy opened up again at 4:00, so she had just time to relax with a coffee at *El Carmelo* on her way back. It felt good to sit down; the long walk and standing made her feet hurt. She examined the package she had gotten at the kiosk. Lino would be delighted to have whatever was inside, but she couldn't help but think about the rum cakes *El Carmelo* used to have. And the éclairs. And the little swan-shaped cream puffs they served with chocolate sauce. Now even their favorite waiter Juan was gone. To Miami? To Angola with the Army? Just another missing face.

In her office she found the letter from Lino in the back of her top desk drawer. A tiny blue square, onionskin folded into less than an inch by two inches. Even though the embassy people were not spies, Antonio would never leave a letter out where someone could find it.

Was it actually against the law to receive a letter from your own husband? It was if the State said it was. It was if the State said one letter a month and you wanted more.

She shut the door to her office and carefully unfolded the fragile paper. This would be only the first of hundreds of readings. Each letter sustained her until the next one. Lino was so relentlessly optimistic; what an amazing soul he was. Even now, after so many years in prison, so many days and nights separated, his positive nature never flagged. She read:

> *Mi amor,*
>
> *I am so happy to be able to send you this smuggled letter. Official letters seem so far apart. But it doesn't worry me because, just by thinking about you, there are so many things to remember - what we have lived together, dreamed, and planned. Just thinking and closing my eyes for a little while is sufficient.*
>
> *I would give anything to be with you. I know it's not possible now, but I feel at peace.*
>
> *I wish I could be in a normal situation, but every day I see more clearly and I feel stronger than a rock. And I am even more in love with you. Don't worry about me. I am healthy as a bull waiting outside the ring for his chance to fight.*
>
> *Your,*
>
> *Linote*

Emy folded the letter and looked around her, out the window at the graceful arches of the arcade across the street, the tower of the cathedral in the distance. How had she known, a young inexperienced girl, that Lino was so special? How had she chosen so wisely? She felt a serenity descend on her, the peace his letters always brought. She knew he was under the same sky, by the same ocean, in the same soul space, right this moment.

42

Emy left the Embassy about seven and decided to stop by to see the Iglesias before she went home. Dr. Alberto Iglesias and his wife Eva had been friends of Lino and Emy since before they were married. Lino had originally done his psychiatric training with Alberto at the Sanatorio San Juan de Dios. Both men had been part of the *Agrupación*.

Other doctor friends of Lino's still in Cuba tried to help her when they could, but somehow she felt most at home with the Iglesias, more like part of their family. The Iglesias had four children; Emy was Godmother to Javier, the second oldest.

Alberto had never been directly involved in the resistance, but he was no friend of Fidel and often provided clandestine medical help or medicines. The family would have to get out soon. It was odd how things had evolved over the years. In the beginning you only got in trouble for being anti-Castro. Now they targeted you just because you weren't enthusiastic enough. Besides, the Iglesias' three sons would eventually reach military age; then they'd be trapped.

Selfishly, she wanted them to stay. She appreciated having Alberto's male perspective on things. Over the years so many people had gone. Her friends and her family, the essence of her life, had been chipped away, cracked and splintered until there was almost nothing left.

She always got a lift from visiting the Iglesias' elegant 1930s apartment in El Vedado, a triplex on Nineteenth Street that also held Alberto's office and an apartment for his sister. Although the building was right in the center of shops and cafes, Emy no longer took pleasure walking through the neighborhood as she had before the Revolution. The store interiors were bleak, the once colorful windows empty and dirty.

Eva opened the door at once. "Emy - what a delightful sight you are. Come in, come in."

Eva was a small cultured woman, a great art enthusiast who had given up her own painting career when she got married. She was a good listener; Emy always knew that whatever she said to Eva would go no further. Eva worried about the prisoners' wives who were alone and fussed over them when they came to the house.

"Believe it or not, I still have some Chilean wine. We'll take it upstairs."

As usual the two women retreated to Eva's special sitting room, high up on the third floor. For some reason no longer remembered, they had nicknamed the cozy space *Coco*. In a comfy chair, surrounded by Eva's books and art, Emy felt completely hidden away from the world. She had spent many hours there with good friends telling stories, teasing one another, and trying to forget the drab world outside.

Now Eva curled up in a faded blue armchair and looked expectant. "Tell me what you've been up to. News of Lino?"

Emy told Eva about her letter and that he seemed in good spirits. She never shared the details of letters. They were the intimacy of her marriage; she kept them to herself. But by the code that had grown up among wives, saying he was in good spirits meant there was no bad news, no new deprivations or punishments.

"And Ileana, how's she doing?"

Since she had applied for an exit permit, Ileana had been assigned to a backbreaking job polishing marble at a workshop in a Havana suburb. She was "paying" for her right to leave by doing humiliating manual labor until the government decided it was enough.

"Oh Eva, it breaks my heart. She comes back every day exhausted. Her hands are raw. I don't know how much longer she can hold up." But Emy knew Ileana would do whatever she had to.

"Where is this marble place?"

"It's in La Lisa. A long bus trip. Of course she was lucky not to have been sent to the country, to cut cane or something. At least she can come home and be pampered at night."

Eva smiled. "And I'm sure Maria does pamper her." For some reason,

Vicki's mother had long ago become convinced that Ileana was delicate; she watched over her carefully.

"Oh she does. She's wonderful. But Ileana's so worried about the kids, and of course her sister."

"It's been nearly a year hasn't it?"

Emy nodded. "She just wants to get there so she can see they're all right and take care of everyone. She's so strong; they need her there."

"How's her sister handling everything?"

"It's hard to know. Ileana hears very little, which just makes it harder. She tried to call around Christmas but couldn't get through."

"Big surprise," Eva said sarcastically. Eva never ranted, but she managed to make her feelings clear.

"You know Eva, I was just as glad. Remember when I got a call last fall from Miami? I thought it would be so great to hear everyone's voice."

"A mixed blessing, I guess."

"Overall, I don't look forward to another one. It's so hard to really tell what the kids are thinking. You know how kids are on the phone."

"Oh yes, I know. Either nothing to say or try to say everything at once."

"And then, poor Mama, she tried so hard not to cry; but she couldn't help it. She asks questions, but not the ones she's really thinking. And what can I tell her? That Lino counts on me? That I miss them all desperately? That's not going to help her." Eva nodded sympathetically.

"I was a wreck after the call. Stood outside the telegraph office in a stupor. Letters are much better; I can read what I want into them. Read them over and over, at the times I most need to."

"But you said the kids sounded good, right?"

"I guess. They sounded like growing kids." Emy straightened up and forced a smile.

"Oh Eva, how can I be so ungrateful? They're growing up fine. Everyone who sees them says they're normal healthy American kids, or Cuban-American, I guess I should say."

"Of course they are." Eva leaned over and patted Emy's arm.

Emy smiled and lifted her glass. "Eva, you are a balm to my soul. I know you have your own problems, but it feels good to let things out sometimes."

Javier barged into the room just then and threw himself into Emy's lap. At eight, he was a natural affectionate boy, and Emy loved to be with him. Rather than make her miss her own kids, spending time with the

Iglesias children made her feel like she was making up a little of what she was missing in Miami. She could look at Javier and imagine her own Po, with long limbs, learning to play soccer like Javier was.

"Javier, *mi amor*, how is school?"

Javier made a face. Since Castro had closed the private schools, Javier attended the government schools, where the propaganda was relentless. He was a good student, but Emy was sure it was confusing to balance his parents' views with what he heard in school. He never mentioned being harassed, but she had heard it from other kids of anti-Castro families.

"O.K., *bien*." He looked at Emy's glass. "Is that wine? Can I taste it?"

Eva nodded and Emy gave the boy a tiny sip.

"Yummm . . . ."

Eva tried to look stern and Emy laughed.

"Now get out of here, my little wino. I'll bet your homework isn't finished."

Emy stayed for a simple supper with the Iglesias. With other people, she would worry that she was taking from what little they had. But she felt so comfortable with the Iglesias that she shared their bounty when they had something good and their meager meals when there was very little.

She was lucky to get a bus back to Vicki's without too long a wait, arriving home a little after ten. Their neighbor Señora Varona was on watch for the neighborhood watch committee tonight. She greeted Emy cordially, but Emy knew she would go inside and note down exactly what time Emy had come home, that she had carried no packages, and that she had been alone.

As soon as she opened the front door, she felt electricity in the air and heard excited voices from the dining room, where they always gathered in the evening. When Emy appeared in the doorway, she saw Maria in the tall mahogany rocking chair, beaming and rocking fiercely. Vicki was perched on one of the straight chairs, sipping from a glass of wine.

Ileana stood in the middle of the room, wine glass raised, radiant.

Her *permiso*. Could she have gotten her *permiso*?

"Ileana - you got it? You're going?"

"Yes!" It was a victory yelp more than a word.

"You must be so relieved." Emy knew her words didn't begin to capture what Ileana felt.

"Stunned is more like it."

Emy's mind reeled, thinking how she would miss Ileana's steadfastness.

She was an anchor, so strong and certain of her beliefs, so good to talk things over with. Vicki was strong in a different way - outwardly emotional and impetuous, but reliable underneath. The three had balanced each other so well over the years. Could a two-legged stool still stand?

Ileana was all too glad to tell the whole story again. The rudeness of the clerks, the long wait, the interview - and her disbelief when they stamped her passport with the exit visa and told her to be at Varadero airport a week from Thursday at 8 a.m.

"I don't know how you'll ever wait another week." Vicki poured Emy a glass of wine.

"Oh I'm not even going to think about it until that airplane takes off." Ileana spoke in her usual matter of fact tone, but Emy had never seen her so animated. Popping in and out of her chair. Raking her fingers through her long black hair.

"Now I hate the thought of leaving Rino," she laughed. "How silly is that? I know he'll be so glad I can go, but still . . ."

"Ileana Puig - stop that!" Vicki jumped up and grabbed Ileana's arms. "Don't you trust us to take good care of him? We'll never miss a visit. Right, Emy?"

"Of course we won't. And Ileana, Rino'll be out in a couple of years. In the meantime, he'll know his children have their mother with them."

Emy felt a lump in her throat. She couldn't help but think of how it would feel to be climbing onto an airplane headed towards her children. She knew it was her own decision. Her commitment to stay with Lino had never wavered, but Lino always left the door open for her to go. In one letter he had said:

> *I have been weak with you about the children, not forcing you to leave. I wish you could be there with them. If you asked me to choose, I would choose that they be with you, not growing up without you.*
>
> *If this next year passes and we don't think any of us will be released, I hope you won't stay here anymore, that you will try to get out of the country.*
>
> *Your,*
>
> *Linote*

As she climbed into bed, Emy looked at the silver frame picture, at Emilia Maria's bright determined eyes. How would her children react when they found out Ileana had come to be with her children? Would they understand how different this was, how Ileana's children had no one else to look after them? She tried not to imagine the almost teenage Emilia Maria asking her grandfather, "If Señora Puig can leave her husband, how come Mami can't do it too?" What would he say?

43

He'd been let out of a dark squalid pit.

"Ay. Pelayo - feel that sun." Lino leapt with relish off the two low steps into the sunny open patio. Behind them, in the dilapidated two story building, their cell was a real room with three beds and a door locked only at night. Down the open air hall was a real bathroom, with supplies to clean it. The rooms and central gathering space had a granite floor, even a TV set.

"It's the Ritz!" Manduco joined the others in the patio, all stunned by their new surroundings. He immediately stretched out on the warm cement to take full advantage of the sun.

Who would have thought these modest living quarters could inspire such exuberance? The old toilet with no seat and the cracked tiles in the wall would have seemed distasteful in their old life; now they were heavenly.

> *Mi cara,*
>
> *We have been moved again, but this time to a place actually fit for habitation. We are in the old women's prison at Guanajay, just 40 kilometers from you, mi amor. The open space and the real bathroom make my heart sing. We can go outside to the patio whenever we want.*
>
> *We organized basketball in the big courtyard. It's still in a high security prison with guard posts all around. But the guards seem to barely know we're here. They lock us up at night and yell once in a while, but inside we congregate and organize ourselves.*

They allow some books, even painting supplies. Ernesto's wife brought his guitar - his home is near here. Listening to his music is such a joy to my senses. Please, bring any books you can when you come. They say there will be visits every month. We will see.

When we pause in our delirium over these small freedoms and luxuries, we wonder what is going on. Is this just for show? Have they really given up on crushing us? Or are they only preparing for something worse? We can only wait and see. It seems too good to be true. We actually had chicken one day, stringy and old, but real chicken-- and bread that wasn't stale.

Of course there is one thing missing and that is you, the other half of my soul, the core of my being. Can I dare hope this is the beginning of better times for us? After so long, it is hard not to be suspicious.

Your,

Linote

The visits did come every month. Couples and families could at last touch each other. Share food and news. A far cry from visits at *La Cabaña*. Even better than *Isla de Pinos*. No walls to separate people. No guards hanging over their shoulders. A little like a run-down boarding school, the students free to roam the grounds as long as they didn't go past the boundaries.

But even during visits, in the joyful hours spent with Emy, Lino worried about what would come next. They had so much to share, such a need to be together. Could they stand the pain if it all vanished?

Manduco was also at Guanajay, so Vicki and Emy made the short trip together. No more fighting for plane tickets and waiting all night at the prison gates. For the first visit, they drove Emy's car, the only one running, and got there at one o'clock for a two o'clock visit. Maybe they could get in early.

Emy had been anxious to see these wonderful new surroundings. But when the guard motioned her through, she ignored everything to run into Lino's arms, to feel his body for the first time in years. She fit right up against his chest as she always had. She was where she belonged; all was right with her world. During the *visitas*, she never tired of leaning against him, rubbing his neck, even just lacing her fingers in his.

A religious wedding was permitted in prison for the first time. Pelayo and Sonia, his girlfriend through all the prison years, were married by the Franciscan Padre Loredo at a makeshift altar in the common room. They were allowed to invite a small group of outside visitors.

Searching for a way to make the day special, Emy remembered a pair of beautiful suede boots that had been left by a visitor from Colombia with a note saying "These are for the day Lino gets out." The boots looked resplendent on Pelayo at the altar in his khaki uniform.

On their next visit, Emy was so excited about Lino's new freedoms that she decided to sneak in a camera to take a picture of him. There was still a cursory inspection coming in and out. She stuck the camera in the waistband of her slip under a full dress and was not stopped. She hurriedly took a picture of Lino and stuck the camera back in her slip.

Then the long arm of petty injustice reached out again. Emy approached the exit at the end of the visit, still smiling at the pleasure of seeing Lino in this bright place. A female guard with long skinny limbs and thinning gray hair pulled her aside. Thinking of the camera still in her waistband, she felt her stomach lurch. Had someone seen her taking the picture of Lino? But the guard just grabbed Emy's bag and dumped the contents on the table.

"*Qué es esto?*" The guard lifted up a rough cotton bed sheet, grey with grime and ripped. Emy was taking it home to mend and wash for Lino. She hadn't even tried to hide it.

"It's simply a sheet. I'm going to wash and mend it." Her voice was crisp. She was depressed at leaving Lino and so tired of these self-important people of the Revolution.

"Of course you are, *chica*." The guard's condescension deepened Emy's irritation. "More likely, you were going to take this home and keep it for yourself."

Steal it? Emy took a deep breath. Way down deep, she knew she shouldn't make waves. It would be useless - and dangerous. But this time she simply could not hold herself back. After all the years, she would say what she really felt.

"*Señora,*" she said in a condescending tone. "At home I am still sleeping on real linen sheets. I assure you I have no need to steal this pathetic rag."

She heard her own words, and her spirit soared for one short moment. Of course it wasn't true. Her sheets were as threadbare as anyone's. But she had stepped out of the shadow of submission. She had refused to blindly accept this endless stupidity.

The guard stood motionless, stupefied by Emy's daring. There was total silence in the hall. Emy could hear a truck start outside.

Then the guard pushed Emy down on a bench with surprising strength and yelled, "Stay there, bitch!"

In a few minutes the Comandante bustled in and led her into a small office. He sat down and motioned her to a stool. He was not as indignant as the female guard; he hadn't actually heard what Emy said. Nevertheless, he began firing questions. "Who gave you the sheet? Why did you put it in your bag? Did you know disrespect to a guard was a criminal offense?"

The room was stifling. As he spoke his wide square fingers drummed on the table, making a slapping sound.

Emy hated confrontation. The flush of pleasure was gone. She was furious with herself for not keeping quiet, for risking arrest, even a prison term, just for one moment of satisfaction. How could she put her visits to Lino in jeopardy? After they had fought so hard for them? She bit her cheek to keep back tears.

For three hours she was questioned, threatened, ignored, questioned again. She felt herself becoming more and more agitated as the accusations came at her. Oddly, she was never searched, and the camera stayed hidden. Emy kept her voice neutral, but she would not admit any guilt.

Finally the Comandante released her. She was to report a week later to *Poder Popular*, the People's Court in Havana where the only judges were common citizens and there were no lawyers. She would be tried for "stealing from the State."

Emy was limp with relief. In the early years of the Revolution, she would have been hauled directly to a cell. Of course in those days she probably wouldn't have dared to speak up.

Still, she was drenched in nervous sweat by the time she and Vicki got into the car. It was already dark, and Emy was glad Vicki couldn't see her anxious face, the nervous red splotches on her skin.

Vicki tried to cheer her up.

"Manduco's like a kid with that basketball team. He loves competition."

"Yea, Lino too." Emy's voice quavered. Vicki squeezed her hand in sympathy and they were silent.

Emy's mind was racing. There was the trial. Worse, she had made herself visible - an easy target for the authorities. With this regime, that could lead to anything: harassment on the street, raids on the house, invented charges. She could be taken into custody even before the trial, abused to make her admit to crimes or inform on others. She knew what she needed to do.

The next day, she destroyed all her personal journals, ripped them to shreds. *I'll never need them to remember these horrid years.* The journals were only her personal reflections; but the house could be searched any time, the journals seized, and used to support trumped up charges. She couldn't risk that. Not now.

She waited all week for trouble to start, but nothing came. *Please just don't make it a prison sentence. Don't take away my times with Lino.*

Sometimes her anger rose up again and she told herself she didn't care about the consequences. Then she lied to herself. *Everything would work out; she hadn't done anything all that terrible.*

One thing she had decided. She would not make trouble, but she would not abandon the core of dignity she had retained all these years. She dressed for court in a linen dress and high heels. She was now working for a Belgian importer, since the Cuban government had forced the Egyptian Embassy to replace her with a secretary-spy. However, her old boss Hamroush came with her to the trial; she felt less vulnerable.

When her case was called, the citizen-judges were clearly uninterested in logic.

"Did you try to exit the prison with the sheet in your bag?"

"I told you, I was taking it to mend."

"We didn't ask what you claim to be doing with the sheet. Do you admit then taking the sheet, stealing a government sheet?"

"No, just borrowing it to mend."

"Were you asked to take it by prison authorities?"

"It was my husband's sheet."

"So the State, the real owner of the sheet, did not ask you to mend it?"

"No."

In an hour of pointless questioning, she never admitted to stealing. At the end she was found guilty and "sanctioned", an ambiguous term the government used when it wanted to give someone a warning. In other words, she had done wrong, but not wrong enough for a prison sentence. *Thank God.*

She would be one month under house arrest, free only to go to work and back. Both police and the neighborhood CDR would check on her. Now the police had something to hold over her head. She was a documented criminal. A high price for her moment of satisfaction.

44

Even inside Guanajay, the prisoners could feel something slowly shifting inside Cuba. Ten years of revolution and repression. Cubans were discouraged, disillusioned enough to question the status quo, if only to themselves. Through visits, letters, even a few magazines, the prisoners could feel the pulse of discontent.

The public had gotten a rare glimpse of the outside world when Fidel, thinking they supported his own Revolution, had allowed coverage of the Paris student riots and the Prague uprising in 1968. Of course access to world news was quickly cut off when the Soviets invaded Prague. But Cubans had seen that people on the street really could object to the status quo and insist changes be made. Such an idea had been unthinkable before.

Then there was the miserable failure of the *zafra,* the sugar cane harvest. Castro had declared with great fanfare that this would be a Ten Million Ton Harvest, the biggest ever. He had rallied - or coerced - millions to leave their homes and jobs to go and cut sugar cane. With all that, the harvest fell disastrously short, a bitter defeat for *la Revolución.*

The atmosphere was ripe for seeking a shift in the status of political prisoners. The word "release" was not spoken openly. But everyone knew that the thousands of political prisoners were not only expensive but embarrassing to Fidel. If he was so beloved, why did he have to imprison so many opponents?

Exhaustion felt great. Lino had played basketball all afternoon. What a fantastic feeling - running, dodging, stretching for the basket. Just using his body. He was still thin, but with a little better nutrition and fresh air, his body had partially recovered from years of inactivity and filth. "Hey, Lino." Eduardo Camaraza collapsed on the cement next to him. "Did you see the copy of *Granma*?" The communist government newspaper had lately been sent into the prison. No explanation.

"Anything interesting?"

"Usual propaganda." Camaraza wiped his face with a ragged towel. "But, it's interesting. You can feel that some factions are questioning our ties with the Soviets, how close they should be. Others want even more ties - and more money. I say throw 'em all out."

Another friend joined them, panting from the game. It was after 6 p.m. but still hot and humid. "You guys look serious."

Camaraza didn't reply directly. He stood up and draped his towel around his neck, then turned to Lino.

"Here it is Lino: little cracks inside the Revolution. They need to widen. We've got to find a way to influence things now, take advantage of these subtle shifts."

Lino nodded but said nothing. He got up, went to shower, and put on his only other T-shirt and his worn workpants. Then he went to a room down the hall. Six other men were gathered there, all important members of the resistance.

This informal group met often, sharing information from every source: someone's brother, a wife's best friend, a cousin's contact in a Ministry. The group focused on strategies for getting the government to shift its policy on political prisoners. Lino always pushed for pressuring the government. He repeated his reasons now.

"Look. We're an ongoing embarrassment. We know that much. We've resisted every attempt to make us disappear." He ticked points off on his fingers. "The moving around, forced labor, isolation, pressure, and then the hunger strikes over ten years in all the prisons." His voice rose. "I tell you, they're looking for a way out."

Manuel wiped his face on his sleeve and moved closer to the window. "Fidel won't admit it, but the outside world knows. There are at least 30,000 of us. And every Cuban knows someone who's been executed or risked their life just to get out."

Ismael took a cigarette from his pack, neatly cut it in half, and put one half back for later. "Clearly Sergio Del Valle wants some new ideas.

He's sent officers from the G-2, we all know that. They've been talking to prisoners in the hallways."

Sergio de Valle was the new Minister of the Interior, in charge of the G-2. When he'd arrived two years before, there was a lot of talk about prison reform. Nothing had happened so far.

At one of their earliest meetings, Alberto had asked the group point blank, "Can we agree on one thing, that we're willing to see our role in a new way? That we'll at least consider trying to influence the Revolution from the inside?"

"What the hell does that mean?" Joaquin groaned.

Alberto ignored the angry tone. "It means trying to influence what goes on, not fight it openly."

Lino jumped to answer. "What are our alternatives? Armed rebellion's a dead cause, has been since 1966. We've kept ourselves ready. I'd fight tomorrow if I could."

"We all would." Antonio looked around for agreement.

"But it's not gonna happen; that road just isn't open. I don't know if there **is** a way to influence the system, but we could at least talk about it. See what we come up with."

Lino looked to Alberto for support. "There are ways to push change from inside the system. Look at what the Czechs did three years ago."

Antonio shook his head. "But what position would look non-threatening enough to Fidel to even talk about?"

"I'm just saying it's worth thinking about. It's not like we've got a lot of options, besides wasting away here."

Joaquin lifted his eyebrows and looked incredulously at the others. "Do you actually think any posture Fidel would accept would work for us? Not in my lifetime."

Lino looked from Humberto to Pepe, trying to stay patient. "If they are truly looking for a solution, then their offers might change on a pretty basic level."

In the end, the group had continued its long intense discussions and had come up with some possible strategies. They had agreed they would not renounce others. And they wouldn't agree to any kind of "reeducation" classes. Either of these would send the message that they had joined Fidel. The question was whether they could accept some agreement to stop actively fighting him.

At today's meeting, Lino brought up a worrisome dilemma. "Say we did want to signal some willingness to change our position, how should we do it? Would a direct approach make us look too weak?"

Manuel shook his head. "Might be better to approach the authorities indirectly. Go through some family connections. I have a brother-in-law pretty senior in the police in Santiago, but I don't think he has much influence."

Pepe spoke up. "Humberto, doesn't your wife have a cousin high up in the Ministry of Transport? Could we funnel something through him?"

Because of Cuba's large extended families, many political prisoners had relatives who had joined the Revolution and were now in responsible positions. In the past, connections like that had been denied or ignored. But paranoia had mellowed over time. It was becoming more common to use family ties to informally test ideas with the government.

Now Ismael shook his head. "Not yet. For now, I'd rather see us try to work with Sergio Del Valle." No one disagreed. They respected Ismael's opinion.

Over the next month, a high ranking G-2 official representing Del Valle continued to visit Guanajay. The prisoners were open about what they wanted. The official gave some ideas of what behavior the government would see as less strident, less rigid toward the system. Some principles were non-negotiable for the prisoners. But the underlying message to Fidel was clear: the prisoners might shift their position if the government shifted theirs.

The answer came in mid-1971 when the government began offering prisoners a plan called *El Progresivo*. Any prisoner who accepted the plan could gradually earn his release through years of work, paid work, in minimum security camps. Each prisoner could decide whether or not to accept the terms of the offer. Lino described them in a June 1971 letter to Emy:

> *Here's the most important thing. They haven't said we would have to renounce anything: our beliefs, our past actions. We wouldn't be labeled traitors. No reeducation classes. But we would have to show that we are dismantling our political organization. You know that would be an enormous step for me, for us. After all we've given up. And of course we absolutely won't inform on others.*
>
> *Basically, they are saying "If you agree to work, you can move towards freedom." They made it clear that meant live in open work*

camps, not prison, and eventually we'd be released. But how do we know they'll keep their word? Have they ever?

I must admit their willingness to pay us is very important symbolically. It's a statement that we are not in debt to this society, that we owe nothing. We work, and we are paid our worth.

I am undecided.

Your,

Linote

Emy tried not to push. She sensed Lino's unease with any plan that meant abandoning all open resistance. He was deeply opposed to everything Fidel had done - was doing - to Cuba. What agreement could he live with?

She asked him during the next visit. They sat at a picnic table, slightly apart from the others. Lino rubbed his forehead with his right hand and sighed.

"I suppose I should be encouraged. It's the first real shift in a very long time."

"But there is something . . .?"

Lino stood, turned slowly, and leaned back against the table. "I'm suspicious."

"You think they don't mean what they're saying?" Emy reached over to rub Lino's back absent-mindedly. She always savored this freedom to touch him on visits.

"I mean they can't be trusted - they **never** keep their word. They've always been cruelly inconsistent, unpredictable. They twist words and promises. They have **no** conscience." Lino reached for the last slice of the small sausage Emy had brought and chewed it fiercely.

Emy silently folded and refolded the paper wrappings from their picnic. She wanted to say something to reassure him, but she knew it would be pointless. She didn't know what would really happen any more than he did.

"*Mi amor*, you have to do what you believe. I've never tried to convince you to abandon your fight. And I'll accept what you do now."

Lino tipped the thermos for more coffee. It was empty. He sighed.

"*Ah mi querida.* That's the hardest thing. To know I have a chance to take up our life again; to be one with you, spend my days and nights with you. He at down next to her again and put his hands on either side of her face. "That lures me. I can't let it pull me beyond what I can honorably do."

"I don't expect you to. You'll know what's right. It'll come to you. And I'll be here. *Siempre, mi vida*. No matter what." She wrapped her arms around his neck and leaned her head into the crook of his collar bone. They sat without moving for a long time.

El Progresivo was practically the only subject of conversation at Guanajay. Some men were inclined to accept; others swore they never would. The group of six gathered on a cool Wednesday evening in November 1971 in a corner of the patio.

Manuel sat next to Lino on the cement floor.

"Lino, I know you're dubious. Can you see any way you might accept the plan?" The others listened carefully. No one else had asked Lino so pointedly.

Lino spoke so low they had to strain to hear him.

"All these years of deprivation, years of our lives given for this idea that we could bring democracy back to Cuba. And now to just walk off . . ." Lino scratched an arrow on the cement with a pebble.

Alberto interrupted. "Not walk off Lino. Shift. Work for ideological change instead of military change." Lino started to speak but Alberto cut him off. "Even if we agree to be less visible in our opposition, we can still work for change in more subtle ways." Alberto rolled up a magazine he was holding and unconsciously tapped it against his thigh.

Manuel looked up. "What good are we doing here?"

"I don't know yet if I'll accept, but I keep thinking we may not get another opportunity like this." Pepe interlaced his fingers and looked down as he spoke. "The government is weak. You know we've pushed them. This plan's not ideal for them either."

Lino's voice was measured, intense. "I just want to be sure we're not taking the easy way out. Convincing ourselves, telling others, that we're doing something honorable when we're really giving in." He shifted to sit cross-legged and put his head in his hands. Alberto and Humberto talked quietly for a few minutes. The others said nothing more as darkness fell.

A few days later Pelayo and Lino were alone in their cell. Pelayo spoke without introduction, "Take it, Lino. Agree to the plan. I'm getting out soon, but you have a very long sentence."

Pelayo continued before Lino could speak.

"I know it's tough. But it could work, if we can still push reform once we're out. Don't be stubborn."

Lino looked past Pelayo and said nothing.

"Lino." Pelayo was normally an easy-going person, but now his voice was hard. "You should be one of the first, not just follow others. You need to clear the way for the rest."

Lino knew Pelayo was right. If he signed up for *El Progresivo*, he would free other prisoners, those who looked to him, to go ahead. If he did not, many other prisoners would feel they couldn't accept either, without being traitors. He thought again of Emy's words: *you'll know. I'll be there no matter what.*

One afternoon a few days later, when most people were asleep, Lino was praying. *God, I have decided to accept El Progresivo.* He stopped, as if waiting for God's help. *This is difficult for me to accept. Will they do as they've promised? If they don't . . . if they renege . . . try to take advantage of us . . . .* Lino could feel his anger pushing through again. *I'll push back with all my force, no matter what the consequences. I won't be railroaded.*

Lino was still for a long time. Finally he felt at peace, as if God deep inside him had said, "I know that, my son." He lowered his shoulders with a deep sigh. How long had he been holding that breath in?

Lino told Pelayo about his decision before supper, and then asked the others to come to his cell that evening. When he announced his decision, Alberto sat up straight on the bed. He seemed surprised.

"What made you decide to accept?"

"A fair question. To be honest, I can't predict whether these bastards will keep their word. But . . . ." There was total silence in the room.

Lino traced the edge of his bed with his finger. "I've convinced myself that accepting this plan is not a surrender. It's a victory. We've forced Fidel to come to terms with us."

"I agree," Ishmael said quickly. He looked pleased.

Lino continued, "Think of what we've gone through. We've persevered with honor; we've endured every kind of duress. In the end, Fidel had to negotiate this release, recognize us as a force. He had no choice. And this agreement preserves our integrity."

Manuel said quietly, "We've all lost people we loved, people we respected, in this hideous struggle. I for one think your decision respects their memory. I'm sure I will accept as well."

Lino wanted to tell Emy about his decision during a visit, but the next one was too far away. He wrote her a long pensive letter:

Mi Rosa roja,

I am going to accept El Progresivo. It is a big step, a difficult one. Will it lead to something? Who knows? I trust only one thing. That I want to be with you. I want your eyes, your kisses. I want our laughs and our banter, our naps and songs and intimacies. Our love deserves everything. The idea of some day being back with you makes me mute with hope, holding my breath until I can hold you again.

I want to protect you from everything, even that part of me that still dreams and imagines miracles. So I must tell you we cannot count too much on this. We will talk a lot at your visit, which I already desire more than you can imagine. I have many kisses waiting here for you.

Your,

Linote

Emy laid the letter down with trembling hands. Could there really be an end to this nightmare? She sat down on her bed and reread the letter. She had no answers. She could only do what she had done all these long years. Take each thing as it came. Ask for God's help. And send her love to Lino.

45

Lino was a paid worker. True, he was a prisoner. He lived in a compound surrounded by fences and guard towers. His jailers could take away everything at a moment's notice. But it was a beginning.

Lino was now in Melena, a different prison, with Manduco. It had a factory right on the prison grounds where they made molded concrete panels for construction. For the first time in ten years, he had paid work: 58 cents an hour. The same wage as on the outside.

He hummed to himself as he left his room in the unlocked dormitory and headed to the dining barracks. He was getting used to being allowed to move around freely, seldom having to deal with guards. A small alarm went off in his head. *Don't get too used to this. You're a prisoner - still totally in their power.*

He had decided to focus on building up his strength with hard physical labor; construction work did that. He could already feel the effects. He was still thin but was filling out as his body adjusted to the work.

He still gave medical care to other prisoners; he couldn't say no to them. Medicine was, after all, his real love. He asked Emy to bring him any medical books she could find, and he studied many nights after work. Someday, God willing, he would be a practicing doctor again. It wouldn't be easy to catch up.

The prisoners who had refused *El Progresivo* insisted they would not "work for Fidel." But if your family had to work for Fidel to buy things for you in prison, then it was the same result. Or was he kidding himself, being sucked in by his longing to get on with his life?

"This is crazy." Lino sat down next to Manduco at one of the long wooden tables in the dining hall. "I actually don't have **time** to read or write. After a day of work, I just collapse."

"*Yo también.* If you'd told me we'd have this problem when we were cooped up in *La Cabaña*, I wouldn't have believed you." Manduco grimaced at the memory.

Lino stretched his long legs under the table. "When you put it that way, I'll stick with Melena."

The food was about the same as at Guanajay; at least here they got a little more protein. They had to if they worked long days at physical labor. God knows, Fidel wouldn't waste food on them unless there was a reason.

Manduco saw a friend Pablo come in and motioned him to their table. Pablo was an engineer who was learning concrete work with Lino. He'd been married by proxy years ago, and he liked to commiserate with Manduco.

"Oh man, I am pooped. I thought being an engineer meant telling people what to do, not laboring like a donkey."

"Or an ass." Manduco smirked.

Lino drained his cup of water and stood up. "Good thing we didn't agree to any 'reeducation' classes. We'd sleep right through."

"Actually that would be just the right thing to do with those classes."

When Lino got back to his cell, he reread a letter Emy had brought him the week before. He had begun for the first time to receive letters from the children, and they were startling in their normalcy. In this new letter, Po announced he was on the baseball team. He wrote:

> *Dear Papi,*
>
> *I'm playing a lot of baseball this year. I'm playing second base. I think it's a pretty good position. I know you played baseball and I wonder what you think. Should I try to develop my pitching? I hope you'll get to see me play when you get here.*
>
> *Your son,*
> *Lino Jr.*

When you get here. God, when would that be? Maybe never. Even out of prison, he might not be able to leave Cuba. Lino had replied:

> *Dear Po:*
>
> *I'm delighted you're playing second base. That and shortstop are very key positions and I would stay there if I were you. You'll get lots of action - a chance to catch some long drives and really make a difference in the score. I always played third base*

but that's just where they put me. I look forward to seeing you
play soon.
 Abrazos,
 Papi

The girls wrote about school, about flamenco dancing, and about clothes. His heart ached not to be there with them, but he felt good that they sounded so natural, so healthy.

In 1972, political prisoners began being sent out in work brigades to live in construction camps on the sites of new schools or new housing. Lino wrote to Emy:

Mi Emilita,

 I don't kid myself. It's still a prison, but we do live in regular worker barracks and there are no fences. That feels good. Of course there are still guards checking the perimeters day and night.

 We are part of a construction crew. I am using the jackhammer for excavation. It takes a while to get used to but I can feel the difference in my arm strength. Maybe next time I see you, I'll lift you up over my head and twirl you around!

 I am going to try to get the training for directing the cranes later on. It would be fascinating. Manduco thinks I'm crazy. He hates heights, says he will try to work on electrical connections instead. We are building a school so at least I am doing something meaningful. But I only look to the future and the day I can come to you. I send you one thousand thoughts of love.

 Your,
 Linote

There were days when Lino felt almost like a normal worker, hurrying to work in the morning, coming home exhausted, showering, then heading to the dining barracks to eat with friends. But always there was the void where Emy and the kids should be.

He had ended up this time in the same camp as Manduco. Others had gone to another camp with no explanation. Lino hated this constant reminder of having no control, of never being told what came next. For some reason the camps were named after agricultural products. Lino was first at Aguacate #2, and then he was transferred to Tabaco #1. His brigade moved every six or seven months.

One Friday evening in the fall of 1973, he sat on the bench long after he had finished eating, watching a group of men playing chess. He should be studying his medical books, but he felt too tired even to walk to his bed in the barracks. Hopefully he would fall asleep quickly and not think too much about Emy and the children. Emy's visits were every month now, but it never got any easier to say goodbye.

Andres Mendoza interrupted Lino's thoughts. Mendoza, a short good-natured man who loved to move between groups and gossip, plopped himself on the bench and held his hands up dramatically.

"O.K. guys, you are **not** going to believe this."

Manduco slapped Andres on the back. "I don't know - sounds like a biggie."

"It is." Mendoza didn't smile but leaned in to the others. "Six guys just got *pases* - weekend passes! They just let them go - no guards, nothing. Honor system, I guess."

"*Pases?*" Lino stared at Mendoza. He felt his heart hammering. "For how long? They can travel?"

"I don't know much. I was talking to Mario and a friend of his got one - a 48 hour *pase*. He's from Oriente and he didn't even know how he was gonna' get home and back in that time.

"Who cares? At least you're free for 48 hours."

"Yea, apparently he didn't hesitate. I guess they tore out of here like hurricanes."

"I'll bet they did." Pablo was half standing. "How do they decide who gets to go? How about guys married by proxy going first? That seems fair. I've never spent the night in bed with my wife, for God's sake!" Lino thought longingly of his own Emy. Once they had spent every night in the same bed, never dreaming it would change.

As word traveled that *pases* were being given out, they all pondered the next steps, ones they had yearned for so long. Where was home? Manduco got his first *pase*. Emy was already saying she wanted somewhere she could stay alone with Lino.

Then Emy wrote to him:

> *Mi querido Linote,*
> *The Huertas have once again become our angels watching over*
> *us. Rene's sisters have invited us to have a home with them. We can*

use the little suite Rene used before he married Raque. I don't think you ever saw the house but it is a very pretty place built in the fifties. I think you met the sisters once. They are so warm and supportive. I was there yesterday. They made me feel that our coming would be their pleasure. They're all in their seventies now but very active. Hortensia is a lawyer and Margarita continues to teach.

Actually, it is brave of them to take us in. They will, of course, be investigated for supporting undesirables, or whatever they call us these days. And the neighborhood CDR will take advantage of this to hassle them more than usual. Ada works with young people through a church - Iglesia de San Francisco I think - which means she is already not very popular with the government.

I spent one night there last week. It took my breath away to sleep in a space where you might actually come and be with me. The suite has a main room, a bedroom and a second room plus a bathroom. More in my next letter.

Siempre,

Emy

46

Lino got his first *pase* six weeks later, on Friday as he returned from the work site. They were always given out at the last minute. No time to tell Emy his turn had come or even to make travel arrangements. He cursed the time he would waste on the bus. Emy would have picked him up if she had known. How typical of the system. Give you a pass but keep you from making the most of it.

Waiting for the bus, he reveled in being out on the road alone, free to do as he pleased at least for these two days. He couldn't believe he would wake up tomorrow with Emy. He would eat when he wanted, talk to anyone, walk out the door when he pleased, wander the streets. Kiss his Emy, entwine his body with hers, drink wine, listen to music, stay up all night laughing and playing.

And then he would say goodbye again. How could he bear it? It would be incredibly stupid not to return. But he let his imagination go for a moment and imagine never seeing another guard, never sleeping again in a barracks full of men.

When the bus came an hour later, it was a pre-Revolution city bus, the painted sides peeled and faded beyond reading. He stepped easily in and got change from the driver. The fare had not changed. How easily he moved in his old ways. How shabby everything looked.

The brown leather seats were torn and patched with bits and pieces of tape, most of their stuffing gone. Lino luxuriated in the novelty of choosing which seat to sit in, whether to open the window. Maybe he would never again be transported like an animal in the back of a truck.

As they neared the city, the bus began to fill up. A sunken looking older woman pulled herself slowly up the steps onto the bus. She was carrying a string bag with a small loaf of bread and holding the hand of a dark-haired girl who looked about seven years old. The child talked incessantly to the woman, who seemed to be her grandmother. The girl turned and smiled at Lino. He had to squeeze his eyes shut and cover his face to hide his tears. His own daughters, his son, were far away. They had already passed through this little girl's age, years of their childhood without him. Would he ever find a way to see them? How much longer?

When he arrived at the main bus stop in Havana, it was after eight and he walked impatiently to Vicki's house. When he strode up to the front door and rang, Maria answered and went pale with surprise.

"*Ay*, Lino." She enveloped him in a hug. "Emy! Emy! *Apúrate*! Come here! Quick!" Emy and Vicki exploded through the dining room door at one time. Lino enveloped Emy in a hug that lasted many minutes. They rocked back and forth, humming in delight. They reluctantly broke apart, and Lino gratefully took the coffee and fried eggs Maria offered him.

He sat in the big leather recliner with his coffee, taking in everything about the room. So this was where his Emy had lived all these years, had written all those letters, had grown and matured, and been there for him.

Emy wouldn't let go of him; she perched on the arm of his chair, her arms around his neck. Lino told about his agonizingly slow bus trip.

Maria stood up and clapped her hands. "*Váyanse para su nueva casa*. I know you're dying to see your own place. You don't have to stick around here and be polite."

They decided to walk to the Huertas. Lino wanted to savor the energy of life on the streets, appreciate the sights he loved.

"I feel like a young bride again, walking in the street with my handsome husband." Emy wanted to shout out, "Here he is - isn't he wonderful?" Lino was oblivious now to the shabby condition of the buildings, the disintegration of the once beautiful city. He just savored the things he had not seen in long long years. A patch of grass, flowers in a pot, a group of boys playing ball.

"You'll love our place - it's so exciting just to call it that, isn't it?" The happy lilt in Emy's voice said it all. "Dolly got us a beautiful damask bedspread - and the Huertas lent us a table and refrigerator, even a hot plate. They've been so great."

Lino let himself sink into the warm pleasure of walking beside her, bodies touching, listening to her happiness bubble. He had waited more than 11 years just to walk by her side down the street.

"You mean you're actually going to cook?" He had always loved to tease her about being the only one in her family who didn't like to cook.

Emy punched his arm gently, "No. But it will be nice to make you your bedtime snack. The sisters said we can eat with them whenever we want." She hugged him discreetly. Even on this first day free with her husband after so many years, she still felt hesitant about too much affection in public.

The Huerta sisters had heard from Vicki of Lino's arrival. They already had the front door open and almost pulled him into the house, hugging him and marveling at his unannounced arrival. Emy knew the neighborhood CDR would be over within the hour to check who was visiting. Then the news would be all over.

The Huertas ushered Lino with ceremony to the third floor suite. Lino looked around the three little rooms. A palace. The elegant bedspread made the bed look like a Moroccan divan. There was a little round table with two stained wood chairs. A tiny sink gleamed. There was even a door leading to a small roof garden. Everything spoke of beginnings, of preparation with love, the two of them in the cocoon they had craved so long. He imagined all the little luxuries - the freedom to wear different clothes, to share his thoughts with Emy whenever they came to him, to have silence when he wished, to use his own bathroom in privacy. He also loved knowing he could leave - walk out, onto the street, upstairs, downstairs, into the garden, to a bodega. No rules, no one watching.

The three sisters had prepared a simple supper and then sent them up to settle in. What a strange feeling, not just to be alone together but to be looking ahead. Where do we start planning for this new life? And underneath, the fear. Are we taking too much for granted? Will all this be snatched away by one of Fidel's mercurial reversals?

All worries were forgotten as they slowly tenderly returned to the delicious rituals of man and wife. They stood a long time in the little roof garden, luxuriating in the knowledge that there was no rush; they had the whole night. They dawdled, savoring the anticipation. Emy felt like a young bride again as she put on the silk nightgown she had saved for years, washed her face, and climbed slowly into bed beside Lino.

"Mi vida, mi vida," Lino's voice was thick with emotion.

Time apart, longing, loss - all disappeared as they touched, softened, merged into one as they always had, as they had on their first night together so many years before.

The next morning Lino wanted to meet Hamroush who had been so kind to Emy, so they walked to the Egyptian diplomat's house. The two men connected instantly. Lino hoped Hamroush could sense the depth of his gratitude, how much his care of Emy had meant to Lino when he could not be there himself.

Lino was upbeat and full of energy, eager to be out and with people. He loved knowing Emy would be everywhere with him, and especially that they would return together to their refuge at the Huertas.

Emy had been invited to a party Saturday night at the house of Gerard Dupuis, the security chief at the French embassy. His wife Nicole had recently arrived in Cuba, and she and Emy had quickly become friends. When Gerard opened the door, he looked confused and almost embarrassed. Emy never came with a man. Then the realization dawned - who this man was. He clasped them both in one wide hug and called Nicole to come see who was with Emy.

Again and again, Emy and Lino basked in people's surprise at so unexpectedly – and after so long - meeting Lino. They explained over and over how no one had known he was coming, how it was only for 48 hours. Lino couldn't bear to have Emy out of his sight; her relief and joy glowed in her face and in every word she spoke. Emy felt incredulous that her two worlds were becoming one; Lino could at last know the people who had made her life bearable all these years.

"Everyone speaks English," Lino reflected as he and Emy walked away from the Dupuis' apartment house just after midnight, his arm tight around Emy's shoulders. "*Mi vida*, you too are speaking it so well. I can see I'll have a lot to catch up with."

Emy gave him a light kiss. "Shhhhh… Don't talk about catching up, *mi vida*, we are only looking forward now. Nothing has been lost between us."

"You're right, Emy. It's only gotten stronger. And you, *mi amor*, you have become not just my sweet angel but my strong fighting angel, always there for me. Always giving me what I need."

Emy fought not to fall asleep that night, not wanting to waste one hour of the time she had with Lino. There would surely be more passes. But in her heart she had learned never to count on anything.

Lino had to be back by 4 p.m. on Sunday. The Dupuis offered to drive him and Emy to the camp. Emy was quiet during the drive, curled in Lino's arms in the back seat. Lino talked with Gerard part of the trip in a mixture of Spanish and halting English. Emy had noticed, today and last night, how Lino made no attempt to share his prison experiences. He would answer questions when asked, but he clearly didn't intend to play the martyr role.

As they neared the camp Lino turned to Emy and took her face in his hands.

"Don't be sad, *mi amor*."

Emy leaned her head to one side, resting it on Lino's shoulder. She had already told him last night, "I won't be sad when you leave. Just nervous. It's coming so close, this promise. But as always, it is out of our control."

The next five years brought many passes; Emy and Lino crammed as much as they could into each one. They went to the beach, to friends' houses, to concerts, on long walks. Emy was amazed at how Lino could fit right into life again. He was not bitter; he looked only to the future, embracing everything new.

They tried to be cautious about what they could hope for. Even if Lino got out some day, no one was allowed to leave Cuba these days. They would be as far as ever from the children. Would Lino be allowed to work as a doctor? Would he even want to? The medical system was in shambles.

Emy knew that Lino's heart ached as he saw and heard what Fidel had done to Cuba, how degraded their country had become, subservient to whatever foreign power offered money. He knew he couldn't fight Fidel openly, but his steel focus never wavered. He needed to do something to help bring the regime down, to bring Cuba back to democracy. His body was becoming stronger; his soul had always been strong. For 15 years he had met everything without fear. Now he was determined to meet the future the same way.

On Manduco's third *pase*, he and Vicki were married for the third time, a ceremony in a real church, Corpus Christi on Quinta Avenida. Vicki at long last had her formal wedding, surrounded by friends, in a long white dress. Lino was the reader. Padre Ascarate, the priest, spoke beautifully of loyalty and steadfast love. To Emy it felt like he was speaking to her and Lino as well, telling them to stay strong a little longer. Vicki's mother had even found a real wedding cake at the last minute and drinks for a reception after the Mass. Vicki and Manduco had waited a long time for this day; it seemed like a preview of life to come.

Lino and Emy lived from one *pase* to another, though they were never sure when, or if, another one would come. They fixed up the little apartment; Lino's own paintings added color to the walls. Friends brought little gifts of decorations or supplies.

Emy loved introducing Lino to everyone. He met Xavier and Marcela Rodriguez from the Spanish auto company, who had invited her so many times and lifted her spirits when she needed it. He got to know Emy's Dutch and Canadian girlfriends and a Bulgarian couple Emy had become very close to.

One evening Emy returned feeling somber from taking Lino back to camp. Why did she always have to say goodbye to her husband? She sat out on the little roof terrace; there was no moon. She thought of their first days together, all the dreams they had. What would their own house have looked like after all these years, if life had been different? Full of memories? Cluttered with the children's things? How many children would there have been? Where would they be in school? Who would be . their friends?

Stop it, Emy! The future is what counts. And the future is soon. She came back inside and climbed into bed, trying to ignore the emptiness of Lino's side.

47

Lino always slept heavily in prison. This night, November 6, 1977, it took him a few minutes to groggily realize he was being shaken awake by Enrique, a slow-moving overweight guard with stringy hair.

Here in the work camps, there were never midnight awakenings. Lino's long trim body stiffened. What did it mean?

He rubbed his hands over his bristled face. He struggled to his feet, towering over Enrique and standing straight and tall as he always did. The years of working in construction had left him in great shape, better at 46 than most of these slouching guards in their twenties.

Enrique spoke with the weary familiarity of seeing thousands of prisoners move through these camps.

"Come on Lino, no sleep tonight. You'll have plenty of time to sleep."

What the hell did that mean? He always had time to sleep. In the 17 years he had been in Fidel's prisons, he was seldom kept awake, even when the guards deliberately hollered and yelled threats. It had been a very long time since anyone had woken him like this. *Why tonight?*

Lino ran his fingers through his hair, willing his hands not to shake. Then he put on his work clothes.

"Bring your stuff."

Oh God, another move. Was everybody moving? Were the others being woken too?

Lino gathered his few papers and books. In the camps, prisoners didn't hoard supplies like they had in prison. The barracks were silent. He and Enrique were the only ones trudging through the dim hall.

Lino was fully alert now. All his doubts about *El Progresivo* came flooding back. Was Fidel reneging? Were all his gains about to be lost? A return to prison? A midnight trial? His mind leapt with a jolt to the opposite possibility. No, they wouldn't release him in the middle of the night. Floundering in a limbo between terror and joy, he shook so badly that he stumbled over a rough spot in the cement floor.

Now Lino and Enrique arrived at the main entrance of the camp. The sergeant, a small balding man in a dirty uniform, came out of a gloomy hallway that Lino knew led to the staff quarters. His name was Martinez. He seemed half asleep and grumpy as he gestured to Lino and mumbled, "Over here." Lino moved in long anxious strides to the small unpainted wooden table where two sheets of white paper lay placed on top of an untidy folder.

"Sign here," said Martinez, now standing behind him.

Lino forced his mind to stay blank, not daring to hope and be crushed. "What is it?" he asked, fighting to keep his voice even.

"Your release papers. We're tired of you." Martinez seemed irritated that he had to explain.

Tired of him! Lino's head felt like it was ballooning out, his insides vibrating. *Focus. Don't show emotion. Don't let them see what this means to you.*

"So sign will you? We've got other things to do." Martinez avoided Lino's eyes. Afraid he would see some sign of triumph?

Lino peered at the paper, concentrating hard to see through the blur of moisture in his eyes. It **was** a release order. He shook his head to clear his thoughts. He read the paper again. He signed both copies, struggling to keep his hand from shaking. The sergeant stepped forward and looked at the signature. Then he handed one sheet to Lino, turned and disappeared down the hallway without a word.

Was this it? Without warning he was free? He had never visualized this moment. He had thought about living with Emy again, not having to count the hours and the minutes from the moment a *pase* began. He had imagined being in charge of his life, planning and working for what he wanted. A real home at the end of every day, food he chose himself, surrounded by people who loved him and respected him. But he had never pictured this exact moment. Now he would never forget it.

Enrique seemed to be waiting for him by the far door. Lino moved towards it, trying not to hurry his step. He forced himself to move slowly. He would not show his eagerness. He drank in the moment. Seventeen long years.

The large wooden gate was almost invisible against the dark sky as it swung open.

"Bus stop down there - you know," Enrique said, pointing to a spot about thirty yards down the road." Then the gate shut and Lino was alone.

Lino looked down the deserted country road; there was a quarter moon. He could just make out the stucco farmhouse with half a roof not far from the camp wall. Nothing else. For a long moment, he lowered his head in disbelief and prayed his thanks.

Then he took a deep breath, stretched his arms up over his head, then down to his feet. As he straightened, he lifted his arms out to the side in an embracing gesture. He was free!

He glanced around again. No one there to see him. He whirled around and let out a burst of song, an old tune from Celia Cruz. Then he straightened up to his full six foot two and started down the road. He picked his feet up higher and higher and began to hum the triumphal chorus from Aida.

Every gesture seemed an experiment. Every move felt different in freedom. He had been on *pases,* but there was a world of difference when you knew you weren't going back.

He found the bus stop and stood erect. This was his choice to stand in this place waiting for this bus. He was in charge. He could change his mind. He could walk. Or run. Or dive into the scrub pine and never come out. Nobody cared. Nobody would pounce.

After a long minute staring into the night, his mind clicked into action. Get to Havana. Get to Emy! His beloved Emy, whose wide green eyes crinkled into a soft understanding smile, even at painful news. Emy, who has waited 17 years with no one's arms around her. Without her children. How could he leave her one moment longer not knowing he was free? Not knowing her painful gamble had paid off, that she had a real husband, a future?

He clenched his fists, willing the bus to appear. When it did, he rushed to board. As the countryside passed, he began a mental list of everything he had to do. Find out about the children. Was there any chance of a phone call to them? Begin the long, probably vain, struggle for an exit visa.

He knew that this time he would leave Cuba if he could, that his family and Emy's happiness had to come before Cuba's struggle. He had to earn some money. Would they let him work at the hospital? He was

46 years old. He had years now to work, to walk the streets, read books, meet friends, lean across to touch Emy - day after day after day, for the rest of his life.

His mind whirred. He was fit. He was still a doctor. He had never stopped practicing. Every day in prison he had concentrated on staying alive and healthy so he could rebuild his life when it was over. Now it could happen. He felt he was about to dive into a warm enveloping lagoon.

He concentrated on looking out the window. They were reaching the center of the city in the thinning mist of early dawn. On his *pases,* Lino had concentrated on getting home, having the most time with Emy. Now he looked around as a person who belonged in Havana. Nothing had changed except by neglect. Fidel had not destroyed this beautiful city. His corrupted Revolution was simply letting it fall slowly to ruins. The University, the *Teatro Nacional,* the Malecon boardwalk along the sea. All stood as before but without repair or paint.

At one stop he saw through the window a beautiful colonial mansion on the corner. He remembered the Rodriguez who had lived there. Now there was a long row of sagging mailboxes for apartments of some sort. It was getting lighter now and a few carts and old cars were stirring. But the stores remained barred and dark. Dark for good or just closed at this hour?

He got off the bus at the main bus stop at Calle 23 and Avenida L and made his way around the side of the building toward the street.

As he came around the corner, he saw a tall blond woman in her early forties standing a few feet away, fumbling with her handbag. She wore a lightweight white sweater with long sleeves pushed up and a pair of navy blue slacks, perfectly creased. She looked out of place in the run-down street with sleepy shabby people stepping around her.

Where had he seen her? Known her? It had to have been a long time ago. Suddenly she spoke. "Lino, *eres tú?* Is that you? It's not possible! *Cómo estás?*" She gave him a warm hug.

It was Mariana from Lino's home town, Esmeralda. She had been his brother Hugo's girlfriend but had left Cuba in the early part of 1960 and they had heard nothing more of her.

Now she put her bag over her shoulder. "I've just arrived this morning, from Venezuela." Lino was torn. He didn't want to stop on his way to Emy. But he couldn't be rude.

"Venezuela?"

"I live there now, have since 1960."

"Surrounded by children?"

She laughed. "No, not me. I'm an actress. The only reason I've come back is to see my family." She pushed the sleeves of her sweater even higher and crossed her arms. "How is Hugo? I think of him often."

"He's married and has eight kids. He's in Miami actually."

"The story of my life. I'm always too late. But Lino, I'm frankly surprised to see you. I thought you'd be long gone too."

Lino smiled and answered quickly.

"Well, I guess I am long gone in a sense." He explained in a few sentences about the resistance and prison and ended by telling her he had just gotten out of prison that night.

"So we've both just returned then."

Lino chuckled. "Yes, we have. In fact, I have the rest of my life to rush off to. My wife lives just a few blocks from here and I'm anxious to see her." *What an understatement.*

"I guess you are." They hugged again, and Lino walked away without looking back.

He found himself almost loping through the streets, even though he knew there was no need to hurry when there was no deadline, no return to prison. He was already getting used to setting his own pace, his arms swinging freely. Ten minutes later he reached the house; it was dark and silent. Emy's bedroom - my God, he would sleep there every night now - was at the back, to the right overlooking the old fountain. He circled around the house, hoping some zealous member of the CDR wouldn't pounce on him for being out at such an early hour. He found the bedroom window, the one with a shutter missing, leaving the window glass exposed.

He didn't have a key; he had always arrived with Emy or someone let him in. He stopped and stood motionless. His darling Emy was right there, lost in sleep, less than twenty feet away. From now on he would be beside her. His hand shook as he bent down and picked up three small stones. He straightened up, paused to steady his hand, and threw one of the stones at the window. It hit the wooden frame with a barely audible click. He threw the second stone and it hit the glass with a tiny ping.

A sudden exuberance washed over him. Why was he being so tentative? Did he think she would scold him for making noise? He grabbed a handful of stones and threw them all at once at the window. They landed with a sound like hail. A light sprang on, and a shadowy form appeared inside the window. The form stood for a moment, disappeared, and returned to open the window.

Emy's gentle round face appeared, creased with sleep and confusion, her hair tangled. A look of concern crossed her face.

"*Lino por Dios! Estas bien?* You got a *pase* already? How long do you have?"

"No, *mi amor, mi corázon.* I am free." He reached his arms towards her. "They released me. *Estoy en libertad.* Come down here. I love you."

Emy raced down the back stairs, unlocked the door, and melted into Lino's arms. She had never cried. Not when Lino was arrested. Not when she hugged her children goodbye. Not as her life passed without them.

Now the tears came. Seventeen years of tears, of longing, of desperation and hope. In a tight embrace that allowed no space between them, Lino and Emy squeezed out all the loss and loneliness of the years apart. They let themselves feel the full brunt of how much they had missed each other. No more holding back, preparing for another parting. No more tearing away of togetherness. This dazzling moment would go on and on.

48

Freedom? Lino wasn't really free. He needed permission to work, permission to travel; he had to report monthly to the police station. Officials could invade his home at any hour without explanation.

"The walls are still there, just invisible." Lino tried to control his growing frustration.

Emy put her arms around him. "At least I'm inside the walls with you."

"You're right, of course, *mi vida*. That is the best part of all." She could feel his body relax a little.

The worst thing was that they couldn't get out of Cuba - couldn't get to their children. They had immediately applied for an exit permit. The authorities were categorical; there were no exit permits, no flights, and no possibilities for leaving. They pushed away their disappointment; they would have to build whatever life they could in Havana. For now.

In spite of the joy of being with Emy, Lino felt a deep sadness that he couldn't give his beloved wife the thing she longed for most, her children.

Somehow the rare times when they talked to the children by phone made the separation more painful. Of course Lino loved hearing their voices. Everyone tried to be upbeat, but Emy was sure the children could tell she was speaking through a giant lump in her throat. No one spoke of their getting out.

On September 9, 1978, Lino and Emy sat in the Huertas living room, Lino reading, Emy drinking her after lunch coffee and talking with Margarita. They were all half listening to a speech by Fidel on the radio. They never listened carefully, but this was an important commemorative day. Emy couldn't remember what was commemorated, nor did she care. But these speeches were sometimes used to announce new policies or a shift in dogma.

Suddenly the room went quiet, except for Fidel's booming voice. Lino and Emy sat frozen.

"Political prisoners have been released by our generosity, many before their sentences were complete."

Fidel had never mentioned political prisoners in public. Never.

"But they continue to be negative, to talk against their country, against our glorious *Revolución.*"

What was he getting at? Why the sudden admission that political prisoners existed, that some had been released? Emy leaned over and grasped Lino's hand.

"If they think the United States is so great, let them go. You. Political prisoners who have been released. Go on - get out! We don't want you and your treason. Your negativity. I say good riddance! This isn't your country. You are not one of us." Fidel droned on.

Emy could hardly breathe. Lino was already reaching for the phone when it rang. Andres Cao spoke so loudly Emy could hear across the room.

"*Lo oíste?* Did he mean it?"

Lino was almost shouting into the phone "Andres, he doesn't say things like this unless it's very well thought out."

Margarita leaned over to Emy. "He's right, what Fidel says goes." Emy gave her a weak distracted smile, still disbelieving what she heard, trying to hear what Lino was saying to Andres.

The next days were chaotic. Visitors streamed in and out of the house; the telephone rang constantly. Special offices were opened in the Country Club neighborhood of Havana for ex-prisoners to sign up for the special permits. They filled out endless forms. Rumors flew from families in Miami to Havana and back.

Now that Castro had opened the door, the United States was making it difficult to get visas. A prisoner had to be requested by a family member who was a United States citizen. The children were not, but by luck Emy's mother had recently become one.

But there was a giant obstacle. Even if all the permissions and visas were granted, there were no flights. Lino's brother Hugo, along with other families in Miami, were frantically trying to set up a charter flight. The bureaucracy was relentless. On the phone, Emilia Maria related how she had told her boss in Miami, the energetic managing partner of a law firm, about the dilemma. His response had been, "Hell, we'll fly our company plane down there - when can we leave?" Emilia Maria had gratefully thanked him, then explained why it wasn't so easy.

Emy remained curiously calm. After Fidel's speech, she had felt a curious click in her heart, telling her this time she would get out. It was just a matter of time. Other families of prisoners were frantic; afraid somehow they would miss their chance, go to the wrong office at the wrong time, and not make it out. Emy just told herself that things always moved slowly. If she panicked, pushed immigration officials too hard, tried to contact visitors from the U.S. to get some news, then something could go wrong. She waited patiently, letting herself imagine the real day, the real trip, the stunning truth of holding her living breathing children once again in her arms.

January 28, 1979. A thin stream of morning sun crossed the floor from the door open to the roof garden. It was still early. Emy had been awake many hours. Hopefully she would never lie in this room again, never again sleep in Cuba. The day had that suspended quality of days when people close to you die or are born. She would do both today. Today her family would be reborn whole.

Her *jabata*, her little bag, sat on the floor, still open. Inside were the only two skirts she owned that were worth keeping, a few shirts, a nightgown, her hairbrush. Two girdles - they'd been available for the first time in years and she couldn't resist. No photos. No jewelry. She'd been tempted to take a little bronze carved box she treasured. And a favorite piece of jewelry, a lapis necklace with a gold chain. No. It just wasn't worth the risk. Not even her wedding ring. She would take nothing that could remotely cause problems at the airport. Everything else had been given away to those who couldn't leave, just as so many people had left things to Emy over the years.

The night before, hopefully Emy's and Lino's last in Cuba, friends had dropped in and out all evening. Most of the old friends were gone. The Iglesias had left years ago. Vicki, Maria, Manduco, and the children had left on the very first flight for political prisoners just a month before. It had been hard to say goodbye to people that Emy knew desperately wanted to come with them. More than 18,000 former political prisoners had applied to leave the country; only 3,000 would eventually be able to go. The others didn't have relatives in the U.S. to claim them. A few people she knew were committed to staying in Cuba; she hoped they would be all right. Her diplomatic and other foreign friends she would hopefully see again.

She dressed quickly in the black and white wool checked jumper, made just for this day from fabric she had saved for years. With it, she had chosen, as a symbol of her lost world, a dark turtleneck she had owned since her school days. She felt odd dressing up with no earrings. No matter. Jewelry was the last thing she cared about today.

They had coffee and bread with the Huerta sisters in the airy dining room filled with sun. Then Lino and Emy enfolded each of them in their arms. It was hard to break away from each hug.

Margarita spoke first, "This isn't really goodbye, you know. You'll always be with us. We'll have you in our hearts."

Hortensia was her usual matter-of-fact self. "Nonsense, even if it is goodbye. This is the way it should be. You're off to find your children. I refuse to be sad for one minute."

Lino laughed. "But you know what they say about kids. You become their slaves. How will we adjust after the way you've spoiled us?" He grasped Margarita's hand. Ada said nothing, her eyes brimming.

Emy fought down the lump in her throat. "Words are impossible . . . You beautiful ladies. You saved my life - our lives - in so many ways. Put yourselves at risk for us. Made us feel cared for." She could say no more. She consoled herself by thinking that saying goodbye to the Huertas would hopefully be the only sad moment they would feel today.

At the airport, they found the twelve other families going on the DC-3 that had been chartered by Hugo and other relatives. They all waited quietly to be processed, each concentrating on their own hopes. *Please don't let anything happen now. We couldn't bear the pain.*

Emy crossed the lobby to say hello to a friend who was on the flight, then looked around for Lino. Where could he have gone? At last she picked him out of a crowd of men a hundred feet away. One man held a microphone that said Radio Nederland. They were journalists.

Panic seized her. He was giving an interview. *NO! Don't say anything. Don't give them any reason, any excuse to take us away, take us off the plane.*

Now the crowd shifted and she couldn't see him. Had he been arrested? Had he said something he shouldn't have? Please God. Don't let him be taken away. Not again.

Then he was beside her.

"Sorry. Those journalists grabbed me. They weren't really here to see me; it's just that we're only the third planeload of political prisoners to go. It's still news."

He realized Emy was shaking all over; her eyes moist with fear.

"It's O.K. *mi amor.*"

"What did you tell them?" Her voice was strained and clipped.

"*Mi cariño*, they asked me only two things. 'Would I fight again?' I said the fighting had been over since 1966. Nothing more."

"*Qué mas?*"

"They asked me how I was treated in prison, and I said I was treated just like every other prisoner. Now none of that sounds very dangerous, does it?"

She shook her head silently. He put his hands on her arms and looked into her eyes. He spoke softly to her, his voice a mixture of sorrow and confidence.

"It's O.K. Emy. We are O.K."

Lino didn't tell her about the government official who had asked him to step outside the airport, then asked him to carry a message for someone in Miami. The message concerned the official's plan to defect on an upcoming trip. Was it a trick? Was the official sincere? Lino would never know. He had said simply that he could carry no messages out of Cuba and turned away.

Emy remained nervous as they passed through the searches and the checking of documents, alert for the slightest frown or questioning look, the turning of one guard to another to consult on some imagined transgression. That was how problems usually began. She was surprised they weren't personally searched, though their bags were thoroughly combed. Lino had covered his wedding ring with a band aid; no one asked about it.

Then they were in the *pecera*, the fishbowl waiting room where she had watched her own children and her parents, ached for them as they waited to leave 18 years before. Where she had mourned Raque's leaving. This time she and Lino were on the inside. One step closer.

After more nervous hours, they were led to the plane. Everyone was silent. Lino and Emy took seats in the middle of the plane. The passengers waited, each in his own bubble of apprehension, the mood of vulnerability ingrained over the years. Anything could still happen.

People had been dragged off planes before. Flights cancelled on the slightest pretext.

Now the doors were closed. The plane lifted off. Emy didn't even look at the green sea below her, at the island where she had spent her life. Growing up, she could never have imagined being so happy to leave it.

All she could think of was how long had they been in the air. She felt rooted to her seat. She finally found the courage to ask the stewardess who confirmed they had been flying for thirty minutes. She crossed herself silently. She knew they had reached the *punto de no regreso*, the point of no return. They could not be forced back.

They were out of Fidel's control.

A tidal wave of relief swept her, reaching into every stiffened nerve and muscle, releasing 18 years of tension and frustration. She was really out. She sat quietly in the luxury of no fear. No vulnerability. She smiled at Lino beside her, kissed him on the cheek. What a casual gesture. What a hard earned right that kiss was. She was only forty years old. He would always be beside her now. He and her children. Her family.

"*Ya todo terminó, mi corázon,*" she whispered. "It's over." Lino looked over at her and squeezed her hand hard. There were no words.

Her thoughts swept ahead to Miami. What had been fear in Havana now turned into nervous energy. She hoped her clothes didn't look dowdy. Lino looked as handsome as ever in a second-hand suit. Would they think him old fashioned, irrelevant? What would the children look like? What would they think? They might be cool and distant. Could she stand it?

Lucia was in high school, and Emilia Maria had already been working two years. Po had graduated last spring from Belen School, where his father had gone - or rather the Belen recreated in Miami. He was in college in Ohio. Would he be able to come meet them?

They were grown up, but they were still her children. Could she learn to parent them? Perhaps her mother held that place for good. Maybe it was too late; they were beyond parenting.

She opened her purse. Inside was a small wooden match box her Bulgarian friend Ivan had given her. She had used it to keep a few soft pressed petals from the roses Señora Bringas had given her on her birthday visit to *La Cabaña* so long ago. This was the only concrete remembrance of those long drab years when the color of a flower had made such a difference. She replaced the box in her purse and took out her brush.

Emy brushed her hair, looked in the mirror, put on lipstick. She closed the purse. Would she seem old to her children? Would they be disappointed? After a few minutes, she opened her purse and began the same routine again.

One thought ran over and over in her head. *I will finally get to know my own children.*

Would they all be at the airport? How soon could she actually touch them? How many torturous hours of waiting in Immigration? How would her parents look?

Lino was uncharacteristically quiet on the trip, deep in his own thoughts. He wouldn't be able to relax, let go of his tension, until he had seen his children, had held them close and knew they were alright.

His greatest hope was to be able to connect with the children. To not be a stranger to them. He and Emy were so lucky to have Jacinto and Emilia. They had believed in what he was doing in Cuba, in their daughter's decision to stay. They would have passed that belief to the children.

He had already decided he wouldn't wallow in bitterness, regretting what he'd missed. He had lost part of his life. But there had been gifts. He had learned to see the real humanity in each person and respect their suffering. He had seen his own limitations and his strengths. Most of all, he had learned on a visceral level what mattered the most in life. And what mattered was being here now, with the future opening up.

He looked at Emy who had her eyes closed. He knew she wasn't asleep, just waiting. What an extraordinary marriage he had. So normal in the beginning, happy but taken for granted. God, they'd had only one year of normal marriage before the violence and intimidation began, before everything fell apart.

When they were separated, constantly under threat, their marriage had changed, become much deeper. As much as he had loved her beauty, the joy of living with her, it became so much more. She had become more mature, with her own ideas, and a depth of compassion and determination he had never imagined.

And dedicated. She had the choice every day of staying with him or going to her children. And she had stayed. She gave him her life; she trusted him. It gave meaning to the idea of marriage for life.

Siempre. He had survived all those years because of her energy and her support, the sharing of pain and dreams.

Now it was her turn. In a few minutes his Emy, his uncomplaining Emy, who had given up everything, would be given back what she deserved. Her parents, her children and family, a life where she could speak out and laugh and be surrounded by people who loved her.

49

L ino - look!"
The ground was suddenly visible, stretches of green broken by
rivulets of tiny cars and trucks on long straight roads leading to Fort
Lauderdale where they would land. They saw enormous clumps of
tile roofs and open playing fields or parks. Now the green gave way to
cement and the runway lay before them.

As the plane taxied to a stop, Lino and Emy craned their necks to
see out the window. Emy let out a gasp. Hundreds of people stood
outside the chain link fence edging the runway! She could make out
individuals, but they were in constant motion; she couldn't recognize the
faces. Was that her mother? No, too tall. Maybe it was Vicki's mother,
Maria. No, Maria wouldn't come to the airport. Her mind fibrillated
with anticipation and the effort of trying to see.

The door opened and warm fresh air flowed into the plane. Emy
realized she wasn't breathing. She grabbed Lino's hand as they moved
down the aisle behind Andres Cao and his wife. What if they got off the
plane and no one recognized them?

They emerged from the dimness into the bright sunshine bouncing off
the runway and the white stucco terminal. They walked together down the
old fashioned metal steps onto the runway, shading their eyes, trying to
see who was there. A hundred yards away, the people behind the fence
were pushing forward. Then one figure simply forced the gate open and ran
toward them, dark hair flying. Lucia. This had to be Lucia. Hugging them
both at once, crying and squeezing and saying "*Mami, Papi*" over and over.

She stopped and held her parents at arms length for a moment, giving them a radiant smile.

"I'm the one who knows you the least - so I needed to get started right away!"

Emilia Maria and Lino Jr. were at the gate. Lino and Emy ran towards them, hugged and kissed them. Emy's parents Jacinto and Emilia were at their side, smiles full of joy, holding on, reluctant to separate from them again. Emy's sister Juani and her brothers, as well as their own families. Kiko, Jorge, and Pepe, everyone pushing into the growing tangle of hugging bodies.

"Oh my God, Lino, they're so big, so handsome these children." Emy tried to stay attached to everyone at the same time.

Emilia Maria has Lino's eyes for sure. Lucia has my eyes but she's built just like Lino - long and lean. Po - he looks so much like his father.

Emy saw nothing but people, people she loved. Not hearing their words but feeling their essence, the presence she had dreamed of for so long. She felt herself whirled from one person to another amid hugs and murmured grateful greetings. She would never remember the airport, the sunshine, the flashbulbs from reporters. Only the breathless fog of being home with her family and friends.

Her parents looked old, tired, but radiant. Even Lino had a healthy glow she hadn't seen in years. Her brothers were there, introducing wives who were strangers, children she had never known. Lino's brother Hugo with his wife and all their children.

Their hesitancy and fear seemed to have vanished the moment they landed on U.S. soil. Lino hardly acknowledged a customs official who fought his way through the crowd and politely explained that there were formalities. The people around the Fernandez family moved as one body into the Immigration offices, the officials trying in vain to detach them. The formalities rushed by in a blur. How different officialdom here was from Cuba!

Everyone wanted to present new family members; the husbands and wives and the nieces and nephews Lino and Emy barely knew existed, now almost grown.

Raque all the way from Georgia, Vicki with Manduco and their boys, the Iglesias and their children. Friends from school she hadn't seen since they were teenagers. Lino and Emy felt immersed in a mix of old lives and new.

"You look just the same!"

"I can't believe how big Javier is."

"So this is the famous Mariana. She's beautiful."

"Susana looks so much like your mother!"

And through everything, trying not to lose physical contact with the kids and Emy's parents.

They would go directly to a Mass of Thanksgiving. After his expulsion from Cuba, Padre Llorente had founded the new *Agrupación* in Miami, a beautiful retreat center on Biscayne Bay.

It was a perfect way to start their new life. From Lino's first days living in the residence, the *Agrupación* had always given a strong underpinning to their lives. Its principles had buttressed them in the darkest hours. Many of the people from the *Agrupación* had become Lino's comrades in arms, his fellow prisoners. He had watched some of them suffer or die in prison. Their wives had supported and comforted Emy. Many had been at the airport to celebrate their freedom and would come to the Mass.

In the end, the immediate family settled in two cars: Lino in one with the kids and Emy with her parents in the back seat of her sister's car. In the car, Lino took off his tie and handed it to Lucia, who clutched it as though it were sacred.

As the car waited to pull onto the freeway, Emy looked in the rearview mirror and saw hundreds of cars coming from behind them. She was stunned. The world had grown, become so complex, rushed onward into the future. How could she ever live in this overwhelming world of 1979? She was sure she wouldn't drive here for a very long time.

The *Agrupación* building was very much like the one in Havana and Lino was flooded with memories when he saw it. After all the emotion, it was a relief to sit now in silence during the Mass. He could look around him and see his family, all in one place. A great sense of peace cloaked him.

The intensity of his prayer startled him. He was glad God could read his soul and feel his gratitude, because no words could ever suffice. The nightmare was over. At last he could build a life, protect and guide his children. Be a father. His thoughts leapt for a moment to all there was to do. Tomorrow they would apply for their Social Security cards, look for jobs, get started revalidating his medical license. He felt confident. He'd been working at Mazorra hospital and was already beginning to catch up with the enormous changes in medicine, especially in psychiatry.

They would become respected people, like they were before the Revolution that had turned them into maggots, traitors, caged animals.

He would no longer be a fifth class citizen but a first class citizen in a place where people just go about their business. Where they don't waste their time on suspicions, scrambling for basic necessities, second guessing every word or gesture.

Emy sat a few feet away, her parents on one side and Emilia Maria and Po on the other. He could reach across and touch them. This would amaze him anew each day. He could touch his wife and children. No wondering and waiting; just decide to touch them, speak to them, share any moment of their lives.

Emy held her mother's hand during the Mass. She wanted to be in physical contact with everyone at once. She knew there would be time for everything, but the old habits would die hard. For too long she had learned to grab anything you could get because it might be yanked away.

She knew people would ask her why she had stayed all those years, would look for bitterness and regret in her. Would they understand how, in an odd way, in spite of the risks and sadness, their lives had been enriched by their torturous odyssey? It had been crushingly sad at times, but how comforting that people had been there to depend on. How much sadder if people had turned their backs, if the risk of guilt by association had made them turn away.

After the Mass they went home. What a simple word. This was home now. They could not be pulled from it in the middle of the night. They could not be evicted by a platoon of militia, or be told which rooms they could use, which possessions they could keep.

The small house on 36th Street in Little Havana had been a bungalow. Emy's parents had added, years before in anticipation of their coming, a second half, making it a side by side duplex. Their arrival had happened so fast that it was still rented, but in a few days it would be empty.

Emy looked around. Every inch of her parents' house seemed precious to her. This was her haven where she would get to know her children and learn to live a real life again. The tiny living room immediately filled with friends and family, some she had seen at the Mass, some at the airport, some only many years before.

She and Lino sat all afternoon, close by the children and her parents. They met friends of the children, new friends of Emy's parents, neighbors and supporters.

Uppermost in Emy's mind was meeting and thanking all those who had helped her children. Tomorrow they would go to Lucia's school and to watch her play basketball. They would visit Emilia Maria's job, meet all the people in her world. Lucia would take them to her after-school job at Woolworths; it seemed the Fernandez were famous in Miami.

When they arrived at the house, Po had pulled Lino into the garage to show him the bedroom he had built there.

They sat on Po's bed. "Papi, we really need to talk about my future." Lino glowed to the center of his being. This was a moment he had yearned for.

"When do you go back to college?" Po had started the fall before at Defiance College in Toledo. "Are you missing classes now?"

"Yes, I mean no. Papi, I'm not going back."

"Why is that, Po?"

Po straightened up and smiled. "Because I've been waiting 18 years to be with my parents. I'm not going to miss one day of it."

What could Lino say? He and Po spent the next half-hour talking about Po's plans, his experiences in Ohio, and what Po wanted to study.

In the living room, more waves of friends had arrived. It was as though some long rambling conversation, begun in a garden somewhere in the old life, had started up again.

Lino's brother Hugo decided to take him to the men's store for his first new clothes since 1960. When he returned, Emy could see how good he felt. He had always loved to dress well and it had been so long. Emy's sister, Juani, arrived with armloads of clothes to share with Emy.

Later his daughters took Lino to a discount department store to get toothbrushes and a razor. To their amazement, Lino took off, zipping down the aisles, loading up their cart with little gadgets, presents for everyone, and snacks. The girls looked at one another nervously. Did their father realize he had to pay for these things? They didn't have much money. To their relief, when Lino arrived at the cashier, he explained to them that some friends had given him pocket money when he arrived. Lino had rediscovered the consumer society.

When they came back, a friend of Juani's had arrived who knew a professor at the University of Miami. There was an opening for a secretary; Emy should go first thing Monday to apply. Lino needed to study full time for his foreign equivalency medical exam; Emy's job would bring health and tuition benefits, plus pay part of her parents' mortgage. The Iglesias had a car they could give them. Even on this very first day, things seemed to be falling into place with astonishing speed.

Food was everywhere: *arroz con pollo, picadillo* and plantains, sweet rum cakes and guava pastries, mangos and papayas, fresh avocados. Things Lino and Emy hadn't seen in decades. Things the people around them took for granted, nibbled on carelessly. An endless supply of rich strong *café cubano* in tiny china cups, doused with heaping spoonfuls of sugar.

Such abundance everywhere! Emy was standing in the kitchen washing a paper towel and hanging it to dry when Lucia came in.

"Mami - what are you doing? You don't wash paper towels. They're made to throw away."

Emy looked from the towel to Lucia in confusion, and then her mind flooded with the realization. She was living in a remarkable unfamiliar world. Her world now.

After supper, Emy had eaten half a rum cake and felt full. So she wrapped it in a little packet and asked Po to put it in the fridge for tomorrow.

"Mami," he said gently. "You don't need to save a half a pastry. We aren't rich, but there'll be more pastries." She felt tears in her eyes at his gentleness.

Emy was exhausted but unable to let this moment go. She felt suspended in happiness, wanting this magic day to go on and on. Even when she could hardly keep her eyes open, she wanted to ask one more question, hear one more of the children's stories. She wanted to talk and talk about the future, listen to everything planned. It would be a long time before she could believe that something planned would actually happen. She had lost the habit of that.

In the end Lino stood up. "*Mi amor, mi familia, mis hijos.* I am a busy man. I must start tomorrow to earn my living, to support my family. I have three wonderful children to put through college." He hugged Emilia Maria, the nearest. "I am going to bed."

"Well you won't have to go far, not in this tiny house," said Emy's mother. "Tonight you will share the girls' room; they're giving up their beds and sleeping on the floor." Emy smiled at the kids. "As long as I can be near enough to touch my children."

"In that case, I may have to sleep sticking out of the closet." Po took a gentle punch at Lucia. He had his room in the garage, but he would move into the duplex next door with Emy and Lino in a day or two.

In 30 minutes they were all settled in the girls' bedroom, Lino in one bed, Lucia on the floor next to it, then Emilia Maria on the floor, and Emy in the far bed. At the door Po and his grandparents blew kisses, reluctant to lose sight of Emy and Lino.

Emy lay awake a long time, her thoughts careening from the surprises of the day to her delight in finding her children so normal and loving. She looked across at Lino, heard his gentle breathing. He was turned toward her and the girls, unwilling to lose sight of them even as he fell asleep.

She would wake up tomorrow and feel her eldest daughter close by. She would walk into the kitchen and find her mother making coffee, her father reading the paper. She might walk to the store with Po and chat with a clerk, trying to lose the habit of weighing her words or wondering who this person really was.

She looked across the room once more and reached gently down to touch Emilia Maria's shoulder. She imagined a sparkling current traveling from her through Emilia Maria, then through Lucia and to Lino. She imagined it reaching to her parents in the next room, to Po in his room. The sparkling current had always been there. It had stretched so far. Now it flowed easily from one to the other. The connection had held.

EPILOGUE
2004

A gentle February sun shone on Barbarossa Avenue in Miami as Dr. Lino Fernandez, tastefully dressed in a blue open-necked shirt and pleated gabardine pants, strode from his car to his front door. He moved with an air of deep contentment, calling to Emy as he came into the house.

"*Mi vida*, what time is the party on Sunday?" The Fernandez were celebrating their 46th wedding anniversary in two days with a barbeque for friends and family. Emy came in from the sunroom where she'd been setting out tablecloths and napkins.

"*A las cuatro. Más o menos*. What time did you tell people?"

"Nothing *mi amor*. I only said I would ask. I always take my orders from you. You are the princess here." Emy chuckled and her green eyes sparkled as Lino kissed her on the neck.

The phone rang. Lucia's new husband, Ramon, wanted to know how much meat to bring for the barbeque. He was a wonderful chef who cooked for all the family parties.

"Just bring a lot; what we don't eat, we'll have Monday." Every Monday the family gathered for dinner at Emy and Lino's.

Emy hung up and carried a small tray to the sunroom, their mid-afternoon coffee and a flowered china plate of sugar cookies. Even today, she was often struck with the simple miracle of living well: cookies on a plate, an innocent phone call, knowing Lino would come home all right.

She sat across the small glass table from Lino, her radiant smile warmer than ever; her deep caring always seeming to fill a room.

"Here you are *mi vida*." She handed him his coffee. "How were your rounds?"

"Fine. Señora Gomez is doing much better. I said she could go home tomorrow if she stayed the same. She hates the hospital." Lino's practice was divided between psychiatry and internal medicine, and he visited his patients every day when they were hospitalized.

When he'd arrived in 1979, even before starting his studies, Lino had taken care of one unfinished piece of business. He had flown to Washington D.C. to beg the State Department for visas for a list of sixty friends, former prisoners who had no family in the U.S. to request their visas. The State Department spokesperson was sympathetic, but could promise nothing. In the end, many of the visas were granted; some of those men would be at the anniversary party.

Six months after arriving in Miami, Lino had taken the foreign physician exam and was again officially a doctor at the age of forty-eight. To start out, he could only serve as a surgeon's assistant, but he felt complete, a part of medicine again. He had made it back to where he belonged.

He started a residency in psychiatry at Miami's Jackson Memorial Hospital, but halfway through he passed the internal medicine boards, which allowed him to open his own practice. He hated cutting short his residency but he needed to earn money. It always bothered him that he hadn't finished the program, so years later he had returned to Jackson and finished his residency as well as running his own practice. On call 24 hours at two hospitals, it had been a tough three years.

There had been many strange crossings of paths over the years. Antonio Gilbert, the young man who had retrieved Lino's letters for Emy when she was at the Egyptian Embassy, had appeared in Miami, and Lino and Emy saw him often. He had died several years ago.

While Lino was at Jackson Memorial, the great exodus from the port of Mariel had begun. Castro had allowed 125,000 people to leave Cuba, provided the U.S. accept a few thousand criminals and mental patients as well. The mental patients were taken temporarily to Fort Chaffee in Arkansas, and Lino was one of the doctors sent to evaluate them. Lino was amazed to find some of the same patients he had treated at Mazorra years before.

Lino sat back and smiled slowly at Emy. "Ah, my lovely bride. No one will believe it's been so long since I gave you my heart in the chapel at *La Coronela*."

Emy laughed and pushed the plate of cookies toward him. She was used to his extravagant compliments, but they still encircled her heart with a soft cushion of continuous love.

Lino was right; the years had flown. The first months in Miami, Emy had felt torn. She needed to help Lino study for his exam and she needed to work to support the family. But she wanted to relieve her parents of their long endured responsibilities. Most of all she wanted to connect with the children.

For Lino the way to knit the family together was to concentrate on reclaiming his profession, become a provider and a contributor to society. Until he did, he couldn't feel he'd returned to real life. Meanwhile Emy stepped softly through the delicate dance of becoming a mother, to children who were nearly grown. Just at a time when teenagers pull away from parents, Emilia Maria, Po, and Lucia suddenly had two sets. They wanted their parents' approval, but they were used to the more liberal rules set by their grandparents.

Emy especially had a hard time with the American culture of the late '70s where boys and girls mixed all through school and had freedoms she could never have imagined. She had to fight the temptation to over-mother, to comment on the girls' clothes (improper by her 1950s standards), or ask why the kids were sitting on the porch with friends at one o'clock in the morning. Unchaperoned. She tried to downplay her disapproval, but it came through anyway.

Habits died slowly; Emy's mother Emilia was a strong woman who'd been the driving force in the children's lives for many years. It was a long time before charge of the children passed completely from her to Emy.

Emy's father Jacinto, on the other hand, had been happy to bow out and hand over his role as head of the household. He had told Lino the very first day, "I love these children, but I'm tired. It's time for you to take over." He was happy to sit back and watch his reunited family.

Emy and Lino had slowly realized just how much Jacinto and Emilia had suffered to take care of the children. Friends and family in Miami had helped out financially when they could, but everyone was scraping by. Jacinto had washed dishes, worked in the fields planting tomatoes, delivered candy to vending machines, and done every kind of manual labor. Emilia did piecework at home; she wanted to be there for the children all the time. Both grandparents had worried as they got older about what would happen if Emy and Lino were trapped in Cuba forever.

It had been a delicate balance, Emy and Lino's first year in Miami. They decided the three generations would live together in the duplex. Emy and Lino wanted to parent intensely, to take away any doubts that they loved their children. But they knew the worst thing would be to treat them like *pobrecitos* - poor things damaged by the circumstances of their childhoods.

They knew they couldn't step in now and remake their children's lives. How could they question customs and permissions in force for years? They could only offer advice, share their standards, and then be quiet. In the end, the children would have to make their own decisions and face the consequences. The acceptance and respect for other people that Emy and Lino had learned through their own painful years alone helped them guide their children now.

In the end, the pushes and pulls were managed. The children, each in their own way, wove with their parents a web of knowing and respect. There were graduations and weddings and babies and graduate schools. There were disappointments, divorces, and changes of careers.

Po became an architect and was married with three children, Lino Jr., Sofia, and Gabriella.

Emilia Maria had stayed at the law firm and gotten her college degree at night. Now she hoped to go to graduate school. She had three children, Carolina, Claudia, and Nicolas. She and her second husband Rafael had been married two years.

Lucia worked her way through her undergraduate degree and then a Master's Degree at the University of Miami. She had two daughters, Cristina and Emily Mary. Now, newly remarried, she was a family therapist in private practice.

Emy and Lino felt lucky. They knew people who'd never been able to connect with their children after long years apart. Emy believed it was because her parents had truly respected their son-in-law and the reasons he and Emy were absent. They had kept alive a vivid picture of Emy and Lino: their personalities, their passions and their foibles. Most of all, they made it clear to the children why their parents were in Cuba. Friends of Emy and Lino, coming from Cuba, made the two of them come alive with stories and their obvious admiration for both of them. The children suffered, missed their parents, and stood in awe of them at the same time. But they always knew they were loved, an important part of their parents' lives.

Emy and Lino had moved to this sunny stucco house with a red tile roof in 1986. After Emy's father died, her mother Emilia lived with them until she died in 1992. Emy's sister lived across the street.

The small kitchen was often crowded with people, doing more talking than cooking. A coffee table in the formal living room held the few family photographs they had managed to send out of Cuba: Emy and Lino's wedding picture, full of sweetness and hope, early pictures of Emy on a pony, Lino Sr.'s first communion. And in every corner of the house, photos of the Miami years. Reunions and family, weekends boating in the Florida Keys, the glorious freedom of travel in the U.S., to Europe, and in Central America.

Most of life was led in the sunroom at the back of the house, eating, talking, savoring the constant comings and goings. Emy and Lino had added a master bedroom and bath on one end of the sunroom, a peaceful retreat in white and pastels.

On one end of the sunroom wall hung a painting by a fellow prisoner, Nicolas Guillen, imprisoned for producing anti-Castro movies. A figure behind bars with black letters scrawling, *Preso por ser libre.* A prisoner for being free. The only crime of people like Nicolas had been daring to remain free in their minds, refusing to surrender their will to Fidel.

"*Abui*, has my Mom gotten here yet?" Claudia, the 14 year old daughter of Emilia Maria, opened the front door and raced into the sunroom, out of breath. She used the kids' nickname for Emy, a version of *abuela* for grandmother. "I was supposed to be back here at 2:00, but the bus took forever."

"No, no, she hasn't been, *cara. No te preocupes* - don't worry." Emy loved to fuss over the children. "Have you had lunch? Shall I make you a little sandwich?"

"No thanks. I ate some pizza on the bus." Claudia gave Lino and Emy each a hug and took two sugar cookies on her way to the phone.

"*Hola,* Nicolas, What are you doing here?" Claudia gave her brother an absent minded hug as he came out of the den. "Don't you have baseball?"

"Not on Fridays," he yelled after her.

Emilia Maria had gotten divorced three years ago, and she and her three children had come to stay in the guest room, spilling into the den, until everything settled down. Even after they moved into their own place, they treated this house as their own. The same thing had happened with Lucia and her children two years before.

While Emy and Lino hated seeing their daughters in pain as their marriages ended, having the grandchildren living in the house had been a joy. Lino always said Emy was the one who suffered most during the prison years, missing her children growing up. Now she reveled in sharing their everyday lives and those of the grandchildren through all the stages she'd missed.

Emy loved to be engaged in the lives of this next generation. Even before the girls and their children moved in, she had spent afternoons picking up kids, dropping them off, picking up others, everyone ending up at her house for snacks and homework until their mothers came to get them.

Spending time with her children, being present for every milestone and crisis: that was her priority. For these 24 years in Miami, life had been filled with the sweetness of giving to her family and having Lino beside her. She was filled with gratitude for all they'd been able to retrieve of this life so long denied to them.

Now Nicolas plopped into the leather recliner. "*Abui*, do we have any oranges?"

Emy handed Nicolas a bowl of fruit, and he retrieved a tangerine and an orange. She set the bowl next to Lino's chair.

"You're just like your grandfather with fruit. Remember Lino, how you went wild eating fruit when we first arrived?"

"No, I only remember fish. Fish. Fish. Every imaginable kind of fish, cooked every possible way. I still haven't caught up."

"I don't think you ever will *mi amor.*"

"Well thank heavens you finally stopped saving every little morsel of food." He looked at Nicolas. "I still remember *Abui's* Mom going through the fridge and cleaning out all her little bites, her *bocaditos*. You wouldn't believe it, a quarter of an egg, one inch of hot dog."

"Oh stop, I wasn't that bad." Then Emy looked serious. "But Nicolas, I will never forget that first day in Miami when I went to the supermarket with my father. I saw this huge aisle just of dog food. And toys. And beds and blankets - all for dogs!"

"*Abui* started to cry, Nicolas, because she saw that dogs in Miami lived so much better than the people we'd just left in Cuba." Lino turned to Emy. "Your father felt so bad that he hadn't thought to prepare you."

The phone rang again. Lino went to answer it, and Nicolas went out to the back yard. Emy was left with her thoughts. Lino's health was so good, considering all he'd gone through. His only problem from the prison years was with his eardrum, shattered during his capture. He worried about eventually losing his hearing.

Had they completely escaped the psychological aftereffects of the Castro years? She often thought they had, but then something would happen. She had never stopped having shadowy nighttime dreams of being followed, of danger lurking, that old vulnerability.

One day, after more than ten years in Miami, Emy had been stopped by a traffic cop. The officer had been an officious type who had demanded harshly that Emy leave the car and hand over her identification. Something in his manner had triggered the old anxiety. The years of militia harassment came flooding back. She began shaking so badly she couldn't take out her papers. It made her realize that some corner of herself would always feel vulnerable. She shivered as she remembered how it had felt. It would never really go away.

Even today I don't confront or complain. I just go along with authority.

Lino stayed tightly linked to the situation in Cuba. Even though he'd physically left, he'd vowed to fight for the return of democracy, and he spent much of his time connecting and supporting resistance groups on the island. When Cuba came up in conversation or the news, Lino's normal easy manner turned intense and focused. He was quick to point out errors in accounts of Cuban history and the Castro regime. Officially he was the International Affairs Secretary of the Cuban Social Democratic party in exile. In 1997 he had spoken at the European Union in Holland about how to help Cuba transition toward democracy. Now there was talk of a conference at the Carter Center in Atlanta.

In 1995, he had attended a landmark meeting in Georgia between ex-Soviet officials, CIA and other U. S. government officials, academics, and former members of the Cuban resistance. The purpose was to finally bring to light the real events behind the Bay of Pigs. It had been an intensely satisfying experience for Lino where he could for the first time understand what had happened and confront the misrepresentations during the 1960s about the internal Cuban resistance.

The three Huerta sisters had come to visit when travel with Cuba loosened up briefly in the early 80s. Emy and Lino had wanted them to stay, but they were content to return home. They had their pensions, their beautiful house, their connections. They had been right to go back; that was their world. Of course they had all died now.

Lino answered the door and came back with a kind-faced man about his own age.

"*Hola*, Moya." Emy gave him a wave. Moya had been inseparable from Lino in the MRR and in prison. In Miami he served as Lino's internet scout, combing Cuba-related sites for news. Soft-spoken and devoted, he arrived every afternoon to discuss his findings with Lino. They disappeared into the den.

Emy searched through her papers for the guest list for Sunday's party. She hoped she hadn't forgotten anyone. It was amazing how close they'd all stayed, at least those who made it to Miami. Some had stayed in Spain or South American countries. Others had never been able to leave Cuba.

They lived surrounded by family. Lino's brothers, Carlos and Hugo, had both come to Miami, Hugo in 1962, and Carlos after Lino had arrived. Although both had died young, their children were always in touch. Emy's sister and brothers, and most of their children, were also in Miami.

Emy and Lino had remained close to the people who had shared Emy's long years alone in Havana: Alberto and Eva Iglesias, whose house had been such a refuge in the early years, Vicki and Ileana and their husbands, and of course Rene and Raque de la Huerta.

Many of the Cuban doctors had gone to other U.S. cities for their U. S. training, although they usually returned to Miami. When Rene and Raque had lived for a time in Milledgeville, Georgia in the late 60s, they had often invited the Fernandez children to spend holidays and summer vacations with them and their nine children. The de la Huerta children had known Emy well from the years she lived at their house. They brought Emy to life for Emilia Maria, Po, and Lucia, regaling them with stories of fun goofy things their mother had done and the tricks they played on her with frogs, which she abhorred. Raque was widowed now and lived nearby.

Vicki would be coming alone. Her husband Manduco had died the year before during a heart transplant, and she had lost her oldest son to cancer. Her youngest son was now a doctor. Despite her losses, she was as bubbly and unpredictable as ever.

Ileana would be there, still elegant and charming. When her husband Rino had made it to Miami in 1975, his old employer Baccardi had given him a job immediately. He was now retired. Ileana had never abandoned the fight against Fidel; she was very active in the organization Mothers against Repression.

Emy couldn't help but think about the people who wouldn't be there: young men executed in the Escambray, prisoners beaten to death or shot in prison, people like Cesar Paez who died of leukemia in prison before he could earn freedom. Thousands who earned their freedom but were never able to leave Cuba, trapped in a bleak unforgiving world. How uneven these lives had been. Some people never had a chance to live; others had grown old with family and freedom.

Emy often joked to new friends, "You might as well know that most of our friends are ex-convicts." And it was true: Pelayo, Andres, Orestes, Eduardo, Vicente. The bonds with these men and their wives couldn't easily be described. But they were as strong now as they'd been in the circulars of *Isla de Pinos* and the *galeras* of *La Cabaña*, outside prison gates waiting for visits, or during the long rides home alone.

Tommy Fernandez had become a good friend. He'd been released before Lino, only to be re-imprisoned for writing an anti-Castro play. In Miami, he had married another resistance fighter and become a Spanish teacher. Emy thought about the many comfortable weekends they spent with Tommy and his wife, Cecilia, at Marco Island on the west coast of Florida.

The slamming front door interrupted Emy's thoughts.

"Mami, are you here?" Lucia came flying into the sunroom, swinging her jacket and flinging off her shoes.

"Right here. Would you like a coke? *un cafecito?*"

"Nothing, thanks." She gave Emy an exuberant hug. "Mami, Wait till you hear my news. Ramon and I are having a baby - can you believe it? At my age?"

Emy felt like she'd been handed a brilliant bouquet.

"Where's Papi? I have to tell him."

"*Mi cara*, how wonderful. Papi's with Moya, in the den. But tell me more. When are you due? How long have you known?"

"I just found out for sure this morning. I couldn't wait to tell you."

Emy felt her eyes becoming moist. *Another baby. Another childhood. One she and Lino would not miss.*

An Overview of Castro's Revolution

At the end of 1958 life in Cuba was spirited and lively. Cubans of all classes lived life to the fullest, socializing, doing business, and enjoying the pleasures of the island's climate, music, and food. Traditionally entrepreneurial, Cubans are known to be determined and independent, seldom still. Nothing pleases them more than discussion, negotiation, and even good natured arguments with others. They had the highest standard of living in Latin America.

As someone would say later, if you were to search for a place where the gray conformity of Communism would easily take root, Cuba was the *last* place you would look.

The rebel forces of Fidel Castro entered Havana in triumph on New Year's Day 1959. He replaced the self-serving and often brutal Fulgencio Batista, a dictator, but one with limited impact on the daily lives of the Cuban people. Nevertheless, Batista's moral corruption had been legendary, and Castro was seen by many as a bright new star, the champion of democracy and social progress. Others were suspicious of Castro based on his personality and his earlier revolutionary activities.

Fidel Castro was the son of a prosperous but uneducated provincial landowner. He was sent to Belen, a prestigious private high school in Havana where he proved to be a good if erratic student. Not all Cubans were aware of how different his leftist politics were from his middle class origins. Those who did have serious doubts about Castro's designs for Cuba could only wait and see.

Elections were promised within eighteen months. They never happened. In the first months of 1959, Castro forces rounded up at least 500 of the worst "war criminals" of the ousted Batista regime, tried them in public forums, and sent them to firing squads. Many Cubans began to question the extent and the savagery of the violence used by Castro forces.

In April 1959, Castro visited the U.S. where he was greeted by cheering crowds, although many people were already suspicious that he might be a

Communist. During his trip, Castro publicly denied the Communist leanings of some members of his inner circle, including his brother Raul.

On his return Castro announced a program of agrarian reform which would make every peasant a landowner. While the new program had clear socialist echoes, it was presented as a humanitarian action. Many Cubans agreed that there was nothing wrong with taking land not being used and giving it to poor farmers who would cultivate it. Unfortunately, much of the land ended up in the hands of the government or of Castro's cronies.

In his new government, Castro placed many of his guerilla leaders with few qualifications. He also included well known Communists and blackballed qualified candidates whose only fault was not being Communist. By July of 1961, Castro had forced the resignation of both the President and the Prime Minister of the Revolutionary government and placed himself in both positions. Castro appointed his brother Raul as Minster of Defense and Che Guevara as head of the Central Bank.

Castro dealt summarily with those in his movement who protested the Communist influence in the new government. In the last half of 1959, the outspoken military commander Huber Matos was imprisoned. Then both Pedro Luis Diaz Lani, the chief of Castro's air force, and the popular Comandante Camillo Cienfuegos died under mysterious circumstances. This brutal response to any shadow of disagreement with Castro would be seen over and over in the years to come.

The press was initially supportive of Castro, but once they began to criticize the composition of Castro's new government, reporters and editors came under increased pressure. In May 1960, the major independent newspapers were closed down or taken over by the government. Many reporters and editors fled the country after threats of violence.

Within the first year a new currency was introduced, and people were given 30 days to turn in their money before it became worthless. However, each person could exchange only a small amount; money that could not be exchanged simply vanished.

As more people became convinced that Castro must be stopped, an internal resistance movement emerged. Several major anti-Castro organizations formed an active underground and supported groups of guerillas gathering in the Escambray Mountains. Even people who had fought with Castro against Batista now joined the resistance. When captured these defectors were either shot on the spot or sentenced to long prison terms.

Relations with the United States deteriorated in 1960 as talks began between the U.S.S.R. and Castro. In June, U.S. oil companies refused to refine Soviet oil and by the end of 1960 Cuba had nationalized U.S. refineries, along with all other U.S. owned companies, banks, and private property. The U.S. responded by eliminating Cuba's preferential sugar quota.

In October 1960, the U.S. initiated its trade embargo against Cuba, and Cuba was referred to in the U.S. as a Communist satellite. Although the U.S. ended diplomatic relations with Cuba on January 3, 1961, it was not until May that Castro referred to Cuba as a socialist country for the first time.

Although Cuba has actually been able to acquire needed goods from many other sources, the U.S. embargo against trade with Cuba, still in place after four decades, has created bad feeling in Cuba and has supplied years of ammunition for Fidel's anti-U.S. tirades.

Governments and individuals alike were astonished at the speed with which Castro had consolidated economic and political power and the ruthlessness with which he eliminated all dissent.

Unlike many Latin American countries, wealth in Cuba was linked to business more than to old land holdings and historic wealth. Cubans were entrepreneurs, and Castro was determined to eliminate the free market. When the government wanted to take over a business, armed soldiers simply arrived to inform the owner that he or she was suspected of being connected to the old Batista regime, of making negative comments about the Revolution, or of simply having friends who had left Cuba.

Many of these owners left the country, expecting to "sit out the storm" in Miami until the trouble blew over. This was a central belief of the Cuban people in the initial years of Castro's regime: the United States would never allow a Communist government to exist just 90 miles from U.S. territory. In the context of the times, the Cold War, such a "menace" was unthinkable, and few Cubans believed Castro would be tolerated. This faith was to prove unfounded.

By the end of 1961, life had been profoundly altered. Citizens had to be very careful what they said, even to neighbors or old acquaintances. Openly religious people were barely tolerated. After September 1960, every block had a CDR (Committee for the Defense of the Revolution) to track the movements of others and gauge whether individuals were demonstrating enough enthusiasm for the Revolution.

The departure of Cubans to the United States and other countries became an exodus. Over the next two decades, more than one million

Cubans would emigrate. In the first two years of the Revolution alone, many businessmen and professionals, including more than fifty percent of Cuba's doctors and teachers, left the country.

Some who left had to sneak out, using great caution, since they had engaged – or been rumored to engage - in anti-Castro activities. Others were allowed to leave but were harassed and allowed to take fewer and fewer possessions as time went on. By the summer of 1962, over 200,000 had fled Castro's regime and 3,000 Cubans a week were leaving for exile in the United States, Latin America, or Spain.

Throughout this period, Cuban citizens and the police played a game in which would-be exiles pretended to be going away on vacation, and police looked the other way. Of course these people were not allowed to take such items as family heirlooms or photograph albums, since they were "only going on vacation." If they wanted to get out, people had to leave not just their wealth, but their memories and personal possessions. Most decided escape was worth it.

The defining event for most Cuban exiles of the 60s was the April 17, 1961 invasion of Cuba at the Bay of *Cochinos* or the Bay of Pigs. This invasion, planned and executed by Cuban exiles in the United States, was encouraged and financed by the Central Intelligence Agency. For very complex reasons, including a change of U.S. Presidents, the U.S. did not provide the support the Cuban exile forces believed was forthcoming, and the invasion failed.

At the time of the invasion, the strong internal resistance movement was available to support the invasion with internal sabotage and support to the fighting troops. Much to the frustration of its leaders, they were kept ignorant of plans for the invasion and never received any signal to lend their considerable force to the plan.

Cubans both inside Cuba and in the U.S. felt betrayed. The spirit of resistance to Castro's regime was mortally wounded. Thousands of anti-Castro fighters had died. Thousands were already crammed into prisons, and many more would arrive shortly.

Castro closed all private schools, and indoctrination was strong in the state schools. New programs were taking schoolchildren into the countryside to work, unchaperoned, for months at a time. Parents felt they were losing control of their children's futures. In December 1960, the Catholic Church began *Operacion Pedro Pan*, an unprecedented program which took 14,000 unaccompanied children out of Cuba to the United States.

Under this program parents, afraid of being trapped in Cuba and anxious that their children not be trapped as well, sent their children out to foster homes and boarding schools arranged by the church. Some of these children did not see their parents until they were adults; others were reunited in a few years when their parents were able to follow them.

In October 1962, the Cuban missile crisis brought the final blow to any hope of unseating Castro with the help of the United States. Faced with irrefutable proof that the Soviet Union was installing nuclear missiles in Cuba, the U.S. government under President John Kennedy issued an ultimatum that they be removed. The world held its breath as the two superpowers engaged in a nuclear face-off. The result was a compromise in which the Soviet Union agreed to withdraw the missiles in return for a United States agreement not to invade Cuba.

In the fall of 1965, in response to growing internal discontent, Castro said anyone unhappy in Cuba could leave. As he would do later at a port called Mariel, he invited Cubans already in the U.S. to come to the port of Camarioca to get their relatives. The response was huge. Thousands of boats were purchased or rented in Florida and brought to Cuba to pick people up.

As the winter weather set in, boat accidents and fatalities increased. Finally U.S. President Lyndon Johnson said that to avoid more problems he would begin *vuelos de la libertad,* freedom flights to bring the refugees from Cuba. The U.S. government rented aircraft from various airlines and began the thousands of refugee flights which would run until 1972.

In spite of heavy subsidies by the U.S.S.R., the economic situation in Cuba continued to worsen. Predictions of state-of-the-art medical care and education, as well as other projects, were not realized or gradually became available only to a privileged few. There was a growing gap between the privileges of government officials or tourists and the goods available to common citizens. In July of 1969, one of Castro's many economic schemes, The Ten Million Ton harvest or *Zafra,* failed miserably, in spite of help from people all over Cuba and several Eastern block countries.

Castro continued to blame the U.S. embargo for Cuba's economic woes. In reality, Cuba traded with many other countries. But trade with the outside world usually improved the lives of top government officials, with very little trickling down to the daily life of Cubans. The greatest improvement in the lives of individual Cubans came from money and packages sent by Cuban-Americans to family members in Cuba.

In the early 70s Castro began sending troops to Angola and Ethiopia to support revolutionary movements there, at the request of the Soviet Union. This Cuban presence in Africa was cited as an impediment to any improvement in U.S.–Cuban relations. Over the years, other attempts were made to open negotiations toward resuming relations but were generally suspended after further Communist or anti-U.S. action by Castro.

In 1979 Castro agreed to let Cuban exiles make short visits back to see their families, apparently believing that the returning exiles would bring stories of homesickness and the hardships of starting over. Instead the returning exiles brought gifts and, more importantly, stories of life in the United States that contradicted government propaganda. Many citizens began to realize they had been deceived.

In 1980 the pressure created by these visits and the increasingly hopeless quality of life inside Cuba erupted. A crowd of would-be exiles stormed the Peruvian Embassy in Havana and requested asylum. Castro said once again, in essence, "OK if these people want to leave, you can bring your boats to the port of Mariel and take them away. Anyone who wants to leave can."

When thousands of Cuban-Americans rushed to pick up family members at the port of Mariel, many found themselves forced to also take criminals, mental patients, or homosexuals, all of whom Castro wanted to get rid of. The "Marielitos" had a harder adjustment than earlier exiles, but most eventually settled in and have done well.

In the 1980s another dramatic exodus began: *balseros*, people who came from Cuba on *balsas* or small rafts. Although some had chosen this route throughout the Castro regime, now people who had missed their chance at Mariel became desperate enough to try crossing the 90 miles of the Florida straits in tiny homemade craft. The *balsas*, looking unthinkably fragile when they arrived on Florida shores, were made of everything from buckets and old tires to pieces of furniture and Styrofoam.

Throughout the late 70s, 80s and 90s, there were numerous attempts, by government groups, humanitarian and church groups, and private individuals, to open a dialogue with Castro. These attempts have had uneven results. A heartening initial contact was often followed by a blatant demonstration of human rights violations. Typically Castro would loosen controls, allowing such innovations as open farmers' markets or the legality of possessing U.S. currency, then reverse his decision and clamp down. Great hope was engendered by the 1998 visit of Pope John Paul II, but further human rights violations have diluted such optimism.

In 1991 the fall of the Soviet Union and other Communist regimes created the expectation – almost the certainty - of Castro's fall. Economic conditions worsened dramatically, but to everyone's surprise Castro remained in power.

By 1996 the number of *balseros* was so high that it provoked a Cuban-U.S. crisis when Castro ordered the shooting down over international waters of two planes belonging to the Brothers of the Rescue, an exile organization that scanned the seas for rafters in trouble. The death of the four occupants of the planes provoked outrage in the United States and led to even more stringent terms for the embargo.

The *balseros* issue provoked another bitter U.S.-Cuban crisis in 1999 when a five year old boy named Elian Gonzalez survived the capsizing of a raft in which eleven other people, including his mother, died. Relatives in the U.S. fought Elian's father, living in Cuba, for custody of the boy, but he was eventually returned by U.S. authorities to his father.

Eventually the U.S. government forged an agreement with Castro to stem the tide. Called the "wet foot/dry foot" policy, Cubans who reached U.S. land can stay and apply for political asylum. If they are picked up at sea, they must return to Cuba. *Balseros* continue to arrive, although exiles and government officials agree that at least half of those who start out are lost at sea. With such daunting odds, Cubans continue to take their chances.

Part of the agreement was that the United States would allow 20,000 Cubans to come legally to the U.S. every year, using visas awarded by *lotteria*. Unlike earlier times, the hundreds of thousands of Cubans who apply for the lottery are not particularly ostracized. There is little to lose in Cuba. They simply wait patiently in hopes of becoming yet another exile willing to leave everything they know because anything would be an improvement over life in Cuba.

There are many views about what will – and should – happen after Castro's death. Will Raul diverge from his brother's path? Will outside governments help economically and under what terms? How strong is the dissident community inside Cuba? What role will the U. S. exile community play?

The next decade is sure to bring significant change. And undoubtedly some surprises.